Drowned Hogg Day

by

Nick Smith

JUSTIN BOOKS ROSELAND

Published in the United Kingdom by

Justin Roseland Books
A subsidiary of www.ool.co.uk
4, King's Meadow, Oxford   OX2 0DP

A CIP record of this book is available from the British Library.

First edition printed December 2016 by Ingram Spark.

ISBN: 978-1-63587-738-0

For Amanda, Robin and Natasha

Contents

Editor's Note

What follows is an edited collection of a series of blogs posted on the internet between 10th November and 30th December 2016. The identity and location of Alex Hogg remain a mystery and all attempts by this editor and the publishers have failed to establish any biographical details. The blogs have been traced to one 'Justin Roseland' but no such person is thought to have existed.

Numerous real-life figures are named in these blogs but each of the figures named denies any knowledge of Mr Hogg or the described events. Any resemblance to real-life figures should therefore be regarded as coincidental.

I would like to thank Michael Gamer, Jim Goddard and Daniela Lipscombe for their wise guidance at different stages of the development of *Drowned Hogg Day*.

Nick Smith (Editor)

The Hoggblog - Thursday 10 November 2016

Doctor admitting it's fatal (8)

I have fifty days to live. I don't mean *roughly* fifty days. I mean *exactly*. My life ends on 30th December 2016.

How can I be so certain? Trust me, I *am* certain….

How will it end? I will be drowned.

I may stay far inland and shun all invitations to swimming galas and hot tub sessions but to no avail – somehow I will be drowned. Perhaps, like Brian Jones, I will be pulled under by some rapacious tradesman, spluttering asthmatically, engulfed by a white wall of chlorinated spume. Or, like Virginia Woolf, I will float seraphically through a knot of lilies and industrial slurry.

Maybe I will make more of a splash, like Donald Campbell, up-ended in *Bluebird* almost exactly fifty years ago, or Captain Ahab, snarled up in his own harpoon-rope?

Should I seek out my fate, stalk my dark bride, like Sir Gawain bidding farewell to his hard-partying pals at Camelot to spend Christmas journeying alone across the badlands of Cheshire? Perhaps if I embrace my fate, I will somehow be spared? Or should I hide whimpering under my antique MFI bed in my tiny room on Osney Island until Isis herself comes crashing across the threshold?

Fifty things to do before I depart this vale of tears:

1. Spend the night with Marie-Claire Goodwin
2. Spend another night with Marie-Claire Goodwin …

That's as far as I've got with my bucket-list. Fifty days may not be long enough to fulfil that first objective, so it would be a mistake to be sidetracked by the usual spurious *carpe diems* of the condemned: the parachute jump, the trek through the rainforest, the pilgrimage to the Stadium of Light (Sunderland, not Lisbon).

A couple of chance meetings have been engineered already this week. On Monday I spot Marie-Claire, sheathed in lycra after her cycle ride from the labs, arriving for lunch in Hall with some professorial dotard and I loiter out of the drizzle in the Porter's Lodge, ready to saunter insouciantly across Front Quad the moment she re-emerges from her repast.

"Hi, Marie-Claire!" I extemporise as our paths cross.

"Hi, er …" she temporises, shaking the rain from her predictably lustrous, black tresses.

"Alex …"

"Sorry, I … good to see you, Alex…"

While I blush, Marie-Claire passes by with hardly a break in her step. If we had world enough and time, I would let things develop naturally. But at my back I hear the Grim Reaper honing his scythe.

Why should a glamorous young geneticist like Marie-Claire even notice me? Oxford is stuffed with scholarly rejects, the city's white, male middle class underclass. Osney Island alone is chokka with the products of Oxford's doctoral sausage-machine. But there is no deep freeze to store us in. We sit on our dusty shelves and the whiff grows a little more pungent each day. We should have been put out for recycling, yet here we still are.

We are scratching out the odd article, introducing ever more fantastical lies to our CVs, pretending that in a slightly different academic "climate", our micro-wisdom could be exchanged for hard cash – OK, perhaps not in Oxford but at some former polytechnic on the banks of the Thames, Trent or Tees. But there are no jobs to be had. The inexorable rise of student fees has done for us. Or so we claim. The truth may be rather simpler, that we simply aren't good enough.

"So, Alex, have you written the play-list for your funeral?"

This is not quite the response I am looking for.

"I'm serious, Phil. I have fifty days to live …"

But Dr Philip Sherborne is too busy chuckling into his pint of Purple Moose.

"Funeral for a Friend? Reg Dwight's finest hour – a bit too gothic? Purcell's Funeral Music for Queen Mary? The *Clockwork Orange* version, obviously. Rather apt for an Alex …"

"Yeah, right … and which droog would you be?"

"A bit of gospel with Led Zep's In My Time of Dying?" Phil is getting into his stride now. "It'll be so cool! Don McLean's The Grave? No, perhaps not. A mash-up of Fauré and Duruflé's requiems? Ziggy Stardust singing My Death Waits at the Hammersmith Odeon?"

"But my death really *is* waiting for me."

"Don't Fear the Reaper?"

"I do, I do!"

Phil finishes his pint with a flourish. Our squash game in the bowels of the Goodhart Building always leaves us pretty thirsty and the prices in the Beer Cellar are far from prohibitive.

"And what's left of our band could bash out Knocking on Heaven's Door with a hundred singalong choruses at the end!"

"Just you dare."

"It'll be massive," Phil muses. "That's the benefit of dying young – a huge turnout. If you peg out at 103, all your friends will be long gone and you'll be lucky to fill a telephone kiosk. Dying now, aged 28, you could have as many as, ooh, ten or fifteen friends and acquaintances turning up for a free sarnie and a chance to sing along to GDP!"

"What a consolation that will be. Just get some more ale in when you've finished cackling. And a few crisps would be good …"

"They don't do vegetarian crisps here."

"Course they will. Cheese'n'onion …"

"No, they're all saturated in animal fat. Can't be doing with those."

"The beer's OK, is it? Only an acceptable number of hops died in order that you might become intoxicated?"

"You can mock!"

"I certainly shall until you finally get that wallet out …"

I should explain that Gross Domestic Product is the name of our band – perhaps you've heard some of our stuff on YouTube? It's domestic in that we all fit in Phil's back bedroom, and it's certainly gross, so we can't get done under the Trades Descriptions Act. I play bass, sort of, and sing a few backing vocals. As you will have guessed, Phil is the front man and general obergruppenführer. We started out as nerdcore hip hop and then got into Swedish doom-metal (think Candlemass, only not quite so cheerful) when Stig, the guitarist, accidentally bought a nyckelharpa on eBay. He thought he was getting a hurdy-gurdy so we should be thankful for small mercies.

Our latest incarnation is as a Rolling Stones tribute band. So on a Tuesday evening, I'm Bill Wyman, all brooding indifference as I meander up and down the bass fretboard. *Maxim* magazine once put Wyman at number ten in its

Living Sex Legends list. When my musical competence was challenged one evening, I did point this out, so now I am known respectfully as Leg End.

Frankly, that's an improvement on most of the nicknames I have collected down the years. With 'Hogg' as a surname, I was never going to have an easy time of it at school. I'm 'Roadhogg' whenever I'm out on the public highways. I was 'Warthogg' through my acne-plagued teenage years and Hoggweed after my friends/tormentors were persuaded to listen to early Genesis. I am regularly exhorted to "go the whole hogg" and to "hoggwash" – my, how I chortle at such merry quips!

Phil returns with two more beakers full of the warm south (well, Cornwall anyway) with beaded bubble winking at the brim, and asks why I'm so sure I'm going to die at the end of the year. But my heart is not in it any more and I decline to tell him. Phil has news of his own anyway. He fishes out his i-phone and gets me to read a message from his ex-wife, Hattie:

Goodbye, Phil. I forgive you for everything. ☺

I try to look as blank as possible.
"So, what do you make of that?" he asks.
"That she forgives you everything?"
"No, the first bit. Why should she say goodbye?"
"Perhaps you should ask *her* that question?"
"I've been trying. Her phone seems to be permanently switched off. It's clear she doesn't want to speak to me. Do you think she's gone abroad?"
"I doubt it. She wasn't fond of flying, was she?"
"I just hope she hasn't done something … stupid."

The thought has crossed my mind too, of course. Hattie is a very volatile girl and she has been in a bad way since Phil walked out on her and their two kids. Jobless, living in various grimy dives in central London, drinking too much. But still heartbreakingly beautiful. Poor kid – she was still just a schoolgirl when Phil took a shine to her.

We stare at our pints for a while in silence, our squash game long forgotten. But it's not long before Phil wants to pick the bones out of yesterday's American Presidential election.

"What are the chances of *any* of us making it through to the end of 2017 with Trump in power?" he asks. "World War Three may be only a matter of weeks away."

I agree that the shock result is an unmitigated disaster for the planet. Phil is never short of a theory to explain the seemingly inexplicable.

"Elections are no longer settled along the old fault lines of wealth, class and religion," he assures me confidently. "Nowadays, the key thing is IQ. Everyone with an IQ over 100 voted for Hillary and everyone below 100 voted for the guy with no political experience, ludicrous half-formed policies and offensive views on almost every subject. Hillary actually secured more votes but in the wrong places, so the dullards won."

"Does that explain Brexit as well?"

"Of course. Almost every disinterested observer was convinced that we'd all be worse off if we came out of Europe – every economist, nearly every politician. Those of us with an IQ above 100 listened and voted Remain. The rest ignored all the arguments they didn't understand and voted according to the usual dictates of xenophobia and blind prejudice."

"My Dad voted for Brexit …"

"Ah, OK. Perhaps there are exceptions to every rule. But it was no accident that the biggest majorities for Remain were not found in the City or the stockbroker belt but in Oxford and Cambridge. That wasn't because of self-interest, it was purely a reflection of intelligence."

"I'll go home and tell Dad he has to leave town immediately."

But when I get back to Swan St, Dad has fallen asleep in front of *Hive Minds* (the Logophiles versus Prime, with the lovely Fiona Bruce in the chair) and I don't have the heart to disturb his reverie …

Friday 11 November 2016

Doubtful as to Gus Poyet but fundamentally generous (12)

RIP Leonard Cohen, that gravel-voiced troubadour and patron saint of the bedsit blues. But back to my own *crónica de una muerte anunciada*. What would it be like to drown? I try to imagine the circumstances in which it could happen to me and draw a blank. I can swim. I will steer clear of beaches and municipal swimming pools on December 30th.

But I'm at a vulnerable sort of age. Shelley was twenty-nine when he drowned, Brian Jones just twenty-seven. I am twenty-eight, twenty-nine on the 2nd of February, if, by some miracle, I live that long. Ho hum …

I have been reading Bill Clinton's autobiography, *My Life*. And why am I poring over the old rogue's sketchy reminiscences? Because I want his money! A million? That'll do nicely, Mr ex-President.

It's not as unlikely as it sounds. My job title is University College Alumni Development Fund Manager. It sounds grand but I'll be straight with you – I'm not the only Fund Manager. There's a team of us dreaming up new ways to twist the arms of anyone who has ever set foot in University College, Oxford. My patch includes the USA and right at the top of my hit-list sits the great man, a Rhodes Scholar at Univ (1968-70). Due to some oversight, we do not *yet* have a WJ Clinton Fellowship in International Relations or even a Chair in International Law. My job is to make it happen. But how?

Clinton's number is not in the phone book or even in Yellow Pages. He has a praetorian guard, shields aloft, fifteen men thick, specifically employed to stop chancers like me getting near his wallet or even speaking to the former Saviour of the Free World.

So I'm reading his autobiography, looking for chinks in his armour. I'll let you know when I find one.

But how has it come to this, begging for crumbs from the great man's table? Why have I made nothing of my own life? Why am I still *here*, in Oxford, amongst the throng of performance poets, Readers in Sanskrit, Inklings tour-guides and literary festival minders? I should be out in the real world by now, not still dossing down in my father's end-of-terrace box-plot. My contemporaries are hedge-fund managers, SEO specialists, online poker players, even captains of actual industry. They escaped from the arms of Morpheus, from the suckling security of their alma mater. But I was too conservative, too risk-averse, too *English*!

And now look at me. My hair has receded faster than a polar glacier. I have the precise combination of genes that makes you resemble a gauche 15-year-old virgin at 25 but a paunchy 52-year-old librarian at 26, omitting 37 years of masculine nubility in the blink of an eye. If only I had thought to take a selfie in my evanescent prime, I could have propped up my eHarmony profile for a year or two but, as it is, my mugshot is only of interest to short-sighted divorcees aged 45-51 and I'm not quite that desperate yet.

Or am I? I did snag a date with a steatopygous hottie back in August, amazed that such a vision of 27-year-old loveliness could think it worth the effort of contacting me. I arranged to meet Megan for lunch on the verandah at the Trout, amongst the peacocks and the Chinese Morse groupies and there she was, a barely-recognisable wrinkly version of the photo over which I had salivated. 27? She looked 54. She may have been hot in 1990 but even 30 seconds in the microwave would not have been enough to warm her up now.

"So here I am once more," she said as I brought the drinks and some teeth-jarring kettle crisps, "in the playground of the broken hearts …"

I almost dropped her white wine spritzer.

"Marillion! *Script for a Jester's Tear!*"

"Looks like we've got something in common," she smiled. And so we had. We dissected 'Grendel', the 18-minute B-side of Marillion's first single, a version of the Old English epic *Beowulf* from the monster's point of view. In an unguarded moment, Megan admitted buying the original single and seeing Fish & co play as market square heroes in Aylesbury.

"So you're not actually 27?" I mumbled, as if surprised.

"No. I'm 49. Is that a problem?"

I was beginning to feel that it wasn't. Women my own age have rarely heard of Marillion, let alone the prog rock titans that dominate my own playlists. Megan's knowledge of prog's heyday in the early 70s was rather sketchy so I regaled her at length with tales of Egg playing Bach's Fugue in D-minor as the warm-up for Black Sabbath and the uneasy mix of Lewis and Tolkien mythologies on *Olias of Sunhillow*. It was the best date I'd had all summer and I was beginning to warm to the idea of being Megan's toyboy, if she'd have me.

"If Fish and Egg had ever teamed up," I quipped, "they would have called themselves Kedgeree."

We swapped piscatorial puns while the peacocks went for their siesta and the date drew to its natural conclusion.

"What if I got some tickets for the Greenslade tour?" I dared to suggest.

"A nice idea, but no, Alex."

"No to Greenslade, or no to …"

"I'm sorry, Alex. You're not quite what I was looking for."

"But …"

The lines round her eyes cracked a little wider as she tried to break it to me gently.

"Don't take it the wrong way," she whispered at last. "But I guess I was looking for someone, well, a little more young at heart."

It will not surprise you to hear that there is no romantic tryst for me tonight. Instead, Dad and I spend Friday evening trying to get interested in the England-Scotland game, despite the complete absence of any Black Cats on the pitch. But why should there be? Sunderland are yet again bottom of the Premier League and in complete disarray. We reminisce on the Gus Poyet days when by some fluke we reached the League Cup Final and even won at Stamford Bridge. But Poyet was sacked and now the club is sinking almost as fast as I am.

Saturday 12 November 2016

Shipwrecked, glad to say? (1, 5, 3)

Megan was right. I am old at heart. I am utterly out of sync with my own generation. While my contemporaries were out clubbin' and dropping tabs, I was watching BBC4 and practising my chipping. Yes, I play *golf*, a game that has been terminally naff for half a century. I have spent much of today hacking my way round Frilford's Blue Course in the rain with a bunch of septuagenarians. I will let you off a hole-by-hole account.

Have I aged prematurely? Still, I seem to have eschewed most of the annoying affectations of my peers. For instance, I never once wore those low-slung bum-revealing trousers so beloved of my peer group. I'd like to think I have never used the word "like" as a random phatic utterance mid-sentence. I have never owned a smart-phone. I even declined to carry a Stone Age pay-as-you-go mobile until very recently – in that respect, I may have been the last remaining refusenik aged 4-40 in Britain.

I wear slippers about the house in the evening and good thick stripey pyjamas in bed. I have developed an unhealthy interest in Victoria Coren Mitchell. I am unapologetically progeric. If I am to die on 30th December, perhaps it is because I have lived out my natural lifespan, like one of those poor kids with Werner Syndrome destined to look and feel like a 75-year old when they are 15.

In a moment of madness, I even secretly voted Conservative in the 2015 General Election, an act that is surely unthinkable for any normal person under the age of 50. I occasionally catch myself wondering whether I should be putting money into some sort of pension. Knowing what I do, would it be ethical to take out a massive life insurance policy? If only I could think of some suitable beneficiaries …

But the biggest gulf of all has been in musical taste. Most people, I am sure, form an indelible attachment to the sounds to which they are exposed at fifteen and continue to listen to that music for the rest of their lives. But while my friends were falling under the spell of *Elephant* and *Absolution*, I had no time for their callow twaddle, still less for the likes of Coldplay and Linkin Park. I was already in thrall to the music of an earlier generation. I had discovered the Golden Age of British Music which stretches from the release of *Sergeant Pepper* in 1967 to *Wish You Were Here* in 1975. If not my America, it was certainly my new-found land and I have lived there quite happily ever since.

So once I am out of my sodden golf-gear and tonight's steak-and-kidney pie is in the oven, I turn to Procul Harum's *A Salty Dog* and relax in the gentle currents of that magnificent Coleridgean narrative:

> We sailed for parts unknown to man where ships come home to die.
> No lofty peak, nor fortress bold could match our captain's eye.
> Upon the seventh seasick day, we made our port of call,
> A sand so white, and sea so blue, no mortal place at all.

Tuesday 15 November 2016

Agreement about unfinished version or passage, to a degree? (10)

Things to do before I die:

1. Spend the night with Marie-Claire Goodwin …

Ah, Marie-Claire … sigh. Jet black hair, jet black eyes. (Yes, I know eyes can't really be black, it's just a *trompe l'oeil*). A slim, wiry, almost boyish figure. The way she sips her muscadet and inspects a canapé says don't mess with me, you muthas. Not that there are many muthas, as such, in the Univ SCR tonight.

Univ? That's short for University College, Oxford, the oldest and finest of the Dark Blues' educational establishments. Balliol and Merton may dispute Univ's claim to primacy, but Univ was founded by William of Durham in 1249, some years before those upstarts were even conceived. William hailed from Sedgefield, not too many miles from my own birthplace. For most of the last 700 years, it was a sleepy finishing school for the Durham gentry but during the twentieth century it reinvented itself as something of an intellectual powerhouse, home to such figures as C.S. Lewis, Stephen Hawking and Andrew Motion. It became a hotbed of left-wing politics – Clement Attlee, Harold Wilson, Bob Hawke, et al – and the Beveridge Report which was to change Britain's social landscape in the post-war period was written in the Master's Lodgings in 1942. Univ is definitely no Porterhouse – it is a cosmopolitan meritocracy of quite frightening intensity. Heaven's breath certainly smells wooingly here.

So how on earth did I get in? Maybe the Durham heritage still counts for something after all. And I wasn't a *complete* failure when I got here. Undergraduate life suited me quite well. It was only after I graduated in 2008 that life took a downward turn. I started an M.Litt. with the best of intentions (on the influence of St Teresa of Avila on Victorian literary culture) but somehow never got the nod to turn it into a doctorate. Most theses are exercises in nit-picking but perhaps there simply weren't enough nits to pick in my tiny niche. The years went by and I even sleepwalked my way through a PGCE year in Norham Road and tried my hand at TEFL before acknowledging my own utter pedagogical incompetence and fear of the classroom. In the darkest days I stacked a few shelves in Iceland before Phil suggested there might be a little part-time work available in my alma mater's Development Office. So here I am once more ...

Tonight we are gathered in the Senior Common Room for the formal announcement of the Annual Fund total. My boss, the gloriously monikered Vladimir Lebedev, is bigging it up for all he's worth:

"... and this year's donor participation total, 31% of all alumni, places us once again in first place in the world rankings ..."

Eat dust, Harvard. Put that in your pipe, Sorbonne, and smoke it.

"...further testament to the warm regard that almost all Univ Old Members feel for their *alma mater* and to the astonishing dedication of my colleagues, without whom ...."

I'd like to take the credit, really I would. But having only been part of the Development Fund team for six weeks, my meagre efforts to date come too late to figure. So far my persuasive charms have earned pledges totalling 20 dollars. My boss, Mr Lebedev, AKA Vlad the Impaler to his many admirers, has trained me up as a phone-pest. Find out what you have in common, he advises me, and build on that. Do not discuss either Iraq War or Trump's buffoonery. Do not mimic their southern drawls or ask whether they are a member of the Ku Klux Klan. Vlad the Impaler is quite clear in his demands, if not his marketing jargon....

"...our propagation planning continues apace and our transmedia storytelling is second to none. The challenge, as ever, is to humanize the brand through actionable analytics and omnichannel ideation..."

Lebedev drones on but at last the back-slapping is over and I sidle surreptitiously over to what I hope is Marie-Claire's blind spot, sending a couple of rickety Old Norse professors tumbling to the threadbare carpet in the process. Marie-Claire turns her coal-black eyes on the carnage.

"This is no time for a re-enactment of the Battle of Maldon!" I jest. And Marie-Claire very nearly sniggers. I could be in here ...

"Hello, I don't think we've been formally introduced, my name's Alex," I offer lamely. Marie-Claire shows no sign of recalling any of our carefully engineered brief encounters to date.

"No, I don't think we have. I'm Marie Claire. Pleased to meet you, Alex."

I scour my addled pate for some sort of inspiration.

"What did you make of that ... speech?"

The question almost dies on my lips but Marie-Claire seems content to catch the ball and run with it.

"I just *love* that accent!" she gushes. "Is he Russian, do you know?"

"I believe so."

"I come over all *Fish Called Wanda*-ish when I hear a Russian accent."

"Gosh. I'm half-Russian myself."

The words are out of my mouth before I can stop myself. I am not even slightly Russian. The nearest I have been to St Petersburg is Seaton Carew Golf Links. Marie Claire looks as though she is waiting for me to declaim a chapter or two of *War and Peace*, Cyrillic script and all.

"... although I don't actually *speak* much Russian," I add hurriedly. "It's just that my mother was a Russian princess, fallen on hard times. So I am technically a prince."

Marie-Claire almost chokes on her asparagus vol-au-vent.

"And, don't tell me, your family lost out during the revolution?"

"Alas so," I sigh. "One day I'm hoping to reclaim the family dominions near Omsk and, er, Tomsk."

"Omsk *and* Tomsk?"

"Yes, they say you can walk all the way from Omsk to Tomsk without leaving land once owned by the Hoggatov dynasty."

Hoggatov? Where on earth did that one come from? And *dominions*? I can't believe she's buying any of this.

"What, like St John's College, Oxford and St John's College, Cambridge."

"No, that's just an urban myth," I scoff. "The Hoggatovs were richer than the tsar himself not so long ago."

"Well, Prince Alexy, you *must* tell me all about it some time."

She turns to go as if a genome is in urgent need of TLC back at the lab.

"I must, I must ..." I'm floundering desperately now, but what have I got to lose? "Perhaps Thursday evening ... I ... I just happen to have tickets for the screening of *Anastasia* ..."

19

"The pop star on *Strictly*? Or do you mean Anastasia Romanov?"

"The very same. A distant relative of mine, in fact," I assure her confidently.

Some other lines from *Macbeth* keep sloshing round my brain:

> I am in blood
> Stepp'd in so far that, should I wade no more,
> Returning were as tedious as go o'er.

How can I backtrack now? I must *be* Prince Alexy. Still, at least I have bought myself some time to research the part properly.

Thursday 17 November 2016

Make wingless noble tiger (6)

So here we are at the Phoenix Picturehouse (formerly known as the Scala and Studio X) in Jericho watching a screening of Kenneth MacMillan's 1971 ballet, *Anastasia*, as revived by the Royal Ballet at Covent Garden. It's not as bad as you would think – the combination of rippling muscle and Romanov opulence is oddly engaging even for a ballet first-timer like me. *Anastasia* tells the story of Tsar Nicholas II's youngest daughter who may (or may not) have survived the Yekaterinburg purge of July 1918.

Natalia Osipova plays Anastasia/Anna Anderson as she tortures herself in an asylum with memories of her gilded childhood and her family's annihilation. MacMillan's ballet was written long before Anna Anderson's death and the discovery that her DNA did not match Anastasia's at all but it does not matter that she was a fraud of sorts – her psychodrama is every bit as powerful if the disturbing "memories" of Rasputin & co are just figments of her deranged imagination.

Perhaps Anna Anderson started in the same way as me, making up a story to impress her gullible friends? Perhaps I too will end up in a padded cell, gibbering wildly about my family's lost splendour. But everyone tells a few white lies to impress the opposite sex, don't they? It makes a change from claiming to be a black belt at jiu-jitsu.

It is the second interval and Marie-Claire and I are enjoying our complimentary thimble of nalivka and the time for pleasantries has passed – Prince Alexy must tell his story.

"My great-grandmother, Princess Irina, was once good friends with Anna Pavlova," I confide. "Or so she told me. Mind you, she was 93 at the time. She and the great ballerina used to go to fancy dress balls in London in the years before the First World War. Irina was a second cousin of the tsar and she married into the Hoggatov family, the richest in all Russia."

"What, richer than the Romanovs?" Marie-Claire asks, pretending to play along with this Walter Mitty figure she has unwittingly agreed to spend the evening with.

"So they say. Think Roman Abramovic and multiply by about a hundred. *That* rich. But it counted for nothing in the Revolution."

"Did your family lose everything?"

"They were lucky to escape with their lives, I think. They jumped on a boat out of Yalta with a few Rembrandts, a clutch of Fabergé eggs, and baby Alexy under their arms.

"Baby Alexy?"

"My grandfather."

"Alexy Hoggatov? You're not thinking of Anastasia's brother, Alexy the haemophiliac?"

Marie-Claire's eyes glitter momentarily. Fortunately, I had anticipated the question.

"Just a coincidence, that. Hoggatov is a name familiar to every Russian, especially amongst the nobility. So Alexy Hoggatov was like John Smith here."

"Is that so?"

"Of course, the name got anglicised somewhat once the family settled in London. It was Hoff for a while but that still didn't sound English enough…"

"So you decided to go the whole hog? The whole Hogg!"

I feel obliged to chuckle.

"We did indeed. It's not the most glamorous of surnames. I was born in England but my father felt some kind of atavistic draw to St Petersburg and he managed to wangle a posting there from this engineering company he worked for. The Old Hoggatov palace had been turned into apartments by now, so my parents rented one of those and I was brought up in one corner of the ancestral home."

"Gosh, how romantic!"

I am not sure she believes one far-fetched word of this but what have I got to lose? At the very least, I may gain some credit for the quality of my story-telling.

"… although almost all of the family wealth had gone by now, they were determined that I should be brought up as a prince. I had my own private tutors who instilled in me a love of books which has stayed with me to the present day. There was a surprisingly big expat community in St Petersburg and I was out skating one day with a young English friend on a frozen tributary of the great River Neva when I fell through the ice and almost drowned. My ankle was severely broken and I have never fully recovered the use of my left foot."

"But you walk perfectly normally …"

"Years of physiotherapy," I sigh. "My parents pooled together every penny of their savings and sent me on a Grand Tour round Europe – Greece Italy, Switzerland, France, everywhere."

"What, all by yourself?"

"No, I had this tutor, more of a minder really, a Monsieur Gothon. He saved me from a lot of scrapes such as when I feel in love with a French girl called Rosalie with the most extraordinary eyes."

Marie-Claire's extraordinary eyebrows rise at this revelation but she does nothing to disturb the flow of my picaresque novella.

"How I loved those eyes! But then I was kidnapped by a religious cult…"

More raised eyebrows.

"No, it's true. The e-Lutherans – an obscure fundamentalist sect for the digital age. I can't think what I saw in them. Their mission was to spam the entire world with the Apocryphal Gospel According to St Thomas. This was the early days of spam, you understand."

"I don't remember finding anything in my InBox …"

"It was in the original Coptic."

"The Sahidic or the Bohairic dialect?" Marie-Claire flutters her eyelashes encouragingly. I am suitably disconcerted.

"I'm not entirely sure …" (Surely this Intermission has gone on rather too long?) "The Sahidic, I think. They wanted me for my knowledge of bandwidths and IFP protocols, not for my ability to transliterate Coptic script."

"I'm not sure Martin Luther would have approved of such an enterprise!"

"It was as if I had temporarily taken leave of my senses, brainwashed by the charismatic leader of the sect, the e-Lutherarch, as he styled himself…"

Where is this coming from? I honestly have no idea. I confess I'd googled a few terms ("loony sects", etc) but most of this is plucked from nowhere. Even I'm impressed.

"I'll tell you all about the weird initiation rites some other time," I promise. "Anyway, the proverbial scales eventually fell from my eyes and I began to feel trapped within this commune of evangelical spammers. Were we all heading for some sort of Waco-style dénouement, I fretted? I felt I needed to take some sort of drastic action …"

But by now the cinematograph is whirring up again, the familiar sounds of Tchaikovsky have given way to some weird stuff by Bohuslav Martinů and Ms Osipova is off again. The rest of my story can wait till who knows when. Marie-Claire sits back in her threadbare mock-velvet bucket seat to lose herself in the spectacle once more. I feel high on a heady mix of nalivka and adrenaline, a king for a day.

Friday 18 November 2016

Queens, perhaps, or old king admitting member (7)

You may have spotted one of my more annoying afflictions, a compulsion to turn ordinary everyday words and phrases into cryptic crossword clues. Please don't take any notice unless you are a fellow-sufferer. It's the legacy of a lifetime spent solving the *Guardian* crossword. There is a strange and terrible beauty to the perfect crossword clue and the English language offers extraordinary opportunities for the compulsive cruciverbalist.

Anagrams are a particular joy. Who does not feel a thrill on discovering that "schoolmaster" is an anagram of "the classroom", for instance? Or experience a moment of exquisite pleasure on learning that West Ham United are leaving Upton Park for "the new stadium", trying to keep pace with Manchester City, the "synthetic cream" of the Premiership? The Old Vicarage, Grantchester is an anagram of "chaste Lord Archer, vegetating" – who'd've thought it? The late, great Araucaria, actually. A novel by a Scottish writer? By anagrammatic miracle, *Ivanhoe* by Sir Walter Scott, of course!

Some people don't feel alive in the morning until they've had a bowl of Fruit'n'Fibre and five mugs of strong coffee. But I'm not truly up and running until the last *Guardian* clue has been solved. Vlad the Impaler's exhortations can wait.

Each of my blogs kicks off with a cryptic clue. Fellow *Guardianistas* will find them all too easy but for the less cruciverbally inclined, I have included the answer within the blog. Enjoy!

My office – well, more of a cubby-hole, actually – is located at the top of Staircase 3 on the NW side of Univ's Main (or Front) Quad. My "working" environment has one notable feature, a west-facing window overlooking the dome of the Shelley Memorial and, beyond that, a section of the High as it curves gently past All Souls and potters towards Carfax.

The domed room, in which Ford's iconic sculpture of the drowned Shelley is housed, was itself designed by Basil Champneys, the great Victorian architect. It echoes the dome of the Radcliffe Camera, 150 yards away, also just visible from my desk. Down on the pavement I see crocodiles of Oriental tourists clicking away with their i-phones, mostly in front of the blue plaque which commemorates the fact that Robert Boyle and Robert Hooke once invented modern Physics on this very spot.

Shelley, of course, dreamed of following in Boyle and Hooke's footsteps as he transformed his undergraduate rooms (in Staircase 1, just above the SCR), into a Chemistry lab, fitting it out with an argand lamp, a rudimentary machine for generating static electricity and any number of noxious chemicals which the long-haired hell-raiser would splash around with careless abandon, prior to his expulsion from the college in March 1811.

Shelley, like me, knew that he would drown one day – you see this conviction in the last lines of *Adonais*, for instance. A defiant non-swimmer, he nonetheless became a keen sailor in later life, making his tiny racing boat, the *Don Juan*, as unseaworthy as possible. On 8th July 1822, there was a great storm over the Gulf of Spezia (probably *not* caused by one of his rain-producing kites) and the self-fulfilling prophecy took no one by surprise.

I shall make no such mistakes. I'm a competent swimmer, covering ten lengths of the old council pool in Gateshead on one memorable occasion, and I have absolutely no intention of setting out to sea in a pea-green boat. If I am to be drowned on 30th December, then death must come to meet me – I will not walk willingly into the icy waves.

My death waits … and I have only 42 days left now. 42 days to discover the meaning of life …

Such thoughts make it difficult to focus on my pedestrian day-job twisting the arms of plutocrats and alumni-turned-drug-barons. In fact, most of my 'prospects' prove to be ordinary folk struggling to pay their medical bills, never mind fund a fellowship or cough up for some new laundry facilities. I hear more tales of abject penury than obscene wealth, and requests for payday loans are by no means rare in the Development Office – naturally, we plead poverty and ring off as quickly as possible.

But I have plans. Perhaps the college's most notorious recent alumnus, Bill Clinton has a net worth of $80 million according to various conservative sources. Surely he can bear to part with just one of his millions for his English *alma mater*? Good luck with that one, my colleagues whisper, especially after *that* election result, but I like a challenge. I have the phone number of the Clinton Foundation in New York and another one for Clinton's own office in West 125th Street – perhaps he is there trying to unpick the Parental Lock on his wife's prized e-mail collection as we speak.

None of my colleagues is back from lunch and I have the office to myself. Gazing at the roof of the Shelley Memorial for inspiration, I key in the necessary digits. Amazingly, there is no recorded message and a reassuring female voice reaches me from across the pond, perhaps borne aloft by a Shelleyan kite:

"Bill Clinton's office – how may I help you?"

"Could you put me through to Bill, please?" Well, you never know, do you?

"I'm sorry, sir. Mr Clinton is not in the office at the moment. What is it concerning?"

"It's a private matter, actually. I'm calling from University College, Oxford. In England," I add, helpfully.

"Perhaps I could take a message for Mr Clinton? Or maybe I could put you through to one of his aides?"

I consider the matter for a moment.

"Yes, I think that might suffice," I say graciously at last.

"Very well, I'll put you through to Hank Mize, one of Mr Clinton's personal aides, if you wouldn't mind holding ..."

After a few beeps I am assailed by a basso profundo Southern drawl:

"Hank Mize ..."

"Ah, Mr Mize, my name is Alex Hogg. I was hoping to catch Bill for a few moments. Yes, I appreciate he is not in the office. I'm calling from his old college in England."

"You want some money?"

I am somewhat taken aback by the acuity of his judgement but I take a breath and plough on regardless.

"No, not at all. It's just that his alma mater is planning to introduce a Fellowship in International Law and it seemed only appropriate that Mr Clinton should have the opportunity to be associated with it in some way."

"So you want some money."

"I ... I ..."

"I'm afraid that is extremely unlikely, Mr Hogg. Mr Clinton has many calls on his funds."

"I don't think he attended *that* many colleges in his youth!"

"... and all his charitable works are channelled through the Clinton Foundation."

"Indeed. I am only seeking a few seconds of his time."

"And what would you say in those few seconds?"

I rack my brains desperately. Absolutely nothing springs to mind. In the end, I have to say *something* and I'm not sure it has quite the desired reassuring effect.

"I'd like to talk about what really happened in his Oxford days."

There is a transatlantic silence that is beyond stony. Hank Mize's words are tinged with permafrost:

"Very well, Mr Hogg, I will pass that message on to the President ... I mean, to Mr Clinton. Good day."

And, with that, the call is terminated. I was way out of my depth there, not waving but drowning. I need hardly add that the Fellowship in International Law has about the same substance as the Fellowship of the Ring.

I am at a critical stage of Level 14 of Candy Crush Saga when my deskphone rings ... no, it couldn't be, could it?

"Development Office, Alex Hogg speaking ..."

"Alex, how're you doing? Bill Clinton calling from the Big Apple."

Either this is a very good impressionist on the line or I really am talking to the 42nd US President. I surprise myself with the faculty of speech.

"I'm well, Bill. How are you?"

"I'm good. My friend Hank here tells me that you are keen to talk about my time at University College. Now why would that be I wonder?"

Why indeed?

"Did he tell you about the Fellowship in International Law?"

"You'd like a *donation*, I imagine ..."

"Well ..."

"What sort of donation are we talking about?"

This is not something I have discussed with colleagues or even thought about. Still, nothing ventured, nothing gained ...

"Somewhere in the low seven figures?" I croak. Amazingly, there is no sound of transatlantic laughter.

"The low seven figures. I see. How low?"

"Oh, quite low. Given a suitable investment strategy, that would fund a fellowship or even a chair in perpetuity." I really am winging it now.

"No doubt. And what can you offer me in return, Alex?"

"Well, that's something we would need to discuss, I guess."

What can we offer him apart from his name on someone's door? It's not exactly a *quid pro quo*.

"It so happens I'm going to be in England on 8ᵗʰ December. I might be able to find a little time in my schedule …"

For some reason I decide to play hard to get.

"The 8ᵗʰ, let me see … that's actually the day of the Alumni Golf Tournament. I doubt if I can …"

"The Alumni Golf Tournament? Perfect! Are you playing yourself, Alex?"

"*Playing* would probably be too strong a word for what I do, but …"

"Put me down for the same tee-time. We can have a quiet word about the terms of this *donation* then."

What???? I am so lost for words, it appears likely that I will never again recover the power of speech. Fortunately, Bill has hung up anyway. I am to play golf with the former leader of the Free World. Perhaps my life will acquire some belated meaning after all?

Monday 21 November 2016

Cures numberless strokes (6)

It has been raining solidly for two days and Osney Island has become one large puddle. Storm Angus has been battering the country although Oxford has escaped lightly so far. I spend a hard day in the Development Office trying to pluck up the college to call Marie-Claire, but I want to postpone the inevitable rejection for as long as possible. The credits had barely begun to roll on *Anastasia* when she was out of the Phoenix and back in the lab to torture some unsuspecting gerbils. There was not so much as a peck on the cheek goodbye. Even I can read the signs.

Bostar Hall is one of Univ's secret treasures, a fusty first-floor meeting room which is only accessible through a maze of staircases and corridors. From Staircase 11 on the Radcliffe Quad, you can take the imitation Bridge of Sighs over Logic Lane and into Durham Buildings. Hacking your way east at first floor level, you eventually reach the vast door to Bostar Hall, a soundproofed and chilly room, looking out over the High St above a charity shop. No one knows who Bostar was or why a hall should be named after him. The college lets it out by the hour to its members for a pittance.

So here we are in Bostar Hall, bashing out a passable version of 'Sympathy for the Devil'. It's not the easiest of Stones numbers to replicate because so much of the familiar sound depends on the piano, the tom-toms and the whoo-whoo backing vocals. GDP is a lot more comfortable playing straight three-chord blues-rock ('Satisfaction', 'Paint it Black', etc) so this is more of a challenge. Ozzie Kay, Univ's Junior Associate Fellow in Eng Lit, is passable (indeed O. Kay) on the keyboards and I have just about got the hang of the chord structure for the bass-line, EDAE, repeated 4 times; then for the 'Pleased to meet you' bit, it's BBE, DAE. Even I can plod through that lot and just about keep time with Rick the Porter on drums. Fast Eddie Prince, AKA Stig Strum, noodles away on lead guitar while Phil struts his Jaggeresque stuff for a notional audience of rock chicks and record company executives:

> I stuck around St. Petersburg when I saw it was time for a change.
> I killed the Tsar and his ministers, Anastasia screamed in vain.
> I rode a tank, held a general's rank, when the blitzkrieg raged and

the bodies stank.

Pleased to meet you, hope you guess my name, but what's puzzling you is the nature of my game?

I watched with glee while your kings and queens fought for ten decades for the gods they made.
I shouted out "Who killed the Kennedys?", when after all it was you and me …

Obviously, the Stones' certainty about Anastasia's fate did not deter Kenneth MacMillan!

I have been deputed to add in the whoo-whoos as we go along and so far I have been well short of ept. If GDP is to become a Stones tribute band, we have a long way to go before we should lay our laurels at the feet of the masters.

"Remind me, who did kill the Kennedys?" asks Stig when we have collapsed in a cacophonous heap. "Was it really us?"

"Well," says Phil, "JFK was shot by someone called Oswald and we do have an Oswald in the band, don't we, Ozzie?"

"Guilty as charged," confirms our ginger-haired keyboard maestro. "We Oswalds have been a pretty nasty lot down the years."

"Oswald Mosley?" I suggest.

"Ye-es. It was all Shakespeare's fault. He invented the prototype Oswald, Goneril's "serviceable villain", sent to kill Gloucester, but failing miserably, as you will recall from 'I am the Walrus'. We Oswalds have been assassins and would-be assassins ever since. Lee Harvey Oswald is the last in a long line. Fascinating character – did you know that as a young man, he taught himself Russian and defected to the USSR after a long and arduous trip across Europe, aged nineteen, all because he sympathised with Marxist ideology?"

"So did the Russians pay him to go back to America and shoot the President?"

"Possibly. Or maybe it was his own private project – we will never know."

Ozzie takes another slurp from a can of Boddington's before continuing.

"And the next most famous assassination in the history of mankind was also the handiwork of an Oswald!"

We consider this proposition for a few seconds.

"Martin Luther King?" suggests Rick from behind his drum-kit.

"No!" snorts Ozzie derisively. "Rasputin!"

"Hang on a sec," says Phil. "Wasn't Rasputin murdered by one of Univ's most distinguished alumni, Prince Felix Yusupov, and a bunch of Russian aristos?"

"That's what Yusupov would have us believe, but most of the historical evidence points to a rather different conclusion. The man who fired the fatal bullet which did for the Mad Monk was almost certainly an Englishman called Oswald Rayner."

"Is all this strictly relevant to band practice?" Stig enquires. "We're paying 50p an hour for the use of this room …"

"Yusupov and his friends were so effete and inbred, they barely knew which end to hold a gun," Ozzie lectures us patiently. "They tried to poison Rasputin with cyanide in the Madeira and home-made cakes but, when that failed, they didn't have a clue. Rasputin escaped into the grounds of Yusupov's Moika Palace, pursued by the hapless gentry. But the bullet which finally killed the bearded madman could only have been fired by an English army service revolver."

"Your friend Oswald, concealed behind a grassy knoll?"

"Behind a snowdrift, perhaps. It's pretty cold in St Petersburg in mid-winter."

"As Alex might confirm," Phil observes, with a knowing wink in my direction. I am suitably discombobulated, but Ozzie does not notice.

"Oswald Rayner and Prince Felix were close friends from Oxford days. Who knows, they may have met in this very room at the inaugural meeting of the Russian Society, set up by Yusupov in 1909. Young Oswald was studying French and German and I guess he had taught himself a little Russian. They were close friends, maybe more, and Yusupov invited him to stay in St Petersburg. When war broke out, Rayner's Russian was pretty good and he was recruited by the Secret Service Bureau, the forerunner of MI6, then posted to St Petersburg, presumably because of the Yusupov connection."

"Why would someone like Rayner want to kill Rasputin?" Stig asks.

"With Tsar Nicholas away at the Eastern front, Russia was being run by the Empress Alexandra, a German, and the sinister Rasputin. They both favoured making peace with Germany and carving up the old Austro-Hungarian and Ottoman empires between them. If so, all the German troops deployed on the Eastern Front would be moved west. With double the manpower, Germany would win the war. Thus it seemed vital to British interests that Rasputin was eliminated."

31

"Did it work?"

"I should say so. Rayner "stuck around St Petersburg", as Jagger puts it, trying to get Yusupov and his pals to do his dirty work for him. Rasputin was picked off in the grounds of the Moika Palace, Alexandra's power was compromised and Russia carried on fighting on the Eastern Front just long enough for the Yanks to join in on the Allies' side."

"So why has nobody heard of your Oswald from Oxford?"

"Rayner was successful not only in shooting the Mad Monk but also in dodging the bullet of personal or national responsibility. Yusupov was determined to take all the credit or blame himself. Ten years later, he wrote a lurid 250-page account of Rasputin's murder and omitted to mention Rayner at all. He even got Rayner himself to do the English translation!"

"So, not just the most effective British spy of all time, but also the most self-effacing?"

"Yes, after the war, he became the *Times*' correspondent in Finland, called his only son John Felix and, when he died in Botley, he took his secret with him to the grave."

"A stirring tale, Ozzie. No wonder they made you President of the Russian Society. Any further assassinations planned?"

"I think I could murder a couple more Stones' standards and then we should call it a night."

"*I* have a cunning plan, actually," says Phil. "I've been talking to a friend who's on the sub-committee that runs the University Parks. They let the parks be used for all sorts of stuff. How about we recreate the Stones in Hyde Park from July 1969? Here, in the Parks, this July coming?"

"I can think of about thirty-seven reasons why not," says Stig, "the first one being we're nowhere near good enough."

"Then it's something to work towards. We'd headline the show but it wouldn't just be us – the other bands who played in Hyde Park that day could also be represented. Rick and I went to see the Twenty-First Century Schizoid Men at the O$_2$ the other week, and they were brilliant. They played the whole of 'In the Court of the Crimson King'."

"Way out of our league," Rick sighs. "We don't even have a *name* for our band."

"Yes, we do. We are the Strolling Dons. Unless you can think of something better ..."

"The Stoning Trolls? Or the Strolling Ones?" I suggest, "if we want a more accurate Spoonerism."

"You know what ..." Stig intervenes, "I'm not sure the general public would get the joke."

"Of course they would," Phil insists. "The right logo, the right image, and you're there. Saturday the 8th is the weekend date closest to the anniversary of the real thing in 1969," Phil explains.

"The Strolling Clones? Wouldn't that work better?" Stig suggests. "Except I think they already exist. If we play in France, we could call ourselves the Gaulstones ..."

"How about we go with Bill Wyman's Rhythm Kings?" I suggest. My co-conspirators barely raise a snort of derision.

Rick seems more impressed with Phil's absurd idea than the others:

"A free all-day love-in? I'd be up for it, lumbago permitting!"

"We'll need to look the part," Phil continues. "I'll dress up as Shelley in a frilly white tunic and recite *Adonais*. Shelley himself drowned on 8th July, of course, so it's the 195th anniversary of that too. We'll need a Marianne Faithfull lookalike and a Marsha Hunt lookalike to sit in the front row and exchange jealous glances."

Stig is warming to the idea at last.

"In terms of publicity, we just need one of us to drown in his swimming pool a couple of days before the event. Any volunteers?"

Everyone laughs but me. I think of pointing out that one of us will indeed have drowned but it will probably be six months too early to have a material effect on the attendance. We play a couple more songs in desultory fashion before Rick has to go off for his night shift. I catch Phil on his way out into Cecily's Court and we head up to his teaching room in 83, High St.

"What was that about me knowing what the weather was like in St Petersburg?" I ask casually.

"I'm sure you would, Alex. Or, should I say, *Prince* Alexy?"

"Prince? Where did you get that from?"

"Marie-Claire was very impressed with your storytelling abilities, I can tell you!"

"She told you?"

"Sorry, was it a secret? I'm afraid that Marie-Claire and I have no secrets from each other."

"You're …"

"That's right. We've been seeing each other for a few weeks now. I think she could be the one, Alex!"

Cecily's Court is deserted. Picking up a large stone from the rockery and smashing it over our lead singer's head has its merits. Being disappointingly British, I try to reason with him instead.

"You said that about Hattie. You *married* Hattie! Was she not 'the one'?"

"Marie-Claire is so much more … sophisticated! Please be happy for me."

Happy? My world has just ended. Ah well, it was due to end in forty days anyway. Why should I care? Phil does not notice my pain.

"Talking of Hattie, she's still missing, you know."

"What about the kids?" I ask.

"Her ghastly sister, Liz, is looking after them."

"Shouldn't they be with their father?"

Phil does not even deign to register this low blow.

"Hattie'll turn up," he insists. "She's *got* to turn up …"

Tuesday 22 November 2016

Grinder crowd (4)

Philip Sherborne and I go back a long way. We were part of the same cohort of Univ English (Language & Literature) students who matriculated ten years ago. Those first few weeks at university are pivotal to the lives of so many young people, especially in social terms – that's when we tend to fall in with the kindred spirits who will turn out to be lifelong friends. But my first impressions of Phil were not that promising. He was tall, lithe, good-looking, with an unruly mop of light brown hair, an aquiline nose that hinted at a patrician background and a surprisingly high-pitched voice which he was unafraid to use in those early seminars and tutorials. He had the sort of confidence that a public school background unfailingly generates.

Phil was everything that I was not. I am what ageing female relatives would describe as "big boned" and others would call "squat". At eighteen, my face bore the stigmata of acne while Phil was fresh-skinned, almost cherubic. I was a proud product of the state school system, brought up to disparage the privately-educated spawn of the idle rich. I lacked the confidence to say a word in those first-year seminars, sensing that my critical faculties were no match either for Phil or indeed any of the other six undergraduates in our year-group.

We knew from the first day that failure was not an option. Our tutor was a wild-eyed Glaswegian, the ageing *enfant terrible* of the English faculty, occupying the very rooms that Phil would one day inherit. Advancing years had not dulled Professor Roy Field's determination to *win*; that is, to gain more firsts (and, failing that, upper seconds) for Univ than any other college could muster in Mods and Finals. If only four out of eight came away with a first, then he would sulk for months at a time and redouble his efforts to school his young charges in the arcane arts of turning a answer into an . The difference between two such essays might be only a single percentage mark but the number of leading alphas you mustered would determine whether you reached the Promised Land of first class honours or not.

Our rite of passage was a first week essay for which we were required to read the collected prose works of Carlyle, JS Mill, Newman, Ruskin and Arnold to determine which, if any, of these grizzled pedants was "central" to early Victorian culture. Well, I don't know if you've tried reading *The Idea of a University*, *Sartor Resartus* or *The Stones of Venice*? I would defy anyone to read more than a page of any of these doorstops without descending into the deepest of comas, yet we were apparently required to read several thousand pages in a single week, then recite our carefully-honed *aperçus* not only in front of a mad Glaswegian, pacing up and down in rapt attention, but also a tutorial partner who, you sensed, had spent most of a gap year living it up in Venice, admiring the aforementioned stonework and ticking off the items on this first-week reading list between tupping the local beauties.

If this was sink or swim, I sank like one of Ruskin's stones. There was no letter in the Greek alphabet that corresponded with the incoherent slop that I somehow scribbled down at the end of a sleep-deprived first week in the groves of academe. Omega minus, perhaps. All I can remember now is that I mispronounced Jeremy Bentham's surname and got JS Mill hopelessly mixed up with his father. I started reading it out at 11.02 and, after an eternity of stuttering inanities, completed the job at 11.05. Professor Field had barely had time to complete four laps of the room.

"Is that *it*, Alexander?"

I had to concede that it was. I slumped a little deeper into my billet, a vast and sagging bean-bag.

"It was brief but …" I could see him desperately trying to locate some sort of redeeming feature. "*Promising*," he concluded, weakly. "Philip, perhaps we could have your thoughts on Victorian culture now?"

Phil, to his eternal credit, had refrained from smirking at any point in my ordeal. Looking back, I'm sure he must have been almost as terrified as I was but, if so, he did not show it. Before he had finished reading his first sentence, Roy was challenging his assumptions and assailing him with counter-examples. It took Phil more than fifteen minutes to complete his opening paragraph, such was the intensity of the cross-examination.

I wanted to dislike this Old Etonian so much and yet it was impossible to do so as he stood up bravely to this pre-planned bombardment. If Roy was trying to knock him down a peg or two, Phil had already mastered the tricky compromise between standing up for his opinions and deferring to the Scotsman's encyclopaedic knowledge of the turgid outpourings of these long-forgotten sages.

When the hour was up, Phil was no more than halfway through his magnum opus. I'm not sure he ever succeeded in finishing the recital of an essay during his whole time with Roy – Phil was a leading alpha man from first to last.

As we negotiated a safe exit from our bean-bags and stumbled out into Cecily's Court, the brash Etonian had some kind words for me:

"I'm sorry you got so little time in there."

"That's OK."

"I guess my rubbish essay rambled on too long and there was no time to go back to yours."

"That really is quite OK."

We went for lunch in hall together and found a surprising amount in common, notably a passion for football. Phil argued that the Italian *Serie A* was the strongest in Europe while I insisted that the German *Bundesliga* was as strong competitive as any. Soon we both joined the Martlets, the college literary society. (I note in passing that the Martlet Ensemble are performing Bach cantatas in Univ Hall tonight, but I shan't be there.)

I saw myself somewhat unimaginatively as Charles Ryder to Phil's Sebastian Flyte. I was in awe of his intellectual prowess and the ease with which he held down a place in the college 1ˢᵗ XI at both football and cricket, and grateful for the few crumbs of friendship that he threw my way. But there was no Brideshead to wrap me in its tendrils – Phil's family home was a surprisingly modest farmhouse with no more than ten bedrooms near Horsham. There were no quail's eggs or poetry-reading debauches. On a Saturday night, we would traipse round town looking for parties we could crash and Wednesday was squash night in the basement of the Goodhart Building. *Et in Arcadia ego*, indeed.

Once he fell in with Hattie, there was a slow but inevitable change in our relationship. To his credit, he tried to pair me off with his little sister, Beth, boarding at Roedean, but she was having none of that. I found few opportunities to hook up with the opposite sex. Oxford was no longer the monastic enclave it had once been, but there were still far more boys than girls and for a 'big-boned' Durham lad like me, the fairer sex was not exactly queuing round the block.

Hattie was still at school when she met Phil. Indeed, she was in the same year as Beth at a private establishment in Wimbledon and performing in the school play when the would-be Lothario first clapped eyes on her. Before long, she was staying over at weekends in college and I found myself parked in the college library when once I had been Phil's willing lineman. But I could hardly begrudge him his good fortune, as Hattie was a traffic-stoppingly beautiful young lady – long blonde hair, huge almond eyes, you know the sort of thing – all the more gorgeous because she was, at that age, utterly unaware of the effect she was having on the male population. In terms of sheer pulchritude, she was way out of Phil's league, and he knew it. But Hattie aspired to the sort of academic success that Phil had already achieved, and she looked up to him almost as much as a hero as boyfriend.

By the end of our first year in Oxford, that relationship was still in its infancy. It flowered in the hot summer of 2006, notably during a post-Mods holiday on Italy's Ligurian coastline. Phil's father had booked this huge villa in a coastal village called San Terenzo. With numerous spare bedrooms to fill, Phil had been encouraged to invite a few friends along. I was flattered to be invited – my idea of an exotic summer location was still a windswept Seaton Delaval, after all. Hattie's parents had forbidden their daughter to go (this was still in the school term) but, thanks to various subterfuges and the promise that she would occupy a single room, Hattie was somehow smuggled onto the plane to Pisa. Phil's younger sister, Beth, who had also just finished her GCSEs, was there, plus another old friend of Phil's from schooldays called Eddie Williamson whom we all ignored.

The Casa Magni was no ordinary holiday let. It was a gleaming white palace with seven arches at the front, looking out over the bluest sea I had ever seen. In front of us lay a beach of the most perfect golden sand, suitably occupied by the most elegant specimens of Italian pulchritude. I asked Phil what the house had cost but he just shrugged. His Dad's fees as a barrister were somewhere north of a thousand pounds an hour so this was just loose change.

At the front of the villa was a weather-beaten plaque. I jotted down the first two lines:

PERCY BYSSHE SHELLEY
CHE DA LIVORNO SE FRAGIL LEGMO VELEGGIANDO

but none of us had sufficient knowledge of the language to translate it. At the time I knew nothing of Shelley (our Mods course had mainly consisted of *Beowulf* and twentieth-century literature and very little in between). I was aware he was a distinguished old boy of my college but little more than that. Phil's Dad, whom we were instructed to call "Tom", said there had been no indication, when he booked the villa, that it had any literary associations. If Shelley had once been there, there was no other evidence of his occupation. There was not a single book on the palatial premises. The carpetless floors were made from vast chunks of Carrara marble and there were busts, urns, gilded mirrors and wall hangings aplenty.

The *nonni* of San Terenzo would take their morning constitutional in the warm Ligurian surf while we tucked into our breakfast cannoli bruschetta on the terrace that overlooked the neat strip of sand between the Casa Magni and the Castello di San Terenzo. Phil and I watched as Hattie and Beth frolicked in the almost waveless sea. Both girls were just short of their sixteenth birthdays but looked much younger than that – Beth in a rather frumpish one-piece that she had had since she was twelve and Hattie in a striking yellow bikini that showed off her athletic brown limbs.

The two girls seemed to be playing some sort of diving game, seeing who could stay under for longest. Beth surfaced after a few seconds but there was no sign of Hattie. The seconds ticked by and Phil leapt to his feet as if he would jump off the balcony and plunge into the water. It was clear that Beth could no longer see her companion and was becoming a little agitated herself. Then, as if in slow motion, a hand and then an arm emerged from the water and waved at the watching world before the rest of a giggling Hattie broke through the surface. She celebrated her victory and shook some of the brine out of her long, blonde locks. But Phil looked drained by the experience, as if he had seen a ghost.

Beth seemed strangely reluctant to mix with her brother and his friends, preferring the company of her parents. While they went for a long drive up into the Apuan Alps, the remaining foursome got up to as much mischief as possible. Even though we had no driving licences, we were somehow able to hire scooters. Mine was a rather sporty Asprilia, the seat barely large enough to accommodate the taciturn Eddie on the back. Phil had chosen a Piaggio Typhoon 50, with Hattie clinging on for dear life behind him. That day we pootled out through the grim container port of La Spezia to the north-western corner of the Golfo dei Poeti.

We parked our scooters at Porto Venere and I jokingly suggested we should swim across to the island of Palmaria, a few hundred yards away. Phil confessed that he could swim no more than ten or twenty feet so instead we strolled up to the Gothic Church of St Peter, perched on a cliff-top, with magnificent views across the bay – we could just about make out the seven white arches of the Casa Magni. On the northern side of the headland was the Grotta dell'Arpeia, AKA the Grotta Byron because Lord Byron had (allegedly) once swum to Shelley's house from here.

As we gazed out of the church window, a pair of bronzed bambinos leapt from a convenient spot above the grotto, executing Daleyesque dives into the lagoon. It was a fabulous sight – two soaring *putti* against the backdrop of rocks and disdainful egrets. Eddie opened his mouth for the first and only time that week to suggest that he would like to emulate the dive and perhaps the rest of us would care to join him. Perhaps we'd all had a few too many glasses of Asti Spumante but this somehow seemed like a good idea. But it took us forty minutes to find our way back through Porto Venere and out to the point from which the boys had jumped. The cliff-edge was roped off and various signs made it clear that jumping and diving were strictly *proibito* but, if the locals could do it, why not us?

There was no sign of the Italian boys now and as we gazed over the lip of the rock, perhaps sixty feet above the lagoon, the water looked an unimaginable distance away. We stripped hesitantly down to our beach-shorts. I don't normally suffer from vertigo but my knees seemed to have turned to jelly. Eddie's face had turned a greenish white as he contemplated the challenge. Phil was urging him on, promising that the rest of us would be close behind. But Eddie was frozen to the spot.

"Looks like Eddie's bottled it and I'll have to go first," Phil said at last.

"But you can't even swim!" I pointed out.

"Maybe not, but I can *dive*!"

And with that he walked calmly to the edge and, before any of us could restrain him, hurled himself off. It was all over in an instant. Indeed, it was a surprisingly competent dive although the splash as he entered the lagoon would not have impressed a set of Olympic judges. We gazed down open-mouthed as he quickly re-surfaced, apparently none the worse for wear.

"Come on in! The water's lovely!" Phil shouted in time-honoured fashion. The three of us looked at each other a little shamefacedly, each trying to compose a suitable excuse. No one inched closer to the precipice. Phil doggy-paddled his way to the shore, exhorting us to follow him in. But we never did. We waited shamefacedly while Phil found his way back to the top. Hattie hugged him, more out of relief than anything. But in that moment something changed in their relationship, I think. Her schoolgirl crush turned into something more with that one act of ridiculous bravado. That night (as Phil told me later) she crept along the terrace to his room and their relationship moved on to a new level. I could see the difference the following day – it was excruciating to see the two of them all over each other. Beth was merciless in her derision for her older brother but the two lovebirds were immune to all embarrassment.

On the last night of our sojourn, Italy played France in the World Cup Final at the Olympiastadion in Berlin. Every bar was a seething mass of Azzurri fans and the roar when Marco Materazzi headed in a 19th minute equaliser from Andrea Pirlo's corner was heard across the bay. The match is famous for Zinedine Zidane's head-butt but it had little bearing on the outcome, a 5-3 victory for Italy in the penalty shoot-out. The bars slowly emptied and the revellers headed for the beach in front of the Casa Magni where an impromptu rave had started. The entire local population, young and old, came down onto the sand and started gyrating to the bass-heavy thud of the music. Unable to sleep, we gazed down on the frenzied throng from the safety of our terrace. All inhibitions seemed to have been shed as the populace celebrated this unexpected national triumph. Some had stripped naked; others seemed to be enjoying carnal relations on the moonlit sand – this was their version of VE Day in Trafalgar Square with just a hint of Dante's *Inferno* thrown into the mix.

While the others flew back to Gatwick, I returned home via Newcastle Airport and saw little of my co-travellers until the first week of October when I returned to Univ. By then, Hattie seemed to have wangled herself a place at d'Overbroeck's, a convenient local sixth form college. She and Phil were now very much an item. But I knew that Phil had no expectation of settling down into a steady relationship at nineteen. Indeed, he had some pretty fixed views on marriage and relationships is general, i.e. that one person could never "own" another and it was everyone's duty to encourage the people close to them to develop in their own way.

"So you'd be happy to share your girlfriend with someone else, if that was what she wanted?" I remember asking him one day in Hall.

"Yes, why not?" he replied, shocking me slightly. Girlfriend-sharing was hardly *de rigueur* in my corner of rural Tyne & Tees which lagged around 50 years behind the rest of England in terms of sexual mores. Naturally, I played it cool.

"Perhaps I'll see whether she'd like to accompany me to the flicks next Saturday evening then …"

"Actually, that's a really good idea. I've been asked over to High Table at Merton and the invitation didn't really extend to Hattie as well. You'd be doing me a favour."

And so Hattie and I found ourselves at the UPP for a showing of *Blow-Up*, a slightly-racier-than-expected movie about the swinging sixties. As Hattie's pale and tiny hand lay on the arm-rest between us, I tried to summon up the courage for an exploratory squeeze. But it was far from clear whether she had left such bait on purpose and, in the end, the "date" elapsed without any significant physical contact – we will overlook the moment when I almost tripped her up as she struggled towards the Ladies through the dark and somewhat grubby stalls.

"I'm sorry, I didn't realize …" I started, as we finally tumbled out into Jeune St.

"You didn't realize what?" Her wide eyes had never looked more innocent in the damp glare of a street-light.

"Oh, I don't know. That photo-shoot with Veruschka was a bit … well, you know …"

"She was *amazing*, wasn't she?"

I had to agree that she was. Having researched Antonioni and his *oeuvre* as part of my meticulous preparation for our tryst, I was ready to wow my charming companion with critical gems on the way back to Kitchen Staircase 1 (all tasteless posters having been carefully sidelined in preparation for her visit) but I was oddly tongue-tied.

"Ah, there's Phil!" Hattie cried, pointing to a shadowy figure further down the Cowley Rd. "I gave him a call from the loos – fortunately, he was through with his dinner and kindly said he would save you the trouble of walking me back to college."

"How very considerate of him!" I murmured, but Hattie had already taken off at a canter. The pair embraced and turned towards Magdalen Plains – should I hurry on after them and feign a jovial indifference? Fight or flight? In the end, I trudged slowly back to college in their wake, taking care to keep a clear hundred yards between us.

It had been an oddly unsatisfactory evening but I took heart from Hattie's willingness to accompany me at all. It did not seem beyond the bounds of possibility that Phil would tire of his protégée in due course and I vowed to be the first on the scene with a sympathetic ear. If Hattie could be netted on the rebound, I would not be too proud to take my chance.

Looking back now, I wonder which of us was the greener? The truth is, we were both little more than children playing at a certain kind of sophistication.

Thoughts of that sweaty evening in the UPP preoccupy me as I drive my battered old Fiat Uno down the rain-sodden M40 to the Great Wen. Phil knows nothing of my mission, i.e. to find out at first hand what big sister Liz knows of Hattie's disappearance. It seems the least I can do.

But Liz Westgrove is one scary woman. Phil makes the sign of the cross whenever her name is mentioned and refers to her only as the Black Widow, even though she has never been married. She is an indeterminate number of years older than Hattie and her favoured colour scheme is black on black. Her long, lank locks are dyed black (with just a hint of purple). Most girls emerge from their Gothic phase at about eighteen but she seems to be stuck in a bygone age, playing 'This Corrosion' by the Sisters of Mercy on a perpetual loop and, one imagines, designing her own coffin. I exaggerate, but only slightly.

'Uncle Alex!' Little Charley races to the door to greet me and I reach down to give him a hug. Considering he hasn't seen his mother for the best part of two weeks, he seems remarkably chipper, but perhaps he is too young to understand. His younger sister, Xanthe, wanders over, a little more uncertainly, her thumb in her mouth.

'Have you brought any presents, Uncle Alex?' she asks, consenting to a half-hearted hug in the process.

'Xannie! Charley! Let the poor man in the door, you two!" Their formidable aunt stands, arms folded, as if guarding the threshold.

"As a matter of fact, I do have a little something," I say.

I give them each a bar of chocolate.

"Thank you, Uncle Alex," they coo in unison.

"Have you seen our mummy?" Xanthe whispers, as she tears the wrapper off.

"No, Xanthe, I haven't. I'm sorry!"

"Oh. She's been gone for *such* a long time. We want her to come back, don't we, Charley?"

Her older brother nods his assent between mouthfuls.

"Chocolate is full of toxins," Liz helpfully points out. "You'd better come in, since you're here, I suppose, Alexander."

Alexander? Why does she insist on addressing me thus?

"You did say it would be OK to visit, Betty," I point out.

"Betty!?"

"If I can call you Betty, you can call me Al!"

But my little ice-breaker falls on deaf ears. I doubt if Liz has even *heard* of Paul Simon. At least I haven't been turned away at the door.

The tiny flat is hopelessly ill-equipped for three residents, I see. There is a kitchen-diner on one side and a solitary bedroom on the other. There's hardly space on the floor for the two rudimentary camp-beds. The walls and curtains are still uncompromisingly black but at least there are no obvious signs of pagan rituals. I am ushered speedily towards a tatty sofa. There is just space for the two children to slot in on either side of me. I have no idea whether it is appropriate to put my arms round each of them – Liz's forbidding manner suggests otherwise.

"Children, why don't you go and play in the back yard?" she says

"Why?" asks Charley. "It's too cold."

"Well, put your coats on then!"

"Auntie Liz is very mean to us sometimes," Xanthe explains *sotto voce*. "Can we come and stay at your house till our mummy comes back?"

The idea of two hyperactive children in my Osney broom-cupboard fills me with alarm but I manage to keep it together.

"I'd really like that, Xan," I say, "but … I'm sure your mummy will be back very soon."

In the end the children are cajoled into their coats and sent out to the concreted area at the back of the flat. There are no toys for them to play with but at least they have their chocolate bars.

"So, no word from Hattie, then?" I ask, as cheerily as possible.

"Not a dickie bird," Liz looks me firmly in the eye and I have little doubt she is telling the truth. "I'm really not coping here, you know."

44

The dust in the flat is tickling my throat and I have not been offered so much as a cup of tea.

"The children need their mother, of course they do," I offer blandly.

"They need their mother and father! If I'd wanted children, I would have had some of my own. Where's that bastard, Philip, when he's needed?"

"Have you asked him?"

"I shouldn't need to. He knows Hattie's gone, doesn't he? You men, you're all a waste of space."

She has a point. We are, indeed, a waste of space.

"Where do you think she's got to?"

"Do you really want to know?"

I try to look encouraging.

"When she dropped off the children that last time, she knew it wasn't going to be just for the day. It was as if she would never see them again. She nearly squeezed the life out of Charley. She did her best to stop me noticing the tears in her eyes. I just thought she was having a bad day, but now I think ..."

"What?"

"It was like she was never coming back."

"Do you think she might be ..."

My question hangs heavy in the late afternoon air. Liz fiddles nervously with the heavy folds of her long, black skirt.

"The police have been round," she says at last. "I suppose we should be glad they're taking it seriously. I think they've made a few enquiries with Hattie's neighbours and had a bit of a scout round her flat."

"And there was nothing?"

"They wanted to know if she'd been a victim of domestic violence. How the hell would I know? I'm surprised they haven't knocked on Phil's door yet."

"How had she been? You know, in herself?"

"She was well. Not as scrawny as she had been. She'd finally managed to put on a bit of weight. Some days she was quite like her old self, I thought."

"She's just naturally slim, surely?"

"You think so? When did you last see her?"

"I'm not exactly sure," I lie. "Easter, I think. I was down in London anyway and Phil asked me to look in, check they were all OK, you know how it is ..."

"Do I?" Liz mutters darkly. But before we can interrogate each other any further, Charley pokes his head round the door.

"I've found a toad, Auntie Liz!"

"And what would you like me to do about it, Charley?"

"Can we keep it in our bedroom?"

Liz gives the boy a withering look but the children have both decided it's time to come in from the cold. Liz looks at me expectantly.

"I guess it's time I should be pushing on," I say. It is clear I am not going to learn much more about Hattie's whereabouts.

"Are you going to bring us some more chocolate tomorrow?" asks Xanthe.

"I'm sorry, I have to go back to Oxford, Xannie. I'll see you and your mummy very soon, I'm sure. And I won't forget the chocolate."

Once out of the flat, I walk round the corner into Marshall Street. Over a graffiti-stained walkway, I spot a scruffy rectangular plaque:

WILLIAM BLAKE WAS BORN ON 28 NOVEMBER 1757
IN A HOUSE WHICH STO D ON THIS SITE

A life condensed to a single event, minus a solitary letter 'O'. Happy birthday, William! I decide to drink a toast to the great man and walk into the Shaston Arms in Ganton Street, close by. Rejecting the Tanglefoot, the Badger and the Hopping Hare, I opt for a pint of the appropriately-named Lethe Ale. The thought of jumping back into the Fiat and hacking back out of Central London on the A40 is unappealing and one pint turns into two. There may have been a third … I wouldn't want to incriminate myself at this point. By this time I have convinced myself that Hattie is definitely dead, lying undiscovered in some dank stairwell. And in 38 days I will be dead too. The barmaid asks if I am all right and I say yes, why ever not? I note that I am the only customer. Solitary drinking is not a familiar experience for me – indeed, I very rarely drink at all and alcohol goes to my head all too quickly.

By the time I have drained the last drop of Lethe to the dregs, toppled off my stool and quit the pub, it's turned quite clarty. Three days on from Storm Angus, the rain is still splattering off the pavements and awnings, as if to say that it has settled in for another night. I have no protection from the elements and by the time I make it back to my car, I am sopping wet. The parking ticket under the windscreen wiper does nothing to lighten my mood. *Ninety quid?* London rates, I guess.

The ignition fires my rusty Uno into action at the fourth time of asking and I battle my way back onto the A40 which looks more like a car park than a major arterial road. I inch along for a mile or two, trying to pick up some traffic news on the radio. It seems that a whole section of the M40 has had to be closed after a lorry has overturned and there is a tailback to the heart of the city. I follow a Diversion sign and find myself heading south through White City. I try to hack my way in a more north-westerly direction but only succeed in getting myself completely lost.

By now the rain is torrential and the wiper-blades are flapping like a demented heron. Water is coming in through the top of the driver's window where I've been too lazy to get the mechanism fixed. I have absolutely no idea whether I am heading in the right direction and, being a man, I have absolutely no intention of stopping at a petrol station and buying a UK map-book or anything sensible like that. The rain has turned to sleet and I sense that I am gradually leaving Metroland behind me and heading out into the backwaters of Berkshire or Buckinghamshire.

To try to keep myself awake, I turn the stereo up to eleven. The lyrics of 'Radar Love' seem apt enough: 'I've been driving all night, my hands wet on the wheel ...'. I feel a deep longing to be back in Oxford. Somehow I'm not far from Wendover on the Aylesbury road (I think) and not for the first time, panic sets in – surely I should be further west? Maybe I can rejoin the M40 near Thame? So I take a left down a road that proves to be rather more minor than I'd anticipated. There is a greyish sheet of slush on the untravelled road. I console myself with the unoriginal thought that nothing lasts forever, even cold November rain.

I decide to give my father a call. Yes, I know, I should stop the car but there's no one about. So I fish the mobile out of my pocket and summon him from his reveries in front of the National Lottery, or whatever.

"So where are you then, Alex?"

"Not too sure, Dad. Somewhere west of Wendover, I think."

"You don't want to be there."

"Yes, thanks, Dad. I don't want to be here either. I'm hoping this road will take me back on to the M40. You don't have a map-book handy, do you?"

"Doubt it. Hang on, I'll have a search ..."

But at this precise moment I am dazzled by the multiple lights of a huge vehicle coming towards me. Some idiot of a lorry driver has, like me, lost his way. In the smear of white light, the cockpit of this juggernaut seems weirdly empty and I fear I am about to be mown down.

I swerve sharply to the left and drive over some kind of unseen obstacle, possibly a brick. I do not hear the tyre burst but the Fiat skews suddenly across the slush.

"Oh, shit," is all I have time to say. At least the lorry has passed safely by. There is a level crossing ahead but we don't reach it, tumbling instead into some kind of drainage ditch. Before I know it, the car is upside down and water is gushing in through the open window and numerous other apertures. My first thought is that this is all wrong; it's all far too early, I can't possibly die yet. But the car is all but submerged and there seems to be no way to force the door open.

Drenched in icy water, I clamber over to the passenger side where there seems to be more room between the door and the bank of the ditch. I am just able to force the door open and squeeze my way out as more water rushes in. I am briefly underwater but I can see what looks like a tree above me, some of its lower branches dangling into the floodwater. I grab one of the branches and haul myself out. I lie on the bank, no doubt in shock, and listen as a train thunders by a few feet away. I feel suddenly very grateful that I crashed into the ditch and not actually on the level crossing. All is quiet again. My head is spinning and I feel a brief sense of euphoria.

The rest of the night is a bit of a blur. Amazingly, my phone still works and I am able to summon a rescue vehicle. My father finds a map and manages to locate a level crossing on a minor road between Wendover and Thame. He drives out to pick me up, like a naughty four-year-old caught scrumping. I'm ferried home and some very modest wounds are patched up. Then I retire shamefacedly to my room.

Wednesday 23 November 2016

Relaxes in solar air-current, first to last (7)

So I have lived to tell the tale, notably to Phil over a post-squash pint.

"And your last words were 'oh, shit!'?" This seems to be the one detail that stirs Phil's interest.

"Yeah, something like that."

"Were you aware at the time that you were quoting Colin Flooks, AKA the great Cozy Powell?"

"What, the Rainbow drummer?"

"The very same. 'Oh, shit' were Cozy's last words when he crashed his Saab 9000 on the M4. He was doing a ton in the fast lane, bad weather, no seat belt, somewhat over the drink-driving limit, talking to his fancy woman on the phone, when one of his tyres blew. 'Oh shit' were his last recorded words."

"No kidding!"

"Sounds like you were attempting a frame-by-frame remake. I should stick to impressions of Bill Wyman, if I were you."

"Well, luckily I was doing no more than fifty at the time, otherwise I might well have met the lorry or even the London train head on."

"It must be a relief to know you've still got a few more weeks to live. How's that big life insurance policy coming along by the way? You have made sure I'm the chief beneficiary, haven't you?"

"You don't take anything seriously, do you?"

"I've been taking your impending demise very seriously indeed. I've located the precise note of gravitas to strike at the Hyde Park gig. We will conveniently ignore your total inability on the guitar and recast you as the Brian Jones of the band, regrettably drowned on the eve of the concert. I've been mugging up on the *Collected Works* of Percy Bysshe Shelley ..."

Phil fishes a copy out of his bag and thumbs through its last pages.

"If you've pegged out in a car crash we can use the last lines of *The Triumph of Life*."

"The one Shelley never finished? Written on the terrace of the Casa Magni?"

By now we are both a little more knowledgeable as far as the Romantic poets are concerned. It turns out that Shelley had not just lived in San Terenzo;

it was his last abode. He raced his boat, the *Don Juan*, with Byron in the Bay of Lerici and drowned close by. But I can't honestly say I like his poetry that much. Phil has found the relevant section.

"That's right. Shelley was halfway through writing *The Triumph of Life* on the day he drowned himself. It would have been his masterpiece, I think, but it's a real car-crash of a poem."

"But cars hadn't even been invented then!"

"Yes and no. Richard Trevithick's Puffing Devil of 1801 was the juggernaut of its day and arguably the first car on British roads. Shelley's triumphant chariot of life rumbles across the Earth like a puffing devil with no brakes, crushing all the poor souls in its path. The dead and wounded are left in its unseeing wake. Here, look at the last stanza he ever wrote, possibly on the very day he died. Shelley is talking to Rousseau, old and crippled, in the wake of this juggernaut ..."

I take the book from him and obediently read out the lines:

> 'Then, what is Life?' I said ... the cripple cast
> His eye upon the car which now had rolled
> Onward, as if that look must be the last

"I've got to be honest, Phil. I don't think *The Triumph of Life* would mean much to a rock crowd, not even here in Oxford."

"You could be right. He drowned just before he could tell us what Life is. And Shelley doesn't even specify whether it's a Triumph Dolomite or a Herald." Phil laughs heartily at his own joke. "Where abouts in Italy are the Dolomites anyway? Perhaps he was pondering on that when he jumped into his rusty old clinker, the *Don Juan*, set the sails at warp factor nine and headed up the coast from Livorno to Lerici on that fateful day in July 1822? But enough of that. What did you make of the Chancellor's Autumn Statement this morning?"

"Eh?"

"With the Income Tax threshold going up to £11.5K in April, you'll be a bit better off. Old Philip has done you proud!"

Philip Hammond, the Chancellor, is a Univ alumnus and some would say a typical product of the college, a decent man, quietly brilliant in various top roles – but perhaps a teensy bit grey.

"One: I don't expect to be *alive* in April. Two: on a college salary, I'm likely to be well inside that threshold anyway. Was there some equally thrilling news for people like you in the super-tax bracket?"

"What, on an academic's salary?"

"So, what *do* you earn these days?"

"If I work all the hours God sends and take every bit of teaching and lecturing that's offered to me, maybe £40K."

"Does that include the royalties on your book sales?"

"Good point. £40,025 altogether. The average price of just a flat in Oxford last year was £320K. How can *any* of us get on the housing ladder?"

"But you did get on the housing ladder," I remind him.

"Only thanks to the Bank of Mum and Dad. I'm just as skint as you are, Alex."

I snort derisively, sup up and splash my way home.

And now the really spooky bit. I hesitate to share this with you because it's just too weird …

In an effort to take my mind off the crash, the might-have-beens and the might-yet-bes, I decide to immerse myself in the weighty tome that is Bill Clinton's autobiography. I've already skimmed through most of the Oxford bit, so I decide to start back at the beginning. And what do I find? On the very first page of his *apologia pro vita sua*, the old rogue tells the story of his father's demise a few weeks before he himself was born in August 1946.

William Jefferson Blythe II was, by all accounts, just as much of a Don Juan as his more famous son. Dad was a sales rep who could not pass a pretty girl without trying to proposition her, succeeding often enough to have been married three times before he met Nurse Virginia Kelley in 1943. Inside two months, WJB II had cleared all his other girlfriends from the path to true love, married Virginia and headed off to war. It sounds as though Blythe Senior, like Shelley before him, had a few scary moments off the coast of Italy as the Americans waded ashore and began their triumphal march to Rome, trampling the Italians underfoot at Monte Cassino and prevailing in numerous other skirmishes *en route*. Billy Blythe was a tank-engineer, no doubt greasing the wheels of this invidious Triumph, bypassing the Dolomites.

Most conquering invaders in history have a sorry record of rape and pillage and there must have been many temptations for the testosterone-fired GIs on the road to Rome. It seems unlikely that Blythe would have let such a chance go by. Who knows how many step-brothers and sisters the ex-President now has, each into their seventies? In these days of ubiquitous DNA-testing, perhaps the truth will yet out. I digress ...

Back home in Hope, Arkansas, young Virginia is anxiously waiting for her bridegroom and WJB II is duly demobbed some time in 1945. Pretty soon, she is pregnant with WJB III, but the young couple has no money and there are precious few jobs in hopeless Hope. So Blythe gets a job in Chicago and finds a house that he will share with mother and baby. We're still on page one of the autobiography:

> 'On May 17, 1946, after moving their furniture into their new home, my father was driving from Chicago to Hope to fetch his wife. Late at night on Highway 60 outside of Sikeston, Missouri, he lost control of his car, a 1942 Buick, when the right front tire blew out on a wet road. He was thrown clear of the car but landed in, or crawled into, a drainage ditch dug to reclaim swampland. The ditch held three feet of water. When he was found, after a two-hour search, his hand was grasping a branch above the waterline. He had tried but failed to pull himself out. He drowned, only twenty-eight years old ...'

A year younger than Shelley, but a year older than Brian Jones, I note. My age, in fact. Of course, it's that last detail that makes me catch my breath, the seizing of the branch above the waterline, the last grasp and gasp of an injured and drowning man. If *I* had been unable to open that car door or unwind the window in time, it could easily have been me clutching at such straws.

Yet here I am, safely on dry land. Have I dodged the bullet with my name on it? Can I, like Baldrick, stuff it in my breeches and look forward to pantaloon'd dotage?

All coincidence, you will say. I am not Cozy Powell or the exiled Shelley, nor am I William Jefferson Blythe II or even Brian Jones brooding by his swimming pool at AA Milne's old house. Yet I am struck by these eerie echoes of drownings past. As fellow traveller Karl Marx put it:

Hegel remarks somewhere that all great world-historic facts and personages appear, so to speak, twice. He forgot to add: the first time as tragedy, the second time as farce.

To which I say: what, only twice!? Once you have fallen past farce, what literary genre do you come clattering into the *third* time around? What depths of bathos should I aspire to as I plummet unmourned to the bottom of some unanticipated lake on December 30th?

Thursday 24 November 2016

Auto-authorization (4)

Ingratitude, thy name is Vladimir Lebedev! My boss is oddly unimpressed with news of my prospective coup:

"So, let me get this straight, Alex ... you got it into your head to ring Bill Clinton?"

"Well, he rang me, actually."

"... and you asked him for some money. How much money, exactly?"

"I didn't mention an exact figure."

"Did you mention a rough figure?"

"I may have done ..." I sense that all resistance is futile. "I may have suggested something in the low seven figures."

"A million dollars? Are you insane?"

"I meant pounds, actually. Think what a difference it could make to the college finances!"

"Think? Did *you* not think at all, Alex? Did it not occur to you that the idea of approaching the President might already have been considered by the Development Office?"

"I suppose ...."

"There have been discussions at the highest possible level. It is a matter of extreme delicacy. It is *not* a matter of a cold call from the office junior. Because that's all you are, Alex, a probationer on trial."

"There's no mention of a 'discussion' on our database and no sign of even a modest contribution so far. Perhaps I just got lucky? Perhaps this just happened to be the moment when he was ready to pay his dues?"

"His *dues*?" Lebedev almost spits out the words. "There are no dues. Mr Clinton was here for a few short months back in the late sixties ..."

"Two years, surely?"

"One academic year. The second year was purely ..."

"Hypothetical? A draft-dodge?"

"... a year spent broadening his horizons in Paris and across Europe."

"Yes, I know. I've been reading his autobiography. Vital background research, I hope you'll agree?"

Lebedev takes a deep breath.

"So how have you left it with Mr Clinton?"

"I think he wants to talk to me about it. In person."

"That would be very awkward. We do not have the budget to send you to America for a *chat*."

"No, he's coming to the USPGA golf day!"

"He's doing *what*!?"

Perhaps I should explain that the USPGA is the Univ Society Peripatetic Golf Association, an informal association for old members of the college convening at a variety of scenic locations across England. It is the more senior of the two USPGAs by about forty years (average age of the players, that is). We have considered suing the rival American upstart USPGA for exploiting our distinguished acronym but that's not really our style.

Ours is the USPGA which upholds the true values of the sport. No shoddy professionalism sullies our travails on some of England's finest golf courses. For us, the five-foot gimme is a normal part of the game – there is no need to prove oneself over so short a range, is there? Most of us would qualify for a telegram from the queen if we were ever to break a hundred. Yet most USPGA members cling to superannuated handicaps of 18 or 24 like badges of honour, clear proof that they could play the game back in 1962, whatever the evidence now.

Despite their advanced age, our members frown on buggies and take great pride in traipsing round all eighteen holes, pulled along by their motorised trolleys, sometimes in a shade under five hours. It's just as well that we have (usually) found a golf club which will conveniently retain its lunchtime kitchen staff till 4 p.m. And by six we will finally be ready to applaud the bandits who have made off with the prizes by the devious expedient of actually playing somewhere near their stated handicap.

Bill Clinton has been invited to every one of the USPGA meetings over the last fifteen years so his first appearance is long overdue. And I am the only person at the Development Office with the slightest interest in golf.

"I think he just wants to explore a few options with me while enjoying the fabulous scenery of Frilford Heath golf course," I explain patiently. "If he says he doesn't want to contribute, what harm has been done?"

"You've absolutely no idea, have you?"

"No, I'm afraid I haven't."

"Have you any sense of how much security is involved in a presidential visit?"

"That's his affair. I haven't invited him for formal dinner in Hall. I mean, I haven't *not* invited him. It just didn't come up. I expect he travels pretty much incognito these days. It's his wife who is the important one …."

"Alex, I'm not sure you have really quite understood your role in this organisation. The college did not give you authorization for any of this nonsense. I'd also like to ask you what caused those bruises and cuts on your face?"

"What? That's nothing … I just had a slight incident while driving."

"Yes, I did hear something along those lines. You wrote off your Fiat on some country lane …."

"The weather was atrocious. One of the tyres burst."

"Had you been drinking?"

I am momentarily taken back by the sheer effrontery of the question.

"I don't think that's any of your business. I am not known for …"

"Had you been drinking?"

"Yes! OK, are you satisfied? The fact that I had consumed a pint of beer earlier in the evening is neither here nor there."

"If you are to work for this college, you need to remember that your behaviour should be beyond reproach at all times. Please consider this as a formal warning."

"Look, I'm not some snotty-nosed student. You can't send me down for gross moral turpitude!"

"No, but I am your boss. Think on it, Alex …"

Friday 25 November 2016

Enthusiastic wolf ravaged avian prey (8)

Hello, Earth! If a tree falls in a forest and no one is around to hear it, does it make a sound? If I publish a daily blog and no one reads it, have I made any sort of splash? Were I to compile a secret diary in a Bohairic dialect and conceal it in the most inaccessible of cubby-holes (like the stone pot of Finest Astrakhan Caviar that was finally fished out of Felix Yusupov's Univ rooms in 1940, according to Ozzie), it would be no more unread than this. My blog is just a click or two away for every internet user on the planet and yet, to all intents and purposes, invisible (however many tags and links I diligently add), hidden in plain sight. So be it. If it is to be my solitary meditation in my last days ... well, world, you had your chance!

Hello, Earth! Today sees the release, at long last, of Kate Bush's *Before the Dawn*, her triple live CD. The centrepiece is *The Ninth Wave* (from *Hounds of Love*), a beautiful and haunting 7-track song-cycle meditating on drowning. This prog rock classic is based on the 1850 painting of the same name by Ivan Aivazovsky, often reckoned to be the most beautiful artwork in St Petersburg. As our Kate says: it is "about a person who is alone in the water for the night. It's about their past, present and future coming to keep them awake, to stop them drowning, to stop them going to sleep until the morning comes." In the accompanying video to the 'Hello, Earth' section, we see her deep under water, one hand reaching up and out towards a lightning-scarred sky. I am reaching out too ...

Around 6.30 in the evening, I am settling down to a good healthy plateful of pie and stodge when there is a knock on the front door. Dad's forgotten his key again, I think, but the rat-a-tat seems a little too decisive for Dad. So I park my plate on a pile of half-read *Guardians* and answer the door. A tall, lupine man in a sheepskin coat confronts me.

"Detective Inspector Hunt, Metropolitan Police." He flashes a laminated card at me. "Would you be Mr Alan Alexander Hogg?"

A thousand thoughts clatter across my synapses. That bastard Lebedev has told the police that I have 'confessed' to drink-driving – how dare he? But how would they even know about my accident? Surely the AA were under no obligation to tell them?

I confirm that I am A.A. Hogg and usher DI Hunt into the back room. My extensive collection of home-made CDs is right in his eyeline.

"That's a lot of music you have there, Mr Hogg," he says, perhaps to unbreak the ice. "You do realize that it is illegal to make copies of CDs you do not own?"

"I ... I ..."

"However, I have not come to talk to you about that. I'd like to ask you a few questions about a lady called Mrs Harriet Sherborne."

"Ah, Hattie, yes!" This comes as something of a relief in the circumstances, but only momentarily.

"Hattie? Was that some kind of nickname?"

"No, just the name that all her friends know her by. Is there any news?"

"No news at all, Mr Hogg. That is why I have come to Oxford. It seemed possible that her husband – ex-husband, whatever he is – could offer us a few leads."

"And did he?"

DI Hunt sighs disdainfully.

"To be frank, I'm not sure Dr Sherborne is taking it at all seriously. 'Hattie's just gone walkabout,' he says. 'She'll be back in a day or two.' That was the gist of his response. Gave me your name, actually. And your address ..."

Well, thanks for that, Phil. You're a pal.

"... so, since I was in Oxford anyway, I just thought I'd pay you a visit and see if you could shed any light on the matter.

"I ... I don't think I can, officer."

Officer! I've clearly been watching far too much American 60s TV.

"When did you last see Mrs Sherborne, sir?"

"Ah, let me see ... I think it must have been round about last Easter. Ages ago."

"And how did she seem on that occasion?"

"She was ... fine."

"Fine? Perhaps you could elaborate?"

"Oh, I don't know. Look, she'd been through a pretty hard time. I think she was finally coming to terms with the fact that her marriage was over. But with no money, no job ..."

"Would you say that she was in good health?"

"She was a lot thinner than she once was. It crossed my mind that she was not eating properly."

"How thin? Anorexic?"

"No, no, she was still …"

"Still what, sir?"

"Well, an attractive young woman. In perfectly good health, I'd say."

"And how would you describe your own relationship with Mrs Sherborne?"

"She was – is – just a friend. Phil Sherborne and I are very close and she is or was his wife. I always got on well with Hattie."

"And you know nothing about her disappearance? Why did you see her last Easter? She and Dr Sherborne were long since separated, I believe. Was he aware of your meeting?"

"I don't recall. Perhaps he wasn't. I was in London and I had a few hours to spare after visiting some friends, so I called by on the off-chance. She just happened to be in."

There is a short pause while Inspector Bucket writes all this down.

"Did you stay at her house while you were in London?"

"I think I may have stopped over, yes. Look, I'm not sure what you're trying to insinuate …"

"I'm just trying to put together some sort of picture, Mr Hogg. Just doing my job. I somehow get the feeling that you are not telling me the full story. Have you had any contact with Mrs Sherborne or her family over the last few weeks?"

"I … I did have a chat with her sister last Saturday."

"You gave her a call?"

"I went to see her. And the children. Look, I'm very concerned. All her friends are."

"As are we, Mr Hogg. As are we …"

Bucket of the Yard leaves and I consume the rest of my pie'n'stodge in silence. The interview has left me a little disoriented. I make a mental note to house my CD collection in a slightly more discreet fashion. How does he know I haven't made copies of CDs that I already own anyway?

It seems clear that the Met are treating Hattie's disappearance as a possible murder case. They have evidently been watching too much American TV themselves. To me it is inconceivable that anyone could have wanted to harm Hattie. I don't think she had an enemy in all the world. Not enough friends when she needed them, perhaps, but no enemies.

So, what *did* go on last Easter, you ask? It was quite an emotional weekend, in fact. I was just coming out of a relationship with a very strange girl called Alice (aren't all Alices strange?) and Hattie was still at a pretty low ebb. We'd had a chicken-and-egg curry at the Star of India round the corner from Hattie's flat and I'd insisted on singing 'Mother and Child Reunion' most of the way back, until a modicum of physical violence persuaded me that enough was enough.

The children had been parked at her sister's place for the night and we just carried on chatting, as you do. There wasn't much booze in the house and after finishing up what was left of the John Smith's, we got on to a bottle of Madeira that she and Phil had brought back from a holiday on the island. Neither of us had ever tasted Madeira, so we decided to test it out and the sweet, syrupy stuff really hit the mark after a heavy Indian.

I did most of the drinking and Hattie did most of the talking. Not just about Phil and her broken marriage, but also about her parents whom I hadn't seen since her wedding day. They run a chain of coffee-houses in Sydney and are way too busy even to chat on Skype, Hattie grumbled. But she got plenty of moral and practical support from her sister, I suggested? Hattie just looked at me darkly, as if I would never quite understand.

Hattie's musical tastes have always been pretty limited but we played Adèle, the Eagles, Mumford and Sons, even some Carpenters. I knew I'd had a few too many because I found myself singing along even less tunelessly to the dangerously prescient lyrics of 'A Song for You':

> And when my life is over, remember when we were together,
> We were alone and I was singing this song for you.

It's never easy to get that last line to fit the tune, is it? (The air-sax solo that follows is rather easier.) We were sat on the floor, swigging directly from this bottle of Madeira and somehow we got to holding hands and I think Hattie put her head on my shoulder. I have a vague memory that at some point, we turned to each other and kind of deliquesced together. For a moment she was the most beautiful woman in the whole world and it seemed somehow ridiculous that I should be inhabiting the same floorspace as her. And then she was kissing me, or I was kissing her, I'm not quite sure which. And then ... and then?

I honestly have no idea. The next thing I remember is waking with a throbbing head and being conscious of the confined space in which I was lying, Hattie's single bed hardly being big enough to contain the two of us. That moment of recognition, that anagnorisis, will be with me for ever. After so many years of vague wondering, there I was, pressed against Hattie's naked back. A quick audit of the numerous points of physical contact suggested that both of us were indeed naked. I remember edging an inch or two back lest my morning glory should arouse Hattie prematurely from her slumbers. My mouth was as dry as the Atacama Desert and the rhythm section in my skull seemed to have been taking lessons from John Bonham. If only I'd had JB's drinking capacity too, I might not have felt half so bad. I remembered the empty bottle of Madeira and it crossed my mind that it might have been drugged, that my memory failure was Rohypnol-related. But the truth was surely more mundane – I had simply drunk too much.

I listened to Hattie's slightly jittery breathing for twenty minutes before my need for a pee became overwhelming. I extracted myself from the crook of Hattie's legs as delicately as I could, pulled on my trousers (from the suspiciously neat pile of my clothes) and stumbled off to the communal bathroom on the first floor landing. I sluiced some approximation of life back into my tongue and throat and tiptoed back to Hattie's bedroom.

I found Hattie awake, sitting up in bed, her hair glistening slightly in the shards of light that criss-crossed the room from the tatty ill-hung curtains. She drew the bedclothes tight across her chest and gazed at me with what felt like unspoken, unfathomable reproach.

"I'm sorry, I …" I started, trying to cover all possibilities.

Hattie patted the space on the bed next to her and I sat down obediently next to her.

"It's OK, Alex. It's really OK."

"I think we may have had a little too much Madeira," I suggested after an uneasy pause.

"*You* did, you mean!"

"OK, *I* had too much Madeira. I can only apologise for whatever may or may not have occurred."

"You don't remember?"

"No, I … God, is that the time?"

I looked in alarm at my wrist-watch which seemed to have survived whatever disrobings and fumblings took place in the early hours of the morning.

"It's half-past seven," Hattie observed helpfully.

"Yes, I know. It's just that I'm due to give some kid an A-level tutorial at nine-thirty. In Oxford."

Hattie digested this information for a moment or two.

"And you couldn't just ring up and cancel it?"

"I don't think I have a number with me."

"I see. Very well, you must go."

Remembering this, a few months on, it all seems spineless and feeble. I did what Hattie said, putting the rest of my clothes on in front of her, stuffing my pants into my trouser pockets as I went. Hattie watched my performance from the sanctuary of her bed and I swear I saw the hint of a tear in her left eye.

"I think we should forget this ever happened, Alex."

"I seem to have forgotten most of it already!"

This was meant as a joke but I'm not sure it came across that way. As I tied my shoelaces, I couldn't help but notice that the duvet had slipped slightly and a greater expanse of milky-white skin was exposed. Was that the hint of an areola? It was hard to be sure in that dawn-light.

"I'm sorry," I said again.

"Please stop apologising, Alex!"

And those may have been the last words spoken between us. Perhaps I said something about being in touch, I'm not sure. But to my shame I left her there and ran off to some paltry cramming exercise with the dim-witted son of a hedge fund manager. Bizarrely, having apologised for my late arrival, I had to give the dullard back a practice essay on John Donne's poetry in which he had attempted to disentangle the sublime imagery of 'The Sunne Rising' – go chide late schoolteachers, indeed!

I did not get in touch that day, or the next. Perhaps I took Hattie's request to forget the whole thing too seriously or perhaps I lacked the confidence to pick up the ball and run with it. Hattie was still technically married to Phil, after all (the divorce had not quite gone through), and there were two small children to consider. Hattie had sworn that she would never set foot in Oxford again for fear of running into her feckless husband (whom she still loved desperately, I am sure) and I was no fan of London or the journey to and fro.

I *meant* to give her a call but as the days turned into weeks, it became too embarrassing to do so. So I never got to find out what happened that night. I imagine that I fell into some sort of alcoholic stupor at some point and Hattie had somehow managed to pull off my clothes and put me to bed. But that is not the only thing I imagine …

Sunday 27 November 2016

Fixed charge includes nothing in common (7)

Sunday is a day of rest and care in the community, so I magnanimously agree to accompany Dad on his favourite walk. We don our hiking boots (just in case it's muddier than usual) and head east from our humble abode, turning right onto the towpath at the Punter. We cross the little network of footbridges at the south-eastern corner of Osney Island and potter along the banks of the Thames as it meanders its way down towards Folly Bridge and the boathouses. We pick over the bones of Sunderland's latest defeat (to mighty Liverpool) and return to the sea-floor of the Premier League in desultory fashion. Cyclists hurtle along the narrow path and seem to take great delight in locating the largest puddles as they splash by, no doubt notching up double points if both of us are drenched in the process.

But we stick to the towpath only as far as the first meander and the tunnel under the railway line. We climb the bank and stroll across Grandpont Nature Reserve. It's a grandiose description of a very modest area of common ground, land that was contaminated by the old gas works and will, with luck, never be built upon. There is no sign of the original Grandpont, a medieval stone causeway across the wetlands of south-west Oxford. At the southern tip of the nature reserve, we take the gap through the trees and cross back over the railway. This little path takes us west and then south into our secret place, our Shangri-La – the Hogacre Common Eco-Park.

Of course, we are a little biased. We Hoggs own almost no acres these days. Our plot of land on Osney Island is the size of a large handkerchief. The colleges are the only landowners in Oxford with whole acres to themselves, but these acres are nominally ours. Once we arrive at Hogacre Common, we feel like kings of all we survey. Most visitors to Hogacre arrive from the east and Whitehouse Rd but we much prefer this westerly approach which affords the prospect of Hogacre's many riches, its orchards, its hazel coppice, its community beehives, wildflower meadow, wind turbines and, best of all, its cricket pavilion-cum-vegetarian café modelled on one of Sir Christopher Wren's designs for a London club.

In my salad days, I did actually play cricket and football here because this used to be the Corpus Christi College Sports Ground. I remember crossing the bridge from Whitehouse Rd for a 3rd XI football match, only to find the entire ground submerged by recent rains. Somehow the other 21 players from Univ and Corpus had been appraised of this news before setting out and I had no choice but to trudge back to college alone. Come to think of it, that was probably the last time I put my name down for any collegiate sporting activity.

Corpus, being a tiny and rather swotty college, eventually found that it had no further need of its own inaccessible, submersible sports ground and struck a deal with Univ. The Corpuscles, as they liked to call themselves, would play their ballgames at Univ's equally low-lying ground on the Abingdon Road while Univ would play a part in the management of Hogacre Common. Phil has been a reluctant member of the committee which has overseen the project to turn the common into a so-called 'Eco-Park'. Phil calls it the Playground for the Loony Left but I love it here.

Despite the recent rains, the common is still passable so we make our way across the old cricket square to the pavilion, now called the Hogacre Café, where we can be sure of a fine pot of tea and the most ethical slices of carrot cake imaginable. It's more of a summer attraction in truth and this is the last Sunday on which the café will be open before its winter break.

Only one other table is occupied when we arrive but we recognise the man who is hunched over a large mug of tea and a laptop. It is the manager of the common, Ben Haydon, a stockily built young man of about my own age with tiny, rimless glasses that magnify his accusing, dark eyes.

"What's up, Ben?" I ask, with all the cheeriness I can muster.

"What do you think?" he mutters, not bothering to look up. "What's the use of a café with no customers?"

"But *we* are customers," I remind him.

"So you are, so you are," he acknowledges. "But aren't you mates with that Philip Sherborne chap at Univ?"

On an earlier visit, we had got chatting and I'd inadvertently let slip that I worked at Univ. I think this chap is now convinced that I am one of the people involved in setting his paltry salary. If Phil had his way, I suspect he would not be paid at all. I nod apprehensively.

"… only I've just had an e-mail from your Dr Sherborne telling me that they've decided to phase out the college's Development Grant for Hogacre over the next five years."

"Well, five years is a good long time," I suggest lamely.

"…so there will be nothing in the kitty to pay my salary. Looks like I'll be back on the painting and decorating."

"I'm sorry to hear that."

"Well, you can tell Dr Philip ****** Sherborne that if I see him any time soon, I'll … I'll …"

"But you're doing a great job, Ben!" I reassure him. "That orchard is growing up into a wonderful community resource. I'm sure that if you put a reasonable case, they'll reconsider."

It's clear that we are about as welcome as an outbreak of Dothistroma Needle Blight this afternoon so we slurp our tea a little more quickly than usual and make our way back out into the afternoon sunshine. Heading west once more and resisting the temptation to test-drive the eco-toilet perched on stilts, we leave this enchanted land past a charcoal burner and follow the rudimentary path next to the Hogacre Stream or Ditch. In summer this can be dry as a bone but it's a *bona fide* river just now, one of many that cross the floodplain. Just to the south and parallel with the Hogacre is the Hinksey Stream but we prefer to follow "our" river upstream. It may be little more than a ditch but the Hogacre was once the boundary between Oxfordshire and Berkshire and, before that, the northernmost edge of the Kingdom of Wessex in the days when the walled town of Oxford was a Mercian outpost. Did rag-tag armies face each other across this little ditch? Did rival kings squabble over this fertile patch of hog-grazing land?

There is little sign of such history now. We follow the Hogacre until it becomes indistinguishable from the Bullstake Stream and turn left into the grounds of the *Fishes*, a public house in North Hinksey. Ignoring the attractions of the adventure playground and indeed of the pub itself, we emerge onto Hinksey Lane where Oscar Wilde and his fellow undergraduates once strove to build a road that would join the disconnected villages of North and South Hinksey. It must have been good preparation for life in Reading Gaol. We walk in silence past the church and turn right on to Willow Walk, one of Oxford's most beautiful paths. But in late November the eponymous willows look bare and brittle as we walk silently back towards Osney. The path comes out at the bottom end of Ferry Hinksey Rd, next to King's Meadow, and from there it is no distance to the school and the little bridge across to Swan St.

The entire round-trip has taken us a little over an hour and I realise that my father and I have hardly said a word to each other in the whole of this period. We have each been lost in our own thoughts.

It's too soon after my car crash nearby for me to contemplate driving to Aylesbury for the Marillion gig tonight even if the Fiat was still viable. I wonder whether Megan will be there, along with all the other pony-tailed 50-something progsters? Instead I settle for watching a documentary on the making of *Graceland* and devouring all 37 sections of the *Sunday Times*. With Phil's comments on *The Triumph of Life* in mind, I turn hopefully to Shelley's prognostications on p.121 of the *Style* section:

Aquarius
JANUARY 20 – FEBRUARY 18
It would be easy to blame recent problems on the careless thinking of others, but, in reality, nobody could have anticipated these sudden and disruptive insane twists and turns.

What, *nobody*? Shelley insisted on the poet's role as a prophet in his *Defence of Poetry* and yet even he seems to have been defeated by the bizarre peripeteias of my final days. Whatever next?

Monday 28 November 2016

Revolutionary puritans murdered Russian (8)

It is clear that the Fiasco is not going to go again any day soon. It is time for a new set of wheels. Fortunately, I know a man who has some to sell or, if I am lucky, give away. Bandmate Ozzie Kay, praelector in nineteenth-century literature and all round good egg, has a Yaris that is surplus to requirements. The college is obviously paying him more than I thought if he can afford a new car, but ours is not to reason why.

"You can't go wrong with a Toyota," he assures me once I have given it a broadly satisfactory test drive. "Their engines require zero maintenance so they are perfect for …."

"A complete idiot like me? Yes, thanks, Ozzie."

"Where was it you turned the last one over?"

"Middle of nowhere, not too far from Thame, just next to a level crossing. Why do you ask?"

"Oh, just curious. You know we were talking about Prince Felix Yusupov and the murder of Rasputin?"

"At band practice, ye-es …"

"Well, your little mishap sounds remarkably similar to an anecdote told by Univ's notorious old boy, Felix Yusupov, in his autobiography, *Lost Splendor*."

"I'll take your word for it."

"No, check it out for yourself. The whole book is up there on my favourite website in all the world. Alexanderpalace, one word, dot org. It's like a set of matryoshka dolls hand-crafted by Fabergé. The further in you go, the more magic you find …."

Suitably piqued, I dial up www.alexanderpalace.org at the earliest opportunity and click on the links to *Lost Splendor*. Just as Bill Clinton's autobiography may be judged by what he chooses to foreground, this is how the fabulously rich Prince Felix starts his story:

> I was born on March 24, 1887, in our house on the Moika Canal, at St. Petersburg. The evening before, my mother went to a ball at the Winter Palace and danced the whole night through. Our friends

thought this was a sign that I would be gay, and a good dancer.

And how right they were, although possibly not in the way that Yusupov intends. The young aristo proves to be as camp as a boy scouts' jamboree, but resolutely in denial throughout his lifetime, including his long and apparently happy marriage to the lovely Princess Irina. Our hero was christened Felix:

> During the christening, which took place in our chapel, the priest almost drowned me in the baptismal font, into which, according to the Orthodox rite, I had to be plunged three times. It seems that I was revived with the greatest difficulty.

Does this near-drowning prefigure the final element of Yusupov's monumental and murderous triptych, the drowning of the monster after poisoning and shooting have failed? Yusupov is (like me, I concede) a great believer in portents of all kinds.

If this remarkable opening was sure to strike me as ominous, then what am I to make of Prince Felix's time at Univ? That's where he finally pitches up after numerous grand tours of Europe, including the witnessing of his elder brother's death in a Parisian duel. Attempting to slum it in Oxford, he insists on being known by the more modest title Count Sumarokov-Elston and is duly given freezing, damp rooms on the High St, not so far from the site of the newish Shelley Memorial. The rooms serve not only as an all-night drinking club for freeloading Englishmen but also as a convenient entry point to the college for those who are out after hours.

Young Felix takes up rowing but finds that golf is rather more congenial. (Maybe he went home to form his own USPGA, the Univ-St Petersburg Golf Alliance?) He has plenty of brushes with the college authorities and this is the bit that Phil must have had in mind:

> Without the personal intervention of the Bishop of London, I would certainly have been expelled ... I was returning from London where I had dined with a fellow undergraduate. In spite of a heavy fog, we were driving at top speed, and we were anxious to be on time as I had already been late twice during the term, and a third offense would have automatically led to my expulsion.

Blinded by the fog, my friend who was driving crashed into the closed gates of a level crossing. The violent collision smashed the gate and I was thrown on the track. I must have lost consciousness, and, as I came to, I saw a light through the fog which grew larger and larger at terrifying speed. I was still too dizzy to realize what was happening, and was only saved by instinctively turning and rolling off the track. The London express thundered by, and the blast sent me head over heels into the ditch. I picked myself up without a scratch, but my friend, though alive, was in very bad shape, with several broken limbs. As to the car, needless to say very little of it remained after the express had gone by. I telephoned from the gatekeeper's cottage for an ambulance, and after taking my friend to the Oxford Hospital I reached my college two hours late. However, in view of the circumstances, I was not expelled.

You may imagine my feelings on reading this extraordinary tale which prefigures the fate of William Jefferson Blythe II and my own in so many ways. What model car was it? Presumably not the same Rolls Royce which ferried the unkillable Rasputin to the bridge over the icy Neva. Where was this level crossing? Alas, Felix does not say. I am naturally convinced it is the very same spot that I visited. And who was the unnamed undergraduate friend? Presumably it is not Eric Hamilton, the closest of his Oxford friends, because he is named in the preceding paragraphs.

Was it instead Oswald Rayner, the Black Country boy who was also to enjoy Yusupov's spectacular largess in St Petersburg? Rayner is only mentioned later on as "a British officer whom I had known at Oxford". We can only speculate on the circumstances in which they met – Rayner was up the High at Oriel, not Univ. As a student of modern languages, it seems reasonable to guess that Rayner joined the Russian Society, the creation of which had been Yusupov's one lasting contribution to university life.

Yusupov studied (if that is not too strong a word) at Univ between 1909 and 1912 and seems to have encountered the "lascivious, malicious satyr", Rasputin, shortly before matriculation, forming an instant hatred for the ambitious starets. This was seven years before the assassination. But did the germ of the idea form in his whisky-addled mind as he lay in his damp Univ bed so far from the comforts of St Petersburg? Did the imposing marble memorial to the drowned Shelley inspire some of the detail of that plan?

Along with a lot of kids of my generation, I remember being force-fed Mary Shelley's *Frankenstein (the Modern Prometheus)* for GCSE Eng Lit and I am struck now by the parallels between Yusupov's portentous narrative and the earlier story (written in late 1816) of a love-hate relationship which concludes with a fatal rendezvous in the Arctic seas, creator and creation locked together in a frozen embrace.

Like GCSE students up and down the country, I memorised the last two paragraphs:

> "But soon," [the monster] cried with sad and solemn enthusiasm, "I shall die, and what I now feel be no longer felt. Soon these burning miseries will be extinct. I shall ascend my funeral pile triumphantly and exult in the agony of the torturing flames. The light of that conflagration will fade away; my ashes will be swept into the sea by the winds. My spirit will sleep in peace, or if it thinks, it will not surely think thus. Farewell."
>
> He sprang from the cabin window as he said this, upon the ice raft which lay close to the vessel. He was soon borne away by the waves and lost in darkness and distance.

To my eyes now, it reads not just as a blueprint for the drowned Shelley's funeral pyre on the beach near Viareggio but for the murder of another misunderstood 'monster' in a frozen St Petersburg.

Was Rasputin's murder best explained as a spurned lover's revenge or did Yusupov grow to regret the creation of this unkillable monster? Was Rasputin truly evil or simply the misunderstood 'wild man' of legend? History, as ever, was written by the winners and Yusupov's account, as translated by the self-effacing English spy who may actually have done the deed, has been generally accepted as a factual account. In reality, Rasputin may well have been an ordinary home-loving boy who devoted his life to prayer and good deeds.

Have I read *Lost Splendor* before? I am 99.9% certain that I haven't. It is a little more plausible that I saw the the movie, *Rasputin and the Empress*, on TV at some point in my childhood. How else am I to explain the strange parallels between Yusupov's early life and the alter ego I created to impress Marie-Claire?

I had wondered at the time where those flights of fancy had come from. It must be that the details of some dreary film have imprinted themselves on my childish imagination.

Looking now at the résumé of the film's plot, so conveniently supplied by Wikipedia, it is clear that very little of Yusupov's life-story is used in the characterisation of Prince Paul (who kills Rasputin). The film was made long before *Lost Splendor* was written, after all. The film does include the haemophiliac Prince Alexy, heir to the Russian throne and subject to Rasputin's faith-healing, so perhaps that was the element that struck me most as I sprawled in front of the TV set during some long-forgotten school holiday?

It's rather harder to account for some of the finer details in my version of the well-travelled young plutocrat from St Petersburg. That scenario in which I escaped from Yalta with a handful of Rembrandts under my arm – what the heck was going on there? The last chapter of the first volume of *Lost Splendor* describes that last journey into exile from, yes, Yalta. How on earth could I have guessed all this?

But there is more. There is one detail in this extraordinary tale which stands out above all others, one detail which chills me like the icy waters of the Neva. The one indisputable fact in this whole farrago of self-aggrandisement and mythopoesis – the date. The date on which this extraordinary assassination occurred. Rasputin was murdered in the early hours of December 30th 1916, one hundred years to the very day before I too am destined to drown.

How can *that* be a coincidence?

Wednesday 30 November 2016

Does something essential rest on these? (6)

Osney is mentioned briefly in Chaucer's *Miller's Tale* as the "nearby town" that Nicholas's Oxford landlord, John the Carpenter, visits, thereby allowing his pretty wife, Alison, to fall victim to the young scholar's charms. Later, Nicholas points to various apocryphal portents to convince the gullible John that a flood of Biblical proportions is imminent and the only way to save himself and his wife is to suspend himself in a tub from the rafters.

Naughty Nick, with his Almagest and his astrolabe, is a role-model for philanderers and conmen everywhere, drawing on a wide range of apocryphal and astrological signs to bend the world to his wiles. Meanwhile, on modern-day Osney Island, subsumed into a rather larger Oxford, my own landlord, dearest Papa, is dozing quietly in his favourite armchair, his collection of zappers on one side and a pile of unread newspapers that is now two feet high on the other.

"Dad, what will you do when the great tidal wave comes and Osney Island disappears under water?" I ask.

"What's that, son?" He half-opens one eye and closes it again.

"You've seen the long-range weather forecasts, Papa. The Environment Agency has got us on Amber Alert already. But the great flood could come without warning one night while we are asleep in our beds."

"It can't be any worse than it was back in 2007, can it?" he snorts. "And please don't call me 'Papa' – I'm not Greek, I'm the Hogg!"

I have not the faintest idea what he is talking about.

In July 2007, as I idled away the summer before my Finals year, the whole of West Oxford was under water. Osney Island, flanked by the Thames/Isis on its Eastern side and encompassed by Osney Ditch on the other three sides, was the first to go as the floodgates were opened, all too literally, further up-river towards Cirencester, and the rest of the Botley Road floodplain succumbed, about an hour later. Even Noah could hardly have experienced quite such a rapid influx of water as Osney's residents suffered that day. The sun was shining in a cloudless sky and many an Osney resident was watching Padraig Harrington fend off Sergio Garcia's challenge in the Open at Carnoustie when suddenly they noticed their carpets becoming a little moist. Within minutes, if not seconds, water was appearing from all directions, through the walls and floorboards. There are two hundred houses crammed onto this tiny island and there is nowhere for the water to go. Frog Island, as it was once known, was underwater for a week. And then suddenly the water drained away, almost as fast as it arrived, no doubt catching a few frogs on the hop.

The impending floods of 2016 could well be considerably worse.

"Why don't we set up the attic for emergency use?" I suggest, although there is barely room in our attic for a medium-sized stash of pornography. "We could get the plumbing sorted out and set up a temporary bathroom-cum-kitchen up there. How do you fancy bathing under the rafters, Dad?"

"Very funny, Alex. You're not the only one who has read the *Miller's Tale*, you know!"

It's easy to forget that my decrepit, mildewy Dad studied at Univ too, way back in the sixties, long before he met Mum. PPE, a solid Second. It wasn't quite the ideal preparation for a future rock star or poet laureate and, sure enough, Dad became a tax inspector instead, the sort of mistake that any of us might have made at that time. As he says, it was a choice between the Revenue and MI6 and he decided he was marginally less likely to get shot at if he joined the Revenue. Dad passed the Civil Service exams and pretty soon found himself in some prefab tax offices back in Gateshead, the start of a happy lifetime spent exploring the mysteries of capital gains tax.

He's retired now, of course. They let you out of the Revenue quite early with good behaviour and the Civil Service pension was calculated according to 1870 life expectancy statistics, so he will be comfortably off until he pegs out some forty years hence, long after the unfortunate demise of his only son has become a distant memory.

The one big disadvantage of retirement was that my Mum couldn't stand having him about the house all day, so divorce followed retirement as surely as night follows day. So now I tell people I'm the product of a broken home. Mum got to keep the house (a couple of miles from Stockton-on-Tees) while my father, footloose and fancy-free, decided that it might make sense to move back to Oxford where he had been so happy as a student.

The fact that his son was already living there may have been a mild disincentive but Dad was not to be deterred and he had just enough money from the divorce settlement to buy himself a modest two-up-two-down on Swan St, on the western edge of Osney Island. A small part of Frog Island became Hogg Island. It's a lovely little house, separated from the Oxford mainland by a little footbridge, on the other side of which is a primary school and, beyond that, the industrial estate of Osney Mead.

Our terraced house has a tiny back garden which slopes gently down to Osney Ditch, one of the many tributaries and relief-channels which meander across the fertile floodplains of West Oxford. This backwater is, like the Hogacre Ditch, little more than a muddy trough most of the time but, when the rains come, it soon transmogrifies into a raging torrent, ready to burst its banks and engulf the neat rows of Victorian terraced homes.

The original Osney, a little further east, was the home of Rewley Abbey in Chaucerian times but that all changed with the dissolution of the monasteries back in 1538. The backwater remained just that for the next three hundred years until the arrival of the Great Western Railway. The iron road cut a swathe through West Oxford in 1851, a great exhibition of technological progress.

The workers for a big programme of railway-building needed to be housed somewhere so Osney Island, then uninhabited, was leased from Christ Church and a symmetrical grid of cheap, terraced houses was designed by George P. Hester. In no time at all the tiny egg-shaped islet was teeming with a thousand residents and twenty pubs. These days there are perhaps five hundred, mostly middle class, islanders and just two pubs, the Punter and the Holly Bush. Osney has been gentrified but it probably has more novelists, poets, artists and musicians per square foot than any other plot of land in Britain. Failed artists and unheard musicians, admittedly, but you can almost feel the thrum of creativity as you wander its bicycle-fringed streets.

Having bought the place from a strange old lady with a brocade hat and a huge fluffy white poodle, Dad lived here on his own for a year and the very thought of moving back in with my father was something that would once have seemed ridiculous, yet here I am. Dad decided he wanted to take a lodger and I happened to be looking for new digs at round about the same time and, let's be honest, the economic argument was a compelling one. At my age, Dad had already married and become the proud owner of his second house, but I can barely *see* the property ladder now, never mind leap on to the bottom rung. Even the flimsiest and tattiest of Osney's two-up-two-downs goes for the best part of half a million these days. Where am I going to find a bank that would lend me that sort of money when I have no more than the derisory "salary" which Univ deigns to vouchsafe to its loyal retainers? So I moved into Dad's spare bedroom for a couple of weeks "while I sorted myself out" and somehow never moved out again.

I cling on to the few shreds of dignity that are left to me. My circumstances are not *quite* the same as the middle-aged man still living with his Mum, is it? I've already proved I can live independently, haven't I? I don't get my socks ironed and my dinner on the table at 6.30 sharp every evening like one thirty-something adolescent that I know. No, I make a point of doing my own ironing once a quarter. Dad does do a lot of the cooking, I confess, but it's not as if he's got *that* many other things to fill up the average day, is it? We rub along OK and I maintain the pretence that I am still on the look-out for a place of my own.

The big disadvantage, of course, is that it kills any prospect of a successful sex-life. What self-respecting girl wants to go out with a 28-year-old man who still lives with his Dad and whose bedroom is only separated from his father's by the flimsiest of partitions? Outright lies and a fantastical autobiography can only keep a girl interested for two dates max. The more outrageous the inventions and prevarications, the bigger the let-down when the truth finally emerges. My best chance, I figure, is to meet a girl who, for purely practical reasons, is still living at home with her parents, and who will *understand* where I am coming from on this, but Oxford is not full of such creatures.

Dad's two great passions in what one hopes are his autumn years are bridge and genealogy. He's a keen member of the Oxford Bridge Club on the Banbury Rd and likes to while away his afternoons playing for threepence a hundred. As most of his fellow-members are in their nineties and a couple are actually over a hundred, he tends to bring home anything up to ninepence of pure profit from each session.

Dad dreams of executing a triple entry-shifting backwash squeeze (or some such) at least once in his life and the house is full of textbooks that fuss over the nuances of the Acol system. It's a world that seems to have moved on very little from the 1920s but he can lose himself in a game of bridge for hours at a time and, to be frank, I'm just grateful to have the house to myself. Dad has an alter ego called the Hideous Hogg, named after a famous fictional bridge player, which he uses for discussion forums and the like. I think he has even had one or two Hogg stories published.

But genealogy is his latest big thing. His mission, predictably enough, is to fill in the Hogg family tree as far back as it will go. The information is all there online these days, census details, parish registers – it's like using the full 848-page Roget's Thesaurus to solve the *Sun*'s Quick Crossword, but he loves the thrill of the chase. He's gone back through six generations without breaking sweat, mainly because the Hoggs are not really a nomadic tribe. We seem to have put down our roots in and around Stockton-on-Tees and undertaken a variety of glamorous tasks – solicitor, funeral director, bank clerk, that sort of thing. Solid yeoman stock and, let's be honest, I'm a pretty solid yeoman myself these days.

But working backwards, the Hogg line peters out somewhat abruptly in the middle of the nineteenth century, round about the time Osney Island made its overnight appearance like a long row of celestial dominoes. We reach one Henry Leigh Hogg who seems bereft of parents of any kind. No doubt he was raised by wolves (or black cats?) before embarking on a stimulating career in marine insurance. After HLH, there's a pretty clear line of Hoggery through to the present day.

"It's so frustrating," Dad whinges. "I should be able to get back to 1750, at the very least. We can see that Henry Leigh Hogg married Violet McDermott in 1874, had a son and two daughters, and died in 1914, on the eve of the Great War, all without leaving Durham, but we've no idea where he came from."

"And you've tried all the available documents?"

"Yes, all the parish registers. Not just Durham, but right across the north-east, in case he moved to Stockton from foreign parts. But there's nothing. I've traced Violet Westlake back another four generations but it's not quite the same thing. She isn't a Hogg."

"No, I can see that must be quite important."

I make suitable cooing noises as yet again he shows me the vast Tree of Hogglife, with its many branches and tendrils snaking out across the grubby sellotaped collection of A3 sheets on which Dad has laboured. But what I'm really thinking is this: does it resemble the Giant Hog(g)weed celebrated by Peter Gabriel on *Nursery Cryme*? Found in the Russian hills and presented to Kew Gardens in an act of misguided benevolence, before running amok across England's green and pleasant land:

Mighty hogweed is avenged.
Human bodies soon will know our anger.
Kill them with your hogweed hairs
Heracleum mantegazziani ...

The sap of the giant hogweed causes phytodermatitis amongst humans, resulting in blisters, scars, and – if it comes in contact with eyes – blindness. No wonder we Hoggs have always been so popular.

But I feel I have more in common with the common hogweed, *heracleum sphondylium*, also known as fools asparagus. Indeed, as a small boy I owed much of my music and sex education to the hogweed. The unkempt gardens of Priory House, where I spent so much of my summer holidays in solitary contemplation, were full of hogweeds, some as much as seven feet tall when in full flower in July. These gentle hemlock-like giants towered over the rest of the undergrowth, their umbels like clouds of tiny white flowers. Uncle Alan showed me how you could turn sections of the thick hollow stems of these magnificent weeds into a musical instrument by inserting a long blade of grass and blowing. Well, it was cheaper than a kazoo.

Unlike the other umbellifers (carrot, parsley, coriander, etc), hogweeds are not really edible – at least for humans – but they do seem to have a narcotic and aphrodisiac effect on insect life. In high summer, the mass of white flowers form a platform or stage on which randy beetles can strut their stuff and mate to their hearts' content. What are those beetles *doing*, I asked my uncle? I forget his mumbled reply, something about making baby beetles, but it was clear even to my young eyes that these little soldier beetles were having a very good time indeed. No wonder the popular name for the species is the hogweed bonking beetle. They would wander about in a stoned state, hook up with a member of the opposite sex, then remain attached even when flying away to investigate the pollen elsewhere. In this state of zonked and erotic distraction, they are easy prey for house martins (or martlets, as Uncle Alan insisted on calling them) that swoop down and hoover up the delicate and tasty couples in mid-air. What a way to go!

Sorry, I digress. Having duly admired all the fronds and tendrils of Dad's Hogg-Tree, I ask casually whether he bumped into Bill Clinton at all back in the sixties.

"No. Why do you ask?"

"Oh, no reason, really. I guess he was slightly after your time. It's just that you both did PPE, didn't you?"

"I heard he used to loiter around the Porter's Lodge mesmerised by the way Douglas, the Head Porter, treated everyone. Ideal prep for someone who wanted to run the free world, I guess. I never met Clinton. But I have to say there were quite a few other Univ PPEists and PPPists who went on to great things in those days."

"What, greater than being a taxman?"

"Arguably so. There was Peter Gibbs who opened the batting for Derbyshire and then had quite a distinguished career as a playwright and novelist. Lovely chap!"

"Never heard of him."

"OK, perhaps you've come across Mike Ratledge?"

"You mean *the* Mike Ratledge, keyboard-noodler supreme and founder member of Soft Machine? He wasn't at Univ, was he?"

"Indeed he was. We got paired up for Philosophy seminars. I remember a long debate on whether Hegel was the clumsy charlatan that Schopenhauer maintained."

"Was he?"

"I can't remember a word that either of them wrote. But it all seemed quite important back then. Mike was a tall, thin lad, quite shy really. He was already into all that avant-garde music. He was up and down, Oxford, London, Canterbury, so he missed a few lectures. But he was a serious scholar too. He wanted to do a postgrad in America but didn't get the paperwork malarkey done in time."

"So he formed Soft Machine instead?"

"I guess so. I didn't see him much after that. I wasn't really into jazz, being more of a Peter, Paul and Mary fan myself."

"What taste you had, Dad! What did you make of the Rolling Stones in those days?"

"Awful racket! You're not still doing their stuff, are you?"

"Phil's organising a big do in the Parks next summer. We're going to try and recreate the 1969 Hyde Park Free Festival, God help us."

"They say Bill Clinton was a big Stones fan …"

"Is that so? Hyde Park would have been just after the end of Trinity Term in '69, halfway through his time in Oxford. Maybe he was there!"

Later, while my father shouts out the answers to Victoria Coren on Monday's *Only Connect*, I retire to my cell with its solitary reproduction of Turner's 'High Street, Oxford' (1810) clinging to the damp wall and contemplate the idea of Bill Clinton singing along to 'Sympathy for the Devil' in Hyde Park in his tie-dye t-shirt and flared jeans. No doubt he would have been puffing at a spliff with an impressionable English rose in tow. I picture them cooling off in the Serpentine and holding hands on the bus back to Oxford.

Thursday 1 December 2016

Murdered Russian porter with two unknown figures (5)

If this is to be my last month on earth and I do indeed die on December 30th, what will there be to remember me by? Where are my *memento mori*? Let's see … £136.47 in my Santander SupaSaver account (earning interest at 0.0001% p.a.), a conviction for cycling without lights (contested all the way to the Crown Court), a brief moment of fame when a wayward Luis Suarez strike smacked me on the bonce, caught in slo-mo on *MOTD2*, and a couple of witty wordplays published on the *Guardian* Letters page, bottom left section. I've been reasonably kind to children and dumb animals and I've refrained from any attempted assassinations although, not being christened Oswald, this was statistically unlikely anyway.

But my great works are still to come. Will it be that my late-flowering talents never flower at all? Will I never be recognised as a misunderstood giant of literary criticism whose insight into the influence of St Teresa of Avila on *Tess of the d'Urbervilles* went unappreciated for so long? I fear I won't be a Man of Letters refusing his Nobel Prize on a point of obscure principle. As for my musical career … well, OK, that was never going to happen, but it would have been nice to play several more notes, possibly even in the right order.

Googlers searching on 'Alexander Hogg' will not find me, only the great map-maker of the early nineteenth century, best known for publishing the journals of James Cook, or the Kiwi politician who became Minister of Labour in 1909. That Alex Hogg, with his squat figure and receding hairline, looks worryingly like the old man I might yet become if I can somehow circumnavigate the great sounding cataract that threatens to engulf me on December 30th.

Meanwhile I see that on YouTube there is a television interview that Felix Yusupov gave right at the end of his life at http://tinyurl.com/h7oxbku. Fifty years on, the old scoundrel was still being asked about the single event which had come to define his life. For the fifty-thousandth time, Yusupov tells his story and, of course, every re-telling is subtly different and unreliable.

But does Yusupov, near death, *ever* tell the truth about what happened that December night in 1916? Now that his old friend, Oswald Rayner is dead and Felix has no need to protect him, perhaps he can speak freely and make his peace with his Maker. I contemplate a screenplay.

My working title is *Yusupov and Rasputin* because the relationship between those two men is, of course, the heart of the story. Both are charismatic faith-healers whose icy gaze in grainy photos still transfixes the viewer a hundred years on. If they had some sort of physical relationship, it is best left to the imagination – they seem to have attracted and repelled each other in equal measure.

Yet if Yusupov was ever "in love", it was not with Rasputin but with Grand Duke Dmitri Pavlovich, his boyhood friend and eventual co-conspirator. Dmitri was an absurdly handsome Guards officer (as well as cousin of Nicholas II) who seems to have encouraged the young Felix to dress up in all his mother's finery in a futile attempt to parade incognito amongst St Petersburg's drinking-dens. No doubt the homesick Felix sent countless *billets doux* from his sodden eyrie in Oxford to his *insouciant chevalier* (too much French? It was the language of the Russian court, after all …) but Dmitri would have been more interested in his preparations for the 1912 Olympics where he finished just outside the medals in the equestrian events.

When it came to the murder plot, Dmitri went along for the ride, both literally and metaphorically, tipping the turbulent priest out of the boot of the Roller and off the Petrovski bridge, but I doubt if his heart was really in it. The scandal may have cost him his military career but advancement in the White Army was of limited value in 1917 anyway. Like Felix, Dmitri got out just in time. Exiled to the Persian front, he managed to escape via Teheran and Bombay before finding his way to that last redoubt of Imperial Russia, Paris, where he dreamt up lucrative business ideas with his latest lover, one Coco Chanel. The first four formulas didn't quite hit the mark but Chanel No. 5 was certainly a winner for the new playboy of the western world.

In the days before the *Sunday Times* Rich List, Felix Yusupov may just have been the richest man in the world. The Yusupov family's land covered 675,000 acres and included highly profitable mining and oil interests. Modern estimates are that Felix was worth around ten billion quid in today's money but that seems a little conservative – it would put him a little behind Roman Abramovich in the yacht-building stakes. While Abramovich and the other perestroika lottery winners have managed to shift their ill-gotten treasures offshore (and to Stamford Bridge) before the rats get at them, Felix was caught a little bit on the hop by the 1917 Revolution. It was a case of how much could you carry out of the country under your arms or, if necessary, sewn into the lining of your baby's nappies, as many of the Yusupov family jewels had to be.

In my version, Yusupov creeps back to the Moika Palace and half-inches a couple of his own Rembrandts. These are intended to fund his life in exile and in the years after the Great War he finds a suitable art-pawnbroker, Joseph Widener. But when the Russian émigré has trouble finding the cash to redeem these priceless works, Widener takes the opportunity to make off with the masterpieces himself.

There's no space for all that in my play, nor for the Nazis' negotiations with Yusupov around 1942 – he claims to have said a firm "no" to the idea of being installed as a puppet-ruler of Russia once the Panzers had laid waste to Stalingrad. I know little of Paris and Stalingrad but plenty about Univ, so my focus is on his undergraduate years: crashing his car, meeting a strange boy with a Brummie accent called Oswald Rayner, sweet-talking the college authorities, entertaining Anna Pavlova in his suite of rooms overlooking Hyde Park, arranging for herds of cows to be shipped from England to St Petersburg, gazing at the Shelley Memorial, dreaming of Dmitri and plotting the perfect crime.

Somewhere in this stew you find the lovely Princess Irina, the porcelain doll who followed dutifully in Felix's wake for the remainder of their tethered lives. There she still is in that extraordinary television interview from their bedroom at Rue Pierre Guerín 38 bis in Paris's 16th arrondissement. The dead-eyed Irina is wearing what looks like a garishly-spotted nightgown, rubbing her hands feverishly as Felix, his eyes well hidden behind some enormous black sunglasses, dutifully serves up his party-piece one last, unconvincing time.

By then Irina has spent fifty years in her Paris salon, chain-smoking and playing solitaire – what story would she have told if anyone had been so insolent as to ask her? *Was* she seduced by Rasputin? Was Felix motivated by sexual jealousy? That's the plot of the 1932 MGM blockbuster, *Rasputin and the Empress,* but the Yusupovs sued the American dream-weavers though the English courts. Yusupov cheerfully admitted being a murderer but the suggestion that he was a cuckold as well was an affront to his dignity. The Yusupovs were awarded 25,000 English pounds in damages, almost enough to compensate for the unfortunate loss of their Rembrandts. It was a salutary lesson for MGM and all those of us who would fiddle with history for our own nefarious ends.

If the London courts are now the destination of choice for billionaires' ex-wives who hope to maximise their divorce settlements, much the same applied to image rights cases in the thirties. I remember Phil's dad telling us all about it on the terrace at the Casa Magni. The key precedent had been set by another Univ graduate, Cyril Tolley, in 1931. Tolley was one of the great golfers of the day, winning the Amateur Championship in 1920 while still an undergraduate and famed for his jousts with Bobby Jones.

JS Fry, the confectionery manufacturers, made the mistake of selecting Tolley as one of the subjects of a series of cartoons created for advertising purposes. The ex-Univ man was caricatured in mid-swing with a bar of Fry's chocolate slipping out of his back-pocket. Tolley sued for defamation and libel, arguing that the cartoon implied he had compromised his amateur status. He was not, repeat *not*, being paid in chocolate bars. The case went up via the Court of Appeal all the way to the House of Lords before a definitive judgement in Tolley's favour. The principle of image rights had been established and Felix Yusupov was one of the first to take a boat across the Channel and cash in on the generosity of the English courts.

But not the last. In my role as self-appointed and unofficial Univ historian, I should point out that a third alumnus of the college achieved a similar and even more newsworthy triumph in 1967. Prime Minister Harold Wilson, a Junior Fellow at Univ in the late 1940s, successfully sued popular beat-combo, The Move, on account of promotional materials associated with the hit single 'Flowers in the Rain'. Once again the offending item was a cartoon postcard, this time depicting Wilson in the bath with his secretary, Marcia Falkender. Wilson duly established that this was disgusting, depraved and despicable (the banner headlines on the cartoon, in fact) and won what proved to be an enormous pay-out. All royalties from the Move's song would go to charities of Wilson's choice in perpetuity, despite the fact that the songwriter, Roy Wood, and the band had nothing whatsoever to do with their manager, Tony Secunda's publicity stunt. This was a verdict which has cost Wood a seven-figure sum (and counting).

So I had better watch what I say about my illustrious forebears at Oxford's Oldest College™, saints the lot of them, even the self-confessed murderers and despots. They can afford expensive lawyers and I don't want to fund anyone's residential fees at the Fletcher Memorial Home. But if you are reading this after December 30th, you will probably need to sue my estate.

Saturday 3 December 2016

Tack back after misplaced hope, like one rejected by Dane (8)

Phil and Marie-Claire have gone away for a "romantic weekend break" to Amsterdam when the call comes.

Dad is out playing bridge at 147 Banbury Rd and I am feeling a little sorry for myself, if truth be told. A couple of cans of Snecklifter Special have slipped down the gullet very smoothly and I am just contemplating polishing off the last one in the fridge. Should I wait up for Match of the Day? The prospect is far from enticing. It's not often that the landline rings these days so I contemplate ignoring it completely, but there is just the chance that it will be the Premium Bond people.

"Mr Hogg? Alex Hogg?"

The voice sounds oddly familiar but I am unable to place it immediately.

"Speaking. Who's that?"

"It's DI Hunt from the Met. You remember that I asked you a few questions."

"Of course …"

"Well, the thing is … there's no easy way to put this, Mr Hogg …."

Fear stalks my entrails as if I were a 1970s BBC radio DJ.

"A body has been found."

"A body?" I whisper. It is as if I have suddenly joined the cast of particularly dire B-movie.

"Yes, a woman's body. In the Serpentine. Now I don't want to alarm you, sir, and this is one of many lines we are pursuing, but …"

"It's Hattie."

"I think it's highly unlikely but it *is* a possibility that we'd like to eliminate as quickly as possible. That's why I'm calling. To be frank, the body had been underwater for some considerable time and there is no quick means of identifying who she is or, rather, *was*."

I have no idea how to respond to this news.

"Under water? I'm not exactly Hattie's nearest and dearest. I'm sure her sister …"

"Yes, we've tried the sister but got no response. And her ex-husband, Dr Sherborne."

"He's in Amsterdam, I believe."

"So-o …"

"You'd like me to come and try to identify the body."

"If you could …"

"Tomorrow morning?"

"As soon as you can. Purely as a matter of routine, so we can cross her name off the list of possibles."

Sunday 4 December 2016

Publisher's flourishes put down (10)

The M40 is quiet at first light, my new Yaris purrs along happily and I have ample opportunity to brood. In my sheltered life, I have had few encounters with mortality. It is some time since the last of my grandparents died and since then I have had few causes to visit the Headington Crematorium. Like most of my generation, I know no one of my own age who has expired, still less in circumstances like this. I don't know what I am supposed to feel. Perhaps I am still in shock?

If it proves to be Hattie on the mortuary slab, how will I respond? What explanation could there be? Did she have some kind of crazy boating accident in the Serpentine? This seems impossible. But the thought that Hattie might have drowned herself is equally ludicrous. Could she *really* have walked out into the lake and taken her own life, like Ophelia or Virginia Woolf? *I'm* the one who's supposed to be drowning but I have no intention of doing so deliberately. Has Hattie, in some weird way, taken my place? Or was I simply misled about the precise date in December 2016 and the identity of the drownee?

The only thing I know about the Serpentine is that it is in Hyde Park and one of the few things I know about Hyde Park is that it was the venue for the extraordinary free concert in 1969 that the Strolling Clones (if such we be) are now trying to emulate. Another odd coincidence? And Felix Yusupov had rooms overlooking Hyde Park in his days of masquerading as an Oxford undergraduate. Irrelevant of course.

My mind is full of absurd literary parallels. What if Hattie has been *murdered*, like Rebecca at Manderley? But who could want to kill Hattie? She had few friends but few enemies either. I catch myself slipping into the past tense – Hattie is still *alive*, I tell myself, and this is all some kind of bad dream.

But *if* she is dead, *if* she has killed herself, who is to blame? I think back to our last, strange, brief encounter around Easter. Should I have tried harder to make something happen then? But surely Hattie was still besotted with Phil? I was just some kind of ersatz-Phil, some temporary solace. It was maudlin, madeira-fuelled madness, and we both knew it. But that image of Hattie waiting for me in bed, her goose-pimpled flesh only partially covered by her flowery duvet, calling me back with her big, reproachful eyes, now seems seared onto my cerebral cortex.

What a toe-rag I was that day. Did I reject and hurt her because she had once unwittingly done likewise to me? When I first knew her, Hattie was already Phil's girlfriend and, even if she hadn't been, she was way out of my league. The only difference now is that she has two children in tow, no money, and a broken marriage behind her. That's the reason men are no longer queuing round the block, the reason why I found excuses for failing to call her back. She's still the most beautiful girl I have ever met. But beauty is no insurance against depression. I should have been there when she needed a friend, when she needed a … a *lover*.

In my time of dying, I do not need this on my conscience.

My eyes well up slightly at the thought of what might have been and I almost miss the White City exit. I will know the truth soon enough now.

Disappointingly, Detective Inspector Hunt has better things to do than turn up at the mortuary himself. Surely a good sleuth should be there to study my reactions at the critical moment, the drawing back of the veil, that macabre anagnorisis? Is he in bed, reading the *Sunday Mirror*?

Instead, a mortuary jobsworth leads me down a couple of corridors. My jelly-legs do not give way beneath me. We arrive in a cold, bare room and some kind of trolley-like contraption is wheeled out, as if bearing a giant Christmas turkey. A simple blue sheet covers the body that I must scrutinise. I make the necessary sign to indicate that I am ready and without fuss the attendant peels back the sheet …

It is not Hattie. It is nothing like Hattie. This poor woman's bloated flesh looks barely human at all, but the long nose and the relatively square jaw bear no resemblance to Hattie's features. I shake my head and turn away.

"Thank God," I whisper.

"Not yours, then?" the man asks, his pen poised above his clipboard.

"Not mine," I say. "Not mine at all …"

I emerge from the sarcophagus and the daylight mocks me with its careless brio. On a whim, I leave the Yaris in the mortuary car park and take a trip on the Piccadilly Line to Hyde Park Corner. Inside forty minutes I am being coughed out of the wheezing tube onto the most distinguished of London's eight royal parks, an oasis of calm in the midst of the bustling city.

I stroll through the Queen Elizabeth Gates and on to a tree-lined avenue.

There is a rose garden on my left. The whole experience seems weirdly familiar, as if I have been here before, sauntering down this very avenue. But I know I have not. When you are brought up in the northern wilds (whence a trip to Newcastle is an exotic treat), London seems like another country. There were no Hoggish day trips to Hyde Park, the British Museum, Bloomsbury or Madame Tussaud's. I am quite certain I have never been to Hyde Park before.

I pass a row of trees on my right, admiring the green-and-yellow plumage of the ring-necked parakeets, and somehow I *know* there is a bandstand behind. My expectations are immediately confirmed. I think of Phil Connors in his Punxsutawney hotel:

Phil: Do you ever have déjà vu, Mrs. Lancaster?
Mrs. Lancaster: I don't think so, but I could check with the kitchen.

Although I cannot quite see it, I sense that the Serpentine is almost upon us. Sure enough, my gravel pathway and a number of others converge at the corner of a spectacular expanse of water. There is hardly a ripple on its glassy surface. The very idea of someone drowning here seems an affront to the natural order. Alone, I palely loiter, while parakeets squawk.

I wonder where they fished that poor woman out of the pond? A couple of small boys are playing with some tiny motorised boats, propelling them hither and thither with their hand-held consoles, under the supervision of their Sunday father. The water is so still, it does not seem much of a challenge. Why, even a paper boat might float serenely across this placid sea. I feel an atavistic urge to find a flat stone and skim it across the lake, but there are no appropriate stones to hand and it might be a little undignified in any case. I am oddly convinced that I have thrown pebbles at this very spot before.

And what of those other Stones? Where did they sing for their supper? The bandstand looks a little too modest to have accommodated Mick's ego, not to mention Keith, Charlie, Bill Perks and a golden-haired young guitarist with the no-nonsense name of Mick Taylor, nervously playing his very first gig as a replacement for Brian Jones who had drowned in his own swimming pool just two days previously. And yet here his bandmates all were in front of this vast lake, trusting to luck that none of the half a million revellers, most of them high as kites, would somehow, accidentally or otherwise, emulate his hero and sink like a Stone ....

Monday 5 December 2016

Fail to declare a stick (5)

Some 24 hours later, Phil, back from Amsterdam, picks up various text-messages and voice-mails and deigns to call round at my bachelor gaff in Osney with Marie-Claire in tow.

I explain patiently that I have done his dirty work for him and determined that his young ex-wife has not, after all, been drowned. I exaggerate the gruesomeness of the experience a little for effect but I figure he deserves it – why is he swanning off around Europe while an escalating manhunt for Hattie is taking place? Shouldn't he be out with a torch, inching his way across Hampstead Heath or Green Park, searching desperately for clues? Failing that, surely some form of thank you would not go amiss?

"The odds against it being Hattie must have been ten thousand to one," Phil says blithely, when I have completed my tale. "I've no idea why they thought it might be her."

"Well, possibly because she loved walking down by the Serpentine. You used to walk there with her yourself!"

Marie-Claire cuffs Phil playfully about the ear.

"You didn't tell me that!"

"I'm sorry, M-C, I'd completely forgotten …"

It turns out that Phil has taken to squiring his latest squeeze around exactly the same haunts as he had frequented with his wife in years gone by. I must admit I'd credited him with a little more style and originality than that. And, as for taking a lovely name like Marie-Claire and reducing it to the bare initials, well, I can only apologise on his behalf.

"Yes, M-C and I were in Hyde Park only a couple of weeks ago when we went to the Schoenberg at the Festival Hall. I was hoping to pick up a few ideas for our Stones gig."

"*Schoenberg*? Are you sure you wouldn't like GDP to have a crack at the Second String Quartet? Is 'Gimme Shelter' no longer a big enough challenge for you?"

"There are a few sides to me even you don't know, Alex. For instance, did you know I once planned to be a lawyer?"

"Yes, I can imagine a career in conveyancing would have paid a little better than academe."

"I figured I could represent all those stroppy rock stars. Punks' attorney Phil, that's me! Punks' attorney Phil!"

"Yes, yes, I got it the first time. Instead you became D.Phil Phil. But *Schoenberg*?"

"It was *my* idea," Marie-Claire says. "I was just trying to pretend I had these high-brow musical tastes. And it seems to have worked!"

The two lovebirds chuckle merrily together and I resist the temptation to improvise a sick-bucket from one of their crash helmets. Why do most women have such unbelievably poor taste in men? What would a ridiculously beautiful young woman like Marie-Claire see in Phil? OK, he's tall, slim, good looking (in a conventional sort of way) and one of the brightest young academics in his field, holding down one of Oxford's top jobs. OK, his family's loaded and he's got a full head of hair, but *apart* from all that? Is it too much to ask that a sensitive, intelligent young lady should see the subtler merits of one such as myself? Or indeed, specifically, *me*? It doesn't help that I'm a couple of inches shorter than most of the women I fancy and that my shiny pate is balding fast, almost as rapidly as my "career" is going downhill, but these things are mere superficialities. In a better world, in a juster world …

But this is the only world I've got, for the next few weeks at least, so I laugh along with my friends.

"*What* seems to have worked?" I hardly dare to ask.

Phil and Marie-Claire exchange glances.

"We-ell …" says Phil evasively. Marie-Claire picks up the baton to save him further embarrassment.

"We're getting married."

"Married!?"

"Er, yes. Is that such an odd thing to do?" Marie-Claire titters nervously.

A second feels like a lifetime as my vocal cords have turned to spaghetti.

"Well, congratulations!" I splutter at last. My words hang icily in the air. "That's splendid news! When's the happy day?"

"We'll probably just creep away somewhere," Phil says.

"Oh no, we won't," Marie-Claire corrects him. "We'll certainly have a bit of a do, possibly on the 30th."

"The 30th?" I gulp. "The 30th of December?"

"Sure, why not? Just a quiet affair, as Phil has been married before."

"I thought he still was!"

"What, to Hattie?" Phil laughs uneasily. "No, no, the paperwork came through, months back – you remember?"

"You don't think the timing is a little …" I try desperately to find the *mot juste*.

"You mean, what with Hattie having gone missing? Well, that does have something to do with it, actually."

"In what way?"

"It's the kids, you see. Charlie and Xan. They need a proper home."

"They've got a proper home, haven't they?! I remind him. "Auntie Liz is looking after them just fine. Besides, you keep telling me that Hattie will be back any day now."

"I'm sure she will. But what if she isn't? I'm their father after all. Trouble is, Hattie's family doesn't see it that way, so there may have to be a court hearing and it would really help if I could demonstrate that there is a stable family situation that the kids would move into. Just until Hattie reappears."

"You mean there's a custody battle?"

"You could call it that."

"That's not the reason for getting married," Marie-Claire assures me. "It's just the reason for getting married *now*."

"It always *was* one of Phil's favourite institutions," I note sweetly.

"If at first you don't succeed …" Phil smiles forbiddingly. "Anyway, we'd appreciate it if a Russian prince could be prevailed upon to …"

"Yes, please, Prince Alexy …"

"Yes, yes, very funny."

"Just to say a few words?" Phil suggests. "Probably not the same few words as last time."

"As best man, you mean?"

"I don't think you'd need a title as such, but …"

"I did mention my slight problem with 30th December, didn't I?"

Phil looks at me blankly.

"You can't get time off work on a Friday? Don't worry, the college is shut between Christmas and the New Year."

"No, it's nothing like that. I did mention it, but you seem to have forgotten."

"You'll have to remind me."

"The small problem that I might be *dead* on December 30th!"

Marie-Claire seems suitably alarmed but Phil treats it all as a big joke.

"Ah yes, the Witch of Endor. How silly of me to forget. What time of day are you expecting to peg out? We could schedule an early start, make sure you fit it in OK before your untimely demise ….”

“Well, thank you for your sympathy, Phil. That’s what friends are for, I guess.”

“Come on, Alex. You can’t possibly believe any of that nonsense, can you? All that Mystic Meg stuff? I could ask Ozzie, if you like. But something like this might be just the thing to distract you from such maudlin thoughts. Then on New Year’s Eve, you can say ‘gosh, I’m still alive, and that was quite a good bash last night, wasn’t it?’”

“We’d really appreciate it,” adds Marie-Claire.

What can a poor boy do?

“Is it going to be some kind of ghastly vegan affair?”

“Yes,” says Phil.

“No, it certainly isn’t,” says Marie-Claire. “It will be a carnival of carnivoraciousness. Plus some veggie-burgers for the groom.”

The two lovebirds wait hopefully for my verdict.

“In *that* case, OK. You know how I love the sound of my own voice. And there *are* forty-seven skeletons in Phil’s closet that still need airing …”

“It’s lucky I’ve brought my chequebook,” says Phil. “Those skeletons need to remain securely buried!”

“So where are you thinking of having this ‘bit of a do’?”

“I’ve given it some thought,” says Marie-Claire. “The Alington Room’s a possibility, I guess. But it’s all a bit fuddy-duddy and conventional. I’ve decided we should hire one of those houseboat restaurants on the Thames…”

“You mean, actually out on the *river*?”

“Yes, the Thames,” Phil confirms. “I thought you would have heard of it.”

“But the Thames is …”

“The Thames is what?”

I struggle to find the words to express an appropriate level of trepidation.

“Put it this way: if you feared drowning on a certain day, would you book a seat on the *Titanic*?”

“Alex, this isn’t the Atlantic we’re talking about. It’s the Thames or, rather, the Isis as it dribbles its way past this fair city. It’s hardly more than a puddle in places.”

“Have you *seen* the Isis this week? If all this rain persists, the levee will break long before Christmas. There will be plenty enough water to drown in. You’ll have to make some other plan! If I’m to be Best Man, you’ll need to stay firmly on dry land.”

Phil and Marie-Claire take their leave and I put on Act II of *Before the Dawn* for what seems like the 50th time since the package arrived from Amazon. Already I know every lilt, nuance and swirl of this reworked version of the *Ninth Wave* suite. This is definitely the music I want to drown by.

And in the evening Dad and I watch *Mr Turner* on Film4. The movie focuses on the last 25 years of JMW Turner's life, long after he painted Univ and the High St, the picture that adorns my bedroom wall. It is a film that seems intent on realizing Turner's worst fears that new technology, i.e. the camera, would render the visual arts redundant. Who knows what digital trickery lies behind those sumptuous and Turneresque film sequences? It is apt that Turner dies as a result of a bug contracted while attending the Great Exhibition in Hyde Park in 1851, the very year that Osney Island was colonised.

Tuesday 6 December 2016

Speculation intrigues singleton when 5-a-side cancelled (8)

To sleep, perchance to dream ... here I am, gasping for air, just below the surface of a swimming pool. My strength is failing and the sides of the pool seem impossibly far away. All memory of how to swim has gone. I break the surface for an instant, gulping in the air and catch a glimpse of Winnie-the-Pooh at the far end of the garden. I have no idea why I am drowning at Cotchford Farm, but drowning I am. I see Mick Jagger and Bill Clinton chatting at a poolside table – why do they do nothing to save me? Is it because I know that my head has morphed into an actual hog's head, possibly even that of a groundhog or the extinct hog-like creature named after the Stones' front man, *Jaggermeryx naida*? Must I endure this torture every day, like Tantalus in his own private hell-pool?

The water engulfs me again but I fight my way back to the surface. Now I am outside college on Oxford's High St. I realise that I am at the very spot that Turner set down his easel. But this is no peaceful, academic scene. A torrent of water is flowing down the High from Carfax, a flood far beyond any that Oxford has suffered to date. How can I save myself? I reach out for a suspiciously familiar life-belt that has been thrown down from the window of Bostar Hall but it rushes by, just beyond my grasp. Too late I realize that the Shelley Memorial, released from its Univ mausoleum, is hurtling towards me, several tons of white marble and wrought iron, somehow borne darkly, fearfully aloft by the current. It seems certain to run me down. But this is no lifeless Shelley – like Hermione in *The Winter's Tale*, he is suddenly re-born. He reaches out his right arm and plucks me out of the water. For a moment I am locked in his cold, damp embrace but then I am released again. Shelley has passed by.

I go down for what must surely be the last time ...

Perhaps someone can tell me why you always wake up at the moment when death seems to turn from probability to certainty? But wake up I do. I sense the proverbial hot sweat on my arms and legs. It's good to be alive, after all. I want to clear my head of these images, so I decide to go downstairs for a mug of tea. As it is 3.57 a.m., I'm a little surprised to find my pyjama'd father already up, studying a sheet of paper. It's the sort of document I have seen many times because he brings one like it home from each evening at the bridge club. It is a computer print-out of all the hands played that session.

"Couldn't sleep at all," he explains. "Board 3 has been bugging me all night. Maybe you can see where I went wrong?"

I don't even pretend to look at the information about Board 3 on the sheet.

"Dad! It's four in the morning! *Hours* before the dawn. I would have trouble playing snap at this time of day so there's no point even guessing. Perhaps I should tell you about the nightmare I just had instead?"

"It's a fabulous layout. Perhaps I'll use it in one of my Hideous Hogg stories."

Wednesday 7 December 2016

Reg confused about returning delta-jazzman (8)

The plans for next summer's Clones in the Park festival are coming along surprisingly well. The University Parks Authority has proved oddly willing to countenance the overall concept and, subject to various boxes being ticked, the cricket square remaining unviolated and assorted Elf & Safety hoops being jumped through, it looks like we've got the free run of a big chunk of land towards the far end of the Parks, where Parson's Pleasure used to be. Even more surprisingly, the imaginatively-named 21st Century Schizoid Men band-members seem happy to go along with the idea and share the set-up costs, despite the fact that we'll be insisting on top billing. No doubt they'll be expecting to blow us away as comprehensively as their predecessors did.

And we've tracked down another tribute band from Leicester called Family Bandstand who, somewhat predictably, aim to recreate Roger Chapman & co's prog-psychedelic sounds, warbling note for note. We've held off from giving them a definite "yes" because there's still an outside chance we can persuade the real Family (or what's left of them now that Ric Grech and various other founding members are dead) to come up for the day. It wouldn't be the first Family reunion, after all.

The Clones have stepped up the rehearsals and there have even been a few moments when it's all come together and, for a couple of bars at least, we have actually sounded something like the band we're trying to imitate. Some would say that you can't go too far wrong with a song like 'Satisfaction' built entirely on a three-note guitar riff – three consecutive notes at that – but the rhythm attack has to be spot on. Rick the drummer and I are getting there. 'Loving Cup' is a little harder to master, especially if you aim for the sound the Stones got on *Exile on Main Street*. But Hyde Park was three years earlier than that and the version they played in 1969 was pretty rudimentary – well, that will be our excuse anyway. Phil has just about nailed the syncopations of 'Street Fighting Man' and is working on his strutting-about-the-stage-like-a-headless-chicken skills.

Anyone can sound semi-competent in the privacy of their own back bedroom. The acid test comes when you've got a bunch of tanked-up punters in front of you, especially in a city like Oxford where the town/gown divide is still as pronounced as ever. So we are all just a little apprehensive as we tune up our instruments and plug in our amps for our debut outing at the Bullingdon Arms. Yes, the Bully, the graveyard of many an aspiring lad-band in the badlands of East Oxford. I've heckled a few garage rock outfits here in my time, so I do have a fair idea what to expect.

Rick is good mates with a chap called Big Dave who is well in at the Bully – well enough in to set up a gig like this, anyway – and Big Dave has let us use some of his toys, notably a dry ice unit. That should give the gig some "atmosphere", we figure, although we may be asphyxiated in the process.

But by the time we are a couple of numbers into our set ("Jumping Jack Flash, it's a gas, gas, gas ..." – an ecstasy of fumbling), the smog is so thick that we can barely see our own instruments, never mind our putative audience. I reflect that we really need to include 'Get Off of My Cloud' in our set-list if we are to exploit the situation's full comic potential.

None of us has any idea how to turn the dry ice machine off and Big Dave seems to have left the building. I try to disperse the altostratus between riffs with a modicum of success and it appears that the pub is now completely empty! All four of the punters who had been huddled round the bar at the beginning of the set have evidently remembered that MasterChef is on TV.

No matter, a scruffy-looking youth and his whey-faced anorexic girlfriend (or boyfriend, it's hard to tell) have just wandered in through the Saloon Bar door and are in the process of purchasing an intoxicating drink or two. It's only 8.45 so one presumes that it's a little early for most of the regulars. I catch a glimpse of Phil hardly going through the motions. It is clear he will need to work on his satanic majesty. Don McLean might well see this as the day the music died, but not for quite the same reasons. To be fair, though, it is not easy to strut your stuff on a stage that's barely big enough for a one-man-band when there are four others (and Rick's drum-kit) to squeeze in.

Halfway through our error-strewn performance of 'Mercy, Mercy', Big Dave re-emerges from the Gents looking particularly pleased with himself. One can only speculate on the cause of his satisfaction but his brow furrows slightly as he spots the accumulated cumuli. It's a long way down to the floor for Big Dave but after a few moments of heavy breathing and incipient angina, he has successfully de-iced the show. Meanwhile, the oik in the leather jacket and his skeletal girlfriend have settled at the pub's most distant table and the girlfriend is attempting to shout something in her partner's ear above the racket we are making. She does not look happy.

Rick lays down a steady hi-hat and we launch into the sub-Velvet Underground sound of 'Stray Cat Blues'. Even a stray cat would be welcome at the door right now. Clint, the landlord, is yawning and staring at his watch – have we established a new world record for the lowest ever attendance at the Bully? Mr Leather Jacket has gone back to the bar for a fresh draught of absinthe. No, on second thoughts, he doesn't want another drink, he's trying to pick a fight with Clint. Clint raises his hands submissively, as if apologising for some omission. I concentrate on an air of Wymanesque insouciance.

'Stray Cat Blues' rumbles to a close and Stig is busy re-tuning his guitar for 'No Expectations' when Clint ambles over towards the band.

"Twenty quid?" he suggests.

"It's all right, mate" says Phil. "We're not expecting to be paid. I can see we haven't exactly drawn in a big crowd for you."

"No, *mate*. I'm offering you twenty quid to stop. You are disturbing the clientele."

"What, that bloke in the corner?"

"Yes, Gary doesn't like anything before McFly," he shrugs. We all chuckle sympathetically. "Twenty quid and a drink each?"

Phil pretends to consider the offer before conceding gracefully. We are now officially a semi-professional band. Even Radiohead probably weren't this successful, this early, on the mean streets of Abingdon.

So, there we are, unplugging the amps and supping the almost drinkable guest ale when who should come in from off the Cowley Road but my father! Behind him, a tall, balding boke with a thick, grey moustache also makes his way in from the cold. Beneath their overcoats, I can see that they are wearing DJs and dickie-bows, not quite the usual dress code for the Bullingdon Arms. They must have come straight from the gaudy at Univ.

My father joins us in our allotted corner and the other man hangs back a little.

"Is it just about to start?" Dad asks.

"Er, not quite," I tell him. "We've actually just finished."

"Finished? But it's barely nine o'clock! That's a bit of a blow …"

"Maybe another time. Look, I really appreciate …"

"It's just that I've brought Mike with me …"

"Mike? Do I know Mike?"

"We talked about him the other day. You remember? Mike Ratledge."

"Mike *Ratledge*?"

"Yes, we got chatting at the gaudy, as you do, and I just happened to let slip that my son was playing in a Stones tribute band. The speeches were a bit dull so we decided to nip over and see how you were getting on ..."

But by now the band has dropped all its instruments in a pile and are jostling for position in front of the great man – all except Rick, for whom Soft Machine are no more than a (slightly puzzling) name from music pre-history. This balding figure does not bear any obvious resemblance to the hippy in shades who once did as much as anyone to "fuse" jazz and rock. But he seems happy enough to play along with the situation, shaking hands firmly with each of us in turn. Phil, who has purloined the twenty quid, is first to the bar to get the former keyboard maestro a drink and (as a bit of an afterthought) one for my father as well. The landlord double-checks that we have absolutely no intention of restarting the gig before pulling a couple of pints and we all settle down for an uneasy chat.

"These boys are all associated with Univ in some way," Dad explains. "Phil here is an English don, just as Alex hoped to be ..."

"Hardly!" I lie.

" ...and Oswald teaches English as well. And Rick there ..."

" ... is just a bouncer on the door," Rick explains cheerily. "But anyone with a drum-kit can transcend the class barrier."

"That's only because drummers peg out periodically," Phil insists. "Rick's our third drummer this year. A bizarre gardening accident waiting to happen."

"We had a guy called Robert Wyatt on percussion in the early years," our distinguished guest observes diffidently. We all nod knowledgeably as if his every drum-fill is etched on our musical mindscapes. "If you wanted someone to lay down a steady four-four beat, Wyatt was *not* your man."

"Rick can't count that far so we prefer songs in waltz-time, as a rule," Phil quips.

We all laugh dutifully and stare into what's left of our pints.

"So when were you up at Univ, Mr Ratledge?" Ozzie asks.

"Sixty-three to sixty-six," he sighs. "God, is it really fifty years since they kicked us out, Reg?"

"Actually, it was a bit of a toss-up whether I stayed in academe or went off and joined Soft Machine. How could I have got that one so wrong?"

This time the laughter is a lot less inhibited. Mike Ratledge seems like one cool dude.

"Did you know Mick Jagger at all?" Phil asks.

"Did I know Mick Jagger? Did I *know* Mick Jagger?" He pauses briefly to place his tankard on the table. "Our lives overlapped in so many ways. We were born a few weeks apart in Summer '43, me in Maidstone, him a few miles up the A2 in Dartford. Both christened 'Michael', like most of our generation. Grammar school boys, both a bit thin and weedy, similar A-levels, both chased after the same girls, no doubt. I got into Oxford; he didn't. I think he's always had a bit of a chip on his shoulder about that. LSE was OK, I imagine, but it wasn't quite Oxbridge, was it? My folks made sure I had piano lessons, flute lessons, the lot. Not sure whether young Michael Jagger learned an instrument at all. I guess he made up for it in sheer *chutzpah*!"

"Yes, that's the bit I'm finding hardest,' Phil admits. 'Mick Jagger was – *is* – one heck of a front man"

"Yeah, credit where it's due, I guess. Anyway, we both went off and formed our bands and bumped into each other on the London scene. And then I got married!"

He looks at us all as if this was the most extraordinary point in his narrative. We wait patiently for him to explain the significance of this momentous event.

"I married this wild American singer-actress called Marsha Hunt."

Most of us continue to look suitably blank.

"Mick Jagger's ex, you mean?" Ozzie chips in.

"She wasn't Mick Jagger's ex in those days – she hadn't even met Mick Jagger. This was 1967. Marsha's career was just taking off and she landed this job on a new stage-musical called *Hair*. It was her Afro which featured on all the posters for the show and suddenly my wife was the hottest girl in London. Everyone wanted a piece of Marsha. She was a lovely lass but it didn't half put a strain on our relationship …"

We nod sympathetically. Being part of Soft Machine and sharing a bed with Marsha Hunt must have been pure hell back in '68.

"And then she met the boy with the big lips from Dartford. The Stones were pretty huge by now while the Softs were playing to rather more of a niche market, shall we say? Mick Jagger had seen the posters, seen *Hair*, and he wanted the girl behind the hair."

"Wasn't he already paired off with Marianne Faithfull?" I suggest.

"Indeed so. But Mick was never the most *monogamous* of individuals, was he? What Mick wants, he gets."

"So it was Mick and Marianne, Mike and Marsha … did you think of getting sponsorship from M & Ms?"

"Thanks for that observation, Reg; no, we didn't. Anyway, it all came to a head round about the time of the Hyde Park show in July '69."

"The show we're trying to recreate," Phil says.

"Indeed. As long as you've mastered all three chords, you should be OK. Earlier that week in '69, I finished a short tour with the Softs and got back to London a bit earlier than I expected. I thought I'd surprise Marsha at the Shaftesbury after the evening show and I arrived at the stage door just in time to bump into her leaving, hand in hand with the aforementioned Mr Jagger. I think it's fair to say that a few strong words were exchanged …"

"You didn't smack him one?" Rick enquires. "Sounds like *someone* had been shafted at the Shaftesbury."

"No, we were all jolly English about the whole thing. I made a gentle enquiry as to what the **** was going on and Mick assured me that "they were just going for a quiet drink, man." Man? I was feeling pretty unmanned by this stage. I suggested to Marsha that I'd see her back at the flat at a certain hour but I could tell by the look in her eyes that I'd lost this particular game. Marsha went off with Mick and I didn't see her again till after Hyde Park. I entertained various murderous thoughts, but did absolutely nothing."

"Was that it for you and Marsha?"

"No, but it was the end of the beginning of the end of our marriage. Marsha was completely infatuated. Mick and Marianne went off to Australia for the filming of *Ned Kelly* but I know he wrote to Marsha every day. In the space of four or five days, Brian Jones drowned, the Stones played the biggest gig England had ever seen and Marianne Faithfull took an overdose of sleeping pills in Sydney. Mick realised just in time what she'd done, just as he had with Chrissie Shrimpton, his first girlfriend.'

'She nearly topped herself as well?" Rick suggests cheerfully.

"Yup. A shame Mick was back in Australia when L'Wren Scott finally lost hope of being a wife and mother or perhaps he'd have saved her too. But July '69 was a pretty intense period for all of them. The memory remains…"

"Metallica, right? Venus in furs' finest hour?" Ozzie always likes to show off his erudition. Mike nods appreciatively.

"Even with Marianne touch and go in some hospital, Jagger was still writing love letters to my wife – serves him right that she put them up for auction all those years later."

"The price of free love?"

"The times were wilder than we were, I'd say. Marianne wasn't the only masochist involved. But *je ne regrette rien*. And I'm still in touch with Marsha. She thinks we should renew our vows. Hey, can I get you another drink, boys?"

A night to remember! But tomorrow will surely be more momentous still…

Thursday 8 December 2016

Clown in town? Have gone with missing President (7)

It is not every day you get to play golf against the former President of the USA. I didn't even have it on my Bucket list! Since his extraordinary offer to come and play, I have been assuming that the re-count in Michigan, Pennsylvania or Wisconsin would inevitably intervene and the great man would send his presidential regrets or that he would suddenly regain possession of his senses and pull a sickie. But the fateful day has arrived and neither of these things has happened. It is to be a "low key" visit we are told, strictly no fanfares and the ex-President will take care of all his own security. Vlad the Impaler has somehow failed to have the whole thing cancelled. Word has it that Bill Clinton is in the country, although no one at Univ is too sure where, and he will show up at Frilford Heath Golf Club at the designated hour, mashie niblick in hand.

It is a surprisingly mild December morning and the serried ranks of stormclouds that have marched across Southern England depositing their freight have temporarily found better things to do. One of Frilford's three courses has been set aside for our exclusive usage and a set of tee-times established. I am to play as part of a threesome with Clinton and the former Master of University College, Lord Houseman, himself an ex-member of Frilford as well as a rugby blue from the days when it was possible for ordinary mortals weighing less than 18 stone to aspire to the Varsity XV.

I am far from sure I'm looking forward to this particular golf game in such illustrious company. It is always a privilege to play with Bob Houseman, himself a USPGA founder member, although even now I still feel I have to mind my p's and q's. But the former President of America? What on earth should I call him? How can I hide my true feelings about Iraq, American foreign policy and the recent farcical Presidential election?

I try to ease the tension in my shoulders by swinging my three wood to and fro. All the other threesomes have long since departed from the first tee on Frilford's Red Course. At last the Presidential buggies trundle down the damp path from the clubhouse, while the Master, pulling his own ancient trolley, struggles to keep pace.

"Ah, Alex, can I introduce you to Bill Clinton? He used to be something big in the States." There is a little polite laughter from the great man. "Mr President,

Alex Hogg used to be one of our most talented young Eng Lit prospects and now we're lucky enough to have him in the Development Office. And he's a bit of a bandit off a nineteen handicap."

"Yes, we've spoken on the phone, Bob. I am particularly looking forward to Alex's company round your fine course." My adequately-sized hand is enveloped in the huge American paw – not quite the full body grip – and I am treated to the orthodontic miracle of the 1000-megawatt presidential smile. "I hope you'll go easy on a couple of old buffers like us?"

"Well, it's just a social event really. I'm sure you'll enjoy Oxfordshire's finest course. Should I call you Mr President too?"

"That's way too formal. Just call me Bill. It sure is good to be back in God's own country! What's the handicap situation?"

"I'm off 16 these days," admits the Master, "and Alex plays off 19. What shall we put you down for?"

"24 sounds about right. What would you say, Dwayne?"

Clinton gestures to the thick-set man in dark glasses gripping the wheel of the buggy behind. Security, no doubt. The big man grunts non-committally.

"You're not a 12-handicapper these days then?" asks Bob.

"Officially, yes, but it's a different game on your British courses and I hardly get the chance to practise nowadays."

The Master winks ostentatiously at Alex.

"24 it is, then. Perhaps you'd like to show us the way?"

Univ's most distinguished alumnus removes the tea-cosy from his chosen weapon. His driver is about nine feet long and has a head the size of a football. Clinton essays a few tentative swings.

"Kryptonite," he explains. "Half the weight of conventional titanium and diamond-hard. I had the guys at NASA run a few tests on it. Even Jordan Spieth will be using it one day."

"We're seriously impressed," I assure him. Perhaps this is going to be fun after all.

After a few final adjustments to his glove and his visor. Bill draws the club back in an enormous arc. There is a blur of kryptonite, an explosion of turf and a few muttered oaths as the little white ball dribbles off the left edge of the tee and into the bushes. Then there is an embarrassed silence.

"Damn, damn, damn!" Clinton mutters. "I'm going to have to use one of my mulligans. I was hoping to save those for later."

"A mulligan?" I ask involuntarily, trying not to snigger.

Clinton carefully tees up a second ball an extra inch off the ground.

"You've heard of mulligans, surely? If you shout "mulligan", you get to play the shot again without penalty." His second strike disappears into the gorse on the right. "Mulligan!"

"I can see I've had a very sheltered upbringing," I sigh.

At the third attempt, the vast club head makes satisfactory contact with its target and the ball exocets 300 yards up the fairway, not far short of the green. It should be an easy par from there. The Master and I drive off in more conventional fashion and the round is under way.

"You're surely not going to carry those clubs, are you, Alex? Why not stick them in the back of the buggy and take a ride with me?"

"That's a very kind offer, er, Bill, but golf is just about the only exercise I get these days. I'll walk, thanks."

"You should try jogging, Alex. How do you think I stay looking forty-two?" he twinkled.

Botox and a regular nasal hair wax, I would guess, but I don't feel I know him well enough yet to offer such an opinion.

"What is your academic area, Alex?" Clinton asks as he motors briskly down the first fairway.

"This and that. Victorian stuff mostly. And a Spanish woman called St Teresa of Avila."

"Hey, wasn't she the gal who was famous for her wet dreams?"

"That's one way of putting it," I agree reluctantly.

"And now you're putting the screws on old members?"

"I'm developing Alumni relations in a variety of interesting ways, one of which happens to involve donations and legacies." This seems to be a little defensive. What have I got to lose after all? "And what do *you* do for a living, Bill?"

Clinton pretends to take my question seriously.

"You mean since the White House? Well, I lecture a bit. I act as an unpaid ambassador for my country. I write my memoirs and support Hillary. I still chase the girls but I'm too slow to catch them these days."

"Unless you're driving a buggy, I take it. Have you got a licence for that thing?"

Bill's laugh booms across the misty fairway. But his chip to the first green is hopelessly topped. It races through the green and into the undergrowth beyond. I know from experience that there is no hope of playing it from the tangle of weeds and gorse roots there. Surely he will call for another mulligan?

The Master comes over to help us search for the ball and the presidential minder even emerges from his own buggy. I glimpse a gun-sized bulge in his hip pocket. I happen to look across at exactly the moment when a pristine white ball emerges from the minder's trouser leg and rolls across a small patch of relatively clear ground amidst a sprinkling of dead leaves.

"Is this it, Mr Clinton?" he drawls.

"Well done, Dwayne. Where would I be without you?"

The man in dark glasses keeps his own counsel on that one. Clinton fetches his pitching wedge and lobs the unblemished ball back onto the green, oblivious to the heather crushed under his left boot. He ambles cheerfully onto the putting surface. By the time he has marked his ball a few times, it has moved so close to the hole that it is no surprise when he one-putts for his four.

"Let's see, is that three or four Stableford points?" he asks.

The first hole is an accurate foretaste of what is to come. Clinton needs several mulligans to get him through the first few holes but it is not that long before he begins to play like the erratic 12-handicapper the Master knows him to be. As he has claimed 24 shots, his Stableford score grows at what would have been an embarrassing rate to any other player.

On two occasions, he "finds" his ball in a convenient spot some thirty yards away from where it has penetrated the undergrowth. To me it is all hugely comical but the Master seems to be simply embarrassed. There is just a chance he will ask the American to play up and play the game and then perhaps we will have an international incident on our hands.

"Written any good reports lately, Bob?" Clinton asks as we make our way down the seventh fairway. I take this as a reference to the Houseman Report on the origins of the second Iraq War, a report that had raked over the entire WMD dung-heap with multi-pronged acuity.

"One was quite enough," Lord Houseman observes quietly. "No one took a blind bit of notice anyway. How long did we spend in Afghanistan?"

The sensible thing would have been to have left it there but I have some strong views on Iraq and it seems a shame to waste them.

"The British press has never really forgiven Tony Blair for that one, have they?"

Lord Houseman takes this as a personal affront.

"They don't seem to realise that our system of government is as good as any in the world. But it's a fragile asset. If we throw too many stones at it, we could find ourselves with a government that is incomparably worse, led by some rabble-rousing populist with no political experience."

"And that justifies the months of propaganda, the distortion of military intelligence, the bugging of Kofi Annan and Hans Blix ...."

"That wasn't us, that was ...."

"The Americans?" chips in Clinton as he emerges from his buggy once more and measures the distance to the pin with his smartphone.

"Well, you tell me!"

"I couldn't possibly comment!" laughs Clinton. "Thank God I'm beyond all that now. You've no idea how much more pleasurable life is when you don't have to walk down the street surrounded by a team of bodyguards."

"So who's the big guy in the rather menacing shades?" I ask.

"Oh, Dwayne, he's more of a friend than a bodyguard. But he does look out for me, I guess."

"Has no one ever had a pop at you?"

"I've been lucky. When you think what happened to Jack and Bobby. No, if someone was going to bump me off, they'd've done it years ago. It's the good lady I'm most worried about. But she's got a thick skin!"

Once again Clinton's laugh can be heard in Wiltshire. "But you can't spend your whole life watching your back. It doesn't half cramp your style with the ladies as well."

Perhaps distracted by his own locker-room banter, Clinton tops an attempted pitch but his ball skips conveniently up to the green and pulls up about six feet from the flag.

"Did you have any girlfriends while you were at Oxford?" I can't believe I have just asked that question.

"Dozens!" he booms. "Back in the summer of '69, as my old pal Bryan Adams still sings, there was no shortage of free love. Yes, the summer of *soixante-neuf*, if you'll pardon my French. But the kids don't seem to be wearing flowers in their hair any more. Back then .... don't tell anyone but I even had a bit of a thing going with Marge from the office. Marge still works at Univ, doesn't she,

Bob? Lovely slim young thing."

"Margot Hesmondhalgh!" It is the Master's turn to laugh. "She's a very well-upholstered and respectable middle-aged woman now, Bill. Truth to tell, she runs the college these days and I'm not sure she'd want to be reminded of any such youthful indiscretions."

"My lips are sealed. And I remember some honey from one of the women's colleges – gee, what was her name? Just a one-night stand and it all ended rather messily but she was a peach."

"It's a shame your autobiography doesn't say too much about your love life at Oxford, "I suggest as Clinton drains his six-footer.

I should have known this moment was coming. How could I have been so dim? My anagnorisis comes on the tricky 16th. Bob Houseman hooks his tee-shot short and a long way left. Clinton's drive traverses the canyon that lies between the tee and the fairway but then slices viciously into a copse of sycamores to the right of a bunker where my own ball has landed. There will almost certainly be no shot to the green from there – at least, not until Clinton finds his ball somewhere else altogether.

"I can show you exactly where that has gone," I say.

"That would be very kind, Alex. Hop in!"

For once, I accept the proffered lift. The buggy is parked next to the bunker and I lead him into the dark glade, pointing to a ball nestling in a clump of twigs. Dwayne waits by the fairway, just out of earshot.

"Alex, are you carrying some kind of recording equipment? A camera, maybe?"

I am genuinely surprised by the question.

"No, of course not! Why would you think that?"

"You know what, I believe you! Dwayne has run a few tests. So we can talk frankly, off the record. What have you got on me, Alex?"

"I … I …"

"What information do you have that you think is so damaging that I would be prepared to write a big cheque just to keep you quiet?"

Even in the darkness of the glade, Clinton's piercing gaze pins me back. I have no idea what to say.

"I was a very young man in 1969, Alex. One or two people at Univ got the wrong idea, altogether. Who have you been talking to? The old Master? The Senior Tutor?"

"I don't want to ..."

"No, I'm sure you don't. A lot of folk have tried to blackmail me over the course of a long career in politics. It's not going to work. There isn't a shred of evidence to back up the stories you've heard. If you or anyone else connected with University College says a word out of turn, well, there will be *consequences*."

"Consequences?"

"Consequences. I think you know what I mean. Now let us finish our game of golf in a civilised manner. I think my ball is still moving ..."

And with that Clinton applies a hefty left boot to his Titleist Pro Vi-x and the ball skitters out of the undergrowth and back on to the short grass next to the bunker. From there, Clinton plays nervelessly onto the green while I miss the ball completely in my attempt to splash out from the sand. Somehow my mind is not quite on the game any more.

The round draws to a close. The Master's golf is simple but effective, generating 35 Stableford points, while mine plumbs new depths of incompetency. I am flattered by a score of 20 points. Clinton, on the other hand, has buggied his way from one cropped gorse bush to another and yet always come out smelling of rhododendrons.

The combination of a generous handicap, numerous mulligans in the early stages, some presidential 'good fortune' in the rough and a late burst of form means that he will finish with a score of 51 Stableford points – a notional 15 shots inside his handicap.

"Do you think 52 points will be enough?" Clinton asks as Lord Houseman is signing his scorecard.

"51, Bill. I can't sign for any more than that. Will it win? Put it this way, I don't think anyone has ever scored more than 38 in the history of the USPGA. So you may be in with a chance."

"I guess I just got lucky," he grins. "Still, only a game, eh? I have to get home to the grandchildren but Dwayne will be around to pick up the trophy."

It has been an extraordinary encounter. Will I go down in Univ history as the man who accidentally blackmailed President Clinton? Should I send him a sworn affidavit that I'll never bug him again. Will he decide, on reflection, that I am simply too big a threat and must be "dealt with"? Will a couple of heavies turn up on December 30th with a set of concrete overshoes? Right now, it does seem the most likely cause of my imminent unexplained demise.

But what has he got to be so embarrassed about? Clinton, famously, did not inhale in his student days. No one would be at all surprised if it turned out that he had indulged in a few illicit substances … well, who didn't, back in the summer of *soixante-neuf*? I google 'Bill Clinton Oxford 1969' and there is surprisingly little there. Surely even the Presidential machine would be unable to airbrush its way across the vast prairies of e-history?

What would the Master and the Senior Tutor have told me? Back in 1968, the Tutor for Admissions was the late John Albery, a Chemistry Fellow who eventually became Master and persuaded Clinton to come back for a high-profile visit in 1994, a few years before his daughter, Chelsea, also studied at the college. Did Albery know where the skeletons were buried? What about Douglas Millin, the voluble Porter who figures so prominently in Clinton's memoirs? Why did they have a private meeting in Clinton's old rooms in Helen's Court in 1994? Was Clinton checking that some inconvenient secrets had been quietly forgotten?

I scour *My Life* for clues. Clinton had won a Rhodes Scholarship and was scheduled to take his finals in PPE in June 1970. Yet "soon after [he] arrived in Oxford", for no clear reason, he is deflected from his structured undergraduate degree onto the altogether more nebulous B.Litt. in Politics, entailing a 50,000 word thesis. Then he switches again, to a B. Phil., also in Politics, and after that all pretence at study seems to have been quietly abandoned.

Later there is the small matter of the draft and Clinton's enrolment, in the Summer of '69, at the law school linked to the Officers' Training Corps at the University of Arkansas. Was that simply a draft-dodging ruse? Clinton evaded the one-way ticket to Saigon all that summer and, at the last possible moment, negotiated a deferral of his law school placement in order to return for his second year at Univ. Clearly, he was a lot safer in Europe and, by the end of 1969, with the introduction of a ballot (for a reduced number of draftees), the spectre of conscription had retreated altogether.

But the second year at Oxford was purely notional. Clinton found digs with some of his American pals in a Leckford Rd "commune" but does not seem to have set foot in college much after September '69, taking the opportunity to further his education in Paris, Amsterdam, Stockholm and a variety of other European capitals.

His Grand Tour took him from Helsinki to Leningrad (as St Petersburg was then known) at the very end of the calendar year, following much the same route as Lenin himself back in 1917 and Lee Harvey Oswald in 1959. There are brief mentions of term-time lectures but no name-check of Univ or its denizens at all. It is as if he no longer has a college – is there an untold story there? A drugs-bust on Hyde Park, perhaps? Was there some sort of drama in mid-'69 which resulted in the bearded American being hauled up in front of the college authorities and told to do one? Was it even possible for a college to send down a Rhodes Scholar? It would have caused major diplomatic ructions.

The truth would probably have been much fuzzier. Perhaps the college told him he was 'no longer welcome' and Clinton told them there was no point in expelling him because he had been drafted and was off to law school anyway. Did he dodge the bullet in Oxford too? Was he allowed back in autumn 1969 on the clear understanding that he would no longer darken the doors of University College?

I find a book called *Naughty Boys: Ten Rogues of Oxford* by Rob Walters. Clinton is one of the ten, along with the likes of Shelley and Howard Marks, the drug-smuggler, an earlier occupant of Clinton's house in Leckford Rd. Walters collates a number of tales told about Clinton's time in Oxford including a story that appears in former FBI Agent, Gary Aldrich's book, *Unlimited Access* (1998) about an accusation of sexual impropriety made against the young Rhodes Scholar during his time in Oxford. Surely Clinton doesn't think I have the inside story on *that*? The story was embellished by the infamous but influential website Capitol Hill Blue whose journalists headed for England in search of a scoop. The 'victim' was traced but declined to co-operate, desperate to preserve some element of privacy. So I will not repeat her name here.

Without her testimony, it is hard to establish the story's veracity. Clinton has not sued Aldrich, Walters, Capitol Hill Blue or any of the other gossipmongers, but I'm wary of giving it much credence. One thing I do feel sure about is that if the college bigwigs had heard of such an accusation, they would have taken a very dim view indeed. Rhodes Scholar or not, the young American would have been told in no uncertain terms that he was now *persona non grata*.

Friday 9 December 2016

Young dog and hard rocking – Candlemas? (9,3)

Band practice this evening. My impersonation of Bill Wyman is spot on. Not Bill as he was in his swaggering, insouciant youth but Bill as he is now, aged 80, riven with cancer, his gnarly fingers unable to complete the simplest of riffs. Rumour has it that my band are looking for a new bass player and I'm not even dead yet. Stig, in particular, deserves to be playing with proper musicians and I know he hates the Stones stuff. Doom metal remains his first love. If Candlemass need a nyckelharpa player for their latest reunion, he'll be on the first plane to Stockholm.

We knock off early because Phil is off to dinner with his prospective in-laws. *Mastermind* is just finishing when I get back to the ranch.

"How about getting *Groundhog Day* on NetFlix?" I suggest as I slump onto the sofa.

"What, *again?*" grumbles Dad. "We must have seen it 27 times."

"Like Phil Connors, you must learn to enjoy the repetition."

"In my day, we watched movies just once, unless they turned up twenty years later on television, in which case we might see them twice."

"Well, it's not your day any more, thank God."

And so we spend the rest of our Friday night curled up on the settee, anticipating all the jokes, chuckling too early, remembering all the other times since 1993 that we have done exactly the same thing. A whole packet of chocolate digestives disappears down our gullets.

I show Dad a book I have picked up from the Public Library, *The Wisdom of Groundhog Day: How to improve your life one day at a time*, by Paul Hannam. It looks at how history repeats itself, daily, in our humdrum diurnal lives and how we can break free from negative repetitions, just as Phil the Weatherman eventually does.

I do not tell him the real reason why I am reading it.

There is a French proverb: *sur la Chandeleur, l'hiver se termine ou renforce*. Will my own life be terminated on 30th December or will I somehow be reborn? It is the Punxsutawney Paradox. Or the Gawain-dilemma. But Sir Gawain had led a life of virtue and restraint. I have not.

I have exactly three weeks left. The axeman is sharpening his blade in some green grotto. But how can I be so certain that I will die three weeks today? You deserve to know. I have held off from telling you the truth because I know you will not believe me. I fear your laughter so be gentle with me.

It was amongst the hottest June days of my adolescence and I was one of a gang of giggling schoolboys who had gone to the Hoppings Fair on Newcastle Town Moor. It was every bit as tawdry as you would expect but carried a hamburgery whiff of danger about it. One or two of my 15-year-old frat-pack took the opportunity to smoke and most of us nursed cans of Special Brew, smuggled in on the bus or requisitioned from an adjacent off-licence. Just grateful that my voice had finally broken, I was far too square and obedient to indulge in any such vice at that age. Nonetheless I pretended to be one of the lads and they indulged the illusion on condition that I adopted a strictly subservient role at all times and only spoke when I was spoken to.

Not much had changed since 1981 when Mark Knopfler wrote 'Tunnel of Love' (although the Spanish City references suggest a Whitley Bay setting rather than the Toon itself) – the carousel and the carnival arcades, the neon burning up above the big wheel, the roar of dust and diesel. But only one of us would-be sultans of swing had a girl to take down the tunnel and it wasn't me. I remember we cheered the hopeful swain and his spotty paramour on their way. Lucky bastard.

Close by the impossibly glamorous tunnel was the ramshackle entrance to a more modest money-spinner. 'Solomon Sage' – that was all the sign said, as though it was somehow obvious what service might be proffered therein.

"Is he a fortune-teller?" a lad called Tony asked the hatchet-faced woman at the turnstile. She laughed derisively.

"It's the real thing, sonny," she said. "Solomon Sage knows your whole life-story. But are you brave enough to hear it?"

We laughed, of course. But one of our number, an earnest lad called John Harrison, fished a 50p coin out of his pocket and, after extracting a promise that the rest of us would wait for him, crossed the threshold into the wizard's cave.

The big wheel kept on turning and we watched promises being made in the shooting galleries. Eventually John, perhaps my closest friend at the time, emerged looking decidedly ashen-faced. Naturally, we pressed him for his verdict but he seemed too shocked to speak. At last he recovered some power of communication.

"Quite impossible! Knew my name, my date of birth, my family, my school, everything!"

We agreed that this was quite impossible but John was adamant.

"He knew my past, my present … and my future."

"So what *is* your future?" Tony asked.

"I … I promised I wouldn't tell anyone. You've got to give it a go, really you have. I dare you to …"

And like a fool, I did, although not before all the others had taken a turn and it would have been embarrassing not to. One by one my pals trooped out looking dazed and confused. There was no hiding place; I too had to take my turn with Mr Solomon Sage.

The booth was surprisingly large once you got inside. The mysterious Mr Sage sat behind a simple table but there was no crystal ball. Instead there was a bookcase full of dusty tomes, so old that you could not read anything on the spines. Mr Sage was no gypsy with earrings and tattoos. He looked like everyone's favourite uncle, with a straggly grey beard and a welcoming smile.

"Sit down, Mr Hogg, what can I do for you?"

I mumbled something by way of reply or greeting and I must have asked him how he knew my name was Hogg.

"I know many things about you, Mr Hogg. Your name is Alan Alexander Hogg and you were named after the children's author, A. A. Milne."

"Well, that's not *quite* true …" I began.

"Although you also have family relatives with those names. Would you like me to tell you when you were born? It was February 2nd 1988. Candlemas, in fact. And Groundhog Day. Didn't the film of that name come out on your fifth birthday?"

I was almost too stunned to speak.

"My favourite movie!" I spluttered at last. "How do you *know* all these things?"

Solomon Sage looked at me for a moment, as if judging whether I was capable of keeping a secret.

"Some of it is in my head and some is written in these books."

He fingered several leather-bound volumes before pulling one out from the shelf. In a matter of seconds he had found the page he was looking for.

"Ah, here we are, Alex. Your past, your present and your future."

"But how do you know my future? How can you know anyone's future?"

114

"This is a book from the future, Alex. It comes from a future when all information is everywhere, when everything that has ever occurred can be recovered and replayed."

"But how can you have a book from the future?" I insisted.

"Our time together is short, Alex. Are you sure you want to spend that time asking such questions? I don't think you would believe me if I told you."

"What does your book say about my future then?"

"I will have a look ..."

I watched him as he scanned the text, jumping quickly from page to page. His shirt-cuffs were frayed and his hands shook slightly as he gripped the book, shielding its contents from me. After thirty seconds or so, he pulled down another book and continued reading, shaking his head slightly. I was conscious that my allotted time was running out.

"Please, Mr Sage," I said. "I'd like to know!"

"There are a few things that it cannot do any harm to tell you. You will do very well in your examinations and you will win a place at Oxford University where you will study literature."

"English literature?"

"Indeed so. But you will find that the study of literature does not offer you an easy path into the world of work. It will take you a long time before you find what you want to do."

"So I won't be a professional footballer?"

"I'm sorry, Alex. You will *not* be a professional footballer." He closed the book with a smile.

"Is that all you can tell me? Surely there is more. How long will I live for?" I was desperately trying to prolong the consultation and had not thought the question through.

"That is not the sort of thing any man should know."

I should have let the matter rest there but I would not. I begged him to tell me how long I had to live, insisting I had a *right* to know the truth. He looked at his watch and swatted my entreaties away but still I would not give in.

"Very well," he said at last. "But you must promise that you will never tell a soul these secrets. It will be very bad for you, if you do."

I promised. It is a promise I am now breaking but, if I am to die, what does it matter anyway? Solomon Sage looked me in the eye. He seemed to be searching for some evidence that I could be trusted with the truth. Finally, with the deepest of sighs, he answered my question.

"The story of your life ends on the thirtieth of December, 2016. That is what the book says."

"But how? How will it all end?"

"You want to know too much. No man should know the manner of his own end. Beware of water, Alex. That is all I will say."

"But …"

"No! I have said too much. There are people waiting. Enjoy your life, Alex. It will contain many good things!"

He snapped the book shut and with that our interview was over. I stumbled out into the glare of the fairground lights. I had opened Pandora's box, eaten of the fruit of the forbidden tree. Like a modern Prometheus, I had stolen the secrets of the gods. Solomon Sage had not wanted to tell me any of this and yet I had badgered him into giving me a date. Of course, it was all nonsense, some sort of legerdemain, I decided. And, for a 15-year-old, 2016 seemed a long, long way off, plenty of time to laugh off these ridiculous prophecies.

It was clear that the rest of my accomplices had had similar experiences, although each was true to his promise. Hardly a word was said. Somehow our appetite for the Wall of Death had shrivelled to nought and it was not long before we slunk off into the cold Geordie night.

I went back the following year. I would have words with Mr Solomon Sage. I didn't know what those words would be, but there would be words. I would grab one of his books and read it for myself. But there was to be no more wisdom of Solomon. Next to the Tunnel of Love, there was only the opportunity to throw ping-pong balls at goldfish bowls, in hopes of winning a stuffed toy. I asked the lady on the stall whether she knew of somebody called Solomon Sage and she just shrugged her shoulders. I began to doubt my own memories – had I somehow hallucinated the whole thing?

When the time came, I told my parents that I wanted to apply to Cambridge, not Oxford. What, after all these years of cheering for the Dark Blues in the Boat Race, my father asked? I could not tell him the reason why. There was a brief stand-off because he had already warned one or two of the folks at University College to expect my application. I should have stuck to my guns, made a futile application to Cambridge and settled for three years at some red-brick alternative. But there was a part of me which *wanted* those predictions to come true. Winning a place at a top university was not my birthright. I had worked quite hard to give myself a chance of getting in to Oxford and I was determined not to be side-tracked by some fairground chicanery, especially if my father's connections might tip the balance. The application was made, the place was won.

If chicanery it was, I never discovered Solomon Sage's secret, nor did I ever see the man again. I've Googled the name – it's as if he never existed. The only Solomon Sage in history (the son, appropriately enough, of David Sage and Bathsheba Judd) was born on August 18th 1737 in Middletown, Connecticut. Profession? Time traveller.

No, I made that bit up. And yet every word that Solomon said was true. There is only one pronouncement left to be verified.

What, you don't believe me? Of course you don't. You are far too sophisticated to give this nonsense any credence. To tell the story at all leaves me open to ridicule, so you can understand my reluctance to confide in even my closest friends and family. 2017 will be my judge. You can laugh at me all you like then. Look, there he is, the man who believed in the power of prophecy, still embarrassingly alive. And if Drowned Hogg Day passes without incident, I will be laughing too. I would love to be proved wrong.

Saturday 10 December 2016

Topless union gear for poet (8)

It's official then. The bastards have hung me out to dry. Phil and Marie-Claire really are tying the knot on December 30th and told everyone that I am to be the best man at their modest nuptial gathering aboard the *Folly Bargères* (sic), departing from Folly Bridge that lunchtime.

The canal barge in question will potter serenely up and down the Isis – hardly an arduous journey, although I am sure the proprietors of the *Marchioness* said much the same thing in 1989. We are unlikely to be rammed by a passing dredger (although you never know, do you?) and I wonder what kind of personal grand folly I will inadvertently perpetrate to precipitate not only my own demise but also that of my fellow passengers? Should I turn the invitation down or simply fail to turn up? Surely that would be the fairest thing to do.

But would it make any difference? If it is written in the stars that four men ride out and only three ride back, that I must drown on that particular day, does it make any difference whether I struggle to avoid my fate or actively embrace it? Sooner or later we all have to die.

Should I have myself admitted to a secure mental hospital and kept under 24-hour surveillance until the day is past? No, I could be strait-jacketed and locked inaccessibly away when, due to a freak plumbing incident and a sudden outbreak of sleeping sickness amongst the supervisory staff, I am engulfed in a roomful of icy water. Whether I hide out at the top of Mount Ararat or take a holiday in the Atacama Desert where it has not even *rained* for several millennia, there is still no guarantee that I won't fall victim to some one-in-a-trillion concatenation of events. Once the President of the Immortals has decided to end his water-sport with me, there will be no effective appeal to some Higher Court of Arbitration.

No, I will steer a middle course and hope the *Folly* does likewise. I shall not encourage my watery nemesis but I will not run away from it either. I tell myself that it is an *honour* to be Phil's best man (again). It may be that I will be the first best man ever to make his speech while wearing a life-jacket.

Sunday 11 December 2016

On the radio, old French rock group causing acute indigestion
(10)

"Sorry, did you say something?" I shout.

"Please turn that racket down, Alex. Come and have a look. Does this man appear at all familiar to you?" Dad asks, no doubt for the second time.

I am trying to cobble together a hummus and Branston bap while listening to *Epicus Doomicus Metallicus* at a cochlea-lacerating 11 on the volume-dial. Dad has printed out a picture of some smug looking old geezer in sideburns and a skull-cap:

"Not a clue. Have you seen the pickle jar anywhere?"

"Look a bit more closely. Do you see any sort of family resemblance?"

This time I devote slightly more than a nanosecond to the contemplation of this image.

"Looks Victorian," I conclude. "Someone trying a little too hard to compensate for male pattern baldness. Seems to be contemplating a particularly lardy luncheon in the middle distance. Lord Palmerston?"

I munch hungrily on my Branston-less bap. There is a look of triumph in my father's eyes.

"This, Alex, unless I am very much mistaken, is your great, great, great, great, great, great grandfather!"

"Well, that's nice," I offer, between mouthfuls. "Ah well, now I know where I got my nose from anyway."

"If I tell you his name, it might ring a bell in your ill-educated brain."

"Try me."

"This man is ... cue drum-roll ... Thomas Jefferson Hogg!"

"Thomas Jefferson Hogg? Hmm, I can't hear any bells ringing. No, wait, there is a faint tinkle in the distance. Wasn't he the chap who wrote *Confessions of a Justified Sinner*?"

"No, that was *James* Hogg, no relation of ours, as far as I know. This is Thomas Jefferson Hogg."

"Was he a slave-owner? A grave-robber? A Whig Prime Minister?"

"Well, he did achieve a certain notoriety for a while …"

"Something even worse than being a Whig Prime Minister?"

"He was sent down from Univ in 1811."

"What, like Shelley? Old Percy was turfed out about then, wasn't he?"

"That's right. Thomas Jefferson Hogg was Shelley's best friend at college and co-writer of the pamphlet on the Necessity of Atheism!"

I do actually choke on my hummus bap at this point. By the time I have poured myself a glass of water, I have recovered most of my composure but bells are now clanging all over my cerebral cortex and there's a display of Christmas lights glittering between my amygdala.

"Wasn't he the chap who insisted on carrying half the can?" I mutter finally.

"That's right. The college authorities sent Shelley down when he refused to confirm or deny that he had written the pamphlet. They were just packing up their kangaroo court when this forebear of ours comes knocking on the door and insists on facing exactly the same question … and then also refusing to answer it! To be consistent, they had to send him down too."

"That's not much of a claim to fame. Did this Mr Hogg do anything else with his life?"

"Well, long after Shelley was dead and Hogg had spent years as a practising lawyer, he was commissioned to write the official biography of the poet. He wrote the first volume and then got sacked because it was all about himself, not Shelley, and included some blatant porkies. A year or two later he died of gout or gallstones or something."

"Chacun à son goût, I guess. Or possibly constipation, judging from the sketch. So why have you only just discovered that he's a relative of ours?"

"I thought I'd reached a dead end with Henry Leigh Hogg, the marine insurer – there's still absolutely no sign of his birth certificate. But we know that he was brought up in Durham, like so many of our ancestors. I'm pretty sure he was Thomas Jefferson Hogg's grandson."

"T.J. Hogg had a family then?"

"He had a daughter called Prudentia, that's all. And as far as the history books are concerned, Prudentia died an old maid, so that particular family line died out. But history also records that when Prudentia was a young woman, the Hogg household was a second home for one Henry Hunt, a charming, penniless chancer. Henry Hunt was the son of Leigh Hunt – surely you have heard of him?"

"Skimpole in *Bleak House*?"

"The very same. Leigh Hunt was a radical poet and publisher, another one of Shelley's pals before he fell on hard times."

"And went to live in a bleak house? Yes, very good …" I groan.

"Well, young Henry was a chip off the old block and in no position financially to make an honest woman of the imprudent Prudentia who had, predictably, fallen for his charms. Even in the more enlightened Victorian households, a baby born out of wedlock was far from ideal. The poor kid was named Henry Leigh, after his father and grandfather, and shipped out to some other household in the extended Hogg family somewhere in the county of Northumberland, with only a career in marine insurance to look forward to."

"This all sounds like wild conjecture to me."

"I still need to dot the i's and cross the t's, it's true. But I *think* we can both be proud to be the distant descendants of the splendid Thomas Jefferson Hogg. What an extraordinary coincidence it is that we should follow in his footsteps and go to the same college. At least neither of us got sent down!"

Monday 12 December 2016

Short Italian food shortages back (4)

I am summoned to Phil's rooms in Univ so that I may discuss wedding plans with the bride and groom, the *folie d'amour* aboard the *Folly Bargères*, but Phil has evidently forgotten the appointment. Marie-Claire is there, tapping away at a text or two, and I'm assured that the great man is expected imminently. I park myself on one of his beanbags and make steady inroads into a bottle of Old Peculier.

"You never did finish that story of your time being brainwashed by the e-Lutherans," Marie-Claire observes between texts. "I looked them up on Google and found absolutely nothing."

I have had a little time to prepare for this moment.

"Maybe you left the hyphen out?" I suggest. "They're long gone, I think. Maybe they digitised themselves and went up into the Cloud? I managed to get myself thrown out when someone said I was plotting to kill the e-Lutherarch."

"Mmm, it all sounds *entirely* credible," Marie-Claire laughs and I fall in love with her all over again.

"So, what are you working on at the moment?" I enquire of the blushing bride, by way of further small talk.

"Giving a bunch of mice a hard time, as ever."

"To any particular purpose?"

"It's based on Sheldrake's morphic resonance hypothesis. We're exploring a barely appreciated influence on adult behaviour – ancestral experience prior to conception."

"What, the things a mother does, *before* getting pregnant?"

"Or the father. From a translational perspective, our results with mice show us that the experiences of a parent, before even conceiving offspring, markedly influence both the structure and function in the nervous system of subsequent generations. We're trying to isolate the genetic components of a phenomenon that has been observed in many walks of life. Dog-breeders, for instance, have noted that if you teach a dog a brand new skill, that dog's offspring may one day demonstrate the same skill without having to be taught at all."

"So the children of a violinist, say, may have a head start in learning the instrument?"

"Maybe. Possibly even the grandchildren. But it's not all good news. The same phenomenon may contribute to the etiology and potential inter-generational transmission of risk for neuropsychiatric disorders such as phobias, anxiety and post-traumatic stress disorder. We've been training mice to fear the smell of roses, then testing their offspring and their offspring's offspring who have never encountered roses at all, to see if they exhibit the same phobia. Sure enough, most of them do. Uh-oh, look who's turned up, smelling of ..."

Phil saunters in, muttering of hebdomadal councils, and the conversation quickly turns to carnations and other wedding paraphernalia. I reach for another bottle of Old Peculier and ask myself a few questions:

1. What if this is just the tip of the iceberg?
2. What if our genetic inheritance compels us to feel the same feelings, think the same thoughts, as our parents and grand-parents?
3. Can the coding skip a generation, two generations, four generations, eight generations?
4. We think of ourselves as creatures of free will and yet 99.9% of our actions are instinctive and habitual or guided by some kind of atavistic impulse. Is what we think of as memory actually not just a store of our own memories but memories hard-wired across the generations?
5. When I experienced an overwhelming sense of déjà-vu in Hyde Park, was it because my mother or my great-grandfa-ther had once passed the same way and had some kind of profound experience there?
6. Most of us have experienced a sense of déjà-vu at some time or other. We rationalise it as best we can, but perhaps our forebears really have been there before?

I remember the first time I set foot in University College. We were on some sort of family trip to see relatives and Dad fancied a trip down Memory/Logic Lane, so we all trooped in to Main Quad. I remember feeling instantly at home there. Was that because I was in a well-tended quad with reassuringly ancient architecture all around me? Or was I genetically programmed to remember the sights and sounds and smells that my father had once experienced?

If that seems rational enough, the whole business about Thomas Jefferson Hogg has, I confess, spooked me. Two centuries have gone by and yet we seem to have so much in common, not just a shared phobia of amphibians, but a whole range of life-experiences. It is almost as if … please don't laugh, gentle reader … as if I *am* Thomas Jefferson Hogg. Minus the sideburns and the skullcap, thank goodness. It would explain a lot: I have never felt quite in sync with the 21st century – all those mobiles and i-pads and whatnot that most people take for granted. Facebook, Twitter … forget it. I was muttering about the youth of today even when I *was* one of the youth of today.

As for sex 'n drug's 'n rock'n'roll, well, the first has generally passed me by, I've steered well clear of the second and even my tastes in music seem curiously retro to my friends – grandad rock, as my mother once described it. While the language of most of my peers is full of four-letter words, I can't abide swearing – I wince whenever someone says '****' – you see, I can't even write it down! I am as repressed as any Victorian, so it would not be so surprising if it turns out that I actually *am* Victorian.

So who was this Thomas Jefferson Hogg chappie? Wikipedia seems the obvious place to start. Let's see: born 1792 in Norton near Stockton-on-Tees. We Hoggs really haven't moved around much, have we? I cycled along Norton's high street with its avenue of trees, its village green and duckpond, quite often as a boy. Norton was an important settlement in Anglo-Saxon times including a large pagan cemetery which predates Christian and Viking influences. Prior to the construction of the Stockton-Darlington railway in 1825, Stockton was a village on the edge of Norton; now their roles are reversed.

Hogg was educated at Durham School, which seems to have had something of a fast-track arrangement with Univ on account of the fact that the college was founded by William of Durham in 1249. So he follows in his father's footsteps, just as I have done, and arrives at Univ lodge a few months too late to appear in Turner's famous painting. Who should he bump into but a precocious young fresher called Percy Bysshe Shelley? The two young men live in each other's pockets until they are sent down in Shelley's second term. The next few lines in Wikipedia are intriguing:

> 'They remained good friends, but their relationship was sometimes strained because of Hogg's attraction to the women who were romantically involved with Shelley.'

But Hogg settles down to a respectable, if unspectacular, career as a lawyer in London and the north of England and marries a woman called Jane Williams, also apparently linked with Shelley before the latter's death, and they have just one child surviving beyond infancy, the mysterious Prudentia.

There seems to be a single surviving image of TJ Hogg – the one my father had printed out – and that shows him aged 65, well into his pantaloon years, so it is hardly fair to judge him on that unflattering profile. I can't help wondering what he looked like at 18 (or, indeed, 28) but it is not easy to knock so many decades off this imposing image. Was he as much of a firebrand as young Bysshe? It sounds as though Jefferson (as his friends called him) also aspired to a literary career but lacked the staying power or the independent wealth which sustained Shelley through his lean years. Or perhaps the Shelley friendship was just a haphazard interlude in a life of deserved obscurity? We'll see.

The Wikipedia page offers so many promising avenues of enquiry that it is hard to know where to start. I decide to begin with Jane Williams. Was she the Jane of 'With a Guitar, to Jane' which I dimly remember from my student days and the Casa Magni? Yes! These are Shelley's lyrical opening lines:

> Ariel to Miranda:--Take
> This slave of Music, for the sake
> Of him who is the slave of thee,
> And teach it all the harmony
> In which thou canst, and only thou,
> Make the delighted spirit glow,
> Till joy denies itself again,
> And, too intense, is turned to pain;
> For by permission and command
> Of thine own Prince Ferdinand,
> Poor Ariel sends this silent token
> Of more than ever can be spoken;

What poor girl could resist such a gift and such a serenade? That final summer of 1822, 29-year-old Shelley and his ever-pregnant wife, Mary, were sharing our accidental beach-house, the Casa Magni, with another young couple, Edward and Jane Williams, although it turns out that Edward and Jane were never actually married at all. Jane was still technically hitched to some other chap, one John Edward Johnson. So the 'Ferdinand' of this beguilingly submissive tribute is Edward Williams, also at a loose end and playing at boats in the Bay of Lerici – what does he know of these shenanigans? Wikipedia claims: 'Jane was successful in her attempts to prevent Edward from suspecting infidelity on her part.' Considering Shelley's reputation with women, that seems a *little* unlikely.

This blossoming seaside romance was somewhat short-lived because, on the 8th July, Shelley and Edward Williams both drowned when Shelley's racing boat, the *Don Juan*, went down in a storm. It is all too easy to imagine the two men at each other's throats, locked in a mortal embrace while their flimsy boat is tossed across the bay. But there is little firm evidence to support such a conjecture – for all we know, they may have been bosom pals to the end.

Back to my computerised tomhoggraphy (sorry!) … it turns out that TJ Hogg was nowhere near Lerici in the Kingdom of Sardinia in 1822. Encouragingly, he did not drown. He was a practising lawyer in Northumberland and Durham and something of a Greek scholar in his spare time. He had turned down all invitations to Italy and hardly seen his old college friend since 1817. Nor had he met Jane Williams. So how did he come to marry the merry widow and become the stepfather to her two children? I must find out more …

… although possibly not on college premises. I am so deeply engrossed in my research that my boss, the fearsome Vlad, has come into my office and is patiently watching over my shoulder.

"I hate to interrupt," he barks and I almost jump out of my skin. "You and I need to have a little chat, Alex."

"Er, OK …"

Vlad looks round as if to check that none of our colleagues is in earshot. He then pauses for effect like a results-announcer on *Strictly*.

"Alex, we're going to have to let you go."

"Right. I see …"

"In fact, I'd like you to clear your desk and leave immediately. You'll be paid up until the end of December."

"But …"

"It's non-negotiable, I'm afraid."

"But I was really beginning to make some progress. Pres …"

"Ah yes, the President."

"I almost thought I'd persuaded him to make a major bequest."

126

"I'm afraid quite the opposite was true. In fact …"

"Has he said something?"

Vlad lets the question hang in the air for a few seconds.

"I couldn't possibly comment," he says at last.

Well, stuff that then. I didn't like the poxy little job anyway. There is something more than a little unsatisfactory about earning close to the minimum wage while ringing up a bunch of rich people and begging for a few crumbs off their table. They can take their job and stick it up some convenient orifice. The fact that I would have been slightly too dead to turn up for work after the New Year Bank Holiday is neither here nor there. Vlad wasn't to know that my world ends on 30ᵗʰ December, was he?

Has Bill Clinton issued some presidential decree from god-knows-where and the college has said "yes, sir, three bags full, sir!"? I doubt it. The truth is probably rather simpler. Vlad never liked me. He never wanted to give me a job in the first place, the bastard. It's a blow to my pride, of course it is. Most of the guys I knew in college have gone on to become hedge fund managers, film makers (the future Tom Hoopers and Armando Iannuccis) and brain surgeons, while yours truly can't even hang on to a job that barely keeps him in tins of spag bol. It is a humiliation.

I'd like to describe a blazing row that culminates in me lobbing my PC out of the window and on to the dome of the Shelley Memorial before I am frog-marched off the premises, but I'm far too English for anything like that. I pack a plastic bag with my stuff and leave, quietly. I wonder if Shelley himself made a little more fuss when he was given his marching orders back in March 1811? History records that he went off and had a good cry on the broad shoulders of his close friend, Hogg, and signally failed to prevent the latter from spoiling his own university career in pursuit of some obscure point of procedural justice.

But why should I take this lying down? Like Shelley, I will mobilise the troops! Instead of turning left and out of the Porter's Lodge, I cross the Main Quad and wend my way through the Radcliffe Quad, past the Master's Lodgings and Durham Buildings and round to Cecily's Court, scarcely bothering to dodge the puddles as I go. Surely Phil will help me in my hour of need? I knock very tentatively on the door of his teaching room even though I can hear some poor girl is being interviewed inside for a place at the college. Another spotty youth is waiting anxiously across the landing. There is a moment's silence until eventually Phil opens his door a fraction.

"Alex!"

"Sorry, Phil, bit of a problem …"

"It's Hattie, isn't it?"

"*Hattie*? No, I shouldn't really have come round, but ..."

Phil looks over his shoulder and turns back to me expectantly.

"It's just that I've lost my job," I continue, lamely.

Phil seems to be at a loss for words. We stand there awkwardly for a few seconds while the Park Fellow in English Literature weighs up his options. He looks at the boy in the tweed jacket who is trying to melt into the background.

"You see, I'm a bit busy interviewing until four o'clock, well, until five o'clock, actually. Do you think you could …"

"Hang on till then?"

"I'm sorry, Alex …"

And with that the door closes on my time at University College, Oxford. I carry my cross home, alone, through streets filled with Christmas shoppers and people putting up reindeer. I wish I had a river I could skate away on, like Queen Matilda besieged in Oxford Castle …

Tuesday 13 December 2016

Churchman the Spanish follow (6)

How did PB Shelley and TJ Hogg respond to the indignity of being sent down back in 1811? One of their contemporaries, CJ Ridley, described the aftermath thus:

> Towards afternoon a large paper bearing the College seal, and signed by the Master and Dean, was affixed to the hall door declaring that the two offenders were publicly expelled … The aforesaid two made themselves as conspicuous as possible by great singularity of dress, and by walking up and down the centre of the quadrangle, as if proud of their anticipated fate.

In their own minds, they had struck a blow for freedom of speech and enquiry. They had published not one but two incendiary pamphlets, one attacking the established Church, the other (the *Poetical Essay on the Existing State of Things*, thought to be lost for almost 200 years and only re-published in 2015) a broadside against the government of the day, its domestic and imperial policies, its suppression of free speech, etc. They ensured their agitprop was displayed in a shop window on the High and seen by their enemies. They went out with all guns blazing, like Butch Cassidy and the Sundance Kid taking on the entire Bolivian army. Shelley and Hogg *asked* to be shot down. Anything less would have been failure, disappointing proof that free speech *was* possible. They left Univ as conquering heroes and headed for London to spread fresh enlightenment to its citizens.

I, on the other hand, go home to No. 8, Swan Street and have a jolly good whinge to my Dad.

"It sounds like you've been shockingly treated, old son," he concludes. "If I had even the slightest influence at college, I'd …"

"Don't worry, Dad. I don't expect you to get me my job back."

"There will be plenty of jobs in the new year."

"Ah yes, the new year …"

Having owned up to my sacking, should I tell him about the much larger axe suspended over my lilywhite neck, poised to fall on the penultimate day of the year? Somehow the time has never been quite right to mention it. Dad's heading off to the bridge club after his tea and I let the moment pass once again. There are some things we all must bear alone.

Not for the first time, I think of Sir Gawain taking his leave of Camelot's Christmas party, perhaps taking a few cocktail sausages to sustain him on his journey, and heading out into the snowy wastes to meet the Green Knight and receive the fatal blow. On December 30th, Gawain is unexpectedly holed up at Sir Bertilak's castle, staving off the advances of his hostess (English literature's first MILF?), and it is not until New Year's Day that he makes his way to the Green Chapel. I take some comfort from the fact that Gawain comes back alive, courtesy of his Teflon-coated neck and his old-school moral code. I take slightly less comfort from the fact that Gawain and the Green Knight are fictional characters.

Wednesday 14 December 2016

Doctor signs on after sea-salts (10)

The pathetic fallacy has come on a long way since John Ruskin coined the term in *Modern Painters*. It has grown up in the school of hard knocks and bumptiously gate-crashed the party of modern literature and popular music. Novelists like Amis and Jacobson rarely bypass an inanimate object or process without attributing some quasi-human emotion or quality to it. Rain never simply rains; it exists to augment the meagre emotional vocabulary of the characters who are caught out in it (says he, staying firmly indoors as the storm batters the fences down outside). Rain defines our anger, our melancholy, our recklessness, even on this relatively temperate island.

Storytellers are like Dr Frankenstein in his laboratory, jump-starting the inanimate world, blurring the distinction between humankind and the non-human. But is this any more than an extension of their original contribution to civilisation, the invention of our very idea of humanity – character, motivation, purposeful action and free choice? Modernism has questioned all those iffy concepts but never quite dislodged them.

Characters in fiction are, by definition constructed out of words rather than flesh and blood, yet they often seem more vividly human than we do ourselves. Mary Shelley and her husband laboured long and hard to bring forth *Frankenstein* and, as far as we can tell, expended rather more care and effort in that enterprise than in the production and protection of their own children. Like Victor Frankenstein, Mary Shelley had to live with the monster she had created and it overshadowed much of the rest of her life thanks to theatre productions and fresh editions. Later books like *The Last Man* sank without trace while the monster lived on.

"Is it still raining? I hadn't noticed …" comments Andie MacDowell in the final scene of *Four Weddings and a Funeral*. It's still raining, Andie. It seems to have been raining for forty days and forty nights. It is rolling in to Oxford off the Cotswolds like a triumphal juggernaut. When the Thames is close to breaking its banks in the vicinity of Osney Island, excess water can be diverted round the west side of the island along Osney Ditch and Hogacre Ditch. But when those ditches are also full to bursting, the water has nowhere else to go. Our back garden in Swan Street, overlooking Osney Ditch, is quickly turning into a swimming pool. Soon the water will make its way in through the back door, through the walls and foundations. We have had years of practice at taking up the carpets and ensuring that all our possessions are at a safe height. It is the price we pay for living in this jerry-built-but-desirable corner of Oxford, conveniently close to the railway station and all modern amenities.

I amuse myself by compiling a PlayList of my favourite rain and flood songs. It is disappointing to discover that my favourite Who track, 'Love Rain o'er Me' is actually 'Love Reign o'er Me' so, with great reluctance I have had to discard that one, but my long list still includes the following classics:

Kate Bush: Cloudbusting
Jackson Browne: Before the Deluge
Peter Gabriel: Red Rain
Peter Gabriel: Here Comes the Flood
The Carpenters: Rainy Days and Mondays
Guns'n'Roses: November Rain
Led Zeppelin: Rain Song
Led Zeppelin: When the Levee Breaks
Eurythmics: Here comes the Rain Again
Phil Collins: I Wish it would Rain Down
A-ha: Crying in the Rain
Bob Dylan: A Hard Rain's Gonna Fall
Rolling Stones: Gimme Shelter
Procul Harum: A Salty Dog
John Parr: St Elmo's Fire
Prince: Purple Rain
The Doors: Riders on the Storm
ELO: Rain is Falling
Roxette: Queen of Rain
Rainbow: Catch the Rainbow

What about a running order? With the Clones' concert in mind, I guess I'd have to start with 'Gimme Shelter':

> The floods is threat'ning my very life todayGimme, gimme shelter or
> I'm gonna fade away …

When the Stones came back to Hyde Park in 2013 they played this, perhaps their greatest song, but it was not part of the 1969 set even though it had been the opening track on *Let it Bleed*. Perhaps we can sneak it into our Clones in the Park set after all?

Next must come 'A Salty Dog', the title track from the number one album in July 1969, clearly inspired by the Rime of the Ancient Mariner and epic in every way. I picture Brian Jones lying contentedly on his pool-lilo, as this tale of shipwreck and redemption blares from his speakers. Did the Stones' discarded guitarist contemplate the iconic album-cover with its life-belt balanced on some choppy seas? Would a life-belt have saved him? In my mind's eye, the album-title morphs into

A SALTY HOGG

and the piratical figure in the middle of the life-belt is replaced by the imposing physiognomy of the ageing, gout-ridden Thomas Jefferson Hogg.

Oxford has already suffered more major flooding incidents in the 21st century than it did in the whole of the 20th. Is global warming responsible? I blame the arrival of Kate Bush in the county. That cloud-busting machine of hers has done irreparable damage to the climate. As for Wilhelm Reich, AKA Donald Sutherland, its inventor, well, you'd have thought he would have learned from his experience at the beginning of *Don't Look Now* and aimed for a cloud-erasure system instead.

Thy kingdom come, thy will be done … Wilhelm and his son, Peter, are not the only Reichs on my mind right now. There's also Robert Reich, whose relationship with Bill Clinton (at Univ and thereafter) echoes that of Shelley and Hogg (and possibly also Yusupov/Rayner).

Robert Reich was the brains and the conscience behind Clinton's first presidential administration (1993-1997). As Secretary of Labor, a key role in Clinton's cabinet, Reich implemented social policies which could almost be described as socialist. Clinton's economic record has stood the test of time in the sense that *Time* magazine named Reich one of the Ten Best Cabinet Members of the century, but he tired of the political merry-go-round and returned to academe in 1997.

And yet I had never heard of the diminutive Mr Reich till now. He has some of Clinton's charisma but none of his gift for controversy. Clinton first met Reich on the boat over from America in the early autumn of 1968 as all that year's Rhodes Scholars were obliged to spend a week on the ocean wave in each other's company, forging some sort of *esprit de corps*. The Rhodesmen were distributed across the Oxford college network but two, Clinton and Reich, were billeted to the same college, Univ.

Both young men were set to study PPE but did not have *that* much in common. Reich was the son of a respectable women's clothing store proprietor and won a place at Dartmouth College where he graduated with an A.B *summa cum laude* in 1968. He had even managed to wangle a date with a formidable young lady from Wellesley College called Hillary Rodham. Bizarrely, the date seems to have involved a trip to the movies to see *Blow-Up*. Great minds think alike, I suppose. History does not record whether the two college kids made out in the back row. More likely, it was the usual comedy of embarrassment and misunderstandings – at any rate, the relationship stopped right there. Perhaps, at four feet ten inches tall, Reich was not quite the grooviest of boyfriends even for a girl with glasses and a dodgy haircut.

Did Reich tell Clinton this story while the *SS Great Britain* sailed serenely across the wide Sargasso Sea? Did it pique the young Arkansan's interest? Did it give Clinton the incentive to pester Rodham into submission in a Yale library in 1971? – he could hardly allow himself to fail where once Reich had succeeded. And how did this shared interest in the geeky girl from Chicago affect their subsequent political partnership? Naturally, they would have us believe that it had no effect whatsoever. But why should that stop us speculating otherwise?

What we do know is that Reich was far from well on the journey over and Clinton took the chance to get to know his future classmate. He turned up in Reich's cabin bearing chicken soup in one hand and crackers in the other. No doubt this proved an economic cure and the two became firm friends.

Some months later, Reich met his wife, Clare Dalton, while both were auditioning for a play in Oxford. Reich missed out on being cast but he had a cunning plan to engineer further meetings with the young Englishwoman – he decided to direct a play of his own and cast young Clare in one of the leading roles. If he had any sense, he would have kept her well out of Clinton's way.

Thursday 15 December 2016

Fawley village's alternative energy after sheep comes back (9)

I have been somewhat preoccupied these last few days mugging up on my distinguished forebear, Thomas Jefferson Hogg. I cling to the twiglet of hope that by understanding the strange life of the old buffer, I may somehow prolong my own. And I have made some alarming discoveries ...

Amongst his many writings, the one that achieved some modest impact was his memoir 'Shelley at Oxford', first published in the *New Monthly Magazine* in 1832 and 1833, a decade after the poet's death. This was a major part of the rehabilitation process which transformed Shelley's reputation from dangerous renegade and failed poet to tortured genius and influential radical. The memoir reads more like a love letter, an elegiac account of a doomed romance.

The first line is telling: 'What is the greatest disappointment in life?' The answer turns out to be Oxford University. Hogg has grown up like Hardy's Jude in Marygreen, excited to be approaching the fabled university:

'I was already familiar with the aspect of the noble buildings that adorn that famous city. After travelling for several days we reached the last stage, and soon afterwards approached the point whence, I was told, we might discern the first glimpse of the metropolis of learning. I strained my eyes to catch a view of that land of promise, for which I had so eagerly longed. The summits of towers and spires and domes appeared afar and faintly; then the prospect was obstructed. By degrees it opened upon us again, and we saw the tall trees that shaded the colleges. At three o'clock on a fine autumnal afternoon we entered the streets of Oxford.'

Indeed, Thomas Hardy, perhaps the greatest of all Shelley's disciples, almost certainly borrowed from this opening for his own tale of academic frustration. Here is Jude approaching the fabled city for the first time:

He now paused at the top of a crooked and gentle declivity, and obtained his first near view of the city. Grey-stoned and dun-roofed, it stood within hail of the Wessex border, and almost with the tip of one small toe within it, at the northernmost point of the crinkled line along which the leisurely Thames strokes the fields of that ancient kingdom. The buildings now lay quiet in the sunset, a vane here and there on their many spires and domes giving sparkle to a picture of sober secondary and tertiary hues. (*Jude the Obscure*, II,i)

Hmm, a slight step up in quality there, I think, perhaps inspired by Hardy's study of Turner's townscapes at the Royal Academy in 1889. While Jude remained the perpetual outsider, Hogg seems to have had little difficulty in securing a place at his father's alma mater, only to find that college life was, academically at least, a sham. Hogg rolled up at Univ in January 1810, some nine months before Shelley, and yet seems to have made no friends at all prior to an accidental encounter with the precocious young novelist from Horsham at Formal Hall. After arguing over the relative merits of Italian and German romances, they become inseparable friends, at least in Hogg's account.

But it is never an equal friendship; Shelley has everything that Hogg lacks – wealth, social position, talent and beauty – and Hogg must besiege him in his rooms (the site of the current JCR) if he is to get any of the great man's company. There is little suggestion of Shelley returning the compliment and paying Hogg the occasional visit. Even when Shelley falls asleep on the carpet, Hogg does not take the hint and leave him in peace. Shelley has accumulated so much scientific clutter that there is hardly room for Hogg to sit down but there he always is, like Boswell or Dr Watson, making a mental note of his friend's genius and eccentricity.

Shelley, fascinated by water and electricity, studies John Dalton's pioneering work on the atomic make-up of water and conceives exotic schemes for harnessing the latest technology (e.g. galvanic batteries) to irrigate the desert regions of Africa. Hogg accompanies him on lengthy rambles into the Oxfordshire and Berkshire countryside, during which Shelley indulges his favourite hobbies of skimming stones and playing with paper boats.

It has been said that he once found himself on the north bank of the Serpentine river without the materials for indulging those inclinations which the sight of water invariably inspired, for he had exhausted his supplies on the round pond in Kensington Gardens. Not a single scrap of paper could be found, save only a bank-post bill for fifty pounds. He hesitated long, but yielded at last. He twisted it into a boat with the extreme refinement of his skill …. (p. 52)

This is an unlikely myth, as Hogg himself admits, but it conveniently foreshadows so many of the later dramas of Shelley's life, from the Serpentine to the Gulf of Spezia.

Jefferson, as he is known to his family, is three months older than Bysshe and at least as widely-read amongst the dangerous philosophers of the day. So who radicalizes whom on their perambulations together around the Oxford countryside? Does Hogg deserve a co-writing credit (at the very least) for the surprisingly innocuous pamphlet on the necessity of atheism? If so, it was to be their last experiment in joint authorship.

Religious toleration is not exactly widespread in quasi-monastic Oxford in 1810-11. Nor are women. Apart from immediate members of their family, Jefferson and Bysshe have little direct experience of the opposite sex. Hardly surprising, then, that they are very much in favour of free love, the exciting new concept they have found in the writings of Mary Wollstonecraft, reflected, in muted form, in her partner, William Godwin's.

The two boys' homoerotic idyll is disturbed not so much by their expulsion from the Magnae Aulae but by the intrusion of a pretty schoolgirl called Harriet Westbrook. After one sex-starved term in Oxford, Shelley glimpses this 15-year-old vision of loveliness at the *Fête Champêtre* staged by his sister's school. Young Harriet quickly supplants the sturdy but slightly dull Jefferson in Bysshe's waking dreams. Bysshe feels guilty about this, so he tries to set Jefferson up with the aforementioned sister, Elizabeth. Egged on by his friend, Jefferson is soon bombarding the unsuspecting schoolgirl (whom he has never met) with *billets doux*. Bysshe and Jefferson dream of a private island on which the four of them will enjoy a life of carefree equality and sharing.

The pragmatic Elizabeth soon tells the clod-hopping Northerner where he can sling his hook while the fragrant Harriet proves to be rather more amenable to Bysshe's blandishments. This is a pattern which will recur throughout the lives of our two young erotonauts. As time goes by, Shelley will discover his inner babe-magnet while Hogg … simply won't.

After their expulsion from Univ in March 1811, our boys decamp to London where Bysshe is better placed to loiter at the school gates and pass on the odd copy of *Zastrozzi*, the slightly racy romance he has penned in his

Eton dorm. How could the 15-year-old Harriet resist? But credit to the poor girl; despite all the talk of free love, she is not going to roll over and surrender the Crown Jewels. Bysshe will have to marry her first. Bysshe has absolutely no intention of marrying anyone. But after a couple of months of fumbling foreplay, Harriet wins the battle. They will elope on her sixteenth birthday in August. Gretna Green, here we come! Or, rather, Edinburgh, for a slightly more up-market ceremony on 28th August 1811.

Harriet's new life of marital bliss lasts approximately two days. After the porridge and the kedgeree, her reluctant husband is already moving the goalposts ...

"Harriet, my love ..."

"Yes, dearest Bysshe?"

Pause.

"Just an idea, my precious ... um, how would you feel if I were to beseech my good friend Hogg to come and join us?"

"What, on our honeymoon?"

"It's just that we had made preparations for a gentlemen's walking tour this summer and all this ..."

"... has rather got in the way?"

"Don't be silly, Mrs Shelley, it's just ..."

"Just what?"

"Oh, I don't know ... let's just forget it. It was an ill-conceived notion."

"No, no, I'm just being silly. Of course we will invite your friend up, whoever he is. If that is what you *really* want ..."

Hogg needs no second invitation. He's at the Edinburgh Coach Station before you can say 'Brokeback Mountain'. Mr and Mrs Shelley's marital love-nest has already morphed into a *ménage-à-trois*. Hogg takes one look at the radiant bride – they have not been permitted to meet before – and he is smitten. Any doubts he has had about his sexuality are instantly banished. Hogg kips on the sofa for a night or two before Shelley informs the landlord that an additional bed must be provided for their sub-tenant. Even so, the honeymoon suite in George Street starts to feel a little cramped for all concerned.

What about decamping to Hogg's lodgings in York? Brilliant! Since the Oxford débâcle, Hogg has been exiled to York to undergo the penance of a conveyancing job in a solicitor's office. Hogg will return to work while the two newly-weds are out romping round the Dales. Each evening they will read improving literature, like Rousseau's *Emile*, to each other.

But somehow the fun has already drained out of the elopement. Things seem to have gone a bit *grown-up*. Hogg's landlady won't countenance such a threesome and suitable replacement digs prove hard to find. Money's too tight to mention. Autumn in York is like winter in London, only drearier. But worse, much worse, is to come. Shelley announces that he is going to have to nip off to London to sort out a few financial matters. A day, two days at the outside. No, dear, he says, you can't come with me – you and Hogg will be fine, just for that short time ... no, don't get up, I can see myself out.

Who knows whether the two 19-year-old boys have had words before the baronet's son naffs off down to London? Perhaps Hogg is simply confused by all the talk of free love and blind to all the body-language of the blushing bride. The days go by and there's no sign of Shelley returning. Hogg assumes there is some kind of 'understanding' between husband and wife. Harriet has finished her course of improving literature. Hogg screws his courage to the sticking place and plonks his size twelves deep into the quicksand.

In my mind's eye, I see Hogg in his dressing gown, chomping buttered toast at the breakfast table in York. Harriet, primly dressed and buttoned up to the throat, is fussing about her chores.

HARRIET:	What will you do today, Mr Hogg?
HOGG:	I will write to Bysshe. As will you, I'm sure.
HARRIET:	(sighing) I can hardly bear to. We have only been married a few weeks. Every day he is away feels like an eternity…
HOGG:	Harriet …
HARRIET:	Mmm?
HOGG:	Harriet … (he shuts his eyes in an attempt to compose his thoughts)
HARRIET:	Are you all right, Mr Hogg?'
HOGG:	(with great difficulty) No, Harriet, I am not all right. A woman of your undoubted acuity cannot but be aware that I have been at great pains to hide from you the depth of my feelings … (he looks at her expectantly; she is lost for words) … but it is

impossible to contain myself any longer. Harriet!'

Hogg goes down on one knee and toast-crumbs fly everywhere. Harriet freezes.

HOGG: I would simply like you to be aware that …if your own feelings were ever to reciprocate my own … and I feel that I have Shelley's blessing in being so forthright with you … then I hope you would not hesitate in … day or night, whatever … you have only to say the word and I'll be …. Oh God, I think you know what I am trying to say! I … I …

HARRIET: (whispering) Mr Hogg … Mr Hogg, I haven't the faintest idea what you are talking about!'

HOGG: Then, for the avoidance of misunderstanding, I feel duty-bound to … to … (unable to continue, he lifts one knee from the bare floorboards and rubs it. Harriet remains well out of reach) …. to be clear. How can I put it? If we had world enough and time, this coyness, lady, were no crime…

HARRIET: Andrew Marvell!

HOGG: I'm sorry, I did not expect you would have …

HARRIET: To his coy mistress!

HOGG: Yes … no …. what I really mean is …

HARRIET: I think I understand your meaning all too well now. Is this what they teach you in Oxford?

HOGG: (climbing to his feet and advancing; she backs away) I only meant …

HARRIET: How could you think such a thing might even be possible? I love Bysshe with all my heart. He is my husband. We have been married a fortnight. No other man shall have me till the day I die.

HOGG: Of course. Please … please, forget …

HARRIET: You are his best friend and yet you would betray him in this way?

HOGG: But … but … Bysshe need never know!

HARRIET: (frying pan in hand now, she squares up to him) So

	it's only a betrayal if we tell him about it? Is that Buffon? Or Plato? My husband will surely be back later today. I think it would be appropriate if…
HOGG:	As it happens, I have an urgent appointment at Norton. I think I should pack my bags immediately and wait outside for a stagecoach.
HARRIET:	Yes, I think perhaps you should.
HOGG:	Harriet, you won't … you won't tell … (she is close to exploding now) Very well! Very well!

Hogg makes a hasty exit stage right. Harriet collapses in a chair, head in hands.

Curtain.

Friday 16 December 2016

Thomas Jefferson to travel back aboard Mercury (4)

Curtains, indeed. Harriet's cries for help can be heard in the most distant unirrigated deserts of Africa, never mind London, and the young poet promptly shelves his cash-grab, racing back to York on the next available phaeton, rehearsing his lines carefully. What? That scoundrel propositioned you? I had not the slightest premonition. Don't worry, dear, he won't darken our doors again … but don't you think you might have humoured him just a little? No, no, quite understandable, the man is a complete cad. We'll double-bolt the doors.

But York has lost a little of its allure by now and so the not-so-newly-weds head off on the wings of Mercury to the Lake District, leaving a note on the mantelpiece saying they are going to Richmond. But the world has already shifted imperceptibly on its axis.

It will be some years before the friendship between Bysshe and Jefferson is partially restored. Hogg must grieve for not one lost love but two. He will need all his stoutness to overcome this disappointment. Still, at least his size twelve *faux pas* will remain a secret between the three of them? In that respect, as in so many others, Hogg is to be sadly mistaken, even though he assumes that he will take his secret with him to his grave.

During the remaining grey months of 1811, numerous letters are exchanged between this awkward threesome, exercises in conciliation and desperation, winging their way to and from Keswick and the later staging posts in the nomadic lives of the young Mr and Mrs Shelley. Here is one such, from Shelley to Hogg:

> I am dismayed. I tremble – is it so? Are we parted, you – I – Forgive this wildness. I am half mad. I am wretchedly miserable. I look on Harriet. I start – she is before me – Has she convinced you? … Will you come – dearest, best beloved of friends, will you come? Will you share my fortune, enter into my schemes, love me as I love you; be inseparable as once I fondly hoped you were … Ah! how I have loved you, I was even ashamed to tell you how … (Letters 1, No. 134)

The love that dares speak its name, at last? Almost fifty years later, Hogg will face the dilemma of how to write up these events in the official biography (or hagiography) commissioned by Lady Wrennie, wife of Sir Percy Shelley, himself the only surviving son of the poet and his second wife, Mary. Lady Wrennie wants to see Harriet airbrushed out of history but Hogg gives Harriet an obstinately good write-up without, of course, mentioning the unfortunate misunderstanding in York.

Hogg does include extracts from Shelley's subsequent letters to him from Keswick, carefully adjusting the pronouns so that the secret of his conduct in York will remain safe (at least until other editors and biographers come to scrutinise those same letters). If that represents a minor breach of the biographer's covenant, Hogg then commits the more major transgression of taking the most explicit of the Yorkgate letters and redrafting them as a 'Fragment of a Novel'. Harriet's name is changed to Charlotte (as in Goethe's *Sorrows of Werther*) and this purple prose is plonked down somewhat later in the time-scheme of Volume 1. Hogg even has the temerity to criticise the 'frigid' style of the fragment in comparison with the Godwinian school of philosophical romance.

Through 1812, Hogg knuckles down to his legal career, now at the Middle Temple, while Bysshe and Harriet travel hither and thither, one step ahead of their creditors, working out some sort of *modus operandi* for married life together. In November, Shelley hunts out his old Univ friend in London and there is a brief, tentative *rapprochement*. Come and stay with us, old chum, Shelley begs.

Faced with Shelley's eloquent come-hithers, Hogg vacillates until February 1813 but eventually the siren call proves too strong. He reluctantly accepts an invitation to join the Shelleys and Harriet's forbidding older sister, Eliza, at their cottage in Tan-yr-Allt, near Porthmadog, in one of the most inaccessible corners of West Wales. But by the time Hogg gets there, the Shelley party has decamped to Ireland, spooked by an incident in which Shelley suspects he is about to be shot by a robber/ghost/assassin (delete according to taste). Like a faithful old retainer, our Jefferson (still only 20, lest we forget) makes his way to Dublin despite incessant rain, only to find that the Shelley caravanserai has moved on yet again.

Now in Killarney, Shelley has somehow omitted to leave a forwarding address for their expected visitor. Sigh. Hogg mooches around Dublin for a few days, thinking dark thoughts. When Shelley hears of his arrival there, he drags

Harriet (now heavily pregnant, of course) back up the east coast of Ireland, only to find that Hogg has given up and trogged off home to England.

I feel Hogg's pain as if it were my own, sodden and shivering in Tan-yr-Allt, abandoned (deliberately?) in Dublin, still mortified to recall the Oxford and York debacles, consigned to a dead-end job. What else could possibly go wrong?

Quite a lot, actually.

Little by little, Mrs Harriet Shelley loses the energy to traipse after her will-o'-the-wisp husband. By the time their first child, Ianthe, is born on 23rd June 1813, she is seeing as much of Hogg as she is of her husband. While Shelley is off talking Platonism with the dewy-eyed Cornelia Boinville in Bracknell, Hogg is keeping the gravid Mrs Shelley amused in Half Moon St. If Hogg's own account is to be believed, he is regularly dining alone with Harriet, taking tea, or allowing her to read to him for long periods without him actually falling asleep. No doubt, Shelley has tipped him the wink once again and Hogg dares to dream, but it seems unlikely that he is any more successful in his suit than he had been in 1811. Hogg is more Prufrock than Don Juan, after all.

Saturday 17 December 2016

Kind green eccentric (5)

It really is happening. It's there in embossed gold – the conjunction of Philip Barry Sherborne (yes, Barry – oh dear!) and Marie-Claire Goodwin in University College Chapel at 11 a.m. and afterwards for luncheon and dancing (!) aboard the *Folly Bargères*. And there's the date in elegant copperplate:

30ᵀᴴ DECEMBER 2016

I briefly admire the subtlety of the triple-underlining. Is this three-line whip for me personally or are all guests to be placed under similar typographical pressure?

30th December 2016 – the day on which the sheltering sky falls in? 30.12.2016. What *about* those digits? Knock a third off the 30 and add a third on to the 12 and what do you get? 2016. Or, to put it another way:

$$30/12 = 20/16 + 20/16$$

It's not quite the number of the beast, is it? It strikes me for the first time that although Phil's initials are the same as Shelley's, he rarely owns up to that unfortunate middle name.

But what's in a name? I was christened Alan Alexander Hogg and for many years was puzzled by the fact that I wasn't generally known by my first name (this caused no end of problems at school). My father insisted that they had put Alan, the name of my father's brother, first for reasons of family propriety, while Alexander, the name of my great grandfather, was always the one they wanted to use. He pointed out that many great men are known by their second name. Certainly, Shelley was usually called Bysshe by kith and kin while Thomas Jefferson Hogg was universally known as Jefferson or even Jeff to his pals. He must have spent years batting off the assumption that he was named after the American President of the same name. "No, no, Thomas and Jefferson are old family names; it's just a coincidence," he would have said, with a sigh. But I suspect he would have been secretly proud of the association.

And I was too when my father finally spilled the beans. It appears that I was actually named after Alan Alexander Milne, whose books my parents both loved. I should be grateful; they might have called me 'Christopher Robin' – I can hardly imagine what *that* would have done for my chances of playground survival. Like most children, my imagination was saturated by the adventures of Pooh, Piglet, Tigger & co, both from the bedtime stories read and re-read to me and from the Disney film, played incessantly until the tape was chewed up by the VHS machine.

So AA Milne became one of the great heroes of my early life, along with Donald Campbell and Kevin Phillips. In later years, I came to admire *The Red House Mystery* (1922) every bit as much as Milne's later work for his young son, but it was to *The House at Pooh Corner* that I see Ozzie has turned for the lengthy epigraph to his new book:

> 'What do you like doing best in the world, Pooh?' 'Well,' said Pooh, 'what I like best—' and then he had to stop and think. Because although eating Honey was a very good thing to do, there was a moment just before you began to eat it which was better than when you were, but he didn't know what it was called.

Those lines were taken from *Pooh Corner's* coda – that final astonishing, farewell to childhood, a chapter whose elegiac power derives largely from its echoes of *Morte Darthur*. When I begged to hear that story one more time, my father would sigh and look for an alternative. The truth was that he knew that he would dissolve in tears (again) long before the end.

What of Uncle Alan, the disavowed donor of half my famous name? I remember him as a kind, eccentric country-lover. But I have barely seen him since the age of ten because he fell out with my father and the two brothers have not spoken since. Uncle Alan, eight years older than his only sibling, was married but had no children and treated me like the son he might have had. We swap e-mails and Christmas cards and I always feel guilty I do not visit him in his big old rambling house near Stockton, especially now that Aunty Janet has died and his own health is becoming increasingly frail. Since retirement from his dental practice, he has struggled in vain to keep the big old house warm and dry. But he's nobody's fool. The last I heard he had applied for outline permission to knock his manor-house down and replace it with thirty flats-worth of sheltered housing. No doubt some modern Rachman had put him up to it but good luck to the old fella, I say. I just hope he has earmarked the best of the flats for himself.

It was Uncle Alan who first introduced me to the delights of the crossword and other kinds of word puzzle. One day he gave me eleven matches and asked me to spell out my name. So I did:

$$A L E X$$

"Do you know what's unusual about this name?" he asked. I looked suitably blank. "It can be spelled out in capitals using straight lines only. Not many names work like that but can you think of another one that does?"

"Alan?" I said at last.

"That's right. Your first name, and mine. But *you* are Al squared. Or Al_2H, chemically speaking. Now see if you can change ALEX to ALAN by moving just three matches."

After a short period of trial and error, I came up with the answer. You need to take three matches out:

$$A L \vdash /$$

And with the odd nudge, you could soon fit them back in again:

$$A L A N$$

It was but a short step from there to a more traditional challenge: change ALAN to ALEX a letter at a time, in just three moves:

```
ALAN
- - - -
- - - -
ALEX
```

Yup, you've got it: ALAN, ALAS, ALES, ALEX. It's actually slightly harder to do it in four moves … how about ALAN, FLAN, FLAX, FLEX, ALEX?)

When I pointed out the ALAS ALES route to Phil one maudlin beery night, he countered that, with my initials, if I were ever to be the unwitting victim of a drink-driving accident, my worldly goods should be distributed equally to the Automobile Association and Alcoholics Anonymous while the offending driver could be charged with AA battery. My, how we laughed.

Should I make a will now? If Scylla or Charybdis pulls me under on 30th December, I don't want it to be any harder for my parents than it needs to be. I should put my worldly affairs in order and make peace with my Maker, whoever He is. But I have so few worldly possessions and a will seems unnecessary. My clothes will be sniffed at by Oxfam. My paltry collection of books is not worth selling. Oxford is so rich in libraries and the internet so fecund that it has been hard to see the point in actually *buying* books. The Yaris is no doubt already worth less than the loan I have taken out to pay for it. I have no pension or savings. My laptop may well pre-decease me, so many viruses does it have. That's about it: my life has negative equity. Perhaps I could hand in the keys and start a new one?

With the floodwaters still rising, the Botley Road has been closed to traffic for a week and I have been holed up on the Island for several days now. Why do all wellies spring a leak inside three months of purchase? The trek to the Job Centre means swishing through the silent streets and returning to Osney with a nasty case of trench-foot. Central parts of the island remain reasonably dry – why could my father not have shown a little more foresight and chosen a property in the middle of Bridge St? – but on the westernmost fringes, we are under several inches of water.

Our ground-floor carpets were all safely lifted in time and we even managed to get the sofa up the stairs without wrecking Dad's back. Amazingly, the gas and electricity still work, so we are able to cook and heat the house. But the smell downstairs is worsening – like boiled cabbage that has been left to stew for several days. A surprising number of neighbours have retreated to second homes or to unsuspecting relatives, leaving Frog Island to the elderly, the infirm and a few poor saps who actually work for a living.

So here I am surfing the net, in preference to surfing the Botley Rd, when I am surprised by a knock on the front door. I descend the stairs, don my wellies and lever the door ajar. On the doorstep, in an outlandish pair of galoshes, is Ozzie.

"Am I in time for a little something?" he enquires.

"We are fresh out of honey and condensed milk," I confess. "But I might be able to do you a coffee. Come upstairs, old son!"

There is just space amidst the clutter of my bedroom for the two of us to hunker down. Ozzie admires the Turner briefly.

"I've come to pick your brains, Leg End ..."

"Pick away!"

"Your boss," Ozzie starts, hesitantly. "Your old boss, that is ..."

"Lebedev? That bastard. Yes?"

"Apart from his bastardy, what do you make of him?"

I have had a little time since my defenestration to consider exactly this question.

"Ruthless. Self-serving. Humourless. Hypocritical. If you've come round to ask me to join his Fan Club …"

"Quite the opposite. You see, Alex, I think he's trying to get me thrown out of college as well."

"How could he possibly do that? You aren't part of his tawdry little fiefdom, are you?"

"No, but he *is* on the College Council. And my Associated Fellowship comes up for renewal in the next couple of months."

"Surely that is a formality?"

"Apparently not. The days of no-questions-asked tenure are long gone."

"But everybody loves you, Ozzie. And that new book of yours on genre has been selling awfully well, I believe."

"It's the book that's the problem."

"I don't follow …"

"It got reviewed in some obscure periodical."

"And they awarded it just the one star?"

"Worse than that. The author claimed that I had nicked all the ideas out of his doctorate."

"And had you?"

"Of course not. I'd never even read the stupid thing. It was written back in 1982, for God's sake, and never even properly published."

"*Properly* published?"

"You can find it online in one of the dustiest, most unvisited corners of the internet. A copy of it was also lodged in the Bodleian, so I'm told, or some annexe of the Bod in Kuala Lumpur. I'd be amazed if anyone has *ever* called it up. I'd certainly never seen it."

"Surely literary criticism has moved on a little bit since 1982?"

"Of course it has. The whole thing's a joke. There are hundreds of thousands of unread doctorates out there, so it's not surprising that one of them, if you go back far enough, has a few superficial similarities to my own book. If enough monkeys rattle away on typewriters, sooner or later one of them produces the works of Shakespeare."

"Then what have you got to worry about?"

"Well … there do seem to be some similarities of phrasing."

"You're being accused of plagiarism?"

Ozzie shrugs his shoulders. He seems close to tears. This is not the first time he has been involved in academic controversy. Prior to his history of literary genre, he created a bit of a stir with an article in an obscure periodical with the title: 'Who *was* Richard Price? The strange discovery of the Gawain-poet in 1824'. The suggestion (hedged in numerous caveats) that *Sir Gawain and the Green Knight* might, just *might* have been a forgery did not go down well with medieval faculties around the world. I remember asking him once (after a couple of ales, admittedly) who he thought really did write *Gawain* and *Pearl* and he put forward the theory that the manuscript that the unknown Mr Price claimed to have unearthed in 1824 was part of the mountain of papers Shelley left behind when he drowned. Shelley? The Gawain-poet? Well, if a teenager like Thomas Chatterton (AKA Thomas Rowley) could get away with forging medieval poetry, how could PBS resist the challenge? So Ozzie does have a bit of form when it comes to literary controversy.

"Do you think it's all just coincidence?" I ask.

"I don't know what to think, Alex."

"My own life seems full of inexplicable coincidences. Why should yours be any different? How did the College Council get wind of all this?"

"Lebedev told them. Said it might come out in the national press."

"Surely not?"

"Someone might leak the story …"

"The press have got much bigger fish to fry. You don't think Lebedev would…"

"Apparently, he reminded everyone that the college must be whiter than white if we are to maximise our alumni donations and benefactions. After the Rhodes Computer Room fiasco, the slightest hint of scandal would set us back years."

"What hogwash!"

"So a little bird tells me that the Council are 'considering' advertising my position."

"Oh, Ozzie, I'm sorry!"

"Except 'position' is too strong a word for what I've got. I'm just temporary staff, paid on an hourly rate for the teaching that no one else wants to do. Some days I have ten hours of tutorials, others none at all."

"I know. It's worse than the zero hours contract I was on at Iceland."

"The public still thinks we academics have a job for life. But tenure is a thing of the past. Do you know that 64% of Oxford lecturers and tutors are on fixed-term or other 'unusual' contracts?"

"As much as that?"

"In Cambridge it's just 13%. But round here we have all the job security of the average manager of Sunderland. If we so much as quibble, our hours can be cut to nothing and there's some other impoverished postgrad desperate to take up the slack."

I decide not to point out that our good friend, Phil, is one of the 36% on a permanent contract or that I am one of the also-rans who would gladly step into Ozzie's shoes. My old pal looks at me plaintively:

"So I've come round for some tips on how to apply for Jobseekers' Allowance."

"I'm going to help you fight this, Ozzie," I say unconvincingly.

"You've read my book?"

"Look, here it is on the table!" I fish it out from under a pile of other stuff. "But I've been a bit preoccupied with other stuff lately ..."

"So you haven't *actually* read it?"

"I was saving it up as a Christmas present to myself. Honest. Cracking title: *A Brief History of Literary Genre!*"

"Not too Hawking-ish?"

"Another Univ old boy! He's not suing you as well, is he?"

"Who knows? It could be another in the long line of ground-breaking lawsuits affecting Univ men. But there are a lot of books these days with "brief history" in the title – it always sells well, apparently. People think they're going to learn an awful lot very quickly."

"So what's in your brief history?"

I try to look as enthusiastic as possible. Indeed, I *am* curious. Ozzie's career to date has been almost exactly what I feel mine ought to have been. But while I boxed myself into a corner with research into the influence of St Teresa of Avila on nineteenth-century literature, Ozzie managed to hit on something which has just got bigger and bigger. And, like all academics, he loves to talk about his work to someone who has at least a glimmer of understanding of what he is on about. So off he goes ...

"My book addresses the question of why genres come and go. Why do they strike a chord for readers and writers at a certain date and then fall completely out of favour? Why were eclogues, for example, hugely popular two thousand years ago and then, like other forms of pastoral literature, dead as a dodo? Who would write or read an eclogue now? Or there's the detective novel, hugely popular throughout the twentieth century and yet almost non-existent before then – why?"

"OK, you've got me …"

"The way we tell stories has changed through time. Writers have gradually told their readers less and less about what is going on. The fundamental question which defines narrative genre is this: do we readers know more or less about what is happening than the central characters? In the earliest narrative genres like tragedy and epic, the readers and listeners were always one step ahead of the main characters, able to see their triumphs and disasters long before the protagonists themselves. This is partly because the same stories were told over and again and partly because writers like Virgil would summarise their story in advance. The audience is, metaphorically, up there in the gods, two or three steps ahead of Odysseus or Aeneas. We've heard it all before but we enjoy the re-telling of these old, old stories. We look forward to the expected peripeteia and we anticipate the hero's eventual moment of discovery or self-awareness, his anagnorisis, with relish."

"Ah, yes, I remember my Aristotle …"

"The old genius had it spot on even though he took, as his primary example, *Oedipus Rex*, a play which was decidedly ahead of its time in this respect. In classical tragedy, and indeed comedy, the audience is one step ahead of the characters at every point – we know all the plots that are being perpetrated and the traps that lie ahead, so we enjoy a sense of dramatic irony and even catharsis when these knotty problems are eventually resolved.

"In simple terms, we, the audience, are one step ahead of the protagonist in tragedy, parallel with the protagonist in adventure and certain kinds of romance, and at least one step behind the central characters when we read a whodunit or other kinds of mystery. This reader-control is the main thing that *defines* each of these genres."

"Surely genres have very different sorts of plot?"

"Not in my book. Take Shakespeare, for instance. What is the difference between the comedies that Shakespeare wrote in the early part of his career and the romances he wrote at the end? Why do we laugh at the comedies but not at the romances? The sort of deceptions and 'practices' that drive the story forward are similar in both and the happy outcomes are more or less identical. So why do they feel so different? Look at *Much Ado* and *The Winter's Tale*, for instance. Both plays feature a man who must be taken down a peg or two before he is allowed to enjoy a happy ending. Both Claudio, in *Much Ado*, and Leontes are fooled into thinking that their partners, Hero and Hermione, have died as a result of their faithlessness and treachery. In fact, each woman is feigning death to teach her man a lesson and the happy ending is triggered by her staged resurrection.

"The big difference between the two plays is that in *Much Ado* we know all about the con trick perpetrated on Claudio while in *The Winter's Tale*, we don't – our perspective is the same as Leontes' so the eventual metamorphosis of Hermione's statue results in as much of a shock to the audience as it does to Leontes. Same plot, very different experience. And that's the main difference between comedy and romance.

"And so to the birth of the novel, so called because it was something the writer had actually had the nerve to make up himself rather than re-cycle. Readers discovered that they actually preferred stories where they didn't know the ending in advance, where there was some element of suspense about what was going to happen. Most of the early novels were adventures, with readers who shared the perspective of the main character, knowing neither more or less than he or she did. Female readers preferred novels which concluded with the heroine marrying her prince but these soon became a little too predictable. It took the genius of Jane Austen to transform that genre."

"But Emma gets her man, doesn't she?"

"Yes, but it's a world away from Fanny Burney and the rest of the eighteenth century lady novelists. Jane Austen puts us inside the mind of her protagonist and yet at the same time, she doesn't. We are never told that Emma loves Knightley or that Elizabeth loves Darcy – no such recorded thought crosses their mind prior to the ending. We learn more of the spark of attraction between the heroine and the pseudo-heroes, Frank Churchill, Mr Wickham and their ilk, than we do of any romantic feelings towards the man they will eventually marry. Jane Austen does *everything* in her power to keep the ending a surprise."

"But the endings are pretty 'obvious', aren't they?"

"Only to the jaded modern reader who has learnt all the tricks of the trade. The challenge of the genre, for a storyteller like Austen, was to make the ending a pleasant and satisfying surprise. The techniques she developed in order to withhold her central narrative secret and to keep the reader in the dark represent a huge turning-point in the history of story-telling. The same techniques lie behind the invention of a new genre, the mystery – *Bleak House*, *Edwin Drood*, Sherlock Holmes, etc – where nothing is what it seems, where the reader knows a great deal less than the detective or the murderer about what is going on, and where suspense is everything, prior to the transformational ending. The challenge for today's novelist is to create an ending which revolutionises our understanding of *every* element that precedes it; character, plot, the lot.

"So a big part of my book is about the ways storytellers tell lies and lead us up garden paths. Austen more or less invented free indirect speech, for instance, where the narrative flits in and out of a character's thoughts and speech-idioms so that we are deceived into mistaking a character's (probably misleading) impressions for narrative "facts". The author-figure is not allowed to tell a lie but novelists have learnt to de-authorise themselves, to melt into the background of their own stories. As readers now, we demand to be kept in the dark, to be constantly surprised."

"How does your old friend, Sir Gawain, figure in this history of storytelling?"

"I was advised to leave him out of this book. But one of the reasons I suggested it might be a nineteenth century pastiche is because it simply would not have been possible to tell the story in that way back in 1390 or whenever it was supposedly written. Keeping the audience in the dark about what the Green Knight and Sir Bertilak are up to – in order to create the surprise ending – would have been feasible in the nineteenth century but not in the fourteenth. If *Gawain* is genuine, it's as much of an anachronism as *Oedipus Rex* was for Aristotle's era."

"So where does genre go from here?"

"Good question. Perhaps the history of storytelling is a bit like the history of classical music from plainsong to Schoenberg's experiments in atonality and chromatic scales. In the end, music-lovers' ears couldn't keep up with that much uncertainty, that much surprise. So we gave up and started listening to pop music instead, with its variations on much more familiar themes and patterns.

"Yes, does anyone actually listen to Schoenberg these days? And how many

154

of us have actually read *Finnegans Wake?*"

"I certainly haven't. Anyway, that, in a nutshell, is my latest book. But what I thought was a revolutionary reappraisal of the entire history of storytelling turns out to be nothing of the sort. Some old doctoral student, now working as a chartered accountant in Grimsby, I believe, came up with much the same set of theories thirty or forty years ago, only nobody took a blind bit of notice at the time."

"What's the name of this chap?"

"I'm not entirely sure. He's still writing reviews under the name of Justin Roseland."

"What, like the golfer, plus 'land'?"

"More likely the Cornish village of the same name. I don't *think* that's his real name. Perhaps I'll find out in court."

Sunday 18 December 2016

Re-mounted main polo-horse (8)

Jobs – who needs 'em? Shelley never had a proper job, did he? Never even *applied* for a job. He relied on pen and ink to furnish him with a living … except that he spent half his adult life trying to cadge a fiver off his father, his indulgent grandfather (what an old rogue he was!) and almost everyone who crossed his path.

Here in my insular eyrie, I have had ample time to immerse myself in the fetid waters of Bysshe's back-story. Is it his fault he's too much of a gigolo? Or does he go out of his way to bewitch as many girls as possible, knowing full well that he would never be able to squire them all?

There seems little doubt that he conquered the entire Godwin household with his winsome smile and a few radical-sounding couplets. Not just sensible Mary and wild, black-eyed Claire but the third of the Weird Half-Sisters as well, the unglamorous, untalented Fanny Imlay.

"Poor" Fanny, as she was so often known, resembles the Cinderella of *Grimms' Fairy Tales* (1812) and Fanny Price in *Mansfield Park* (1814) – an uncomplaining doormat for her marriage-hunting step-sisters. But, unlike her fictional counterparts, Fanny Imlay never gets to marry her prince.

Mary Godwin is the one with the good looks, the sweet manner, the vivacity and the intellectual accomplishments to attract the earnest but inconveniently married young poet. Having been brought up in such a liberal and unconventional household, Mary sees Bysshe as a kindred spirit and perhaps as a potential means of escape from the hothouse of her family life in Skinner Street. Claire Clairmont, her less gifted and less obviously attractive step-sister, also sixteen, is happy to chaperone Mary in the days and weeks that follow their first meeting in June 1814 and turn a blind eye to their intensifying relationship, even on visits (it is rumoured) to Mary Wollstonecraft's grave. Claire must bide her time and hope that her turn will be next. Orphan Fanny sits at home, embroidering.

By the end of June, Shelley is telling Godwin of his love for Mary and, to the poet's surprise, the old advocate of free love is appalled. Godwin cannot condone the pursuit of his only daughter, aged just sixteen, by a married man.

Soon Shelley is no longer welcome at Skinner St, there are furious rows, threats of suicide and Godwin even enlists the pregnant Harriet Shelley in his attempts to nip the romance in the bud. This is not a winning move. On 28th July, Godwin gets up to find a letter propped up on the breakfast table. Not only has Mary eloped with her lover to Calais and beyond, but Claire has gone too! Harriet has the good sense to reject Shelley's magnanimous invitation to join them in Switzerland. No one thinks to invite poor Fanny.

This rehearsal for exile lasts a mere six weeks before the money runs out and the intrepid threesome are back in Kentish Town to face the music. Shelley's marriage is irreparably broken, for all Harriet's attempts to forgive and forget, and Shelley only hears of the birth of his son and heir, Charles, by post. Mary is pregnant too by now; she and Claire are no longer welcome at Godwin Towers in Skinner St. Shelley, beset by women and their babies as well as his numerous creditors and bailiffs, begs Hogg to come and save the day and/or join his commune of like-minded souls.

Hogg duly trots down from Norton and is quickly assimilated into the Shelley ménage. His role is to entertain the increasingly bed-bound Mary while Bysshe, with Claire now his constant companion, is out negotiating with lawyers and money-men, or simply *out*. It is clear to all four of them what Shelley has in mind and Hogg, still a virgin (one presumes), hopes that his lottery numbers have come up at last. Mary, depressed by the realization that she can never have Shelley all to herself, is flattered by Hogg's attentions and encourages him to hope, at least. But does she really fancy him? I suspect not. Only just seventeen and about to have a baby, the last thing she needs is a physical relationship with her lover's best friend.

From a distance of two hundred years, we watch the children play. It's all a little bit like the *Adventures of the Famous Five*. Bysshe is, of course, Julian, tall, good-looking, the natural leader of the group – some years later he will dramatise his relationship with Byron in *Julian and Maddalo* – while Mary is pretty, obedient Anne and Claire is a natural as George, the obstinate, gender-confused, name-changing rebel of the group. But does Hogg have what it takes to play cheeky, dependable Dick, doing his best to cheer Anne up whenever she is in low spirits? Or is his natural role as Timmy the dog forever biting on the rough end of the stick?

But it's even rougher for poor Fanny, famous only for carrying herself off in October 1816 to a random, Swansea hotel (the Mackworth Arms) and killing herself in a suitably unimaginative way, with a draught of some dull opiate. Poor Fanny! Poor, poor Cinderella! While Mary and Claire had, in their different ways, an outside chance of pinning the butterfly down in mid-air, Fanny had none.

Stuck at home in Skinner St with her tut-tutting mother and step-father, Fanny begs to be allowed to join the great Shelleyan adventure in Bristol and beyond. She would be no trouble, she promises. Shelley, always on the look-out for fresh votaries and vestal virgins, would no doubt have said yes but Mary and Claire will hear nothing of it. Fanny's last hours are still the subject of much conjecture. Does she make one last desperate plea to Shelley himself? It seems so. She has no bargaining chips except empty promises and pathetic threats. Does he slam the door on her inarticulate infatuation with a little too much force?

Shelley takes Fanny's threats sufficiently seriously to follow her to Swansea and, it seems, sweet-talk his way into her rented room. Is he too late? Does he even check Fanny's pulse? Our hero seems to have been more concerned with locating a suicide note. Not only does he fail to call the alarm or summon a doctor, he tears off the incriminating half (one assumes) of Fanny's valediction and skulks off into the night and out of Swansea. It is left to the hotel proprietors to discover the anonymous corpse and what is left of her last will and testament.

Despite everything, Fanny is identified and her next of kin is contacted. Mortified, although not quite as mortified as his inconvenient step-daughter, William Godwin forbids the whole of his extended family from going to Swansea to identify the body. Let the Welsh bury the English dead! Not one member of her family sees Fanny interred. Relatives are told she has gone to Ireland and then, later on, if anyone is so foolish as to ask, that she has died of a severe head-cold. It is as if poor, illegitimate Fanny has never lived at all.

The truth is that love-lorn suicide had become a little bit *passé* by 1816. A generation earlier it had been all the rage. It was almost a badge of honour amongst the beau-monde to have thrown yourself off at least one London bridge in the last years of the eighteenth century. Why, even the great Mary Wollstonecraft, having given birth to Fanny and been rejected by the baby's father, Gilbert Imlay, made two attempts to kill herself, first with laudanum and then by hurling herself into the Thames one rainy night. A stranger fished her out but may not have received much thanks. A little over a year later, she gave birth to her second daughter, Mary (by Godwin), and died of septicaemia a few days later. Godwin's memoir of their short, passionate time together, combined with the circumstances of her death, transformed the public's perception of her.

But by 1816 the bottle of laudanum in the garret room had become an embarrassing cliché. Too many vaporous and vapid teenagers had taken the easy way out. But Fanny Imlay's inconvenient life was over before it had really begun.

Which brings me, of course, to the tragic demise of Mrs Harriet (*née* Westbrook) Shelley, just a few weeks later.

While the modern Prometheus and his entourage (Mary and Claire) have been enjoying Lord Byron's grudging hospitality in Geneva, dreaming up *Frankenstein*, etc, the discarded Harriet is left to bring up Ianthe and Charles in one of the less fashionable corners of London.

Ianthe and Charles? At this point, I need hardly point out some alarming parallels two hundred years on. For Harriet, read Hattie (who was indeed christened Harriet, I believe, although it is not a name I have ever known her by). As far as I am aware, Hattie knows nothing of the Shelley circle and yet she too has children called Xanthe and Charley. Those are popular names nowadays and one could put that down as coincidence if it were not for the other still more alarming parallels. But you can dot the *i*'s and cross the *t*'s for yourself; I will simply summarise what history tells us of the last days of Harriet Westbrook.

It is hard to say when or indeed whether Harriet, now just turned 21, hears about Fanny Imlay's lonely valediction. The news may have exacerbated her depression and sense of isolation. Or it may simply be another coincidence and Harriet's precipitate action is triggered more by the undeniable evidence of her latest pregnancy, this time without any input from her estranged husband. Harriet has been brought up as a good little middle-class girl and within such bourgeois circles there is still considerable shame attached to motherhood outside wedlock.

There was retrospective talk of a Mr Smith, a soldier perhaps, said to be her new partner, but there is virtually no evidence that such another man actually existed. She takes to calling herself Harriet Smith but that was probably no more than a ruse inspired by a reading of *Emma* (published 1815) in which the well-meaning Harriet Smith pays a high price for mixing with her social superiors. The most common surname in England is a convenient one to hide behind in her last days.

Pregnant, desperate and having left the children with her parents, Harriet walks out of her final lodgings in Elizabeth St in early November 1816. Six weeks later, what is left of her is fished out of the Serpentine in Hyde Park, identifiable only from the ring on her finger. There has been no manhunt in the interim period – her absence has gone almost completely unremarked. News travels fast, they say, but evidently not in those days. Shelley has absolutely no idea that his wife is missing until after her body is recovered. He finds out that he has been widowed, not from Harriet's family or from any official body (the Metropolitan Police had not yet been invented, of course) but from his publisher, Thomas Hookham. Yes, his *publisher* and only then because he had made a casual enquiry after her welfare a few weeks previously.

These days, such a story involving a prominent rap artist (say) would dominate the front pages for a week or more. But in 1816 there is no vilification of the estranged husband. The *Times* mentions the death of a "respectable woman with an expensive ring on her finger" but there is no indication of her identity. The coroner records a verdict of "found drowned" but there is no very lengthy inquest. Harriet is brushed under the carpet as quickly and effectively as Fanny Imlay before her.

But Harriet does leave us a suicide note, addressed to her sister, Eliza, free of any poetic redaction. Here is a transcript:

> To you my dear Sister I leave all my things as they more properly belong to you than any one & you will preserve them for Ianthe . Hog bless you both My dearest & much belod Sister
>
> Sat. Eve.
>
> When you read this letr. I shall be [no] more an inhabitant of this miserable world. do not regret the loss of one who could never be anything but a source of vexation & misery to you all belonging to me. Too wretched to exert myself lowered in the opinion of everyone why should I drag on a miserable existence embittered by past recollections & not one ray of hope to rest on for the future. The remembrance of all your kindness which I have so unworthily repaid has often made my hert ache. I know that you will forgive

me because it is not in your nature to be unkind or severe to any. dear amiable woman that I have never left you oh! that I had always taken your advice. I might have lived long & happy but weak & unsteady have rushed on my own destruction I have not written to Bysshe. oh no what would it avail my wishes or my prayers would not be attended to by him & yet I should he see this perhaps he might grant my last request to let Ianthe remain with you always dear lovely child, with you she will enjoy much happiness with him none My dear Bysshe let me conjure you by the remembrance of our days of happiness to grant my last wish – do not take your innocent child from Eliza who has been more than I have, who has watched over her with such unceasing care. – Do not refuse my last request – I never could refuse you & if you had never left me I might have lived but as it is, I freely forgive you & may you enjoy that happiness which you have deprived me of. There is your beautiful boy. oh! be careful of him & his live may prove one day a rich reward. As you form his infant mind so you will reap the fruits hereafter Now comes the sad task of saying farewell – oh I must be quick. God bless & watch over you all. You dear Bysshe. & you dear Eliza. May all happiness attend ye both is the last wish of her who loved ye more than all others. My children I dare not trust myself there. They are too young to regret me & ye will be kind to them for their own sakes more than for mine. My parents do not regret me. I was unworthy your love & care. Be happy all of you. so shall my spirit find rest & forgiveness. God bless you all is the last prayer of the unfortunate Harriet S——

Is it too late to grieve for poor Harriet now? I shed a tear anyway. "Hog bless you both"? Surely that is not what she intended to write?

When does Harriet's sister, Elizabeth, receive or find this note? Does she raise the alarm or wait calmly for a body to be discovered (or not) in the fullness of time? Who else sees the note, and when? Is an active decision taken *not* to tell Shelley until it is too late? These questions remain unanswered.

And what of Shelley when he discovers her fate? Does he weep tears of remorse at her funeral? Does he retire to a monastery to rue his appalling treatment of the schoolgirl he seduced, married and abandoned to her fate?

Does he heck. *Je ne regrette rien* has become the poet's motto.

And whither Charles and Ianthe? Would they stay with Auntie Eliza and their grandparents? "My dear Bysshe let me conjure you by the remembrance of our days of happiness to grant my last wish – do not take your innocent child from Eliza who has been more than I have, who has watched over her with such unceasing care. – Do not refuse my last request…"

Naturally, Shelley decides that *he* should take custody of the children. The Westbrooks are suitably appalled by the proposal and outright war is declared. M'learned friends (possibly including Hogg) advise Shelley that "ownership" of the children does not *automatically* revert to the father in such circumstances, even when the father is the son of a baronet. The case will still have to be argued in court. Shelley's family solicitor, Longdill, tells him that, to win custody of his children, he will need to demonstrate a stable domestic environment. He must make an honest woman of Mary, something that William Godwin has been pressing him to do since the day they met.

If Shelley was sceptical about the institution of marriage before his union with Harriet, he is even more certain now that matrimony is anathema to him. Wild palominos could not drag him to the altar a second time. And yet, and yet … if that is the way to spite the Westbrooks and assuage his fatherly guilt …

Mary, pregnant, exhausted and under pressure from all sides, is in no position to save Shelley from himself. She knows (or hopes) it will make no difference to their relationship – Bysshe will remain the least uxorious man alive. But perhaps society will view her in a slightly different way? Who would not want to be "respectable"?

And so Bysshe and Mary are married in St Mildred's Church, just a few short weeks after the interment (in a small cemetery off the Bayswater Rd) of the drowned and unlamented 'Harriet Smith'.

The date of the nuptials of two of the greatest figures of English literary history? No, it cannot be possible. *30ʰ December, 1816.*

Sunday 18 December 2016 (2)

Promoting Oscar, the Roman co-respondent (5,3)

Yes, that's right, Shelley marries Mary on Monday 30th December 1816, in St Mildred's Church, Bread St, one hundred years to the day before Rasputin is launched into the icy waters of the Neva by Felix Yusupov and his hapless cronies, and two hundred years to the day before … I cannot bring myself to write the words.

So let's check we have this right. My old college's most infamous alumnus marries on the same morning as its next most infamous old boy commits *that* murder a hundred years on? Has no one spotted this before? I reach for the 600-page *History of University College* by Robin Darwall-Smith – surely this "coincidence" is noted there?

Both Shelley and Yusupov feature prominently in this meticulous tome and yet the significance of this shared date has unaccountably slipped beneath the radar. As the world's media seizes on the centenary of Rasputin's assassination in the next fortnight, surely this strange concatenation will be noted? Or will I take the secret to my own grave?

Amongst this mortal triumvirate, I do not want to play Lepidus to Mark Antony and Octavius. (Lepidus? No, me neither …) If the tendrils of time bind me to these past dramas, surely I correspond to TJ Hogg, not Shelley, and to Yusupov, not Rasputin. Neither Hogg nor Yusupov died on December 30th, nor did they drown at a later date. Both grew old in relative peace. Suddenly, I feel a lot more hopeful. Perhaps that fateful date *may* not be Drowned Hogg Day after all?

It is often said that we must learn the lessons of history if we are to avoid making the same mistakes again. I ought to spend what time I have during my enforced and watery exile scrutinising the evidence. What exactly happened one hundred years ago and indeed two hundred years ago? Are there some crucial clues I've missed? Clues that would keep me safely on dry land on the sixth day of Christmas?

Even the most detailed Shelley biographies provide scant detail of the events of December 30th 1816. We learn that Bysshe and Mary were invited to dine (for the first time since their elopement) at the modest Godwin family home in Skinner St on the previous evening. One can only speculate on how this exercise in Sabbath Day *rapprochement* must have gone – it would take more than a shotgun wedding to dissipate the years of mutual suspicion and frustrated hopes. The atmosphere may well have been frostier inside than out as 1816 prepared to bid its own farewell. Godwin's teeth would have been as gritted as the roads outside. Did Shelley, remembering *Zastrozzi*, sniff the celebratory Madeira, just in case? Did the cakes appear a little tart that night in the gloomy recesses, not of the Moika Palace, but of Godwin's fusty mansion?

It is not unreasonable to assume the consumption of Madeira, at least. Throughout the eighteenth century, the tiny island of Madeira produced a surprisingly vast proportion of the world's wine. The addition of distilled alcohol meant that it could be shipped around the world and remain unspoiled and drinkable. Madeira was a favourite of Thomas Jefferson and it was used to toast the Declaration of Independence. During the Napoleonic Wars, it was impossible for England to import wine from France or its colonies and Madeira enjoyed something of a monopoly.

Hogg mentions his college friend's love of sweet cakes in *Shelley at Oxford* but it is left to another mutual friend, Thomas Love Peacock, to provide a more telling picture of the Shelley circle in *Nightmare Abbey* (1818). The plot of *Nightmare Abbey* revolves around the hero, Scythrop Glowry (Shelley's) unwillingness to make up his mind which of two young women (based on Harriet and Mary) he is in love with. Scythrop 'drank Madeira, and laid deep schemes for a thorough repair of the crazy fabric of human nature' (end of ch. 2). In the end he plumps for Marionietta despite plenty of opposition:

> But when Marionetta hinted that she was to leave the Abbey immediately, Scythrop snatched from its repository his ancestor's skull, filled it with Madeira, and presenting himself before Mr Glowry, threatened to drink off the contents if Mr Glowry did not immediately promise that Marionetta should not be taken from the Abbey without her own consent. Mr Glowry, who took the Madeira to be some deadly brewage, gave the required promise in dismal panic. Scythrop returned to Marionetta with a joyful heart, and drank the Madeira by the way.

At the end of this bibulous tale, Scythrop, rejected by all his women, is determined on suicide yet again, by one means or another, and calls for his butler, Raven. These are the final lines:

> Raven appeared. Scythrop looked at him very fiercely two or three minutes; and Raven, still remembering the pistol, stood quaking in mute apprehension, till Scythrop, pointing significantly towards the dining-room, said, "Bring some Madeira."

For those who were half in love with easeful death, a fortified wine had clearly become the accessory of choice. Did Felix Yusupov read *Nightmare Abbey*? Was the whole murder plot against Rasputin a strange homage to his illustrious forebear at Univ?

So soon after Christmas 1816, it isn't clear who would have come to St Mildred's on a Monday to speed the happy couple on their way. We can be fairly sure, I feel, that Sir Timothy and Lady Shelley would *not* have swept up in the brougham from Field Place, and even sister Elizabeth would have been barred from attendance. Shelley's doting grandfather had died the previous year, so it is probable that there was not a single representative of the Shelley clan on his side of the pews. Peacock and Leigh Hunt would surely have been there and perhaps Hogg too – we know that he had returned to London in November and mixed in all the same circles.

On Mary's side: Fanny was dead and Claire, the stroppiest of Shelley's marionettes, had stayed behind in Bristol, confined by the imminent birth of Alba/Allegra, the long-awaited consequence of Byron's grudging sperm-donation. Claire's cynicism about the Shelley nuptials is apparent from the fragmentary memoir she wrote some sixty years on, after all the other players in this melodrama had passed on.

Monday 19 December 2016

Carry us up over some assassin (7)

"That may be the last squash game for a little while," Phil tells me as we knock back a second pint of Purple Moose in the Beer Cellar. "As a hen-pecked husband, I won't be able to get out so much and something has got to give."

The news is no more unexpected than the result of tonight's game.

"I'm sorry, Phil. It wasn't much of a challenge this evening."

"Have you won any games this year? Just asking …" he winked.

"There was a straight sets win in May, wasn't there?"

"I was on one leg that night. Since the ankle got better, it's been, well, a bit too *easy*."

"It'll be even easier when I'm dead."

Phil yawns.

"Dead? Yeah, right. Have you booked the crematorium? Might be worth it at this time of year."

"Your sympathy has been greatly appreciated. Actually, do you mind if I ask you something, Phil?"

"Ask away."

"Have you ever noticed any similarities between your life and that of Percy Bysshe Shelley?"

Phil looks at me quizzically for a moment and then laughs heartily.

"Shelley? I wish. I haven't written a poem since I was thirteen."

"You've got the same initials. You both grew up in Sussex and went to the same college."

"But Shelley was thrown out!"

"OK, it's not an exact match. But your love life has been decidedly Shelleyan…"

It takes me a couple of pints to lay out my case. Phil fights me all the way but even he is forced to concede that there are some odd similarities.

"It's bizarre," he concludes. "Almost as bonkers as your theory that you are going to die on Friday week."

"The two things are connected, don't you see?" I insist. "I seem destined to repeat most of the mistakes of my ancestor, Thomas Jefferson Hogg, and you are getting married two hundred years to the day after Shelley married Mary!"

"I'll be straight with you, Alex. We fixed that date precisely *because* you had told me how significant it was for you. It's not random. I hoped it would make you focus your mind on something more positive. But I do see now why you were so concerned about Hattie's disappearance."

I tell him about the trip to Hyde Park and the sense of déjà vu I felt there. Phil has a simpler explanation, that I am over-thinking the Bill Wyman role and appropriated too many of the stories of the Stones' 1969 gig.

"So we're all living through some kind of weird Groundhog Day," he concludes, sceptically. "With me in the Phil Connors role?"

"Punks' attorney Phil, that's you."

"Actually, there is one odd parallel you may not have considered. Does the name Benjamin Haydon mean anything to you?"

"You mean Ben Haydon from the Hogacre Eco Park, the guy who's been bugging you for years?"

"There was another Benjamin Haydon. He was in the Mike Leigh film, *Mr Turner.*"

"Remind me."

"Haydon was the painter with delusions of grandeur that Turner lent money to. Haydon couldn't pay him back because everyone hated his art."

"So he was. I saw the movie a couple of weeks ago, in fact."

"What a film it is! Anyway, I already knew about Haydon because he was best mates with John Keats. Keats even dedicated a couple of sonnets to him."

"So he did." I make a mental note to check this out when I get home.

"Haydon did a life mask of Keats exactly two hundred years ago, December 1816. It's in the National Portrait Gallery."

"But Keats and Shelley didn't mix that much," I say – it's my turn to play the sceptic.

"They were both on the invite list for Leigh Hunt's dinner parties in Hampstead. As was Haydon. If I remember right, the first such *soirée* was in January 1817, a few weeks after Shelley married Mary. Maybe Hogg was there too? But Shelley and Haydon were chalk and cheese. Shelley, the militant atheist, spent the whole meal making fun of Haydon's Christian beliefs. Haydon scribbled all the nasty details down in his diary and vowed revenge."

"A dish best served cold?"

"Indeed. And twenty years after Shelley drowned, Haydon published those diaries to raise some much-needed cash. Not long before he shot himself."

"This doesn't sound a lot like the Ben Haydon we know from Hogacre."

"Well, I haven't checked his TwitterFeed, if he has one. But what's in a name, eh?"

This does not seem like the right time to tell Phil about my recent encounter in the Hogacre café.

"I don't suppose you'll be inviting him to your wedding bash, will you? It would be a shame if someone scuppered the Folly Bargères!"

We both laugh heartily at the idea. Some of Phil's healthy scepticism has rubbed off on me. How else can I deal with the suspicion that my own paltry life is, in some respects, a comical replay of the events of 1816? And then there's all that Russian stuff to deal with as well ...

What would it have been like in the basement room of the Moika Palace, St Petersburg, December 29-30 1916?

Here the hapless five-man death-squad would have assembled – the fey plutocrat, Yusupov, and his childhood pash, Grand Duke Dmitri Pavlovich, together with the cyanide-bearing Dr Lazovert, the token politician, Vladimir Purishkevich, and the hapless Sergei Sukhotin, whom no one can remember asking along. Of these, only one, Sukhotin, has seen military action and I picture him arriving back from the front, swathed in bandages, here to do his imperial duty in a different way.

Did each man bring his own weapon to the party? A blunderbuss here, a musket there? I doubt it. Grand Duke Dmitri might have had a weapon or two. He had been enrolled in the Horse Guards at birth and, as an equestrian, finished 7th in the Stockholm Olympics of 1912, but his experience with firearms was probably rather more limited.

It is also hard to envisage Dr Lazovert unearthing an arquebus or a flintlock to defend himself against the devil incarnate's laser-eyes. Given how the night panned out, it appears that his skills as a poisoner were roughly on a par with his efforts to cure Prince Alexy's haemophilia with aspirin.

Was it Lazovert alone who concocted the famous cakes and doctored the Madeira? Or did all five men make a symbolic contribution to the preparations, wearing pinnies and wielding rolling pins as if in an unconvincing episode of

Celebrity Bake-Off for Comic Relief? Yusupov's *Lost Splendor* is far from clear on this point, as indeed on most others. How many people in St Petersburg did *not* know what was cooking in the Moika Palace that night? Possibly just Rasputin himself. Even the reclusive Tsaritsa Alexandra had got wind of it, it seems. Did she make a last-ditch effort to put the frighteners on this mötley crüe? Had anyone tipped off the local constabulary? Did the fragrant Irina, safely despatched to the Yusupovs' winter palace at Yalta, know of her role in the conspiracy?

And, of course, the million rouble question, why on earth did the cassocked cleric go alone at midnight to the home of his most outspoken critic? Did he believe his own PR ("no bullet can kill me …")? Did he anticipate some kind of threesome with the porcelain princess and her closeted, corseted husband? Was it the promise of a ride in FY's Silver Ghost that clinched the deal? Why did he give his tainiks the night off?

But perhaps we are giving Felix's beguiling tale too much credence? Maybe Rasputin did not come to the Moika of his own free-will but was frog-marched there or beaten senseless in his own apartment? There may have been no cakes and Madeira at all. Oswald Rayner, Stephen Alley and their cronies may have done the deed quietly and efficiently and delivered a stiff to the Moika, enabling the Russians to take the credit with as big a splash as possible. But this was a conspiracy that has produced surprisingly few conspiracy theories.

In Yusupov's account, the unkillable starets is poisoned several times over and then shot in the heart at point-blank range, only to rise again from the dead and escape through a locked door into the snowy grounds of the palace, pursued by the feckless fivesome trying to find the firing mechanism on their rusty flintlocks. Enough shots are fired to wake the city and by the time old laser-eyes is shot and killed a second time, the Keystone Cops have arrived to ask what all the fuss is about. Just high spirits, they are told. Suitably reassured, the constabulary leaves them to it. Yes, that seems pretty plausible.

Even with the bullet from an English service revolver lodged in his brain, Rasputin seems to have moved yet again from his resting place in the snow (despite being pronounced dead a second time). A larger contingent of cops comes and goes, presumably blindfolded. Yusupov later hams it up for all it is worth:

'As I reached the top of the stairs, I saw Rasputin stretched out on the landing, blood flowing from his many wounds. It was a loathsome sight. Suddenly, everything went black, I felt the ground slipping from under my feet and I fell headlong down the stairs.

'Purichkevich and Ivan found me, a few minutes later, lying side by side with Rasputin; the murderer and his victim. I was unconscious and he and Ivan had to carry me to my bedroom.' (*Lost Splendor*, ch. xxiii)

There Felix is, the sleeping Bride of Frankenstein, like Elsa Lanchester in the 1935 film.

Eventually, Rasputin is bundled into the boot of the Roller and carted off to the Petrovski bridge. The tyre tracks in the snow, there and back, leave incontrovertible evidence of what has occurred so no one will feign surprise when the icy corpse is washed up on the banks of the Neva a day or so later.

In the early hours of December 30th, there is a second or third visitation of the forces of Law and Order and Purishkevitch makes an unprompted confession ("The shots you heard killed Rasputin. If you love your country and your Tsar, you'll keep your mouth shut" – Yusupov's dialogue needs a little more work, I feel).

But it is unlikely that anyone apart from the police keeps their mouth shut in Petersburg that day. Even the tsar, cowering under his bunk-bed 400 miles away in Moghilev, would have heard the word. His wife is having fainting fits at the news in her boudoir at the Alexander Palace, begging the police to arrest the villains. But they do the sensible thing and dither. Rasputin has been murdered and everyone knows whodunnit. But there is no will to arrest and prosecute the culprits. If Felix and his friends gambled on that, they judged the public mood well.

That mood would have been very different had the populace known that the assassination was really the work of some opportunistic English spies. Having stage-directed the whole farce and administered the necessary coup-de-grâce, Oswald and his friends melt away into the night and (no doubt) leave town on the next available train, happy to return to lives of relative obscurity in England. A brief report appears in the *Times* a couple of days later, courtesy of Reuters:

170

A NOTORIOUS RUSSIAN MONK

Petrograd, Jan 1: the body of the notorious monk Rasputin was found on the bank of one of the branches of the River Neva this morning. An inquiry has been opened.

It is almost as brief and neutral as the report of Harriet Westbrook's washed-up body a hundred years before.

The champagne corks will have been popping in the War Office but there is one English reader in less jubilant mood. Gerard Shelley, enjoying a quiet New Year with his parents in Sidcup, must have choked on his egg soldiers. This Shelley, no relation to Percy Bysshe or his family, has been Rasputin's one true advocate on these shores, defending the so-called Mad Monk from a wide variety of calumnious attacks. The young Jesuit first meets and befriends Rasputin while staying with friends near St Petersburg in 1915 during his gap year. He returns to Russia the following summer and hooks up with Rasputin for boating trips on Lake Ladogo (exactly a hundred years after Shelley, Byron & co had been boating on Lake Geneva, dreaming of monsters and unkillable vampires). Young Gerard warns Rasputin that the English are out to get him, but evidently to no avail.

To Gerard Shelley, the Russian with the floating hair and the wild, staring eyes is an Old Testament prophet, a mystic, a noble savage, not the foul-mouthed peasant of popular repute. On hearing the news of his death, Gerard Shelley rushes back to St Petersburg in time for the February Revolution and the chaos that ensues. In the end, he escapes on a train from Moscow to Finland, hiding under the seat in women's clothing while his fellow travellers sweet-talk the Red Guard.

Eight years later, Gerard Shelley publishes not one but two books on his travels to exotic lands, *The Blue Steppes* and *The Speckled Domes*. The latter is not a critique of the star-spangled design of Univ's Shelley Memorial but it paints a very different picture of Rasputin from the one peddled by Yusupov and dutifully translated by Rayner himself. By 1952, while Yusupov is composing *Lost Splendor*, Shelley has become the third Archbishop of the Old Roman Catholic Church of Great Britain – not quite the Illuminati or Opus Dei, but not so far removed either.

If the murder of Rasputin was intended to prop up the Romanov dynasty, it had precisely the opposite effect. Alexandra lost her confidant, then her freedom and very soon her life. She was canonised by the Russian Orthodox Church in 2000, an honour not bestowed on Grigori Yefimovich Rasputin. Her reliance on the peasant-mystic with the questionable hygiene has often been compared to her grandmother, Queen Victoria's, dependency on her ghillie, John Brown, also the victim of a whispering campaign in court circles and beyond. This is far from accidental. Alix's mother, Princess Alice, died when she was six and Victoria then took responsibility for her upbringing as a future queen at a time when she was leaning ever more heavily on her own noble savage. Losing her chosen mentor and spiritual guide, Rasputin, in the early hours of December 30th 1916 was a blow from which the Empress never had a chance to recover.

Tuesday 20 December 2016

Something went well for Lady Bracknell's daughter? (4)

After an extremely soggy trip to the pseudonymous Jobcentre in George St, I am tipping the water out of my wellies, drying my feet and hunting vainly for a pair of clean, dry socks and some trousers. It seems clear that my father has nabbed all my clean pairs of socks but since I know he is at bridge club, that is no problem. I can simply retrieve them from the chest of drawers in his room.

Imagine my surprise, dear reader, as I wander into my father's bedroom, clad only in my boxer shorts, to discover my father in bed. And not by himself! There, sitting up under the covers like some long-married couple on a Sunday morning, are my father and some floozie. Perhaps "floozie" is not quite the right word. The lady occupying the right-hand side of my father's narrow bed, in obvious danger of falling out, looks barely younger than my Dad. She is wearing a relatively low-cut nightie which reveals rather more wrinkly brown flesh than I want to see at this hour of the afternoon. There is a hint of blue-rinse in her hair and I can see that she is fumbling round for her glasses.

It's not often you catch your own father *in flagrante*. I must confess I'd rather assumed that such days were well behind him. The important thing, I sense, is not to act as if this is anything out of the ordinary. I take in the scene for a second or two – my father open-mouthed, his eyes pleading for … what?

"Oops, I'm sorry! Just wanted some socks!" I mumble at last and return to my own chambers.

As I find sufficient clothes to achieve a level of respectability, I can hear similar activity taking place next door. It is clear that there will be no further nookie this afternoon, if indeed there had been any prior to my unfortunate intervention. I really do not want to consider whether such things are even *possible* at my father's age, at least without some kind of chemical assistance. Parents can really embarrass you sometimes.

I expect to hear the creak of the stairs and a slam of the front door but instead there is a knock on my own door. My father and his now fully-clothed partner troop in a little shamefacedly.

"Look, I'm really sorry, Dad," I begin. "I didn't realise you were in the house…"

"It's OK, Alex. No, really. Have you met Gwen?"

"I … I don't think so."

Gwen and I shake hands as if we had just agreed to divvy up the old Austro-Hungarian empire.

"I met Gwen at bridge club," Dad says.

"I thought you had been spending rather a lot of time there recently!"

"Have I?" My father considers this proposition for a moment or two. "Yes, perhaps I have. Gwen has got me playing Precision for the first time in my life!"

"Well, careful you don't wear out your welcome with random Precision!" I suggest.

"My welcome? What on earth do you mean?" My father and Gwen exchange anxious glances. "Gwen's daughter has invited us to spend Christmas down at her house in Bracknell …"

"But, surely …"

"So you will have this house to yourself at that time, as long as you promise not to hold any wild parties and trash the place."

It is my turn not to get the joke.

"Father, I am twenty-eight. I don't think I will be advertising a rave on Facebook."

"But you will be all right, won't you?"

"I would refer m'learned colleague to my first answer. I'm nearly twenty-nine. Of *course* I will be all right. A little damp and cold, perhaps, but maybe you will leave me a shilling for the meter."

"You could go and stay with your mother."

"No, I shall endure this pagan festival with my usual stoicism here in Oxford. Besides, I have my best man duties to perform on the 30th."

"Well, that's good. Only, the thing is …" My father seems to be searching for the right words.

"Yes, Dad?"

The two wrinkly lovebirds swap further conspiratorial glances.

"I have suggested to Gwen that she might come and live here. Not right now. In the New Year."

"What, in this pokey little rabbit-hutch? Do you think it will be above water by then?"

"Who knows?"

"There is barely enough room here for the two of us, never mind three!"

My father and his slightly podgy paramour both wince.

"Yes, it would be rather crowded …"

The penny drops.

"You want me to move out, don't you?"

"No, Alex, it's not like that at all. Not straight away. But maybe in time you'll find somewhere else that's more suitable for a chap of …"

"Of what? My *age?*"

My father shrugs his shoulders and sighs. Gwen looks as if she is hoping that the ground will swallow her up, however high the water-table might be.

"Don't worry, Dad, I'm out of here. I know *exactly* where I will be after December 30th. I shan't be a waste of space in Swan Street."

"I'm sorry, Alex, I didn't want you to find out like this."

"Like what?"

"Well, you know." He gestures to the adjoining room. We all shuffle a little uncomfortably.

"You are forgetting the most important thing, Reg," Gwen says at last.

"What's that, pet?"

"The news you've had …"

"The news? Ah, yes. We've had some sad news, Alex. In fact, that was the reason Gwen came home with me this afternoon. I was a bit upset."

"Yes, I could see that, just now."

"There's no need to be sarcastic."

"So what was this sad news?"

"It's your Uncle Alan."

All sorts of possibilities flash through my mind in an instant.

"Is he … ill?"

My father looks at Gwen again. I feel a freezing sensation in the pit of my stomach.

"He's *dead*, isn't he? But I heard from him only a fortnight ago. Tell me it's not so!"

"I'm sorry, son. A severe chill, it seems."

"And you hadn't even got round to telling me!"

"That's not fair. This is the first chance I've had."

"My wonderful Uncle Alan, dead? He was ten times the man you will ever be.

175

And you didn't think to even let me know!"

"Alex! *Alex!*"

But it is too late. I have stormed out of my own room and stomped down the stairs as noisily as is possible barefoot. I throw on my waterlogged wellies and a coat and exit Oates-like into the cold December rain. With any luck, I too will be carried off by a severe chill, if apoplexy does not get me first.

Wednesday 21 December 2016

Am I OK? Broken home to go to … (5)

Long before he settles for the quiet life of a jobbing lawyer, Thomas Jefferson Hogg dreams of being a writer. Unlike his itinerant friend, Shelley, he has no gift for poetry, but he hopes that his narrative skills will compensate for that. A year or so after his expulsion from Univ and a little while after his unequivocal rejection by the 16-year-old Harriet, my forefather finds time, in between his mind-numbing conveyancing work and his study for the Bar, to work on what he hopes will be the first of many novels. And unlike most of us, he actually finishes it. And even less like you and me, gentle reader, he finds a publisher.

Hogg's novel, *Memoirs of Prince Alexy Haimatoff*, supposedly translated from the original Latin by the fictitious 'John Brown' (his faithful Scottish ghillie?), is completed in 1812, when Hogg is still just twenty, and printed by Shelley's publisher, Thomas Hookham, in the autumn of 1813.

Yes, the memoirs of Prince Alexy Haimatoff. The title seems scarcely credible to me as it echoes the very name I gave myself in trying so vainly to impress Marie-Claire only a few short weeks ago. The obvious conclusion is that I must have encountered this text somewhere before, or perhaps simply the title, and the name has seeped into my subconscious, although I have no clear recollection of ever having seen such a book before. Unlike *Pride and Prejudice*, also first published in 1813, it is not a novel that has been reprinted a thousand times in a hundred languages (it sank almost without trace). But it seems reasonable to suppose that there is a copy somewhere in the college library. I must have picked it up one day and registered its unusual title, possibly because later editions are attributed to Hogg and I would have been impressed by the family name.

The alternative explanation, that some filigree of DNA coding has been passed down the family line and inspired both of us to adopt the same *alter ego*, does not bear thinking about. Even atavism has its limits.

If any copies from Hookham's original imprint survive, I have not been able to trace them. The 'first editions' of *Prince Alexy* that you will encounter these days are from the Folio

Society's reprint of 1952 which features a number of startling wood-engravings by Douglas Percy Bliss. The dust jacket tells us that only two copies of the original are known to exist but does not say where. I have been reading it alongside Prince Felix Yusupov's memoirs, also written (in French – perhaps his Latin was not quite up to the task?) in 1952 and published as *Lost Splendor* in Britain and America in 1953.

It is hard to believe that the two texts are not the creation of the same fetid imagination.

It is certainly possible that Yusupov could have encountered the Folio Society's dusty tome while he was brushing up his own memoirs in 1952, even if he is unlikely to have encountered the *Memoirs of Prince Alexy Haimatoff* during his chilly sojourn at Univ between 1909 and 1912. It is a little fanciful to imagine him purloining the college library's only copy and devouring it in the shadow of the brand-new Shelley Memorial. Did it inspire the very first inklings of the plot to kill the ghastly Rasputin?

Yusupov was not a great reader of English novels, as far as we know – perhaps he never encountered Hogg's one and only novel. If so, we must flip the question on its head: how did Thomas Jefferson Hogg come to write a novel which so accurately foretells the life story of history's second most famous assassin and a Univ graduate to boot?

Prince Alexy Haimatoff is a romanticised version of the college friend Hogg thought he had loved and lost in the Battle of York. Many of the episodes in the *Memoirs*, notably the initiation rites in the haunted chapel, are a lightly fictionalised version of anecdotes that Shelley had told about his own life. Is it simply that Shelley himself became a figure of fascination during Yusupov's lonely vigil at Univ? Should it then be surprising that Prince Felix emulates Prince Alexy as well? But the resemblance seems to go well beyond mere second-hand emulation.

Let us consider just a few of the similarities. Both these princes are born in St Petersburg, Felix amidst the soon-to-be-lost splendour of the Moika Palace and Alexy in rather more mysterious circumstances, a prince who does not know the identity of his parents. At a young age, Alexy is despatched to Lausanne in Switzerland under the care of a French clergyman called Gothon to commence his princely education. Like Felix after him, his teenage years will take him across Europe and beyond, surviving a series of improbable escapades in

Paris and other "exotic" locations, overcoming numerous temptations, pitching up in England and encountering a charismatic supra-religious figure who seems to challenge his very identity.

Both Alexy and Felix are somewhat sickly children, they say. Alexy's ankle is severely sprained as a baby when his nurse falls on some ice and this disqualifies him from any sporting activity thereafter. This sedentary life was "not without its inconveniences; by never suffering fatigue, I became effeminate' (p. 30). Felix's childish sickliness leads him in a similar direction:

'I was ashamed of my skinniness, and longed to find a means of fattening out. Then, one day, I happened to see an advertisement which gave me high hopes. It extolled the merits of Pilules Orientales, a French patent medicine warranted to turn the flattest breasted lady into a harem beauty of opulent charms. I managed to get bold of a box of these pills and took them on the sly, but, alas, without result.' (ch. 5)

Never mind the HRT, it is not long before Felix is dressing in his mother's clothes and parading around the streets and clubs of St Petersburg. Did he really pass muster as the most glamorous girl in town? Felix insists this was the case but it seems more likely that the denizens of that demi-monde were happy to humour the gender-confused young plutocrat.

The Yusupov boys, Felix and his older brother Nicholas, are also taught by a "kindly" Swiss tutor, Monsieur Penard. Alexy, meanwhile, embarks on a grand tour of European cultural centres and arrives in Florence where a fellow-student called Schwartz is in love with a girl named Viola whose brother, Corvini, has treated her shockingly and accused Schwartz of seducing the girl. Schwartz feels compelled to challenge the brother to a duel with pistols and asks Haimatoff to accompany him as his second. Alexy is forced to witness his friend being killed. Corvini has the first shot and misses. Schwartz then fires directly upwards in a bid to end the proceedings in a peaceful fashion but his adversary, unaware that the miss was deliberate, now shoots and kills him.

Fast forward a hundred years and Felix's elder brother, Nicholas, falls in love with a girl who, inconveniently, is already engaged to an officer in the Guards regiment. Nicholas and the girl become passionately involved but Nicholas is unable to prevent the wedding taking place, despite dining with the girl on the evening before her nuptials and planning an elopement. The married couple honeymoon in Paris but Nicholas is unable to restrain himself from pursuing them there (rather like Hogg in Edinburgh) with Felix in tow, attempting to ensure that the matter does not get out of hand. Felix neglects to intervene as the jilted bridegroom challenges Nicholas to a duel and kills the first-born heir to the vast Yusupov fortune. Felix is not present but learns later what occurred:

> It had been agreed that the weapons would be revolvers, and the distance thirty paces. The signal was given, Nicholas fired in the air; his adversary fired at him and missed him. He then insisted that the distance be reduced to fifteen paces. Nicholas agreed, and again fired in the air; the officer took careful aim and killed him instantly. Thus ended an encounter which was not a duel but a murder (ch. xii).

Nonetheless, Felix is now the sole heir of the Yusupov empire and the weight of perceived responsibility that goes with it. Not long afterwards he meets, and forms an instant dislike to, Rasputin, and then knocks on the door of University College, Oxford, in order to conclude his gentlemanly education.

Hogg, meanwhile, has his Russian prince sent not to an English but to a sinister German university (a precursor of Mary Shelley's Ingolstadt), where the spartan collegiate life is plainly a reflection of his Univ experience. Just as the closed minds of his tutors and college officials had been a grave disappointment to the 18-year-old Durham boy, so Prince Alexy is alarmed to discover that there is no opportunity for free thinking and scientific investigation as the 'university' is actually a front for the Eleutheri, a fanatical cult based on what Hogg knows of the Illuminati.

The head of this university is the Eleutherarch, a man who commands the unquestioning obedience of his followers. Hogg repeatedly uses the same word, "mysterious", to describe this cult figure as Yusupov assigns to Rasputin. Like the Russian starets, the Eleutherarch has a mesmeric effect on his young followers and his ultimate objectives remain obscure.

The Eleutherarch tells Prince Alexy that he must endure a novitiate of three years before he graduates and becomes a fully-fledged member of this arcane society. Alexy agrees to these terms, swears an oath in Latin and is forced to endure a series of tests and initiations. He studies hard for a year and is summoned back to the Eleutherarch's office where, to his surprise, he is accused of excessive pride and weakness as far as the female sex is concerned.

Is he prepared to swear another oath of total obedience to the Eleutherarch? He is given three days to think about this but his mind is made up:

> In the evening I could bear this suspense no longer. I concealed a dagger under my garments, and wildly ran to the university. I inquired for the Eleutherarch. He was alone in his study. As soon as I entered, I bolted the door, seized him by the neck, brandishing my dagger ... The venerable man, with a serene countenance, bared his breast, and pointing to his heart, said, 'Strike there, Alexy; thy blow will then be effectual.' I trembled in every limb. 'Nay, if thy hand is unsteady, let me guide it,' he continued, taking hold of my hand, and raising it, as if to strike. The dagger fell to the ground. I could not endure his penetrating gaze; he saw the nakedness of my soul; I covered my face with my hands (pp. 128-129).

So much of this foreshadows the black comedy of the December night in the Moika Palace – the bolted door, the secretly armed assailant preparing to murder his spiritual leader, a man he both admires and loathes, the sense that the victim has both anticipated and accepted his fate, the homoerotic undercurrents, the penetrating gaze that deflects our hero from his task, and so on.

There is one key difference, of course. Prince Alexy cannot bring himself to finish the job whereas Rasputin does not survive his ordeal. Reprieved and surprisingly lenient, the Eleutherarch promises to keep the incident to himself and sends the young prince down for a year (a rather shorter sentence than the one imposed on Shelley and Hogg, we note). Alexy must go to England and there his story concludes after a series of further adventures and a disappointingly conventional marriage.

So much for Thomas Jefferson Hogg's literary revenge on the college officials who had expelled him in 1811.

The *Memoirs of Prince Alexy Haimatoff* basked in well-deserved obscurity after its publication. It earned one solitary review and that by Shelley himself in the *Critical Review* of December 1814. If he was attempting to do his old college pal a favour, it was of a very mixed kind and Hogg must have laughed at some of Shelley's criticisms, including this one:

> But we cannot regard [Bruhle's] commendation to his pupil [Alexy] to indulge in promiscuous concubinage without horror and detestation ... He asserts that a transient connection with a cultivated female may contribute to form the heart without essentially vitiating the sensibilities. It is our duty to protest against so pernicious and disgusting an opinion (*Prose*, p. 304).

This is a bit rich coming from a man who has recently abandoned his pregnant wife and moved in with not one but two teenage girls.

But there is no doubt that *Prince Alexy* gave Hogg a certain kind of street cred when the time came for him to be introduced to Mary and Claire. If he seemed a little dull and conventional in person, the novel was the proof of an exotic imagination and a commitment to liberal ideals, including Godwinian free love. The girls were happy to conflate the stolid legal clerk and his fictional *alter ego*, soon dubbing the new lodger 'Prince Alexy' rather than 'Mr Hogg'. In their more private moments, Mary took to calling him 'Prince Prudent' and Hogg was happy enough to accept the moniker – indeed, he subsequently called his own daughter, my great-great-great-great-great grandmother, Prudentia.

There is little reference to Hogg's own state of mind during the Hans Place days at the end of Volume 1 of Hogg's eventual *Life of P.B. Shelley* (1858, like *Lost Splendor* 36 years after the star turn's death), and little sign of the notes he must have written to his bedridden "dormouse", Mary. But we do have Mary's many missives to her gallant prince during her pregnancy and after the loss of her baby. Here is one from 7th January 1815, not long before the premature parturition:

> My affection for you, although it is not now exactly as you would wish it will I think daily become more so – then, what can you have to add to your happiness, time which for other causes beside this – phisical causes – that must be given – Shelley will be subject to these also, & this, dear Hogg, will give time for that love to spring up which you deserve and will one day have.

That dreamed-of day never comes, despite Hogg's gauche opportunism and Shelley's undoubted connivance. Mary's first thought when she loses her baby is to send for Hogg but the *ménage-à-quatre* was never likely to survive that bereavement and Mary has little difficulty fending off Hogg's increasingly tentative physical advances thereafter. Perhaps his heart is never really in it. I suspect he is still more than half in love with poor abandoned Harriet who, like Hogg in the preceding years, now spends much of her time contemplating the young poet's gilded goldfish bowl from the outside, alternately horrified and entranced by what she sees. Perhaps Hogg recognises Harriet as a kindred spirit, a fellow outsider.

Through the winter of 1814-15, Hogg trots dutifully to and fro between Shelley's neglected leading ladies, hoping for a morsel of affection here, a crumb of comfort there. If he can't have Shelley to himself, one of these sleeping satellites would make an agreeable substitute.

Of course, very little of this figures in Hogg's whimsical biography, ironically berated for including too much of Hogg and too little of Shelley. Hogg's commission from Lady Wrennie (Shelley's daughter-in-law) was for a hagiography, especially in its account of the Shelley-Mary "romance" which, it was hoped, would out-schmaltz the Browning version. Too honest and yet not honest enough, Hogg was summarily sacked before he could embark on Vol. II. From Lady Wrennie's perspective, the first volume read more as character assassination than apotheosis.

Was Hogg envious of his old friend's posthumous success while he languished in obscurity? The same could be asked of Yusupov. However many times the Russian émigré told his story and however much he overplayed his own role in the assassination, the more Rasputin's fame grew and his diminished. His own vituperative character assassinations had precisely the opposite effect from the one intended, elevating his subject to ever greater fame. He was right all along – the old devil really was unkillable.

Friday 23 December 2016

Solo organisation, relatively speaking (5)

It is the eve of Christmas Eve and I have gone "home" to Teesside for my uncle's funeral. Embarrassingly, Dad has stayed in Oxford, claiming an unspecified prior engagement in Bracknell. While I know they have never seen eye to eye, this seems to me like a shocking betrayal – how can you be too busy to attend your own brother's funeral?

Priory Hall, near Stockton, is much as I remember it and yet irremediably diminished without my Uncle Alan. I feel a bit like Pip going back to Satis House, rattling at the rusty gates and noting all the signs of neglect. The hogweeds have got the place surrounded. Give them another twenty years and it will have become impenetrable.

The sale of Priory Hall has gone through and we can see the lorries of the developers already parked outside the property. But Uncle Alan seems to have made special arrangements with his solicitors that, in the event of his demise, the old homestead should be allowed to play host to this cheerless send-off. So here we all are, following the obligatory Mummers' play at a local crematorium, chewing on our ham sandwiches and wondering how many glasses of fizzy white wine we can put away without compromising our ability to drive home for Christmas. There is quite a good turn-out but, apart from Mother and the odd relative, only a few folk that I recognise.

I have just loaded up my tiny plate with a second helping of vol-au-vents and egg sarnies when I am accosted by a vaguely familiar-looking chap of my own age. He has already been pointed out to me as Uncle Alan's solicitor.

"You don't remember me, do you?" he says.

"I'm sure I do …" I try in vain to place the man.

"We both had a bit more hair when we were young. John Harrison."

I picture him with a full head of hair.

"J.K. Harrison! Of course! I'm sorry, John, I …"

"No need to apologise, Alex. I thought I'd see you here. I am … I *was* your uncle's solicitor. I know how much you admired him. It's a sad day indeed."

John Harrison was my best friend when I was about fourteen, at just about the time when one stopped having best friends any more. I remember him as a bright lad, if a little bit spotty and nerdish. Like me, he was into crosswords at a surprisingly young age and we used to swap clues that we had found inspiring or baffling. I don't think we ever made a conscious decision to *stop* being good friends – it was just that we took different options for GCSE or discovered girls instead. Probably not the latter in my case – indeed, I'm not quite sure that I have "discovered" girls even now. Anyway, we drifted apart and John went off to do his A-levels somewhere else and I haven't seen him since.

"A solicitor, eh?" I say. "Of course I remember you. Still doing the crosswords?"

"You bet. I was down in London a few weeks ago for the *Times* National Crossword Championships."

"Did you win?"

"Nah. The top guys are solving three fiendish cryptics in twenty minutes or so. It's all I can do to get through them in an hour."

"An hour for *three* puzzles? Sounds impossible to me."

"Just a matter of practice. I do a couple every lunchtime, between sandwiches, me against the clock."

"So, let's see. You did a law degree and after that ..."

"Articles, then joined a local firm of solicitors. Very dull."

"Jarndyce & Jarndyce? Markby, Markby & Markby?"

"Procter & Harrison. At the sign of the hedgehog."

"The hedgehog? You've lost me there."

"*Hérissant*. French for 'bristling'. Harrison, *hérissant*, I should have a family crest done. A rampant hedgehog."

I contemplate this ghastly proposition for a moment and decide to humour him.

"Me too. Only mine would be the sign of the *ground*hog."

"A far mightier hog, I suspect! I'll hedge my bets while you go to ground!"

We snort with laughter, like the hog(g)s we are. It is a surprise to find myself having quite so much fun. I enquire whether John's firm has been handling the sale of the property or the will. It turns out to be both.

"We're good old-fashioned all-purpose lawyers," he sighs. "A finger in every pie. With planning permission in place, this old ruin has fetched a bob or two, I can tell you."

"How many bob?"

"I would tell you. But I have just come from a meeting of the executors and an initial reading of the will. I don't think it would be indiscreet to let you know that you are a beneficiary of the will."

"*Me?*"

"Yes. Is that so surprising? You're aware that your Uncle Alan had no children. He had to leave his money to someone."

"I can't deny that a couple of thousand would help me stave off the most persistent of my creditors."

"It will be rather more than a couple of thousand, I think. I should be able to give you a ballpark figure in a few days, although it will probably take some months to value all the assets, pay off the taxman, etc."

"So, I shouldn't expect to see any actual cash before, say, December 30th?"

John Harrison looks at me as if I am completely barking.

"December 30th? But we're into the Christmas holidays now. Even if I was working on the case all day every day and Mr Taxman was doing likewise, then there would be no possibility of sorting it out within that sort of timescale. These things take months, years even. What's so significant about December 30th, anyway?"

"Oh, it's nothing, really. It's just that I *might* not be around after December 30th."

"You're thinking of emigrating? That wouldn't affect a legacy ..."

"No, it's just ... it's just that it would be nice to have some serious cash in my pocket so that I could enjoy the Christmas season in some style. Live like there's no tomorrow ..."

"Yes, but why December 30th, specifically?"

"Let's just say that I have reason to believe that I may suffer a certain misfortune on that day."

My old schoolfriend gives me the funniest of looks. Perhaps he even understands what I am saying. I wonder whether he would consider trading the answer to his question for some specific information about the size of my legacy. But before I can broker any sort of deal, we are interrupted by my mother who seems to have drunk rather more of the lukewarm Asti Spumante than is strictly wise at her advanced age.

"Ah, friends reunited?" she suggests, a little too loudly.

"You remember John, do you, Mum?"

"I remember *all* your friends, Alex. I always knew John would go far. He had that extra spark, that determination."

"Oh, I don't know about *that*, Mrs Hogg," John blushes.

"Unlike me, you mean?" I enquire. My mother laughs it off.

"Well, let's just say that he has found himself a nice solid job where he can charge people £200 an hour for his services ..."

"*Two hundred quid?*" I gulp. How can *anyone* earn that much, I wonder? John soon puts her straight.

"I'm sorry to disappoint you, Mrs Hogg, but it's actually nearer three hundred pounds an hour these days."

"I suppose the divorce *was* a little while ago now."

"Yes, inflation is a wonderful thing, isn't it? But I shouldn't stand round here chatting when I could be off fleecing the poor and luring the unwary into pointless litigation. I must do some networking!"

"Thanks, Mum," I grumble, as John edges politely away. "We were having quite a nice little conversation till you came along. It sounds like I'm going to inherit a few quid in Uncle Alan's will."

"But the old buffer couldn't stand any of us, could he?"

"I used to get on rather well with him, actually. He was someone who took a real interest in my intellectual development."

"I shouldn't speak ill of the dead, I suppose. Not until the coffin has been firmly nailed down anyway! But Alan turned out even more pedantic than your father. If that's possible ..." She reaches for another glass from a passing tray.

"That stuff is stronger than it looks, you know ..."

"Oh, give us a break, Alex. It's a funeral! There aren't many pleasures left in life! Things could be worse, I guess – I could still be married to your dad. Thank God he's not here. What's the old fool up to these days?"

I tell her all about Gwen and the random precision of his new love-life, as well as my imminent ejection from Hogg Towers on Osney Island.

"Well, you're a big boy now, Alex. Or you should be. It isn't healthy to be living with Dad at your age."

I am tempted to respond in kind but, like Donald Trump, I reflect that Bill Clinton has said far worse to me on the golf course.

"It's all a bit *Steptoe*-ish," Mum continues.

"Indeed. Let's just say that, if I had been earning three hundred pounds an

187

hour, I might have found alternative lodgings by now. The fact is, I wasn't. And now I'm earning sweet FA ..."

My mother considers my predicament for a moment ...

"Well, I suppose you could always come back to the frozen North ..."

"What, to your place?"

"I haven't got room, of course, but ...."

"It's a kind offer, Mum, but ... well, let's just get through Christmas first, shall we?"

I have agreed to sleep on the sofa and enjoy at least *part* of the Yuletide snoreathon with the old bat. It is not a prospect I'm relishing, if truth be told. If it proves even more ghastly than expected, I can always claim that I have to return to Oxford to fulfil my responsibilities as MC on Phil's stag night.

Sunday 25 December 2016

Poetic middle name – a foolish mistake, one gathers (6)

Christmas Day is spent watching my mother slowly drink herself under the table. Gin has indeed been my mother's ruin but I guess she is old enough to make her own decisions. There is no point immolating a turkey for the two of us, so we "treat" ourselves to a boeuf bourguignon from M&S before microwaving a gin-soaked Christmas pudding for afters. I decide against revealing my fears of an imminent demise and we settle for bellowing along to Perry Como's *Greatest Hits*.

The gin has certainly loosened my mother's tongue. Is there anything more excruciating than listening to a parent lamenting their love-life or lack of it? Parents should not be allowed to have love-lives or even the slightest interest in the opposite sex. But even now my mother does not seem to have quite exhausted her vestigial interest in the opposite sex or her incredulity at the fecklessness of men in general.

Mum tells me in lurid detail how she spent quite an upbeat fortnight with Jack, a former county bowls champion, only to discover the hard way that he preferred the company of an 80-year-old with wobbly dentures (a "shameless hussy", if my mother is to be believed). Another transient beau called Brian had wilfully concealed the fact that he had had a triple heart-bypass and was likely to peg out at any moment – he didn't, but Mum wasn't taking any unnecessary chances on that score. Internet dating seems to offer an inexhaustible supply of puffing dotards and my mother is committed to finding "the one". At least it gives her something to grumble about on Christmas Day.

In a moment of maudlin solidarity, I tell her about Hattie.

"She's been missing for *two months*, has she?" my mother concludes. "She's probably been kidnapped and trafficked as a sex-slave to Eastern Europe."

"I think it mostly works the other way, Mother. But I guess we shouldn't discount it as a possibility …"

"And you had to check out a body they fished out of the Serpentine? How ghastly for you!"

"It was a relief, actually. I really thought it might be her."

"Did you have *feelings* for this girl?"

"For Hattie?" I laugh. "There was a time, but …. well, she was way out of my league."

"How do you mean?"

"Well, she was simply gorgeous. A perfect ten, as they say. And then she was married, so I didn't think about it any more."

This is not strictly true, I realize. I have been thinking about Hattie for years. Every time I meet a nice girl, a six out of ten or a seven out of ten, I think of Hattie as she was then and – surprise, surprise – things don't quite work out. But even after the marriage to Phil broke up, I was always too scared of getting my fingers burned all over again.

"Hattie *was* gorgeous, you say," my mother probes. "Did she lose her looks when she had the children?"

"No, she just looked older, sadder somehow. To me she looked just as beautiful as ever."

"Having children changes everything. Men just don't see you any more. It's as if you have an invisible force field around you. I remember when I had you …"

"Yes, thank you, Mum. I know what a catch you were; I've seen the sepia-tinted photos."

"And yet I allowed myself to be caught by your father," she sighs.

"Well, I wouldn't be here otherwise. And a very good Dad he has been too. I think you only really appreciate that when you are an adult yourself. You realise the sacrifices that your parents have made, how they put up with your tantrums and your taste in music, how much it all *cost* …"

"I'm sorry, Alex. Your father had his good points, of course he did. It was just very easy to lose sight of them when he was out playing bridge or golf. And now he's found someone he can actually play bridge with? Well, good luck to the old fool, I suppose."

So I tell her about Dad's family tree and the link he's discovered to Thomas Jefferson Hogg. She's never heard of him, of course, but I tell her all the stories anyway, including the curious parallel between the sad life of Harriet Westbrook and my own recent experience.

"So your great-great-whatever it is-grandfather propositioned this poor girl on her honeymoon, did he?"

"It seems so. Mind you, he propositioned most of Shelley's relatives, girlfriends and wives at one time or another until, with Shelley in his watery grave, he finally got to marry one of them. But Harriet was the one he really cared about, I think."

"Then why didn't he marry her when Shelley went off with Mary and the other girl?"

"Because she was still married to Shelley? Because he hadn't got his career sorted out? I don't know. But he did see a fair bit of her in the years before … before she drowned."

"It's a wonder he ever forgave himself. Men, eh?"

"Yes, we're a bad lot. Still, it's nice to have someone interesting in the family tree."

"Well, if I wasn't so busy with the dating websites and keeping this place from falling down around me, maybe I'd have time to find out about my own family line. I wish I knew a bit more about my Grandad for instance."

"Grandpa Jones you mean?"

"No, my mother's father. He died long before I was born but it sounded like he'd had an interesting life. He was French, I think. But he got out of Paris in the 1930s when the Nazis threatened and washed up in Cardiff."

"Paris, eh?" I chuckle. "His name wasn't Yusupov, by any chance?"

"No, of course not. His name was Nicolas … but what was his surname? I remember it was a bit odd, like the name of a town in Cornwall."

"St Just-in-Roseland?"

"No, along the coast a bit. *Helston*, that was it, but without the H. Nicolas Elston. Granny called him Nicky. Drank himself to death, I think."

Why does that name ring a bell? I rack my addled brains. We sit in silence for some time. My mother seems strangely agitated and I have rarely seen her consume alcohol at such speed before. Talk of her grandfather's untimely demise does not seem to have acted as much of a deterrent.

"What's up, Mum?" I say at last, not really expecting her to tell me.

"Alex, I have to tell you something." A slight slur but she is still just about intelligible. "It's only fair … at this time …"

"You mean, at Christmas?"

"No, at this time of grieving …"

"What, for Uncle Alan? But you never liked the man!"

My mother puts her glass down on a side table and gives me the oddest of looks. The wind howls in the chimney. The tears begin to flow. I have never seen my mother cry before.

"I did once …" she whispers at last.

Thursday 29 December 2016

Only drunk outside, tee-total biographer of eminent Victorians (6)

I have the long drive south to try to digest the news.

I think back over the days I spent with Uncle Alan and his anagrams and his matchsticks. Those bonking beetles. The idea of my mother and Uncle Alan, her brother-in-law … one Hogg and the wrong Mrs Hogg … making the beast with two backs is too ghastly and implausible to contemplate. Just once, I asked? Just three times, my mother admitted, not daring to look me in the eye. Did Dad find out? A shrug of the shoulders. He knew. He never said anything but he knew.

Should I confront the old fool with the news? What if he never knew at all? I don't want to be the one to tell my father that he has been cuckolded and his only son is not his son at all. Besides, he is still my Dad. He has earned the right to be called 'Dad' after three decades of scraping a in that role. We've had our differences and I've dismissed him as a bigoted dinosaur on dozens of occasions but the fact is we are still making each other cups of tea and lusting after Victoria Coren Mitchell together. We may not share quite as many genes as I had originally thought, but does it really matter so much?

And what of my name – Alan Alexander Hogg? Was I really named after the esteemed owner of Cotchford Farm? Or was I always an 'Alan' in my mother's eyes … at least until Dad guessed the truth?

Somewhere around the Nottingham exit my thoughts turn to my mother's odd recollection of her grandfather, Nicolas Elston, the Parisian émigré. Elston! Wasn't that the name Felix Yusupov went by in his Univ days? Count Sumarokov-Elston. Yes, that was it. He didn't want to be Prince Felix in this strange new environment. Being a mere count would allow him to stay under the radar. And once he and Irina and their baby daughter had escaped the clutches of the Bolsheviks, they did wind up in Paris. But they had no further children, as far as I am aware. Perhaps Felix had a mistress? In Gay Paris of the post-war period and early 1920s, it would have been rude *not* to.

The idea is ridiculous, of course. The man was plainly a homosexual. And yet, and yet … he did father one girl, after all. Could I possibly be Felix

Yusupov's great-great-grandson? I am as sceptical as you are, gentle reader.

Maybe if, against all odds, I am still alive in the New Year and inherit a few bob from Uncle Alan, I will fork out for a DNA test. But how would we get some Yusupov DNA to compare it with? Perhaps there is some kind of Parisian registry of births? Dad could tell me where to look.

Now I'm back home in Oxford and my newly-ex-father is nowhere to be seen. Well, I say "home"; I am acutely conscious that I am expected to leave our little tin shack on Frog Island so that Dad can indulge in a spot of free love. But what is the point of traipsing around town looking at grotty bedsits when I may have only days left to live? I would much rather do something *useful*. So I set about researching Ozzie's plagiarism case. It's not too difficult to track down the prehistoric doctorate that Ozzie is supposed to have copied. Ah, here it is. I skim over the abstract:

Suspense in the English novel from Jane Austen to Joseph Conrad

Abstract: Because of critical neglect, there is no established terminology to describe techniques of suspense. Borrowing from Aristotle, Koestler, and others, a new body of concepts is suggested and importantly, a distinction of tense is established, between types of suspense which relate to the narrative past, present, and future.

The classical world's intuition of a connection between mental uncertainty and the physical state of hanging has conditioned Western man's notion of narrative suspense until a comparatively recent date. Eighteenth-century theories of the sublime helped to create an understanding that suspense was not necessarily painful.

Through an analysis of novels by Jane Austen, George Eliot, Dickens, Hardy, and Conrad, an attempt is made to identify and evaluate the most common suspense strategies in the period's popular genres, notably the Austenian romance, mystery, and tragedy. The Austenian romance is compared to the detective story in that narrative presentation is determined by the need to control the reader's expectations, and to achieve an ending which is both satisfactory and surprising.

I can see that there are a few tenuous links here to Ozzie's book but the whole emphasis of this ancient thesis is radically different. It isn't a history of genre. It's a nuts-and-bolts analysis of the nineteenth-century novel. I download the doctorate itself and spend a very congenial hour or two dipping into it. It comes from a golden age of literary criticism, mixing the structuralism of the likes of Todorov and Frye with the more radical post-structuralist theories of Barthes and even the dreaded Derrida. But it is a work that is also somehow out of time, exploring a byway of the jungle of literary theory that has not been glimpsed before or since – it is *sui generis*.

I wonder if the author ever tried to get it 'properly' published and, if so, what the commissioning editors at OUP and CUP would have made of it? Sorry, son, we really don't know how to *position* this. Or maybe: come back when you've got a proper job. But there were no jobs in academe in the early 80s and this quirky tome languished in the Bodleian stack where it no doubt sits to the present day. How many other thousands of doctorates have suffered a similar fate?

But here's the rub. On the left-hand side of the Oxford University Research Archive webpages, you can see the figures for Views and Downloads. At the time of writing, 27 people have viewed the summary-page and just four have gone on to download the actual thesis. I can't tell how long this resource has been here but it seems to have been wearing a cloak of invisibility.

As it happens, I know a chap called Graham who works in the university's IT department, so I drop him a line, expecting him to plead ignorance or confidentiality. But no, he says the information is freely available to anyone who asks. So I get him to check up on the access-history of this particular document. And what do you know? All those four downloads of the thesis have taken place in the last two months. In other words, long after it could have had any influence on the writing of Ozzie's book.

What about the original hard copy, sitting somewhere deep beneath the earth, possibly in the lost city of Atlantis, I ask? Can one find out how often it has been summoned up? Of course! Every movement has been tracked for the last twenty years. Et voilà – the original Bodleian copy of *Suspense in the English Novel* has not been requested by a single reader in the whole of that period.

I call Ozzie to tell him the good news.

"Yeah, I'd come to a pretty similar conclusion myself. I could see that the online version had only been accessed by a handful of readers. But someone can always claim that I found it on another website."

"What other website? It doesn't exist on any other website. It barely exists on *this* website!"

"God, I hope you're right, Alex. I don't suppose it's going to be enough to satisfy Vlad the Impaler, but it's a start. Who knows, maybe I'll get a new contract after all. Anyway, where are we off to tonight?"

Tonight is the Stag Do. Some might sample the fleshy delights of Riga or Ljubljana, others might go paintballing in the wilds of the Surrey stockbroker belt. But Phil just wants us to go out for a curry and a few jars of ale before an early night and his big day tomorrow. So we're going to Chutneys Indian Brasserie (with optional added apostrophe) and then to the Royal Blenheim, just off St Ebbes (ditto). It'll be half a dozen nearly middle-aged men behaving not particularly badly.

The poppadoms prove to be a bit limp but we are hardly the Bullingdon Club and the meal passes without significant incident. Most of us repair to the Blenheim but Phil only stops for a single pint, pleading the need for some beauty sleep before his big day. I am tempted to remind him that his first stag night was a *little* more reckless, especially the last bit on Hampstead Heath.

The rest of the stags soon go back to their wives, leaving just me and Ozzie, the only poor fools without partners to minister to our every need. One pint of Ecky Thump soon leads to another. Ozzie proposes a toast to James Joyce who published *A Portrait of the Artist as a Young Man* a hundred years ago today. I remind him that it was a hundred years ago this very night that his namesake, Oswald Rayner, shot Rasputin somewhere in the grounds of the Moika Palace.

Ozzie laments the fact that he has never tasted Madeira, so we decide to order a couple of shots of that particular amber nectar from the bar – alas, they've never heard of it. It seems the heyday (or, at least, the monopoly) of Madeira is long-past.

"Isn't there the Madeira Stores on the Headington Roundabout?" Ozzie suggests. "They should sell the stuff …"

"Mmm, a bit too far," I decide.

But keen to toast the triumphs of Oswalds past, the two of us repair to a Tesco Express on St Aldate's and find a bottle of the aforementioned tipple on "special offer" at just £13.99. We successfully pool the necessary funds (just!) and sheepishly take our solitary bottle to the check-out. But such purchases are clearly not unusual in these parts at this time of night and the check-out girl gives us not so much as a knowing glance as she clocks up the sale.

It is approaching midnight now and the pavement is slippery with incipient frost but when we take a slug of Madeira straight from the gaudy bottle, it tastes surprisingly smooth and warming. The bottle goes to and fro a few times and I am beginning to feel a little light-headed.

"I think Oswald Rayner is buried in Botley Cemetery," Ozzie surmises. "What say you to the idea of trotting along there and seeing if we can find his grave? This rocket-fuel should keep us going along the way."

"Also too far," I decree. "If you mean the war graves tucked away behind the Best Tiles and Bathstore, I don't think we'll find him in there. That's just soldiers, not spies."

On the corner of Speedwell St, I am sufficiently *compos mentis* to spot a poster glued precariously to a lamp-post:

A-WASSAILING WE GO
Thursday December 29th, 10 p.m.
HOGACRE COMMON ECO-PARK,
Off Whitehouse Rd, South Oxford
Join us in the tradition of Wassailing the orchard, with mulled apple juice, cider, singing, Morris Dancing with Cry Havoc, and a roaring fire.

"Hogacre Common, my ancestral kingdom! Have you ever been there?"

"Never heard of it," says Ozzie. "And what the hell is "wassailing the orchard"?"

"Some kind of pagan fertility ritual, I guess, a song and dance to make the apples grow next year. I think we should go and join in!"

"What, with Cry Havoc and the Morris dancing?" Ozzie shakes his head. "I'm with Oscar Wilde on that one. Do you think they'll let loose the hogs of war?"

"At least those veggies won't be roasting one. Unlike Phil and Marie-Claire tomorrow, from what I hear. Come on, let's do it. The night is yet young," I point out, somewhat inaccurately.

So off we gambol. We head south down the Abingdon Rd towards Ozzie's flat in Lake St and turn right into Whitehouse Rd where the old Oxford City football ground has been turned into yet more college accommodation. We swig Madeira as we go – its cloying sweetness proves strangely moreish. We consume the whole bottle in less than five minutes, passing it to and fro like a sconce challenge. It is more than enough to make a Hogg whimper. A drowsy numbness pains my sense, as though of hogweed I had drunk, like those zonked beetles.

Friday 30 December 2016 – Drowned Hogg Day?

Island produced a terrorist organisation (7)

A distant church bell sounds and I see from my watch that it is midnight. A snatch of Metallica's 'For whom the bell tolls' comes unbidden to my mind's ear. It is the day I have feared for so long. It is Drowned Hogg Day.

A confession: the rest of the night's events are a little bit of a blur. An evening of sustained alcoholic consumption is not something I am used to these days and I have had little practice in being drunk. By the time I have forced down the last of the Madeira, sozzled is most certainly what I am and I may even have thrown up at a convenient spot outside the White House – the pub, that is, not the Clintons' second home.

As we lurch into Whitehouse Rd, I have a dim recollection of the conversation turning to Vlad the Impaler. I tell Ozzie it's all right for him; he hasn't actually lost his job as a result of the college Development Director's Machiavellian ministrations, whereas I have. Ozzie reminds me that we are actually going right past his house. There it is, on the corner of Hodges Court. It being after midnight, we contemplate ringing his doorbell and running away – that's how drunk we are. But Ozzie has a better idea:

"What about some graffiti? I've been doing a bit of home improvement over the festive season and I've got some spray-paint left over."

"A few choice swear words on Vlad's front door, you mean?"

"No, something a little more artistic. This is Oxford, after all."

"How about some Shelley? My name is Ozymandias, king of kings. Look on my works, Vlad the Impaler, and despair?"

"Ozzie who?" My partner in crime looks at me blankly. The drink has evidently gone to his head too.

"Ozymandias – you know, Shelley's famous sonnet."

"We don't want to get done for plagiarism, do we?"

"But Shelley's been dead for almost two hundred years!" I point out.

"Not Shelley. We might be sued by the guy who did the graffiti on that Hernes Rd development a year or two back. He spray-painted half Shelley's sonnet on forty yards of boarding. It was brilliant – they even had guided tours going there just to see the graffiti ..."

It is possible I have dreamt this whole conversation up. The plan is quite ludicrous but Ozzie soon scurries off to fetch the paint while my job is to stay put and make sure Vlad's house doesn't do a runner before Ozzie gets back. So there I am, loitering with intent, when a light goes on in an upstairs room. The curtains are not drawn and I see Vlad himself, in his dressing gown, walking about.

I should do a runner myself but I stand transfixed, possibly even impaled to the pavement, as Vlad comes over to the window, gazes out and sees me standing underneath the lamp-post. Time stands still as he opens the sash window.

"Alex! Kakogo chyorta! What on earth are you doing there?"

I search for an answer to this very reasonable question but find none.

"You're shivering!" he observes. "Look, you'd better come inside and warm up."

"No ... no ..." I start, but Vlad is already on his way down the stairs to open the front door. The only sensible thing to do is to leg it but I am now the owner of two vast (if not quite trunkless) legs of stone. I remain transfixed by his icy gaze for some seconds.

At some point I regain the power of perambulation and follow Vlad into his lair like a lost puppy. The only thing in my mind is that I must avoid throwing up again. That seems a tall order so I settle for the easier target of not chundering all over his sleeping wife, assuming he has one. I feel my stomach churn in the warmer air. Vlad is mumbling away about something but I am unable to catch what he says as I follow him up the stairs. He turns to me on the landing.

"You're absolutely plastered, I can see. If it's about the job ..."

It is all about the job, of course it is. And somehow I am down on my knees, pulling pathetically at his dressing gown, begging, whimpering, mewling. Just give me another chance. Please!

Vlad tries to brush me away and somehow I end up pulling at the sash which is holding his dressing-gown together. The gown gapes open and it is apparent that he is wearing nothing underneath. I am inches away from ... no, this must all be some terrible nightmare. Surely Ozzie will arrive and save me. As Vlad struggles to recover his modesty, I cling beseechingly to his knees.

Aeons pass as Vlad wrenches himself clear of my embrace and I regain my feet. What is that in your coat pocket, Vlad asks? I glance down. It is the empty Madeira bottle – somehow, I have failed to discard it. I take it out and wave it in the air. Perhaps the bottle is too opaque for Vlad to be sure that it is empty and perhaps he thinks I am likely to get drunker still. For whatever reason, he tells me to give him the bottle. For equally obscure reasons, I demur. How else to explain a situation in which we are both struggling for possession of an empty wine bottle? But that is what we proceed to do.

And that is when disaster strikes. My memory of what follows is relatively clear.

Somehow I manage to wrench the bottle from his grasp. Not expecting to win the battle quite so easily, my arm frees itself and the bottle swings upwards and across, before catching Vlad around his jaw. The bottle smashes on impact and I drop what is left of it. But the impact has caused Vlad to lose his balance and/or consciousness. I stand helpless as he falls heavily down the stairs and onto the stone flooring below. I wait for him to pick himself up and come at me again, but there is no sign of further movement.

Because the scuffle has been so half-hearted and my brain so addled, it takes me a moment to comprehend the significance of this scene. Vlad is pretending to be hurt to scare me. Still he does not move. My legs have returned to their Ozymandian state but eventually there is nothing for it but to follow Vlad downstairs. As I near the body, I see a hunk of glass protruding from his neck. Blood is oozing from that wound and a number of others. At that moment, for the first time, I glimpse the possibility that I have killed my old boss. It was a freakish accident but my mind is already racing with various dire scenarios. I am in deep, deep trouble.

I wish I had a river I could skate away on …

December 30th was supposed to be my dying day. Has there been some celestial clerical error? Was *this* the death the chronicle foretold? Will I spend the rest of my life behind bars, wishing I was the one who died on a cold stone floor in Whitehouse Road? But there are no wailing sirens, no hysterical wives, only a cold and eerie silence. I am by the front door. I try to focus on Vlad but feel certain it is too late to help him. I must get out of this place. It is my only chance.

In my rush to escape, I completely overlook the fact that my fingerprints will be everywhere. The evidence will be overwhelming. Lynda La Plante's services will scarcely be required. I have just the neck of the bottle in my own bloodied hand. To my astonishment, my legs now know how to run. But before I have reached the end of the front path, I see Ozzie crossing the road in front of me. He has a paint-pot and a brush in his hands.

"I wouldn't go in there, if I were you!" I say or at least croak. Ozzie looks at me in astonishment. It is almost as if he has guessed the terrible truth. But I have no intention of waiting to find out. My instinct is to get home as quickly as possible, but I cannot go via the Abingdon Rd and round past the station. Even at this time of night, there is too great a risk of being seen by some driver or passer-by. So I turn right out of the house and head off quickly west instead. I half-expect Ozzie to follow me and haul me back but I dare not even look over my shoulder.

After a few seconds, I reach the crossroads with Marlborough Rd and briefly contemplate turning right again but I decide to stay on Whitehouse Rd – this is a familiar part of town, after all. It is as if magnets are drawing me to Hogacre Common. I fork left past the Adventure Playground. Before I even reach the refurbished footbridge over the railway line, I hear the sound of wassailers in full swing. Apple trees in wassailing range are no doubt resolving to bear fruit in 2017. There are lights on in the old cricket pavilion but I see that most of the latter-day pagan revellers are now outside, watching Cry Havoc jigging to and fro, their handkerchiefs in the air, while a small band of folk musicians are playing a tune I happen to recognise, even in my inebriated state, as Old Tom of Oxford.

I have no time to wonder what my esteemed ancestor, Old Tom of Oxford, would have done at this point. No doubt he would have turned quickly round and made alternative plans, certainly after he discovered that the ground on the far side of the bridge was largely still under water. Perhaps if I blend in with the revellers, I may establish some kind of alibi for the evening? I splash along the track for a few yards until the Morris men (and women) are clearly in view.

But one of the musicians is all too familiar – it is Stig Strum! So *this* is what he gets up to in his spare time when he is not imitating Keith Richard! There he is with his nyckelharpa while an accordionist and a fiddler pick out the tune. Stig is in motley garb with some kind of cap-and-bells arrangement on his head. As far as I can tell, he has not seen me.

But Stig is not the only figure I recognise. There's Phil's old adversary, Ben Haydon, the long-suffering manager of the Hogacre Project. He is dressed all in green and his arms are outstretched with apples hanging down in clusters. The Morris men jump to and fro, circling this jolly green giant, sticks clashing and handkerchiefs twirling. It is every bit as ridiculous as it sounds. Ben is facing directly towards me and it becomes clear that he has seen me in the distance.

But there is no reason why he should recognise me in this light. I turn away from the main path and jog away across the sodden turf, travelling clockwise around the perimeter of the eco-park. The ground is so marshy that icy water is washing over the tops of my shoes but I plough on regardless. The music is a little fainter now and I am fairly sure no one is following me – perhaps I have not been seen at all.

My plan, of course, is to cut across to Grandpont and join the Thames towpath as it makes its way north to Osney Island. But first I must traverse the Hogacre Stream by the little wooden crossing-point at the north end of the eco-park. Usually this would be a simple matter, even by moonlight, but when I reach the crossing, it's clear that I face a major challenge. Thanks to the recent rains, the stream has risen above its normal banks and flooded the surrounding land. Much of the water has turned to ice. The crossing is just about visible under a few inches of ice on the surface of the stream.

There is no going back now. I tiptoe across the ice as delicately as I can. My right foot goes through the thin sheet but there is something firm beneath. Then my left foot goes through it and there is nothing below. Suddenly I am falling, falling, into the Hogacre Stream.

My forehead hits the edge of the bridge as I crash through the icy crust of the river. In that instant I know that I am going to drown and my frozen corpse will be found by tracker dogs first thing in the morning. I will be consigned to an unmarked grave with quicklime shovelled on top, the only fate I deserve. Please God, do not let it end this way.

And yet I do not die, not yet anyway. This is not the River Neva, after all, just a glorified drainage ditch, a bit like the one I found myself in when the Fiat crashed. I flail wildly for a few seconds and splutter on a few mouthfuls of muddy water but I am soon able to grab at the undergrowth that is half in, half out of the stream. I haul myself out on the Mercia side, sodden and shivering.

I feel the gash on my forehead with my finger-tips. There is a little blood but no great sign that I will bleed to death. I feel light-headed, not just drunk but delirious. I must get home before I pass out and die of hypothermia. There is sufficient moonlight to see the familiar route home. I follow the path by the railway and cut across into the Grandpont Nature Reserve where the ground is slightly higher above flood-levels. Soon I am able to follow the Thames Towpath back towards Osney Lock.

As I approach the little bridge that will take me onto Osney Island, I am alarmed to see that there is a light on in the lock-keeper's cottage. Desperate to be seen by as few people as possible, I turn left before the lock and follow the little footpath through to Osney Mead. There will be no one on the industrial estate at this time of night. This way I can get home without passing a single residence. I am soon turning right at King's Meadow. Past Electric Avenue, I turn right again onto the footpath that skirts the West Oxford Community School and leads to the little bridge linking Frog Island to the western world.

I am clammy with cold but adrenalin continues to course through my grateful veins. Astonishingly, there is no helicopter overhead strafing the fields with its searchlight and no siren is wailing. I stumble on the bridge's icy surface but do not fall. My heart is laughing, screaming, pounding. I am at the gates of delirium but I know how it will end. I will be crossing the bridge when I see my father, an ineffable smile on his face, on the doorstep of our honeysuckled home...

But I am not Peyton Farquhar and this is no Owl Creek Bridge. Nor is my father there to offer his benediction. He is in the arms of a different bridge partner. I turn the key in the door and close it clumsily behind me. I am tearing my sodden and frozen clothes from my body as I negotiate the stairs in the darkness ...

And that is all I remember. At some point I must have passed out for the next thing I know it is morning and I am lying head down on my bed. I find I am still wearing a t-shirt and a sock, but nothing else. Wintry sunlight summons me to the new day.

Momentary confusion turns to despair as I realize it is still December 30th, still my dying day or (the very best I can hope for) the day I am arrested for the murder of my old boss.

For an instant, I feel sure that last night was all some kind of dream but the cuts on my forehead and the blood on the duvet are real enough. To say that I feel wrecked hardly suffices – this is wreckage on a *Titanic* scale. My brain seems to have been flattened by a steamroller and my stomach is as fragile as a Fabergé nipple-ring.

I know what I must do with all possible haste: check online for flights out of the UK, head for Brazil (well, it worked for Ronnie Biggs) and establish a new identity as a lifeguard or football pundit. If only I had had the foresight to purchase a fake passport! The airports will surely have been alerted by the time

I get there. What about the tiny airport next to Kidlington? I could be there in twenty minutes. Perhaps I can hop on a plane to Jersey and then take it from there?

But several hours have elapsed since my accidental slaying of Vlad and still there is no one battering at the door. Perhaps Ozzie has ignored my suggestion and set foot in Vlad's house? With luck, he has removed some (all?) of the incriminating evidence, shut the door and crept off home. If so, the corpse might lie there for days before it is discovered by an astute postman or a neighbour with well-developed olfactory powers.

Should I go round and check? No, that would be pushing my luck. More likely, Ozzie, being the fine upstanding citizen that he is, has summoned the police and is currently "helping them with their enquiries". I don't want to call his mobile but perhaps it is safe to try to ring him at home? No better plan presents itself, so I make the call to his home number. No one picks it up. In the end I manage to leave a reasonably casual message asking him to call me back "about the wedding".

The wedding! OMG, the wedding! If I am *not* going to attempt to leave the country strapped to the underside of a Boeing 787 Dreamliner, surely I should try to carry on "as normal" and fulfil my Best Manly duties? My heart sinks at the prospect, almost setting off my fragile stomach *en route* to the ground. I gave my word to Phil and Marie-Claire that I would do it. I might as well do something useful with my last day, after all.

The wedding ceremony is to take place in University College Chapel and, if I am to get there in time for kick-off, I will need to move fast. As I try to hide the bruising on my face and throw on my hired togs, I search my conscience for some sign of remorse. A man has died. OK, I didn't set out with the intention of killing him – it was a complete accident – but a tragedy has occurred which could have been avoided if I hadn't got drunk and connived in the ridiculous notion of defacing someone's property. How can I live with myself? But after a thorough audit of my befuddled state, I can locate very little regret, only an instinct for self-preservation and the hope that somehow things will all blow over.

I gulp down a life-saving cuppa made from half a jar of Nescafé and am just about ready to leave. But there is someone outside the front door. A thousand possibilities trample through my hippocampus until a letter plops onto the doormat. I pick it up, noting the Procter and Harrison stamp and the pretentious hedgehog logo, but there is no time to digest it now. So I stuff it into the inside-pocket of my morning suit and head off into town on foot. I note in passing that the Botley Rd has *not* been sealed off by a police cordon. People are going about their business apparently oblivious to the date on the calendar and it is actually quite a bright day, albeit with a fierce Arctic wind blowing.

I traverse the puddles in Frideswide Square and walk briskly past the boarded-up Central Library considering my defence. Surely the jury will see that I was merely the unwitting medium through which History (the capital letter is important, I think) repeated itself. It was a hundred years to the very day, perhaps to the very minute, since the murder of Rasputin. I did not *choose* to be cast as a latter-day Felix Yusupov. Perhaps Ozzie (like Oswald Rayner before him) duped me into playing out this charade? No, we have both been fitted up. It is clear who is to blame, m'lud – History, that serial offender! History should be locked away, for all our safety, especially on 30th December 2116.

It's an unusual defence, I grant you.

I take some comfort from the observation that neither Yusupov nor Rayner paid any obvious penalty for their misdemeanours despite their evident guilt. Perhaps I too will go unpunished?

I arrive at Univ with about five minutes to spare. The bridegroom is fretting like an old mother hippo just outside the chapel. The Chapel! Like Gawain, I have journeyed here at the death of the old year, just about ready to embrace my fate, whatever that might be. At least it has not been painted green.

"Where on earth have you *been*, Alex?" Phil bellows across the quad.

"It's only four minutes to," I point out. Out of the corner of my eye, I see two men dressed in black skulking in the doorway of Staircase V. One of them bears a strange resemblance to Dwayne, Clinton's minder at Frilford. Surely not? There is no time for such a thought.

"But you're the Best Man," Phil is saying. "A fat lot of help you've been. Still, at least you can do a bit of ushering, now that you're here. There is no time to tell you the extraordinary news. Here are the rings, by the way..."

So I do a spot of ushering, sending latecomers to their allotted sides. There is a good turn-out on Marie-Claire's side but relatively few of Phil's kith/kin seem to have made it. I think of Shelley's wedding two hundred years ago today – surely this will be a somewhat happier affair?

The person I really want to see, of course, is Ozzie, but there is no sign at all of him. I picture him clapped in irons in the dungeons of Oxford Castle. Perhaps, like Sydney Carton, he has taken the rap for his feckless friend. Is that the extraordinary news?

The college is in most respects still on its Christmas recess, so, apart from the lurking heavies, we have the place to ourselves. The ceremony is an unremarkable affair conducted by the Rev. Andrew Gregory, the red-headed college chaplain. Ozzie was due to play the organ but one of Marie-Claire's relatives fills in at short notice and we are able to plough through a couple of rudimentary hymns. The bride looks exquisite in a simple white gown, her hair artfully raised at the back to reveal her long, elegant neck – Phil is a very lucky man. In a different world it might have been me marrying this sweet, brilliant woman. OK, a *very* different world …

I produce the simple gold rings at the appointed juncture. A special marriage licence has been procured from the Lord Chancellor of the Privy Chamberpot, or some such, and the two lovebirds sign it in front of the assembled throng. Then there is the interminable ritual of the photographs, tastefully arranged against the ivy-clad backdrop of Front Quad, right under Shelley's old rooms, before we all troop off to Folly Bridge. Let the revels commence!

The *Folly Bargères* looks like a huge and flimsy paper boat, tugged at its moorings by the passing torrent. It looks no match for the Isis in the aftermath of some of the worst flooding that Oxford has seen since global warming began. The icy north wind will be at our backs as we lurch erratically towards Iffley Lock and on towards Sandford, Radley and Abingdon. At some point we will turn around and fight our way back against the current and the wind. I can only hope that the *Folly* has a little more clearance than Shelley's life-size paper boat, the *Don Juan*. It seems like a strange kind of madness that I should be on such a boat on such a morning.

Fifty years ago today, Donald Campbell gazed out over Coniston Water and wondered whether conditions were right to make his long-postponed attempt at the world water-speed record aboard *Bluebird*. He knew that the slightest gust of wind would put him at mortal risk while travelling at 300 mph. Every day that passed was draining his funds but the winds were plainly too strong on December 30th 1966. Five days later he lost patience with the English weather and made his bid for glory anyway. *Bluebird*, like Icarus, flew too close to the sun. Campbell's body lay undiscovered until 2001 when diver Bill Smith was inspired to look for the wreck after hearing the Marillion song "Out of This World", written about that tragedy.

As Best Man, am I *de facto* captain of this ship? At least, I don't have to steer the thing. A somewhat tubby man with a straggly beard and a jaunty beret seems to be taking on that job, so I have a quick word with him before anyone embarks.

"Is it all right to go out on the water today?"

Captain Pugwash grunts ambiguously.

"Yeah, should be just about OK," he says at last. "And we'll never be more than twenty yards from the shore, will we? But we might have to take it in turns with the life-jacket."

His wheezy chuckle reveals his nicotine-stained dentures. I thank him for his reassurance and resist the temptation to ask him whether he stoppeth one of three wedding guests. While most of us have covered the short distance from Univ on foot, the happy couple have hired a limo which pulls up close to Folly Bridge. Most of the revellers have climbed on board the barge by now but I wait onshore until the guests of honour have reached us.

"So what was that extraordinary news?" I ask Phil as he sweeps by with his bride on his arm. He and Marie-Claire exchange glances.

"You'll find out soon enough," he smiles. Soon I am the only one left ashore. I feel it is the point of no return. I take a deep breath before stepping aboard the boat and making my way to the main cabin where the tables are set for the wedding feast. The pungent aroma of the hog roast assails me. I am not over-fond of pork at the best of times and, with the lurch of the boat on the water and the residual effects of a night on the Madeira, I am already struggling to hold it together.

There is a brief delay while various items of food are ferried aboard by the shivering serving crew. We are almost ready to set off when I see there is a last-minute arrival at the makeshift jetty. It takes me a little while to focus and make out who the latecomer is. It's Ozzie! He does not have a police escort. Never have I been more elated to see anyone in my life.

Having kissed the bride and enjoyed a brief moment of banter with Phil, Ozzie comes over to join me in my quiet corner of the cabin. He is utterly unencumbered by members of our fine constabulary and there is a smile on his face.

"What a complete twat you are, Alex!"

I nod in agreement.

"What's happened?" I croak.

"I've just spent the night in the JR, that's what's happened."

"You mean …"

"Yes, Vlad is in poor shape. His CT scan showed some concussion and some pretty deep wounds from that broken madeira bottle. He lost a lot of blood."

"But he's OK now?" I cannot believe my good fortune.

"He's fine. We had to wait all night to get to the front of the queue but the scan revealed nothing untoward in the old cranium. He had to have a few stitches in his jaw and he may be left with a bit of a scar but nothing too drastic."

"I thought he was dead, Ozzie!"

"Ah. I did guess that might be the case. What the hell happened in there?"

"I should think Vlad has a better idea of what happened in there than I do. I was completely off my face."

"Serves you right for knocking back 80% of that Madeira."

"I feel sick even remembering it."

"Vlad went through various phases in the course of the night. Shock, anger, relief, a desire for murderous revenge, gratitude that I'd found him and called an ambulance …"

"Am I going to do time for this?"

"No, Alex. It's OK. It shouldn't be OK, but it is. Vlad's recollection is that you were waving this bottle about and he made this stupid decision to try to get it off you. You held on, Vlad lost his grip, the bottle swung round and smacked him on the jaw, shattering in the process."

"Strangely, that's how I remember it too. Pretty feeble glass if you ask me."

"And somehow he ended up slipping on the polished floor and toppling down the stairs. He is suffering from the delusion that you did *not* push him or intend to hurt him in any way."

"So he's not going to press charges?"

"I suggest you go round with a crate of the finest Madeira and apologise profusely, not just for your drunken bottle-waving but, rather more significantly, leaving him in a heap at the bottom of the stairs. Why didn't you call an ambulance yourself?"

"I wasn't thinking straight. I thought he was dead. How was I to know that he'd do a Rasputin and rise again? My first thought was to get out of the door and catch the first flight to Rio, a Rembrandt under each arm."

"Yes, you did seem to be in a bit of a hurry when I saw you. Turns out it's your lucky day."

"I did bash my head on the ice."

"You should get that checked out. Do you want me to run you to A&E?"

"For some more tomography? Not this time, Ozzie, but I owe you one."

"You owe me half of that bottle of Madeira, certainly. It's been a long old night but a productive one from my point of view. During all those hours in A & E, I talked him through the whole plagiarism thing. He was surprisingly reasonable about it and accepted there was plenty of evidence that I'd never even seen this ancient thesis, not that it has much in common with my masterpiece anyway. As he said, it was never personal; he was just looking out for the good of the college."

"That's great news! And history doesn't quite repeat itself!"

"History? What's history got to do with it?"

"Well, it was you who lectured us on assassins called Oswald, wasn't it?"

"Yes, but ..."

"Think about it. It was a hundred years to the day, no, to the *hour* since Rasputin was murdered, not by Prince Felix Yusupov but by his young English friend, Oswald Rayner ..."

"So you're saying I could have gone in to Vlad's house, discovered the old fool was alive and kicking and finished him off myself?"

"While I would have carried the can for it!"

"A brilliant plan, Alex – or should I say *Felix*? – I'm only sorry I let you down in the execution. Perhaps I'm not cut out for the life of an assassin, after all."

"So you've still got your fellowship and I should roll up to the office first thing on Monday morning?"

"Er, no, I don't think he was going to go *quite* that far. You had just turned up at his house blind-drunk and nearly killed him. I should give it a couple of weeks, or decades!"

"Ha. I wouldn't want the ghastly job back anyway!"

Originally, President William Jefferson's poetic spirit, one hears
(6)

It is now well past mid-day and I am still alive. I have not been struck by a thunderbolt or been the victim of a revolutionary outrage. The *Folly Bargères* shows no signs of hitting an iceberg and I have yet to feel an overwhelming urge (like the Duke of Dorset in *Zuleika Dobson*) to hurl myself into the Isis. I still feel like I could throw up at any moment with each lurch of the barge but I have given myself strict instructions to consume no further alcohol. Instead, I am cradling a flute of cranberry juice and trying to look compos mentis. Lunch is a buffet affair and I restrict myself to the plainest of hog-free viands and victuals for fear of tipping a delicate pH balance one way or the other. I find myself talking to Marie-Claire's father, a philosophy don, about the latest incumbent of the White House and about Araucaria, the Tiger Woods of crossword-writing.

Phil gives me a nudge and I remember that, despite the bride's initials, I am supposed to be the MC around here and there are speeches to be made. So I call the assembled throng to attention and invite the bridegroom to take the first knock. Phil thanks everyone he has ever met in his life, one at a time and in great explanatory detail, before reciting a sonnet he has written for his radiant wife. It really would be a shame to throw up in the middle of this, so I concentrate on checking that the rhyme scheme is satisfactorily Petrarchan (it isn't). Marie-Claire blushes appropriately and then delivers her own far pithier take on the whole business of getting married in the twenty-first century. Her dad also gets to wax philosophical for a while, advising his new son-in-law to brush up on his snooker skills.

After the warm-up acts, it is, of course, my turn. A Best Man can be as rude as he likes, as long as he's funny and has first-hand experience of some of the more embarrassing moments in the bridegroom's life. I am fairly confident my carefully-honed mixture of wisecracks and anecdotes will knock 'em dead as I rise groggily to my feet and retrieve my speech from my inside pocket.

Or rather, I don't. The document I pull out is not a speech but the letter I have grabbed from the doormat in Osney. I scrabble around in all my other pockets but there can be little doubt about it – in my drunken panic this morning, I have completely forgotten to bring my script. What on earth was I going to say? My mentis is not compos at all. It is a tabula rasa, a palimpsest. I cannot remember a single word.

Everyone is chuckling politely at what they take to be my comic buffoonery. But all I can do is own up.

"I'm sorry, folks. I seem to have left my speech at home. All I have is this letter from my solicitor." More laughter. "No, really, this *is* the only thing I have!"

"Well, you'd better read us that, then!" some wag shouts out. It turns out that this proposal reflects the mood of the baying mob. I make various gestures designed to indicate that this is a ridiculous idea and/or I have gone down with TDS (Temporary Dyslexia Syndrome) but my audience will have none of it.

"Come on, Alex. No speech, no fee!" Phil smiles. "Besides we all want to know how your solicitor plans to get you off on those embezzlement and heresy charges."

In the end, there is nothing for it but to rip open the letter and find out what is written inside. I'm hoping it's just a perfunctory couple of lines announcing that Procter & Harrison have been appointed as executors but I discover that there are actually a couple of sheets of densely-printed text.

Dear Alex [I start],

Firstly, it was good to see you again, albeit in such unfortunate circumstances…

[I explain briefly that my uncle has died]

> I am writing to you in some haste for two reasons. The first is to convey confirmation of the fact that you are the primary beneficiary of your uncle, Mr Alan Jeffrey Hogg's will. You will appreciate that it is still a little too early to give you a precise indication of the size of your inheritance but a conservative assessment, based on the recent sale value of his property and scrutiny of his other investments, suggests that you should expect to receive a sum in the low seven figures …

[This gets an inevitable "ooh" from the audience. I take the opportunity to catch my breath.]

... the low seven figures, certainly at least £1.3m. I should be in a position to provide a little more detail in terms of the provisional valuation of assets and timescale early in the New Year and we will proceed with probate with all due haste.

[All around me, wedding guests are cheering. They seem to be genuinely pleased at my windfall. I try to think what I could do with all this money but absolutely nothing comes to mind.]

The second matter is rather more personal and pressing. Alex, I owe you a huge apology. It was only after we spoke at the funeral that I remembered a practical joke I had played on you all those years ago. I had almost forgotten it and assumed you had long since done likewise but your casual remark that you were expecting some form of catastrophe on 30th December tells me that you have not.

In short, you are *not* going to die on 30th December. At least, I have no reason to expect that you will, and I was the person who was responsible for this fear in the first place. I am truly sorry. It was all a consequence of my own relationship with my uncle, Fred, and my youthful fascination with locked door mysteries and impossible challenges. Uncle Fred used to travel round the country plying his trade at various fairs and festivals. He was a regular at the St Giles Fair in Oxford, for instance. His *nom de plume* was Solomon Sage and he used to tell people's fortunes. Depending on his assessment of the paying customer, he'd peer into a crystal ball, pretend to read a palm or scrutinise an astrological chart, although he had a healthy scepticism for all those predictors. In reality, he picked up on all the physical and conversational clues that were available to him – it's amazing how much you can guess about someone just by looking at them. The more he practised, the luckier he got and most customers left his booth convinced they had been given some sort of insight into their future.

I knew that our whole gang was going to the fair that year and I was pretty confident that I could persuade some or all of my classmates to have their fortune told. I collected a few mugshots with my digital camera and compiled a dossier of all the information I could possibly find, before handing the whole thing over to Uncle Fred. With most of the boys, I only had things like date of birth, favourite football team, and so on, but in your case, I had several pages worth, because we had been the best of friends for some time and I had got to know your family. I knew your heroes, your ambitions, everything. It was obvious you'd end up at your father's old college, a real no-brainer.

But Uncle Fred did far too good a job – how could he fail with such a big advantage? The tricky bit came when you asked how long you would live. That is not a question anyone should ever ask but when you are young you think you are going to live for ever. He refused to tell you but you pressed him and pressed him (at least, that's what he told me afterwards) and in the end, because there was a queue of paying punters waiting in the wings, he made up a date. To him, December 30th 2016 sounded an impossibly long way off, and I'm sure it did to you too. When we spoke about it at the time, you seemed to shrug it off and I tried to convince you it was all rubbish. I did not guess that it would be preying on your mind in years to come.

Uncle Fred died in 2008 so I am apologising on behalf of the two of us. It was a stupid trick to play. I must track down other classmates on LinkedIn or Facebook and make sure none of them is labouring under a similar misconception.

So as well as a seven-figure sum, I grant you a new lease of life! Happy New Year!

Yours, etc,

John Harrison

It is hard to believe that I am able to read this entire letter aloud without collapsing in a quivering heap. The news seems too good to be true. All those years of needless worry and suspense! But even now I am already rewriting my life-history – how could I possibly have believed such a prediction? The putative reader of these Hoggblogs will have pooh-poohed such an idea from the outset. You're right, it was ridiculous, I never believed a word of it, did I?

As I struggle to hold back the tears, the wedding party stands and applauds me. Phil and Ozzie leave me bruised with their celebratory high-fives and backslaps and the kiss I get from Marie-Claire lasts a micro-second longer than decorum demands of a bride. Mine has been an unusual prothalamion but the applause shows no signs of abating and I have no idea what more to say. In fact, the clapping seems to have intensified and turned into a gasp of surprise. An irrational panic seizes me – has my audience suddenly realized that my flies are undone? – but most of all I just feel nauseous and dizzy. It is vital that I get out of the cabin immediately before I throw up. Attempting to wave apologetically, I stumble out through the nearest door to the stern of the boat, vaguely conscious that that is the right end to be. No one has followed me out, which is a great relief.

I crouch over the guard-rail and heave convulsively. What little I have eaten and drunk disappears into the greeny-grey waters of the Thames. Fortunately, this is a very quiet stretch of the river and there are no witnesses to my embarrassment. We are still careering downstream at some pace, having recently passed Sandford Lock. The banks are thickly covered with bushes and a row of pylons in the distance disfigures the South Oxfordshire skyline. The icy air does not seem to be making me feel any less nauseous and I decide to stay put until I am ill a second time. I feel so rough I can hardly bring myself to contemplate the good news I have just received. I should feel elated and astonished as a curse is lifted and I suddenly have a bit (OK, a lot) of money in the pipeline. And yet, and yet …

I don't know which comes first, the voice or the touch on my shoulder. But the combination of the two at a moment when the *Folly Bargères* is pitching left and right are almost enough to send me flying overboard. I grab the rail and hang on for dear life. It can't be! I haven't heard that voice for nine months or so. It is the last voice I expected to hear today. I must be dreaming!

Even as I turn round, I am convinced that this must be a cruel trick played on me in my delirium. But the evidence of my eyes is clear enough. It really is Hattie, alive and well. I am completely lost for words. But that is not the only shock. Hattie is wrapped up snug and warm in a thick winter's coat and in her arms she is cradling a baby, swathed in so many layers that I can barely see its tiny face. For an instant I wonder whose baby Hattie could possibly be looking after but there is something so natural about the two of them that there can be only one possible conclusion.

"Alex!?" Hattie whispers at last. "I'm so sorry to shock you like that. Are you not well?"

Somehow I manage to recover the power of speech.

"Hattie, how marvelous to see you! How truly, truly wonderful to see you! We thought you were …"

"Dead? Oh, I'm so sorry, Alex, to let you think that. You don't know what it was like. I had to get away from London. I felt I was going mad. I didn't want anyone to know where I was, not even Liz, not even … you."

I gaze at mother and baby, shaking my head. I am conscious that there are tears in my eyes and I wipe them away.

"There's no need to apologise," I start.

"I just wanted to go somewhere where I could have my baby and decide what I was going to do next. I went to Ireland and stayed at the house of an old college friend called Jenny. I owe her so much. And now there is a new person in my life. Also called Jenny!"

As if on cue, the baby gurgles and splutters. I feel sure that the infant should not be out in the open air on such a winter's day but I am no expert on childcare.

"Jenny is a lovely name," I offer lamely. "But …"

"But what?"

In the end I cannot resist the obvious question. In my heart of hearts, I already know the answer. Hattie gazes at me for a moment as if to ask how foolish I can possibly be.

"Who do you *think*, Alex?"

There is no bitterness or recrimination in her voice, just a steely calmness. I search in her eyes for some sort of confirmation. The truth seems almost beyond comprehension.

"Me!?"

"It's all right, Alex. I know it was just a drunken fumble."

"Is it really nine months since that night?"

"It was March 25th. Not a night I'll forget in a hurry."

"March 25th?"

The date my forefather got sent down from Univ. Shelley too, of course.

"Part of me wanted to keep it a secret from you for ever. But having a baby changes the way you think. I knew I had to tell you. You are the father, after all. So here I am."

I am suddenly conscious that there are numerous eyes gazing at us through the cabin window. Am I the last to know about all this? The tears are flowing freely. But this is no time for self-consciousness. I must hold my daughter.

Hattie intuits this and hands the baby across. I have to surrender my grip on the guard-rail in order to take the baby and support her against my chest. It is hard to put into words my feelings – it is the most extraordinary moment of my life. I had never wanted to have children, never felt capable of being responsible for a child and yet, now that the moment has come, I know that it is the best thing that has ever happened to me. And considering the other things that have happened to me in the last half hour alone, that is quite something.

The number of eyes pressing at the cabin window has doubled and I do not feel well enough to perform as I should for such an audience. I sense that Hattie feels similarly uncomfortable. She has many other people to see and a baby is a star performer at any wedding. We agree that we will go back into the cabin separately and later, when the fuss has died down, we will find a quiet moment to reflect. I need a little time to think, that's for sure, and it's easier to ponder out here than it will be inside, especially now that the party is starting in earnest.

Honestly, I did not see this coming! Perhaps *you* did, reading astutely between the lines. If so, I applaud your perspicacity, but it may just be a sign that you have read too many Victorian novels and confused them with real life. My personal peripeteia seems suspiciously neat and yet I can't help but reflect that it breaks the pattern of history. Hattie has *not* succumbed to the fate that seemed implicit in the story of Harriet Westbrook.

Hattie didn't weigh down her pockets with stones and walk out into the Serpentine, like her predecessor. An unexpected pregnancy now does not entail the same social stigma as it did two hundred years ago. No one on the *Folly Bargères* is treating her as a pariah – on the contrary, Phil and all his friends are cooing over her as if she were the prodigal son. Even Marie-Claire seems genuinely happy to be upstaged. She is secure that Phil is now hers and the reappearance of his ex-wife is a blessing, a load off everyone's mind, not that Phil had seemed overly concerned in the first place.

As baby Jenny is passed blithely from one set of hands to another, cooing and wriggling in time-honoured fashion, I feel a little resentful. That's *my* baby you are treating like the cabaret! How can I possibly have developed such paternal feelings in the space of half an hour?

But what of my feelings for Hattie? She has regained the bloom in her cheeks that she had before she married Phil and I see now that she has dressed in the brightest of clingy frocks for the wedding, showing off her spectacular, maternal figure. Am I in love with her? I am certainly in lust. And what about her feelings for me? After nine months of living with the consequences of my carelessness, I could hardly blame her if bitterness and resentment are the predominant emotions she feels. It's clear that she has told no one the name of the father as there are few furtive glances in my direction. Perhaps everyone is too drunk to guess.

Before we know it, we are safely back to Folly Bridge and the party is adjourning. I jump ashore, an undrowned man. Plenty of folks are heading over to the Univ Beer Cellar where a few bevvies have been laid on. Hattie is busy wrapping up Jenny against the winter cold.

"Do you think we could head off somewhere?" I suggest.

"Somewhere far from the madding crowd?"

"No, the *Madding Crowd* has shut up shop. How about the *Royal Blenheim*?"

So the three of us make the short walk up St Aldates and along Cornmarket to the second of the two pubs named after Hardy novels by the late, great Noel Reilly. St Aldates is surprisingly busy. Someone on a bicycle has been struck by an old Stag MK11 – the cyclist looks to be in better shape than the Stag's wing-mirror but an ambulance is standing by.

As we pass Carfax, I see close behind us a young man in a wheelchair being pushed by someone who is a dead ringer for the second of the two men I glimpsed at Univ. Perhaps it is just the incongruous shades he is wearing. Hattie and I lug the carry-cot complete with Jenny and all her clutter through the doors of the pub. I sort out some drinks while Hattie gets herself organised in a convenient corner.

"Are you in a rush to get off somewhere else?" she asks. "That's not the first time you have looked at your watch!"

"I'm just glad to be alive!"

"What on earth do you mean?"

And so I tell her – the whole Drowned Hogg Day story. If I spin it out long enough, the midnight hour really will strike and I will have survived. I feel reasonably confident that the alarm clock will not ring tomorrow to reveal that I am trapped in the Oxford equivalent of Punxsutawney, if only because I don't actually *own* a radio-alarm. The predictions were right all along – December 30th is indeed the day my life ends … and a new one starts. I have gained a family and a fortune in the space of half an hour.

"So … what are your plans?" I dare to ask at last.

"I might move to America and find myself a log cabin big enough for myself and three growing children …" Hattie looks at me askance. "Or I might stay in London – Charley and Xan are settled there, after all. But I hate London. This is the place for me. No wonder you've never left! How does anyone leave Oxford? Trouble is, I can't afford to rent a one-bedroom flat here, never mind actually *buy* something."

"I could lend you a fiver," I offer generously.

"A tenner might help us all get here on the Oxford Tube," she laughs.

Actually, I think I can do rather better than that," I say. "Now that I have come into my great expectations, I feel it is time I became a man of property. I will buy you a house."

"Don't be ridiculous, Alex!"

"What's ridiculous about that? When I woke up this morning, I didn't have a penny in my pocket and I'd quite like to return to that blissful state as quickly as possible. If I can do a good turn along the way …"

"You're serious?"

"Ah sure ahm!"

"Very well. On one condition."

"Which is?"

"That you come and live there too. Jenny needs a father and the other two could do with a man about the house. Or does the idea fill you with dread?"

I am forced to admit that the idea does not fill me with dread at all. It fills me with the deepest possible joy and anticipation. Hattie shakes her head in bewilderment. And for once in my life I do the right thing. I lean across, slowly and deliberately, and kiss her full on the lips. I lack the words to describe the magic of that moment. If this is my groundhog day, I will never tire of this. No frog transformed into a prince ever felt happier than I.

Perhaps sensing that she is no longer quite the centre of attention, Jenny starts to cry in her little carry-cot. I wonder that a sound so loud could come from such a tiny pair of lungs. Hattie plucks her daughter out of her swaddling clothes, checks to left and right and unfastens the bodice of her dress. As her right breast is released from the confines of her maternity bra, I catch a glimpse of its plump softness before Jenny latches greedily on. I too long to be pillowed on my fair love's ripened breast. Reading my mind, Hattie chuckles and I blush.

"This day was perfect," Hattie tells me. "You couldn't have planned a day like this."

"Well, you can. It just takes an awful lot of work."

"Jenny has two parents now. But we should have had ten times more fun making this baby!"

"Is it too late to catch up now?" I hardly dare to ask. Hattie seems unembarrassed but doubtful.

"How gentle can you be?"

"What, a clodhopping fool like me? I'll give it my best shot!"

"Well, you'd better call a taxi, then. My room at the Old Parsonage should be just about big enough for the three of us ..."

As Jenny continues to chomp and dribble contentedly, I go outside in search of mobile phone reception. Snowflakes tumble on me, the first of 2016, and I think again of Phil Connors and Rita, breaking the cycle at last. At the end of St Ebbes, I catch another glimpse of the cripple in the wheelchair and I make a mental note to count my many blessings. The night is only just beginning ...

Editor's note

As many readers of these posts will now be aware, Alex Hogg collapsed suddenly at around 10.45 p.m. on 30th December 2016. Emergency services were called to the Old Parsonage Hotel on Banbury Rd but paramedics' efforts were unproductive and Mr Hogg was pronounced dead on arrival at the John Radcliffe Hospital an hour later. Preliminary examinations were not successful in determining the cause of death and a provisional attribution of SUDS (sudden unexpected death syndrome) is likely to be revised in due course.

Mr Hogg's family and friends have been advised of this sad news and arrangements for Mr Hogg's funeral and a memorial service will be announced in due course.

In Mr Hogg's pockets was found a copy of Keats's *Selected Poems* and the draft of a crossword. The latter may serve as a cryptic epitaph for the last 50 days of his life.

A crossword for 30th December, linking numerous alumni of 11 15 Oxford, including 22 ac who married 24 ac on 30th December 1816, 10 (AKA Prince 9), 19 who killed 8 on 30th December 1916, and 17 (×2).

Across

8 Revolutionary puritans murdered Russian ... (8)

9 ... and another porter with two unknown figures (5)

10 Thomas Jefferson to travel back aboard Mercury (4)

11 Agreement about unfinished version or passage, to a degree? (10)

12 Does something essential rest on these? (6)

14 Doctor admitting it's fatal for 8 and 22 ac (8)

15 Queens, perhaps, or old king admitting member (7)

17 Clown in town? Have gone with missing President (7)

20 Topless union gear for poet (8)

22 Poetic middle name – a foolish mistake, one gathers (6)

23 Publisher's flourishes put down (10)

24, 25 Fawley village's alternative energy after sheep comes back (9)

26 Tack back after misplaced hope, like one rejected by Dane or 14 (8)

Down

1 Re-mounted main polo-horse (8)

2 Short Italian food shortages back (4)

3 Cures numberless strokes (6)

4 Relaxes in solar air-current, first to last (7)

5 Enthusiastic wolf ravaged avian prey (8)

6 Doctor signs on after sea-salts (10)

7 Only drunk outside, tee-total member of 23 set (6)

13 On the radio, old French rock group causing acute indigestion (10)

16 Speculation intrigues singleton when 5-a-side cancelled (8)

18 Promoting Oscar, the Roman co-respondent (5,3)

19 Carry us up over some assassin (7)

21 Make wingless noble tiger (6)

22 Originally, President William Jefferson's and 22 ac's poetic spirit, one hears (6)

24 Grinder crowd (4)

Appendix 1

A fragment of Thomas Jefferson Hogg's unpublished autobiography has been found amongst the papers left by Alex's uncle, Alan Hogg. In this section he describes a tea-party involving Jane Williams and Mary Shelley some time in 1823...

It was amongst the more embarrassing events of my adult life, if not quite on a par with the day of the unfortunate misunderstanding with Harriet. Jane and I were by now on intimate terms but as Jane was still officially grieving for the loss of Edward, we had kept our relationship secret from our closest friends, even from Mary who had been the unwitting matchmaker.

Jane, in turn, was completely unaware that I had once aspired to partake of Mary's bed in the days when we shared a house at 13, Arabella Rd. Although Mary was no longer my dormouse and I was no longer her Prince Alexy, there was still an element of unfinished business between us, especially now that she was a widow, albeit one that was prematurely aged by grief. I did what I could to ensure that the three of us were never alone in private conversation but that day soon came unbidden. Not long after her return to England in 1823, Mary called unexpectedly at Jane's home one afternoon and found not just Jane, strumming idly on her guitar, but also your humble friend in residence.

"Mr Hogg! I did not expect to find you here!" she said on entering the drawing-room. I struggled in vain to find a suitable explanation for my presence. Jane was rather less circumspect.

"Dearest Mary! I owe you the most heartfelt of thanks. It was so kind of you to put me in touch with Mr Hogg. I would have known almost no one in England otherwise. Jefferson and I have …"

I recall that Jane looked across at me, as if for my blessing, and I must have blushed deeply. But she carried on anyway.

"We have become the *closest* of friends," she said, reaching for my cold hand, "and we owe it all to you!"

Mary looked at each of us in turn and tried to force some sort of smile but I was not deceived. She never truly forgave me for stealing Jane from her. Her coldness towards us in later years is a source of the deepest regret.

In an effort to change the subject, I asked Mary if she had made much progress in sorting through the mountain of papers and unpublished work that Bysshe had left.

"It will take me ten years or more, I suspect," she replied. "But I have a pamphlet with me which I believe you may have seen before, Mr Hogg."

From her portmanteau, Mary pulled out a grubby booklet and handed it to me.

"Ah, yes, the Poetical Essay on the Existing State of Things," I said. "*This* is the publication for which Bysshe and I should have been sent down, not that mild-mannered piece on atheism. This polemic is truly seditious!"

"Indeed!" Mary responded. "I cannot put this in his Collected Works. It can *never* be published again. Just look at those first few lines!"

I turned over the introductory pages, skimming past the dedication to Harriet W---b---k, and recited the opening section; indeed, I might have done so from memory as Bysshe and I had laboured over every word of it in his rooms at Univ:

> DESTRUCTION marks thee! o'er the blood-stain'd heath
> Is faintly borne the stifled wail of death;
> Millions to fight compell'd, to fight or die
> In mangled heaps on War's red altar lie.
> The sternly wise, the mildly good, have sped
> To the unfruitful mansions of the dead.
> Whilst fell Ambition o'er the wasted plain
> Triumphant guides his car ...

"Ah, the triumphal car," I chuckled. "Wasn't that in his final unfinished poem, the *Triumph of Life*?"

"Yes, indeed, but in a less incendiary form."

"Little had changed. He was still at heart a revolutionary."

"I have found something even more extraordinary," Mary went on. "Some poems Bysshe wrote in Middle English!"

"What, like Chaucer, you mean?"

"No, it's intended to be a more Northerly dialect, I think. It's full of alliteration. There's a dream-vision thing called *Pearl* and an Arthurian tale. There's no title to it but I think it should be called *Sir Gawain and the Green Knight*."

"*Was* there a Green Knight?"

"Who's to say? There are a few echoes of poor John Keats's poem, 'La Belle

Dame Sans Merci'. Anyway, I've found some old parchment and I'm writing the whole lot out neatly."

From her portmanteau she retrieved the oldest notebook I have ever seen, neatly stitched together and inscribed with monastic rigour. With my limited knowledge of medieval script, I could barely make out the opening words:

> SIÞEN þe sege and þe assaut watȝ sesed at Troye,
> Þe borȝ brittened and brent to brondeȝ and askeȝ

"Do you think you could help me get it published somewhere as if it really were medieval?" Mary enquired.

"That is surely impossible!"

But this was a challenge I could hardly resist. Ever since the *Posthumous Fragments of Margaret Nicholson* forgery of our first term at Univ and the invention of John Brown, the "translator" of Prince Alexy, I have loved a good hoax. Mary too had passed off *Frankenstein* as the work of the polar explorer, Robert Walton. This would be a more arduous venture but, succeed or fail, highly diverting. If Thomas Chatterton, a schoolboy with little poetic experience, could successfully pass himself off as a medieval poet for a while, surely Shelley, with our support, could do better still?

We needed an intermediary figure, a John Brown or a Robert Walton. Another plain English name seemed expedient. It was not long before Mary and I had invented one Richard Price, a denizen, like me, of the Middle Temple, called to the bar in 1823 and the unlikely 'discoverer' of our mildewy manuscript (a "Temple-haunting martlet", as Mary called him, forgetting that she had once applied the same soubriquet to me). Mary continued with her transcription and we started to look for a gullible publisher. Various communications went via the fictional Mr Price's pigeon hole at the Middle Temple and I picked up any correspondence there. On the very few occasions when meetings were unavoidable, I pleaded an inability to leave the confines of the Middle Temple and met visitors in a room starved of natural light. I even took to wearing a hairpiece that covered my own middle temple. Had my visitors encountered me at a social gathering that same evening, I doubt whether they would have recognised me again.

Before long, the very persuasive Mr Price had managed to talk his way into a job as Editor of a new edition of Thomas Warton's *History of English Poetry*, which covered the 11th through to the 16th century. This, we decided, was the perfect medium for Price's exciting new discovery. We tested the water with a small section of Shelley's cod-medieval masterpiece in the 1824 edition of Warton, complete with an Introduction by Price that Mary and I laboured long and hard over.

By this date, Mary had found her true vocation as a literary editor, perhaps the greatest the world has yet soon. After her husband's untimely demise, she had been the custodian of a million scraps of paper, each crammed with spidery scrawlings overlaid with amendments, additions and furious deletions. She took these unreadable fragments and pieced them together like one of John Spilsbury's jigsaw-dissected maps to create the *Collected Poems of Percy Bysshe Shelley*, a literary Monster conjured from wisps and ether. If that manipulation of manuscripts was her true life's work and her greatest act of procreation, our medieval jest was but a transient divigation. Mary's calligraphic skills were unsurpassed and she loved to construct the illuminated letters at the commencement of each stanza or fit.

Mary took great delight in the many arts of forgery; I recall that she was also instrumental in the counterfeiting of a passport for an acquaintance who wished to travel abroad. Each piece of parchment was aged with alchemical care to the point where it was susceptible to disintegration. The ink was faded almost, but not quite, to the point of illegibility. Warton's *History* was Mary's style-guide and furnished my partner in crime with many examples of the lettering, punctuation and other orthographic features to be found in an authentic early-fifteenth century manuscript.

Within London's literary circles where everyone knows everyone, a few questions were asked in the years that followed. Who *is* this Richard Price? A barrister at the Middle Temple? Well, *I've* never heard of him! As the mutterings multiplied, we decided to kill off our unmarried and childless Mr Price in 1833 (a convenient bout of dropsy), leaving the rest of the *Gawain*-manuscript (as we called it) in the hands of his unsuspecting publishers. It remained one of the many secrets I shared with Mary. We determined to stay silent about our imposture and, whichever one of us should survive the longer, that personage should be responsible for correcting the historical record. Since Mary's untimely decease in 1851 I have postponed that confession. But my duty will be fulfilled when the secret is revealed with the publication of these memoirs shortly after my own death.

As I saw little of Shelley in the last five years of his life, I have no idea when he found time to compose these extraordinary poems. Such was Shelley's ability to work on many pieces at once even Mary had been unaware of her husband's experimentation. He had evidently begun to practise his Middle English skills with short experiments called *Patience* and *Cleanness*. We considered discarding these awkward pastiches but Mary enjoyed her calligraphic labours so much that they were included in the final collection. There was a longer poem called *Pearl* which, I confess, I never quite understood.

But it was the extraordinary narrative of Sir Gawain and the fearsome Green Knight which captivated us. In planning our deception, the problem was not that Shelley's poetry was unconvincing; it was rather that it was *too* compelling. No writer of the period, not even Chaucer, could have created a story of such depth and complexity, such masterly control of its readers' expectations, such *surprise*. One or two early readers compared *Gawain* to *Frankenstein*, especially in the way the central character must set out across unknown, wintry lands in search of a murderous, hideous, unnamed monster. But no one went so far as to suggest that the same author or authors might be responsible for both works. Yet to me, numerous aspects were unmistakeably Shelleyan, especially the wife-sharing machinations.

After much debate, we also declined to give the author of these poems a name. Mary convinced me that the lack of an appellation made all her monsters more frightening and extraordinary.

So far our *jeux d'esprit* has still not been rumbled! I can only attribute that fact to Shelley's astonishing invention of his own Middle English dialect. Some say it has a little in common with Langland's *Piers Plowman* but this invented language is more courtly and Frenchified. No matter that the dialect exists in no other document – it has its own ring of alliterative authenticity. We had succeeded where young Chatterton had ultimately failed. I feel sure that, once the truth is known, the public's appreciation of Shelley's genius will be still further magnified.

On another visit, on which I was accompanied by Jane herself, I enquired whether Mary had found any time to work on a second novel of her own, following the astonishing success of *Frankenstein*?

"Why, yes, as it happens, despite all my editorial duties," she said. "Do you remember our trip to the Sibyl's cave near Naples, Jane? Of course you do. It has given me the idea for something. What if we had found some prophetic writings there? A vision of life in the twenty-first century after some terrible catastrophe has struck. A great flood or a plague of some kind. I am calling it *The Last Man*."

"The Last Man in Europe?" I suggested.

"Not just Europe. It is about the only man left in the whole world and how desolate such a creature would be. Somewhat like Frankenstein's monster after he has been spurned. Although it is set two centuries hence, it is really about Bysshe and me and Byron and all our poor friends."

"Not *another* novel about Shelley," I sighed.

"Well, his ridiculous father won't let me write a biography, so this will have to suffice. In my modest way I am trying to finish the *Triumph of Life*. What about you, Jefferson? Will *you* put Bysshe in another piece of fiction?"

I indicated that I had absolutely no intention of writing another novel.

"*Another* novel?" Jane shrieked. "I didn't know you had written a novel at all, Jefferson!"

"Oh, it is nothing," I insisted.

"Mr Hogg is the author of *The Memoirs of Prince Alexy Haimatoff*," Mary divulged. "Did he not tell you that?"

"He did nothing of the sort. Jefferson!"

I could not but feel a little pride so I told her something of Prince Alexy and the "translation" by John Brown, Esq. Mary was good enough to confess that much of her own *Frankenstein* was inspired by my earlier novelistic bagatelle, from the St Petersburg opening through to the murderous embrace of the protagonist and his ghastly alter ego.

"I wish you would write another book. For me!" Jane shrieked. "I shan't stay friends with you unless you do!"

Perhaps she said these words in jest; I am not sure. It was one of many challenges she issued in the days before we married. To prove I was no stick-in-the-mud, I had to embark on a Grand Tour of Europe, all on my own. It took me two hundred and nine days and, believe me, I counted off every single hour of my lonely exile. I suspect I was even more of a stick-in-the-mud when I returned unbloodied from my knightly quest.

So perhaps it was all Mary's fault that Jane also challenged me to write a prophetic novel like Mary's, set in the twenty-first century.

"But I know nothing about the twenty-first century!" I remonstrated at first.

"You knew nothing of Russian princes either," Jane insisted. "Imagine it is one of our distant descendants. I am sure his life will be much like your own. You don't have to publish it or even put your name to it – just write. We can put it in a drawer for our grandchildren to find after we are gone …"

If I wanted to make my home with Jane, I had little choice but to accept the challenge. It was not quite as severe an ordeal as Gawain's, after all. In the weeks that followed, prior to embarkation from Dover, Mary and I passed our time in the *terra incognita* of the 21ˢᵗ century. We exchanged ideas of how our distant descendants would live and die, what contraptions they would have, where they would eat and drink. I decided on a setting that might change relatively little in 200 years, the Oxford that I had known as a callow young man, but it was still an undertaking that would stretch my imagination beyond its natural capabilities. Mary's *Last Man* was, in this author's humble opinion, her true masterpiece but my paltry effort was never destined for publication. Like these memoirs, it will remain locked in a drawer until after I have departed this vale of tears.

I picked up my pen early in my continental expedition and tried to begin the process of writing. I stared at a blank page for many days. You will not believe me when I tell you that the first line came to me in a dream one night as I too sojourned on the shores of Lake Geneva:

"I have fifty days to live …"

Appendix 2: Crossword Solution

Answers to clues not included in the crossword:

11 Nov: steatopygous;   12 Nov: A Salty Dog;
24 Nov: Fiat;   26 Nov: Hogacre;
 5 Dec: baton;   7 Dec: Ratledge;
13 Dec: chapel;   17 Dec: genre;
20 Dec: Gwen;   21 Dec: Moika;
23 Dec: uncle;   30 Dec: Madeira

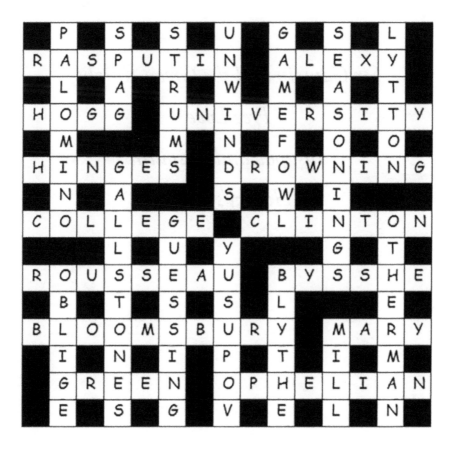

Four Plays - Afterplays
The 30/12/16 Tetralogy

Sir Gawain and the Green Knight

Free Love

Yusupov and Rasputin

Hillary's Term

Sir Gawain and the Green Knight

Cast

Sir Gawain	King Arthur's young nephew and possible heir, idealistic but untested, shy, devoted to Shelley, determined to prove himself and enhance the honour of the court – in short, the hero of the piece. This part is best played by a female actor in principal boy mode, but this is not essential.
Sir Lancelot	swashbuckling ladies' man, Guinevere's masochistic lover, faux-legend (because he alone can read), over-confident, cowardly
Merlin	very ancient wizard, living as a hermit in a cave, unpredictable, embittered, omniscient, still capable of flashes of magic
The Green Knight	a figure of mystery, a 100%-green giant with long wild tresses, frightening and dangerous; he morphs into:
Sir Bertilak	courteous but unpredictable lord of his own manor, uxorious, sport-loving, ceremonious, apparently hospitable
Queen Guinevere	(much younger than Arthur), desired by all, black-clad dominatrix, the power behind the throne, lover of Lancelot and many others (they wish)
Shelley	A farmer's daughter, anti-chivalry, etc, plain-speaking, plain-looking, gradually blossoming as Gawain's love-interest
Bella(donna)	Sir Bertilak's wife, breathtakingly beautiful and dangerous, the deadly nightshade that clings to Gawain, much classier than Guinevere but, finally, no more than a cipher
George	A schoolboy at knight school
Gringolet	A pantomime horse (optional, non-speaking)
Doubling:	The play can be performed by three men and two/three women, with Lancelot also playing Bertilak (and/or the Green Knight) and Guinevere also playing Bertilak's wife.

Scene 1: Arthur's court (front of stage)

Camelot, 29th December 715 AD, evening. General hubbub from behind the curtain, desultory mandolin-playing, clinking of glasses, crackers being pulled, etc.

Enter Guinevere in killer-black dress and coronet, pursued by Lancelot.

LANCELOT   Gwinny, Gwinny!

GUINEVERE   It's Guinevere, Sir Lancelot.

LANCELOT   Gwinny! How can you say that? After the nights of passion we've shared! (PUTS ARM ROUND HER)

GUINEVERE   (PULLING AWAY WITH DERISORY SNORT) Nights of passion? You really must learn to keep that fevered imagination of yours in check. You are no more than an ant – no, a small badger – in my eyes.

LANCELOT   (ON KNEES, TUGGING AT HER SKIRT) You can't deny what's happened. The night we spent in the dungeon, the time you had me on the torture rack …….

GUINEVERE   All forgotten. If, indeed, they occurred at all.

LANCELOT   Look at these scars (DISPLAYING HIS LACERATED ARMS). The men think that was from fighting a monster called Grendel, but we both know the truth. Gwinny, please! One more night!

GUINEVERE   (SOFTENING SLIGHTLY) Ah, Lancey, my little badger ….

LANCELOT   I long to feel your stilettos deep in your chest, your crimson fingernails piercing the skin of my back………

GUINEVERE   Difficult to combine the two, but ……

LANCELOT   Your whip. Your tassels. Your mask.

GUINEVERE   You see, it could have been anyone!

LANCELOT   Your coronet, suspended on my ……..

GUINEVERE   What a repulsive image. Arthur is expecting me. I must go and behave like a queen.

LANCELOT   It's been fifteen days. Fifteen days of non-stop partying! God, I hate Christmas. All that jollity, all that waste. We're down to the last few twiglets. Nobody will miss us if we aren't there. Just give me an hour, you know you want to. Half an hour. I can be very quick!

GUINEVERE   (PULLING AWAY AGAIN) So I've noticed …….

LANCELOT	Come back, Gwinny! I'll do anything you ask. I'll lick the piggery clean. Again. Any quest, any favour!
GUINEVERE	Not tonight, my little badger. Maybe tomorrow, maybe never. (BEGINS TO LEAVE)
LANCELOT	Gwinny, come back! This is so typical! You know what? You're a ..... you're a SADIST, that's what you are!
GUINEVERE	(EXITING) You should be so lucky, sunshine!

Scene 2: (full stage)

Shelley, the farmer's daughter, dressed as a skivvy, is pottering around the stage with a cloth and a duster, looking miserable.

Enter Gawain, adjusting his dicky-bow anxiously – he is dressed for a posh party. Each sees the other but pretends they haven't. Gawain continues to fret anxiously in front of a mirror. At last he turns to Shelley who has been studiously ignoring him.

GAWAIN	Oh, didn't see you Shelley, do I look OK?
SHELLEY	Of course you do.
GAWAIN	Not mutton dressed as lamb?
SHELLEY	I think it's only *girls* who can look like mutton dressed as lamb.
GAWAIN	(ANXIOUSLY) Yes, of course. Obviously. But do you think I look all right.
SHELLEY	I think you look ridiculous, Gawain.
GAWAIN	I'm glad I asked.
SHELLEY	But no more ridiculous than the rest of the knights of the sodding round table. How many evenings have you been at it?
GAWAIN	Fifteen. It *is* Christmas.
SHELLEY	The Hula Hoops ran out two weeks ago. You'd all kill for a Ferrero Rocher.
GAWAIN	True. Just one goblet of mead would be good.
SHELLEY	It's a bunch of clapped-out old chauvinists telling each other their tales of days gone by. Quests and jousts. Dragons slain. All that bollocks.
GAWAIN	But it's not bo .... it's the stuff of legend. I just wish I had

	similar tales to tell.
SHELLEY	Well, I'm glad you don't.
GAWAIN	But I'll never be accepted as a true knight unless I do something heroic, like Lancelot and Mordred and all the others.
SHELLEY	Mordred? Hah!
GAWAIN	Look, I'm supposed to be the king's nephew. Uncle Arthur is desperate for me to live up to the family name. I shouldn't be partying. I should be far away, rescuing damsels in distress, slaying dragons, possibly even finding the Holy Grail itself. Then I'll be able to look the other knights in the face.
SHELLEY	Well, good luck with all that then.

Pause. Shelley resumes her dusting.

GAWAIN	Look, what's wrong, Shell?
SHELLEY	Please don't call me Shell. It's Shelley.
GAWAIN	But I always used to …
SHELLEY	We were children then.
GAWAIN	I'm sorry, Shelley. Tell me what's the matter?
SHELLEY	Oh, I don't know, just everything. Being a woman in a man's world.
GAWAIN	Yes, it must be awful.
SHELLEY	You don't know the half of it.
GAWAIN	(QUIETLY) I wouldn't be so sure about that.
SHELLEY	How could you? You're one of the knights of the round table. While I have to do odd jobs to make ends meet, like clearing up after your so-called festivities.
GAWAIN	Don't you earn enough from looking after Merlin? That's a full-time job.
SHELLEY	Tell me about it! You should see his chamber-pot in the morning.
GAWAIN	I'd rather not, thank you.
SHELLEY	Well, you don't have to, do you, Gawain? He's a horrible old man. Just because he's 143 doesn't mean he no longer has a responsibility to take baths or stop his beard from becoming

	infested with rats.
GAWAIN	I thought you'd decided to become a teacher.
SHELLEY	I have, but I've got to finish the bloody PGCE first. It's my first teaching practice next week. It's a pretty frightening prospect. I know those boys. They'll eat me alive.
GAWAIN	They'll be knights themselves one day. You can set them on the right track.
SHELLEY	But I'm a woman – what do *I* know about anything?
GAWAIN	You're wiser than any man, Shelley. Really, you are.
SHELLEY	Oh, Gawain!
GAWAIN	You know I think the world of you.
SHELLEY	Even though I'm just a farmer's daughter and way below your station in life.
GAWAIN	But you can *read*! Do you know how many of the knights can actually read?
SHELLEY	Just old prance-a-lot Lancelot, I think. Reading wasn't on the National Curriculum before he went to Knight School.
GAWAIN	And you can draw! I've got all your pictures on my wall.
SHELLEY	Drawing doesn't pay the rent.
GAWAIN	I know. (SIGHS) I think the party is just starting up.

Rock music is heard in the distance.

SHELLEY	Off you go then, like a good little boy. Perhaps you'll meet a nice young damsel.
GAWAIN	But Guinevere is the only woman invited!
SHELLEY	I was being ironic. Maybe you're right. What you really need is a quest. Something to make you a man.
GAWAIN	A man?
SHELLEY	A real man, like your Uncle Arthur wants. Don't worry, Gawain, something'll turn up …

The music gets louder. Curtain.

Scene 3: (full stage)

The morning after (30ᵗʰ Dec): the debris of the party is untouched. A bleary Lancelot, in pyjamas and flamboyant dressing gown, picks his way across it, munching loudly on a piece of toast and marmalade, scratching his backside, etc. Enter Gawain, still dressed as he was the night before, visibly shell-shocked.

LANCELOT   Chin up, Gawain old son, worse things happen at sea! (GAWAIN DOES NOT SEEM TO HAVE NOTICED HIM). Not such a bad party, all things considered. (STILL NO REACTION) No need to take it like that. (MUNCHES TOAST)

GAWAIN   Tell me it was all just a bad dream, Lancelot!

LANCELOT   It was all just a bad dream. (UNFOLDING NEWSPAPER)

GAWAIN   Was it? The alternative is too horrible to contemplate. Did no one else see a gigantic green knight here in the castle?

LANCELOT   That bit was certainly real.

GAWAIN   And he challenged us all to a game. One of us would swing an axe at his unprotected head, then the green knight would have the chance to do the same in return a year and a day from now?

LANCELOT   Sounded more than fair. A year and a day. You would definitely want to have your turn with the axe first.

GAWAIN   And *I* was the idiot who volunteered!

LANCELOT   Yes, I was a micro-second too slow sticking my hand in the air, you lucky so-and-so!

GAWAIN   And I chopped off his head!

LANCELOT   The perfect go. Ten point zero all round the room. We were all proud of you.

GAWAIN   And that should have been the end of it. He'd been decapitated, after all.

LANCELOT   Game over. And yet …

GAWAIN   And yet he picked up his severed head ……

LANCELOT   (appearing very surprised) No!

GAWAIN   He *didn't* pick up his head?

LANCELOT   (CHEERFULLY) No, that's the bit you're imagining. Once the head has been severed from the body, there's no way back. Not even for a jolly green giant.

236

GAWAIN	So it was all just a bad dream? He's dead?
LANCELOT	Yup. (THEY LOOK AT EACH OTHER FOR A MOMENT)
GAWAIN	(RELAXING DRAMATICALLY) God, that's a relief! You know, I really believed that I was going to have to go along to his place and have my head chopped off! The mind can play funny tricks on you, can't it?

There is an expectant pause as they look at each other again. Eventually Lancelot can keep a straight face no longer ....)

LANCELOT	(COLLAPSING IN MIRTH) Gotcha! Can't believe you fell for that one. Sorry, old son, couldn't resist it. *Of course* it happened. What can I say? Bad luck, old chap!
GAWAIN	Bad luck? Do you think there's no hope?
LANCELOT	Well, I'm making the naïve assumption that you're like the rest of us *homo sapiens* and your head is attached to your body by means of various bones, sinews and arteries and when your neck is exposed to the full force of a sharpened axe wielded by some weirdo colossus on steroids – well, there can be only one possible outcome. Lights out, nurse. Unless ......
GAWAIN	Unless?
LANCELOT	Unless ...... unless you die of natural causes in less than a year. Might be your best strategy.
GAWAIN	So, based on your experience of these things, there's no hope at all?
LANCELOT	Absolutely none. Still, look on the bright side. You can have a really cracking last year, unencumbered by any worries about the year after. Wine, women ..... more women. You're in an enviable position.
GAWAIN	You think so? I rather thought I'd spend the year doing good works and improving myself. Learning to read, like you. No other man round here can read a word and ......
LANCELOT	An extremely *bad* idea!
GAWAIN	For instance, what was that book you were engrossed in the other day?
LANCELOT	You mean *Beowul* ..... beer, the *Good Beer Guide*? Not worth

	learning to read just for that. Look, Gawain old son, we can all help to make your last few months a bit more bearable. Who's that totty you've got the hots for?
GAWAIN	Totty? That's not my ...
LANCELOT	I've seen you. Eying her up when you think no one's watching. You know, that farmer's daughter,whatsername. Shelley? Can't see it myself. Still, takes all sorts. I could put in a good word for you ....
GAWAIN	No!! (EMBARRASSED PAUSE) No, thank you – I'd really rather you didn't.
LANCELOT	You're right, you could do a lot better than that! Anyway, can't sit around here nattering – I'm booked in for a hot wax this morning and then I'm off to see the wizard, the wonderful wizard of Camelot – not! Ta-ra! (EXIT)

Gawain addresses the audience directly:

GAWAIN	Don't take any notice of Lancelot – Shelley's gorgeous. Well, you've seen that for yourselves. And we did have something going when we were both kids – you know, swore we'd be sweethearts when we were a bit older, that sort of thing. She's probably forgotten all that now but it meant a lot to me. (EXIT)

Scene 4: Merlin's Cave

Merlin is not the wizard he once was. He's now 143, with a long, straggly beard down to his waist, gnarled features and long, bony fingers, an older version of Albert Steptoe with a tall pointy hat, in fact. His cave is dank, dark and cobwebby with a few Gothic accoutrements.

Merlin enters, carrying a magic wand and a stuffed dog which he places on a table (or chair) right. From a range of about six feet, he tries to perform his magic. Each time he does so, there is a suitable sound effect, but the stuffed dog remains exactly as it is and Merlin becomes ever more frustrated.

MERLIN	Abracadabra! (WAVES WAND) Dammit, why didn't that work? Wrong incantation, I guess. Hocus Pocus! (WAVES WAND) By

the power of slugs and snails and puppy dogs' tails! (WAVES WAND) Shazam! (WAVES WAND) It never used to be this hard! Am I getting too old for this caper? Shazam! (WAVES WAND) Did I already try that one? I know the spell has a 'z' in it somewhere. Alacatraz. Zanzibar. Alzheimer's?

Unseen by Merlin, Shelley enters, carrying a fold-up ironing board and iron. She is Merlin's relatively new live-in carer. She sets up her ironing board back stage and she will proceed to take female clothes from a pile of washing and seek to iron them.

SHELLEY	I'm sorry, Mr Merlin. Do you mind if I get on with some ironing while you're doing your magic practice?
MERLIN	Well, actually, I do m…
SHELLEY	Only there's nowhere else to do it in this cave, is there? There's no privacy at all!
MERLIN	It's suited me perfectly well for 143 years! How can I be expected to concentrate if you're clattering around?
SHELLEY	May I ask what you're doing, exactly?
MERLIN	I'm using my magic powers to transform Inish there into … into …
SHELLEY	Yes?
MERLIN	(MUTTERING DEFEATEDLY) A python.
SHELLEY	A parrot, you say? A dead parrot?
MERLIN	No, a python. A stuffed python.
SHELLEY	A *python?* What use is that? It'd only go round constricting people and asphyxiating them. Why waste a perfectly good poodle?
MERLIN	No reason, I just need the practice.
SHELLEY	(SIGHING) You know what the doctor said, Mr Merlin. You need to retire from all this wizardry nonsense. It's bad for your blood pressure. I've got your statins. (SHE WAVES A BOTTLE OF PILLS AT HIM) You need to put your feet up and let me look after you in your twilight years. That's what a live-in carer is for!
MERLIN	Twilight years? I won't allow any twilight in here. I plan to

	live forever – I'm a magician after all.
SHELLEY	Yes, Mr Merlin, of *course* you are! (OPENING THE BOTTLE) Just eat these.
MERLIN	(WAVING HER AWAY) I don't need your pills. I make my own potions!
SHELLEY	(RESUMING HER IRONING) I wanted to be a wizard when I was a little girl, you know.
MERLIN	A witch, you mean?
SHELLEY	Well, that's the trouble, isn't it? A *wizard* is a pillar of society, trusted adviser to the king, all that malarkey. A witch, on the other hand, is a figure to be feared, an evil temptress, an outcast, someone to be thrown in the ducking pool. What sort of career option is that for a girl? It's sexism in its purest form. I had to give up on my dreams of wizardry and become a skivvy instead. It was either that or be a dulcimer player …
MERLIN	(DREAMILY) A damsel with a dulcimer in a vision once I saw!
SHELLEY	… and a skivvy gets a groat a week, twice as much as a dulcimer player, so here I am. Only now they call it "live-in carer". God, I hate ironing. (holds up a blouse, still visibly creased) That's hopeless. (HOLDING UP THE PLUG END OF THE CORD) The sooner someone invents electricity the better, I say. And where are all *your* clothes? Don't any of them need washing and ironing?
MERLIN	Well, I …
SHELLEY	To my knowledge, you haven't changed that cloak for the four years I've been working here! No wonder it's a bit whiffy! How long since you last changed it?
MERLIN	(AFTER SOME COGITATION) About 86 years, give or take.
SHELLEY	What!? You haven't taken your cloak off for 86 years?
MERLIN	Except when I have a bath, no.
SHELLEY	And how often do you have a bath?
MERLIN	(PROUDLY) Once every nine years. Hygiene is very important to a wizard.

There is a loud knock on the door, startling both Merlin and Shelley. Merlin shrugs.

MERLIN   Enter!

In comes Lancelot in wintry clothes. He and Merlin embrace uneasily. Unseen by Merlin, Lancelot holds his nose briefly.

MERLIN   Lancelot! Am I glad to see you! This young lady is making my life a misery.
SHELLEY   Well, thanks a bunch!
LANCELOT   (REMOVING HIS CAPE) And I'm glad to see you too, Merlin, old friend. How are you keeping?
MERLIN   Terrible. Living for ever is a horrible burden, you know. And you don't come as often as you used to.
LANCELOT   Being a senior knight is pretty time-consuming, you know. I've been busy, busy.
MERLIN   Goblet of anthrax?
LANCELOT   Ummmm, I think not. I just want to fly a few ideas past you, throw you a few curveballs.
MERLIN   I'm 143, Lancelot. I'm not sure I'd be able to catch them.
LANCELOT   Shelley, if you wouldn't mind ...
SHELLEY   Wouldn't mind what? Oh, I see. You'd like me to ... er, yes, Sir Lancelot.

Shelley edges off stage back left, curtseying ironically as she goes.

MERLIN   Sit down, sit down, son! (THERE IS NOWHERE OBVIOUS TO SIT). Don't worry about the ironing. Sit on that. (he does) What's the prob?
LANCELOT   I don't know where to start. Being a knight, Camelot, what's it all for?
MERLIN   You *know* what it's for.
LANCELOT   I don't, not any more. Will I ever be king? There was a time when I dreamt of doing good deeds, uniting a nation, bringing together the Angles and Saxons, welcoming the odd Viking trade delegation, possibly even putting up with the Celts and those ghastly French types.

241

MERLIN	All laudable ideals, my boy.
LANCELOT	But the Angles, the Saxons, the Vikings, they *all* hate us. Camelot is not the centre of a happy unified kingdom. I blame the fiscal policy. Asking poor people to give us a groat every week, then having a draw each Saturday.
MERLIN	It's a complete lottery.
LANCELOT	But hardly any of it goes out in prizes. The rest of it goes to "good causes", we say. The peasants can see it's just paying for Mordred's holiday cottage on the island of Avalon. Camelot has become a fortress to keep out the barbarians at the door. And inside those fortified walls, everyone is plotting to dethrone the king.
MERLIN	Except you. You're just sleeping with his wife.
LANCELOT	Arthur doesn't mind that. I think he rather likes it. I've seen him hiding in the wardrobe once or twice while … (he winks ostentatiously) … it's a sign of true nobility to be willing to share everything you have, even your wife.
MERLIN	Says the man who has never been married.
LANCELOT	I'm the one person Arthur trusts. But I know he's just clinging on to power. Fragile coalitions here, secret pacts there, just so he can stay atop the greasy pole a little longer. Power for the sake of power. I'm tired of propping him up, Merlin.
MERLIN	Why not take a holiday? Somewhere exotic? Stonehenge, for instance?
LANCELOT	And as for Mordred … Arthur's own nephew! More plots than a whodunit writer. He'd stab me in the back in the twinkling of an eye if I let him. Ghastly man, and yet people respond to his fascist rants. Do you know what he wants to do?
MERLIN	Yes.
LANCELOT	… he wants to seal up all the doors of Camelot so no one can get in and no one can get out. The Round Table as a closed shop. No new knights coming in and taking the old knight's jobs – it's positively medieval!

MERLIN	Medieval? I wouldn't say it's as up to date as *that*!
LANCELOT	Couldn't you put a spell on him, Merlin? For old time's sake? I'd be forever in your debt!
MERLIN	You already are, after that business with Guinevere.
LANCELOT	For ever in your debt *again*. Please!
MERLIN	I'll, er, see what I can do. (CONSULTING HIS WATCH) But don't forget I know exactly what you're thinking, Lancelot.
LANCELOT	You do?
MERLIN	You know I do. You may be Arthur's great white hope, his blue-eyed boy, but I see through all that. No one has been plotting more than you. But remember: what goes around, comes around.
LANCELOT	I don't know what you mean.
MERLIN	I think you do. (SHOOING HIM OUT OF THE DOOR) It's the witching hour, I'm afraid, and I'm expecting some other visitors, so …

Both exit. Blackout.

Scene 5:. Schoolroom (full stage)

We are in a prep-school for the sons of knights. We see a single boy, George, sitting at an old-fashioned school desk, waiting for the lesson to begin. He is ogling a magazine called *Mediæval Bæbes*. There is a din of other boys talking and arguing. He puts the magazine quickly inside the desk as the teacher comes in. The din lessens only slightly.

Enter Shelley, in gown, with pile of dog-eared exercise books.

SHELLEY	Shurrup the noise, 3G …… (JUST AS MUCH RACKET AS BEFORE – NO SIGN THEY'VE NOTICED HER ARRIVAL) SHUT IT!!!!!!! (GRADUAL GRUDGING SILENCE). Right, some Geography homework to give back ….. (THROWING EXERCISE BOOKS OFF THE FRONT OF THE STAGE AS SHE SPEAKS) Stonehenge should be right at the centre of the map of the world, Tarquin. Eh? (LISTENS TO THE IMAGINARY TARQUIN) No, you can't sail off the edge of the world. Neville …… no map at all; George (HUBBUB INCREASING AGAIN), ten out of ten.

GEORGE	Thank you, Miss.
SHELLEY	And where was your homework, Sidney? Stop tweaking Neville's ear or … (WEAKLY) or you'll be in big trouble. Right, shurrup the lot of you. It's a very important lesson, today. If you are to become Knights of the Round Table – hard to imagine, I know – then, it may be the most important lesson of all ……
GEORGE	(TO IMAGINARY NEIGHBOUR) She's going to tell us the quickest way to like kill people and run away again.
SHELLEY	Today it's the cross-curricular subject of courtly love. It's part biology ……
GEORGE	The birds and the bees at long last! Cool!
SHELLEY	Part sociology, part psychology, so listen carefully. Courtly love, or *l'amour courtois*, as the French call it ….
GEORGE	You didn't mention modern languages, miss!
SHELLEY	Yes, thank you, George. Courtly love is …. how shall I put this … a secret special feeling between a man and a woman. Yes, Neville? (SHE CUPS HER EAR). Like Mum and Dad? No, probably not like your mother and father, Neville.
GEORGE	(ASIDE) Depends who his father *was*, doesn't it?
SHELLEY	(WHILE WRITING BULLET-POINTED ARISTOCRATIC, RITUAL, SECRET, ADULTEROUS, LITERARY ON THE BLACKBOARD OR VIA A POWERPOINT SLIDESHOW) Courtly love is always **aristocratic**; it's the love shared by knights and ladies of noble birth, none of your riff-raff.
GEORGE	So it might be a top knight – Sir Lancelot, say – and, um, a *queen*, just fr'instance?
SHELLEY	An unlikely example, Tarquin, but yes. The lady might well be of higher birth. Anyway, courtly love is full of little **rituals** – handkerchiefs being dropped, little jobs being performed, sonnets being written, and so on. The lady is the master, the man the servant who satisfies her every whim ….
GEORGE	And what does the *man* get out of it, miss?
SHELLEY	Would you please stop interrupting, George! Sidney, take that paint-brush out of your ear and give it back to Gareth. Courtly love is secret. It must not be declared to the world.

	If the world finds out, it's all over. Number 4 – I hope you're all making a note of this! (GEORGE SCRIBBLES FURIOUSLY) – courtly love is **adulterous**. Number 5……
GEORGE	Hang on, miss, what's "adulterous"?
SHELLEY	It means …erk … it means it takes place between two adults. None of you lot are old enough. What's that Tarquin? (CUPS HER EAR AGAIN). Is it when a man creeps into a lady's bedroom while her husband is like safely out of the way, and they …… certainly *not*, Tarquin! The courtly lovers exchange small gifts, read poems, etc, as I said before. In fact, that brings me to the final point: courtly love is always **literary**.
GEORGE	Lots of talking in French!
SHELLEY	Quite probably, yes.
GEORGE	And do we *have* to do all of this when we get older? Ugh! (HE BLOWS A RASPBERRY)
SHELLEY	George, don't do that! It *can* be a little messy, I agree. But I think you'll find there are a few compensations, which you'll understand when you're a little bit older. What's that, Sidney? No, 69 is just a number. No, Neville, there's no need to demonstrate with Gareth. Right, I think that's everything there is to say about courtly love – I *won't* be mentioning it again. So, who can sum up the lesson for me?
GEORGE	(HAND SHOOTING UP) Miss, miss!
SHELLEY	Anyone? (LOOKING ROUND FOR OTHERS TO VOLUNTEER, THEN RELUCTANTLY) All right, George?
GEORGE	Courtly love is a quasi-legitimisation and sublimation of an apparently transgressive social practice involving the pseudo-reversal of gender-based norms, a tokenistic semiology and eventual reinforcement of masculine hegemony and existing socio-economic paradigms. And it's a great chance for us lads to get our leg over.
SHELLEY	Yup, that's about it.

Scene 6: Guinevere's boudoir (front of stage)

Guinevere is draped on a long couch in bath-towel, coronet and shades. She sips from a purple cocktail, complete with umbrella and all the trimmings. Sir Lancelot is patiently painting her toe-nails an even more lurid shade of crimson.

LANCELOT	Thursday?
GUINEVERE	(WEARILY) Shiatsu.
LANCELOT	Friday?
GUINEVERE	Tae-kwondo.
LANCELOT	The weekend?
GUINEVERE	(STUDYING HER FINGERNAILS) Feng shui.
LANCELOT	What, *all* weekend?
GUINEVERE	It's a feng shui workshop. Don't forget the little one!
LANCELOT	Bloody Japanese imports. When *am* I going to get to see you, Gwinny?
GUINEVERE	Sometime, never.
LANCELOT	Gwinny, I dream of you over me, like some gigantic golden eagle, about to sink your talons deep into my lilywhite flesh, the blood oozing ……
GUINEVERE	(BORED) How poetic!
LANCELOT	I want to shout our love out from the rooftops!
GUINEVERE	(FREEZING) I would have you flayed and thrown in a vat of boiling oil.
LANCELOT	Now you're talking!
GUINEVERE	No, seriously, Lancey, my little badger, if you so much as breathe a word of our harmless little trysts, I'll… I'll…
LANCELOT	Yes …. ?
GUINEVERE	I'll … doh! How do you punish a man who loves being punished?
LANCELOT	(CHEERFULLY) Keep trying? I'll tell you what would be really wicked…… (HE WHISPERS IN HER EAR AND A SMILE SPREADS SLOWLY ACROSS HER FACE AS THE LIGHTS FADE)

Scene 7: Up on Prog Rock (front of stage)
Shelley, well wrapped up against the chill wind (sound-effects?) is up on Prog Rock sketching. She is just finishing her last sketch. As she gathers her stuff and begins to cross the stage, a dainty embroidered handkerchief falls unseen to the ground from her back pocket. Simultaneously, Gawain appears suddenly from behind her.

GAWAIN	Shelley! I think you just dropped this! (PICKS UP THE HANKY AND HANDS IT BACK TO HER)
SHELLEY	(TAKING IT) God, how embarrassing, I hope you don't think ....
GAWAIN	(GENUINELY PUZZLED) You hope I don't think what?
SHELLEY	Well, you know, that I dropped it on purpose or anything.
GAWAIN	(STILTED, KEEPING HIS DISTANCE) Good lord, no, I saw it slip out quite accidentally. (EMBARRASSED PAUSE) What a .... what a nice day it is!
SHELLEY	Bloody freezing! (THEY LAUGH NERVOUSLY. PAUSE.)
BOTH	Lovely. Super. Sorry, after you ......
SHELLEY	(EVENTUALLY) No, I was just saying what a lovely view you get from up here on Prog Rock.
GAWAIN	(TRYING TO ADMIRE IT) Ye-es.
SHELLEY	Kestrels, merlins, red kites, martlets, great auks, all sorts, depending on the time of year. (THEY WALK A FEW STEPS) Look at those skylarks – what blithe spirits they are!
GAWAIN	I suppose so.
SHELLEY	I'm sorry, Gawain. Here's me rattling on about the beauties of nature when you've got that terrible *thing* hanging over you.
GAWAIN	(UNCONVINCINGLY) Oh that! The axe? Nearly forgotten it. Long way off. 297 days.
SHELLEY	Gosh, is that all? Time flies when you're ......
GAWAIN	Having fun?
SHELLEY	No, no, I didn't mean ...... you know what I mean!
GAWAIN	I do indeed, but I'm not. (FURTHER EMBARRASSED PAUSE). Shell?
SHELLEY	(too quickly) Yes?
GAWAIN	Shell ...... (LOOKING ANYWHERE BUT AT HER) I wouldn't have the nerve to say this if it wasn't for the fact that I have so little time left .....
SHELLEY	Yes, yes ......
GAWAIN	And I'm pretty sure I know what the answer's going to be. And I don't want to say anything that's likely to put our friendship at .....
SHELLEY	Look, just spit it out will you!? (they face each other now; their eyes lock)
GAWAIN	Shelley, I ...... (FREEZE)

SHELLEY   Oh, Gawain!

Suddenly she can bear it no longer and rushes towards him, dropping her
sketchbook as she goes. She kisses him passionately, despite the clashing of noses,
and he's just beginning to respond with a little more freedom when she pulls away.

GAWAIN   You knew!

SHELLEY   Oh, Gawain, I've always known. (THEY KISS AGAIN IN UTTER
                 JOY)

GAWAIN   (BREAKING AWAY BRIEFLY) I hope you didn't think I was being
                 too forward?

SHELLEY   No, Gawain, I can safely say that thought never began to even
                 contemplate crossing my mind.

GAWAIN   Only I really don't know if I'm going to come back from this
                 ... this *thing* ... alive. Come December 30th, I'll be dead. I feel
                 I have to make the most of every moment that's left to me.

SHELLEY   We will, my love, we will.

GAWAIN   You mean, you'll marry me?

SHELLEY   *Marry* you? Good lord, no. But I'm certainly up for a bit of
                 how's your father. Oh look, a convenient grotto ...

They scamper off the stage, hand in hand, Shelley leading the way.

Curtain.

Scene 8: (in front of curtain)
Shelley is marking some schoolbooks. George rushes in.

GEORGE   Miss, miss, I need your help.

SHELLEY   What on earth's the matter, George?

GEORGE   Haven't you heard? Sir Lancelot's gone missing. It's been a
                 couple of days now. The Queen has offered me a reward of a
                 silver farthing if I can find him.

SHELLEY   He's probably nipped off on another quest.

GEORGE   Isn't a bit cold for quests?

SHELLEY   Last year, he told us how he defeated Grendel, the sea monster.
                 And now he says he's been challenged for a re-match by
                 Grendel's mother.

GEORGE	Grendel's *mother*?
SHELLEY	You're right, it does seem a bit unlikely. Maybe he's called in on King Pele the Grail Guardian and saved his daughter, Elaine, from a vat of boiling water in which she has been imprisoned by a magic spell for several years. Again.
GEORGE	How did this Elaine survive for several years in boiling water?
SHELLEY	Search me. Lancelot is always a bit vague on some of the key details.
GEORGE	Help me find him, miss!
SHELLEY	As it happens, I definitely heard some strange sounds coming from the pig-sties.
GEORGE	Oink, oink, perhaps?
SHELLEY	No, sort of like a man suffering. Listen.

They stop to listen and in the distance there is the sound of Lancelot groaning. Shelley tries to lead George by the hand and find a way through the stage curtain but George hangs back.

GEORGE	I daren't go and have a look in case it's a troll.
SHELLEY	There's no such thing as trolls, George.
GEORGE	Or a werewolf! I think it was that pig-sty over there.
SHELLEY	No harm in taking a look inside …

Shelley and George go to back half of stage via centre curtain. There is a scream from Shelley. No one is visible as the following conversation is heard.

GEORGE	Why hasn't he got any clothes on?
SHELLEY	George! Cover your eyes!
GEORGE	Spoilsport!
SHELLEY	OK, let's get these ropes untied. How long have you been here, Lancelot?
LANCELOT	(WEAKLY) Two days. Why didn't she come for me?
GEORGE	He's gone rather blue.
LANCELOT	It's been sub-zero. I was almost gone.
SHELLEY	Come on, Lancelot, put this round you. Let's get you back to a warm fire.

249

Shelley re-emerges from front of curtain and addresses the audience.

SHELLEY   We've found him. You can all go home now. Nothing to see
                here. You're certainly not going to see Sir Lancelot *completely*
                starkers?!

GEORGE   (ALSO RE-EMERGING BUT LOOKING BACK) But he's not
                completely starkers, is he miss?

SHELLEY   Well, OK. He may have been wearing a small gloved puppet.
                I didn't really see.

GEORGE   A gloved puppet? Is that what it is?

SHELLEY   Yes. (sheepishly) A badger. (GEORGE SNIGGERS). This is a
                serious business! But it's just as well he's wearing it. I'm afraid
                frostbite seems to have badly affected his other extremities.

Enter Guinevere, out of breath.

GUINEVERE   Oh God! Am I too late?

SHELLEY   It's all right, your majesty. We've found him. He's OK.

GUINEVERE   There's been so much happening, I ... I ...

SHELLEY   Yes, your majesty?

GUINEVERE   (DEFEATED FOR A MOMENT, THEN STANDING TALL AND PROUD)
                I don't know what you're sniggering at, young man. Sir
                Lancelot had behaved very badly and he needed some firm
                discipline. As his queen, it fell to me to impose the necessary
                punishment. Now, is there anyone else who requires similar
                chastisement?

GEORGE   No thank you, your majesty (edging towards exit).

GUINEVERE   If I hear a word from anyone! Shoo! Shoo! (she shoos George
                and a very reluctant Shelley off-stage and exits behind them).

Scene 9: Camelot's Courtyard

Enter Shelley, pulling Gringolet, the pantomime horse, Merlin (in his tallest
pointy hat) and Gawain, struggling under the weight of his armour and protective
clothing.

SHELLEY   Now, are you sure you're wrapped up warm enough, Gawain?

GAWAIN   I can hardly breathe under this lot, Shell.

250

SHELLEY	There's a ridge of low pressure coming in from the north, according to the shipping forecast. And you've got your packed lunch? You'll need to make sure you're eating properly.
GAWAIN	I don't think it's going to make much difference when the time comes.
MERLIN	You really don't have to do this, Gawain.
GAWAIN	But I want to. No one has ever let the Round Table down before. How could I be the first? I made a vow.
SHELLEY	(TRYING TO EMBRACE HIM) Oh, Gawain! I'm not sure I can bear to let you go.
GAWAIN	(BRAVELY) Don't worry, Shell, I hope to be gone for just a few days.
SHELLEY	(ALMOST IN TEARS) You'll miss all the Christmas festivities! Oh, Gawain, we'll pray for you!
GAWAIN	Thank you. (THEY KISS, RELUCTANT TO LET EACH OTHER GO.) Shelley, dearest, whatever happens ... well, I will always love you.

Sir Lancelot, wearing his best Christmas jumper, saunters in.

LANCELOT	Ah, Gawain. It is Gawain, isn't it? Auf wiedersehen, old son. King Arthur would have come down to wish you the very best of luck ...
GAWAIN	I sense a "but" coming on ...
LANCELOT	... but he's busy writing his Christmas speech. You'll miss that.
GAWAIN	The king's speech is as much a part of Christmas as turkey and mistletoe.
LANCELOT	We are both proud and envious of you. Yours is one of the most momentous and dangerous quests that ever faced the Knights of the Round Table. I wish I were going myself ...
MERLIN	Well, off you go, then.
LANCELOT	... but I can't do everything. I must conserve all my energy for my life-or-death struggle with Grendel's mother next year. It is time for younger men to go in search of glory. You will bring great honour to this court.

GAWAIN	(GENUINELY OVERWHELMED) It is an honour to represent you all.
LANCELOT	(SHAKING HIS HAND LENGTHILY) Gringolet is a wonderful horse. (HORSE NEIGHS). He will not let you down. And our cartographers have drawn you the very best map possible ….
GAWAIN	I have it here. (HE GESTURES TO HIS BREAST POCKET)
LANCELOT	… although unfortunately the Green Chapel is not actually marked on it …
GAWAIN	I'm sure I'll find it.
LANCELOT	… or indeed anything much else.
GAWAIN	I can always ask. I'm not due there for about a week. Not till dawn on the 30th, a year and a day after the first blow.
LANCELOT	And a very fine beheading it was too. But we too are making a comparable sacrifice. The king has decided to postpone the start of our Christmas party until you come back or until … well, you know!
GAWAIN	That really wasn't necessary.
LANCELOT	Send us a postcard! Chin up. Good luck, my boy.
MERLIN	(TO SHELLEY) He'll need a bit more than that.
GAWAIN	Goodbye everyone!

Gawain mounts Gringolet with great difficulty and the horse attempts to bear him off-stage, followed by the other three.

Scene 10: In Sir Bertilak's castle

Boxing Day, Sir Bertilak's castle. Gawain, still wearing nearly all his clobber, is enjoying a glass of wine, constantly replenished before he has had the chance to make much of a dent in it. Bertilak and Bella also have glasses but they are rarely seen to drink. Each is attired in (medieval) evening dress (much smarter than Gawain) and Bella looks particularly striking in her classical low-cut gown, elaborate hair-do, jewels, etc. As she replenishes his glass, she leans extravagantly over Gawain. He tries hard but fails to avert his gaze.

GAWAIN	This is most awfully kind of you, Sir … Sir Bertilak, did you say?
BERTILAK	No, no, not at all. It's the least we can do at Christmas, especially on a night like this.

BELLA	I'm sure you would do the same for us. I don't think we've met before. My name is Lady Belladonna but you may call me Bella (OFFERS A HAND TO KISS, BUT HE CLUMSILY ENDS UP SHAKING IT, NEARLY SPILLING HIS WINE IN THE PROCESS).
GAWAIN	Delighted to meet you.
BELLA	Let me pour you some more wine. It's from an island on the edge of the world called Madeira.
BERTILAK	And you can call me Bertie – Bertilak is such a mouthful. Make yourself at home. If I were to make a wild stab, I would guess that you are from the court of King Arthur.
GAWAIN	Yes, I …
BELLA	And perhaps you are out on one of those famous "quests" we've heard so much about?
GAWAIN	Yes, I …
BERTILAK	… but you were temporarily lost …
GAWAIN	Yes, I … (pause, but this time he is not interrupted) I was looking for the Chapel of the Green Knight … (MUCH NODDING OF HEADS)
BERTILAK	Ah yes, the Green Knight. (CHUCKLING) Odd chap, eh Bella?
BELLA	(SHARING THE JOKE) He certainly is, Bertie!
GAWAIN	You mean, you know where he lives?
BERTILAK	Why, it's not two score leagues from here! What's that in kilometres?
BELLA	It's not half a day's journey! We can give you precise directions. Have some more Madeira, my dear.
GAWAIN	(GULPING) That's very kind of you, only …
BELLA	When are you expected?
GAWAIN	Oh, not for three or four days, but …
BELLA	Then why not stop here as our honoured guest until you have to go?
GAWAIN	No, no, I couldn't possibly …
BERTILAK	(much more sinister, suddenly) No, we absolutely insist! (SOFTENING AGAIN) You must treat our castle as if it were your own, Gawain. Everything that's mine … (BELLA LEANS OVER TO REPLENISH THE GLASS AGAIN; GAWAIN CAN'T TAKE HIS

	EYES FROM HER CLEAVAGE) … is yours. Just help yourself. And tomorrow we go hunting! There's wonderful sport to be had.
BELLA	As long as you avoid those nasty hunt saboteurs, Bertie.
BERTILAK	It's ridiculous, isn't it? As if we are going to suddenly wipe out the entire population of British bears, lynxes and wolves!
GAWAIN	Of course not.
BERTILAK	So you'll join me and my men tomorrow morning for some sport?
GAWAIN	To be frank, Bertie, I'm absolutely cream-crackered. I'd rather just have a lie-in.
BELLA	(EXCHANGING GLANCES WITH HER HUSBAND) That's very understandable, isn't it, Bertie? I shall still be here. I can, um, look after our guest. (MORE WINE-POURING)
BERTILAK	Well, Gawain, if you insist …but anything we bag while we're out hunting will be our gift to you, our guest of honour.
GAWAIN	But what can I give in return?
BERTILAK	Well, I don't know. Anything you have bagged in the same period? (LAUGHS) No matter. Let's go on through to dinner, Gawain, and you can tell us all about this little "quest" of yours …. (SHEPHERDING HIM OUT)
GAWAIN	It's quite a long story, I'm afraid. It was last Christmas time and we were all having a bit of a do and along came this large, green knight, not sure of his name, and … (AD LIB AS HIS VOICE TRAILS AWAY OFF-STAGE)

The curtain closes, the lights go down and then up only slightly as the curtain reopens. It is three days later (29th Dec 716). Gawain is snoring on the couch, still in most of his armour. Enter Bella in a flimsy nightie and negligee, held in place with a green belt, possibly singing 'I got you, babe'. She tiptoes towards the couch and leans across the sleeping figure.

| BERTILAK | (OFFSTAGE) Honey, I'm home! |

Bella panics and falls on top of Gawain who wakes up. She struggles to retain her dignity but the green belt finishes across his face. She hurries off-stage on the other side. Lights up. Bertilak finally comes in waving his sword excitedly.

BERTILAK	Gawain, you lazy so-and-so! Still in bed! Call yourself a knight?
GAWAIN	(HIDING THE BELT BEHIND HIS BACK) I'm sorry, Bertie. Didn't hear the alarm. Have you finished hunting already? Did you catch a bear?
BERTILAK	No, but we finally nailed this pesky fox. (HE HOLDS UP A MANGY FOX-PELT) You know, the one that has been leading us a merry dance the last three days. This trophy is all yours.

Keeping one hand awkwardly behind his back, Gawain does his best to accept the prize.

GAWAIN	I am humbled and honoured once again. Your generosity as host has known no bounds. I am sure it will be even tastier than that badger you bagged yesterday. I shall be for ever indebted to you.
BERTILAK	Have you nothing for me? No trophies you can trade?
GAWAIN	Embarrassingly few. Just three night-night kisses (STILL HIDING THE BELT, HE DELIVERS THE THREE KISSES, SLOWLY AND DELIBERATELY, INDEED WITH A REVEALING PASSION).
BERTILAK	Steady on, Gawain, this is just a manly thing!
GAWAIN	Sorry, Bertie, didn't want you to be short-changed. And this will be the last time. I must arrive at the Green Chapel at dawn tomorrow.
BERTILAK	You seem to be hiding something behind your back. Do you have something to exchange after all?
GAWAIN	(after a pause, showing the belt) I ... I ... it's nothing really.
BERTILAK	My wife's belt? What is the meaning of this?
GAWAIN	Um, it has no meaning at all ...

He is relieved to see Bella enter, slightly more demurely dressed now.

BELLA	Dawn?! Good morning, husband dearest. And Gawain, are you to leave us today? Surely you will stay with us a few days longer.
GAWAIN	I couldn't possibly impose myself ...
BELLA	Nonsense! I have enjoyed our little tête-à-têtes. I feel we are just getting to know each other.

BERTILAK	And it's icy cold at the moment – you'll catch your death!
GAWAIN	(SIGHING) I might well do that.
BELLA	A few more days can't do any harm!
GAWAIN	(WEAKENING) I ... I ... (looking from one to the other). I tell you what, can I ask the audience?
BERTILAK	It'd mean using up one of your lives ...
GAWAIN	(ALARMED) Would it? Oh, I see. Won't take a moment. (HE STROLLS TO THE FRONT OF THE STAGE AND ADDRESSES THE AUDIENCE DIRECTLY.) OK, audience, what should I do? Should I (a) fulfil my appointment with the Green Knight at daybreak tomorrow, (b) pootle off from here but go straight back to Camelot and say the Green Knight didn't turn up, (c) stay here as a grateful guest, keeping well away from Bella, then head back to Camelot, or (d) stay for a while and enjoy a little "courtly love" with Bella while her husband's out? OK, hands in the air, please – (a) head off for my date with the Green Knight? (counts hands, if any), (b) toddle off back to Camelot? (COUNT AND REACT), (c) live it up with Sir Bertilak? (count). And finally (d) get my end away with the bootilicious Bella? (COUNTS AND ATTEMPTS TO PUT THE RESULT IN PERCENTAGE TERMS, THEN GOES BACK TO BERTILAK AND BELLA.) OK, it seems that XX% of the audience ...
BELLA	(VERY ENTHUSIASTIC) That's quite a high percentage.
GAWAIN	Yes, XX% think I should ... I should ...
BERTILAK	(MORE FIERCELY) Yes?
GAWAIN	That I should ... go for (d). But that would be utterly wrong. If being a knight has taught me one thing, it is that you must be true to the vows you have made. (AUDIENCE BOOS?)
BELLA	Even if it costs you your life?
GAWAIN	Even so. I'm going for (a). I'm off to the Green Chapel.
BERTILAK	Final answer? You've still got 50/50.
GAWAIN	Final answer.
BERTILAK	That's a brave decision. Audience, give Gawain a big hand. (PAUSE, LOOKING AT WATCH) OK, let's take a break now. We'll be back in a few moments to find out whether Gawain made the right decision or not.

Scene 11: At the Green Chapel

30th December 716 AD, dawn. Time for the dry ice machines, if the budget stretches that far, to suggest the bleakest of wintry scenes and the Green Knight's grassy dell and grotto or "chapel". First we see Gawain, in full armour plus Bella's belt, then Gringolet, being reluctantly led. Gawain is scrutinising his map and scratching his head.

GAWAIN   What do you think, Gringolet? The six-figure grid reference is definitely about here and you can see the green chapel symbol on this new map that Sir Bertilak gave me. But there's no chapel here. Gringolet?

Gringolet shrugs his shoulders (if he has any).

GAWAIN   Well, you're a fat lot of use. (CHECKS HIS WATCH) Perhaps the Green Knight is dead and gone? He did look as though he was suffering from verdigree and a year is a long time. Perhaps my magic love-taken (INDICATING BELLA'S BELT) has warded him off? Or maybe I'm just a bit early? I think I'll ask this chap....

Some improvisation may be necessary to allow Bertilak time to disguise himself as the Green Knight but eventually a figure emerges from the murk. Gawain slowly realises that it is the Green Knight. And tries belatedly to hide behind Gringolet.

GREEN Kt   Sir Gawain, welcome to the Green Chapel!
GAWAIN   (SHOWING HIMSELF) Ah, good morning, Mr ... Mr ... I'm sorry, I don't think I ever picked up your name exactly.
GREEN Kt   I am the Green Knight.
GAWAIN   Yes, yes, I know, but ...
GREEN Kt   ... and I am glad to see that you have fulfilled your promise.
GAWAIN   Well, I, I, aim to ...
GREEN Kt   ... enough of the small talk, I think. It is time for you to face the full weight of my axe.

The Green Knight displays his enormous (rubber) axe, touching the blade with his index finger. He winces and licks the blood off his finger, then waits expectantly, but Gawain seems rooted to the spot.

Green Kt	Come on, come on, we haven't got all day!

Slowly and very reluctantly, Gawain goes down on his knees in front of the Green Knight and leans his head forward.

Green Kt	I can't even see your neck through all that armour!

Shaking visibly, Gawain slowly removes his helmet and adjusts his armour so that his neck becomes visible. He bends down again, looking at the ground. The Green Knight raises his axe high above the target.

GREEN Kt	Ready? (NO REPLY) Are you ready, Sir Gawain?
GAWAIN	I am ready.
GREEN Kt	Right. On a count of three. One … two … THREE!

He brings the axe down rapidly but Gawain, who can't see it, jerks away from the impact and the Green Knight stops the axe an inch or two above the target. Gawain gets up, feeling his neck.

GREEN Kt:	How disappointing! I really thought better of you, Sir Gawain.
GAWAIN	I'm sorry, did I move slightly?
GREEN Kt	Just a little. I don't think that's really in the spirit of the game, is it?
GAWAIN	Well …
GREEN Kt	No, it definitely isn't. I must ask you again to prepare to meet your fate. The wheel has come full circle.
GAWAIN	(KNEELING ONCE MORE AND DISPLAYING HIS NECK) I will be brave. I will be brave.

The Green Knight raises the axe once more, emphasizing its huge weight. With a roar he begins to bring it down but once again Gawain flinches away from the expected blow. The Green Knight stops dead in mid-swing. Gawain jumps up again.

GREEN Kt	This really is not cricket!
GAWAIN	I'm sorry, Mr … er … Green Knight. It's just that I could have sworn that I saw something moving. Just over there. Hard to be sure in the morning mist …

GREEN Kt	I can assure you that we are completely alone. I am disappointed in you, Gawain. The honour of the Round Table is at stake.
GAWAIN	I know – I've let King Arthur down. I've let myself down. But it's quite a stressful business, having your head chopped off.
GREEN Kt	Tell me about it! You just have to pick yourself up and move on.
GAWAIN	I'm grateful for your advice, really I am. It's always good to talk to someone who has been there and done it before you. (UNCTUOUSLY) Should I say my prayers again?
GREEN Kt	Look, don't push it, sunshine. It's time to meet your Maker, whoever He may be.
GAWAIN	(SIGHING) This really is it, then …

For a third time Gawain goes down on his knees, bares his neck, etc. He closes his eyes and mouths a prayer as the Green Knight laboriously raises his axe. With a blood-curdling roar, he begins the downswing and this time Gawain stays completely still. The rubber axe just skims Gawain's neck on the way past before burying itself in the stage. The Green Knight struggles to dislodge it from the imaginary turf. Gawain opens his eyes. Disbelievingly, he finds that his head is still attached to his body. He feels his neck and finds the spot where the axe has passed. There is a small wound and he licks the blood from his fingers.

GAWAIN	Gosh, I'm still alive. I'm still alive!! I'm sorry – did I flinch again?
GREEN Kt	No. I have taken my turn. You are free to go. The honour of the Round Table has been upheld.
GAWAIN	I'm not dead!
GREEN Kt	You're nicked, that's all. And it seems you were right – we did have an audience!

Through the dry ice comes Shelley, racing towards him, then George, with Merlin wheezing somewhat behind. Shelley embraces Gawain so violently that she is in danger of causing more damage than he has sustained so far.

SHELLEY	Gawain! You're still alive! My hero! I love you. Still alive – I'm so happy.
GAWAIN	(WINDED) Shelley? What on earth are you doing out here in this god-forsaken place? Have you been following me?

SHELLEY	(UNCERTAINLY) No-o.
GAWAIN	These are the Badlands of Cheshire. There are ogres and dragons and professional footballers at every turn. It is far too dangerous a place for any girl!
SHELLEY	I know, I know. But how could I bear it, watching everyone opening their presents on Christmas Day, knowing that you were out in the ice and snow, perhaps freezing to death ...
GAWAIN	(GUILTILY) Ah, yes ...
SHELLEY	... so I begged Merlin to help me. He said "abracadabra"...
MERLIN	Shazam, actually.
SHELLEY	... and teleported us all here.
GAWAIN	Teleported?
SHELLEY	That's right. Isn't he brilliant?
MERLIN	Well, no one has yet invented a satellite-based tracking system so I had to improvise. Sometimes the old ways are the best. Anyway, here we are, just in time for your ordeal.
SHELLEY	Oh and George came too. (GEORGE WAVES DIFFIDENTLY) Not sure why.
GAWAIN	That's nice.
SHELLEY	You're bleeding, Gawain! It's lucky I thought to bring an Elastoplast. (SHE PRODUCES THE TINIEST STRIP OF ELASTOPLAST, UNPEELS IT AND PLACES IT LOVINGLY ON GAWAIN'S NECK) There!
GAWAIN	Thanks, Shell. But I've absolutely no idea why I'm still alive. That enormous axe, my lilywhite neck – what went wrong, Mr Green Knight? (THE GREEN KNIGHT SHRUGS, SHAMEFACEDLY) Was it a matter of poor technique? Did you have trouble seeing the target through all this dry ice?
GREEN Kt	(MORE MENACING, WRENCHING THE AXE UP AGAIN) Look, I'll have another go if you're not careful!
MERLIN	I think you've got some explaining to do, young man.
GREEN Kt	Indeed I have...

The Green Knight takes off his mask, his wig and other aspects of his disguise to reveal the fact that he is in fact Sir Bertilak. His voice reverts to Sir Bertilak's. Meanwhile Bella emerges through the gloaming on the other side to join the party. Gawain and Shelley watch open-mouthed.

MERLIN	As I thought, Sir Bertilak! But who put you up to this? It was Morgan le Fay, wasn't it?
BERTILAK	(CHUCKLES NON-COMMITTALLY) Arthur's wicked half-sister, disguising herself as my beautiful Belladonna? If that's the story you wish to believe …
MERLIN	What alternative is there?
BERTILAK	Perhaps I am sent here by one of your gods to show you the meaning of true honour and fidelity? You are very lucky indeed that it was Gawain who was left to represent you …
SHELLEY	Gawain, my hero!
BERTILAK	… I suspect that anyone else (GESTURING TO THE AUDIENCE AS WELL AS THE CAST) would have fallen short in the face of so many temptations. Gawain stayed three nights in my castle and was subjected to the most beguiling of temptations (LOOKING AT BELLA) …
SHELLEY	Oh, he was, was he?
BERTILAK	… but he resisted them all. His virtue remained intact. There was just the slightest of slips at the end.
SHELLEY	Oh, there was, was there?
BERTILAK	… when Gawain accepted a very small token of affection, the belt he is wearing round his waist. That tiny slip corresponds to the wound on his neck.
BELLA	Lady Shelley, you are a fortunate young woman indeed.
SHELLEY	Don't I know it!
GAWAIN	So you'll marry me now, Shell?
SHELLEY	(BREAKING AWAY FROM HIM AND FREEZING FOR A SECOND) You stupid boy – of *course* I will!

She hugs and kisses him passionately while the cast [and audience?] cheers, then there is a group hug and general celebration. Gawain pulls off the green belt and throws it over his shoulder, perhaps into the audience.

GAWAIN	I don't suppose the Green Chapel is licensed for wedding services? Merlin can put on his Druidic robes …
MERLIN	I was defrocked, I'm afraid. I wonder if there is a lesson we should learn from all this?
BERTILAK	There are many lessons. Man is part of nature not set against it.

If you destroy the green things, the flora and the fauna, nature will come back ever stronger. After winter comes spring. You should give up your superstitions and quit searching for some imaginary ideal – the truth is all around you. Don't treat strangers and foreigners as enemies. Live in peace with your fellow man.

SHELLEY   Yes, yes, that's all very well but there's a party going on back at Camelot. We need to do some serious celebrating. It's time to get legless because Gawain is not headless. Merlin, could you teleport us all back there?

MERLIN   (TAKING OUT HIS WAND) I'll give it a go. Shazam!

Blackout.

Curtain

AUTHOR'S NOTE

Music to accompany this play, written and recorded by Gross Domestic Product, may be heard at http://tinyurl.com/hna94gc (copyright © PriSm records)

Free Love

Free love has this, different from gold and clay,
That to divide is not to take away...

Shelley, *Epipsychidion*, 1821

This short play recreates the events of December 30ᵗʰ 1816 from the perspective of Claire Clairmont.

Dramatis Personae (in order of appearance)

CLAIRE Clairmont,	Mary Shelley's half-sister
William GODWIN,	author of *Political Justice*, etc
MRS Mary Jane GODWIN,	second wife of the author
Percy Bysshe SHELLEY,	poet
MARY Shelley (née Godwin),	Shelley's second wife, author of *Frankenstein*
Leigh HUNT,	poet and publisher
BESS Kent,	Leigh Hunt's sister-in-law
Thomas Jefferson HOGG,	college friend of Shelley's

The scene is the modest drawing room of William Godwin's rented house in Skinner St, London, around lunchtime on December 30ᵗʰ 1816. Although the décor is showing its age, there are numerous bookcases filled with books – literature of all kinds, philosophy and science, in English and a variety of European languages, reflecting Godwin's broad scholarly interests. Towards the back of the stage, there is a medium-sized table, covered in a white linen tablecloth. On it, there are the makings of a frugal wedding reception. At the front of the table is a multi-layered wedding cake. Dining chairs are placed round the rear of the stage.

Initially, the curtain is closed to conceal this scene.
An old woman, dressed like a widowed Queen Victoria with a walking stick, walks slowly up through the auditorium and climbs uncertainly on to the stage. It is Claire Clairmont.

CLAIRE: Just me left now then. Why did I not drown myself all those years ago, like Shelley? Now they are all dead – Shelley, Byron, Hunt, Hogg, even Mary has been dead for twenty years. But still I must wander the earth like Frankenstein's monster, for ever exiled.

I have never told my story. Mary wrote her novels and her prefaces and her biographical notes – she turned Shelley into a saint. I did not have her gift for language and no one would have believed me anyway. But now there is no one left to gainsay me and – who knows? – it may help me find a little peace before I die.

My name is Claire, Claire Clairmont. Yes, the 'scarlet woman' who bore Byron's "love" child and lived in occasional sin with Shelley – ah, it is all so long ago! Looking back now, there was one day, one event which was at the heart of that blackness. December 30th, 1816, the day Shelley and Mary got married. And I wasn't even there!

This was our family home in Skinner St and here are my mother and stepfather.

Claire sits on a bench front left as the curtain opens to reveal the drawing room and the wedding cake. Mrs Godwin is hurriedly bringing in fresh dishes from the wings, while Godwin in a slightly frayed suit is helping ineffectually. Wedding bells are ringing from a nearby church.

MRS GODWIN: They will be here any second! You're not helping, you know …

GODWIN: Don't fuss, dear. They know to wait a few minutes.

MRS GODWIN: Look at this oxtail – how could the son of a baronet eat that? What will Shelley's friends think of us?

GODWIN: Shelley's friends, if he still has any, were not in church and will not be here. There will hardly be anyone.

MRS GODWIN: And where is poor Jane? Why is she not here?

GODWIN: Jane? You know we must call her Claire now.

MRS GODWIN: Jane, Claire, she is still my daughter. I could bear it if

	she were here.
GODWIN:	They say Claire must look after my grandson in Bristol.
	And that she is not very well.
MRS GODWIN:	Do you believe that? (NOISES OFF)
GODWIN:	No matter. They are here.

Godwin goes to open the door. Shelley carries Mary on stage back left, as if over the threshold. Both are dressed for their wedding but very soberly so. Mary is in noticeably higher spirits than Shelley. He puts her down abruptly, and they greet each other without obvious signs of affection. Meanwhile, Claire offers the following commentary.

CLAIRE:	The happy couple! The notorious poet and atheist, Shelley, and my sister, Mary. I say "sister" but she was not really that. William Godwin was my mother's second husband – I never knew my true father. And Mary never knew *her* mother, the great Mary Wollstonecraft, because she died giving birth to Mary. So the widowed Godwin married again and found himself with three daughters, not one. We all grew up here in this scruffy house in Skinner St – there was no money even to pay the rent. Mary was always the pretty one. I don't think my mother liked that ...
GODWIN:	(EMBRACING HIS DAUGHTER) Mary! You make your poor old father so proud! How did you get to be so beautiful?
MARY:	Nonsense, Papa.
GODWIN:	My heart was pounding as we walked down the aisle together. I don't think there can ever have been a more beautiful bride. You are a very lucky man, Shelley.
SHELLEY:	(SHAKING HANDS TENTATIVELY WITH GODWIN) I know.
GODWIN:	And welcome to our humble abode!
SHELLEY:	It has been a long time.
GODWIN:	Indeed it has, but let us not talk of that today.

They freeze as Claire rises sharply and waves her stick at them.

CLAIRE:	I think perhaps we should. None of us has set foot in our home for two years! Why? Because my stepfather made it plain we were not welcome – and especially not Shelley, the evil seducer of his 16-year-old daughter, father of her bastard children, malign corrupter of every girl he met. One small problem – Shelley's money might save Godwin from bankruptcy. And Shelley is finally doing the decent thing – no wonder my stepfather is so happy!

And I was happy too, for one brief instant, the instant Shelley first invited himself here on the pretext of introducing himself to the great William Godwin. Look at the man! (SHE STROLLS ROUND SHELLEY, POINTING AT HIM WITH HER STICK) Look at his eyes, his cheekbones, his lustrous hair, his bearing, his graceful manner. We three girls all fell in love with him in that single second, here in this room. But Mary was the prettiest and the cleverest … what chance did her sisters stand?

And now they all pretend that nothing has happened. |

They unfreeze.

MRS GODWIN:	But there are some people at the door. (SHE BUSTLES OVER TO OPEN IT) Ah, Mr Hunt and Bess and … I do not believe I know you, sir?

Leigh Hunt enters, with his sister-in-law Bess Kent on his arm, while Jefferson Hogg follows diffidently behind.

HOGG:	My name is Hogg, madam. Jefferson Hogg.
SHELLEY:	(ANIMATED AT LAST) Jefferson! Thank you for coming back! Hogg, this is my new father-in-law, Godwin, and Mrs Godwin, of course.
HOGG:	(BOWING) It is very kind of you to welcome us into your house.
SHELLEY:	And you too, Hunt. My oldest best friend and my

	newest best friend. How I would have gone mad without you both, especially these last three weeks.
HUNT:	I only wish we could have done more.
SHELLEY:	(TO GODWIN) Hunt is going to publish my 'Hymn to Intellectual Beauty'!
HUNT:	No need – you have married her instead! (SHELLEY ALONE LAUGHS, LONG AND HARD)
SHELLEY:	And he and Hogg are helping with the court case.
GODWIN:	Ah, the court case. Drinks, everyone, we will start with a drink. (GESTURING TO HIS WIFE) Dearest …

Mrs Godwin scuttles round, serving small glasses of madeira to each person, while Claire takes her chance.

CLAIRE:	The court case. And so we approach the heart of the matter. Shelley wants custody of the two children of his first marriage. To win the case, he must show that he is respectably married and can offer a stable, family home. In the next few days the case will be heard by Lord Eldon in Chancery. This whole charade serves that end…
GODWIN:	So let us drink a toast to the bride and groom (glasses are raised) …

There is some half-hearted clinking of glasses and confused echoes.

GODWIN:	I am sure that some more guests will be with us in a minute and we will be able to enjoy this extraordinary cake. Is your friend Peacock coming, Shelley? Or Haydon?
SHELLEY:	Who? … I'm not sure …
GODWIN:	I saw that none of your family was in church.
SHELLEY:	It was all such short notice … Horsham is a long way …
MRS GODWIN:	(LAUGHING AWKWARDLY) Do they even know about it, Mr Shelley?
SHELLEY:	I … yes, yes of course … but (GESTURING ROUND THE ROOM) it would have been difficult …

MRS GODWIN:	Because our house is too small?
GODWIN:	Now, now, Mary Jane! Let us all be happy. For today, at least.
MRS GODWIN:	But where is my daughter? I have not seen her for so long. What have you done with her, Mr Shelley?
SHELLEY:	I have done nothing with her! (ALL FREEZE)
CLAIRE:	Not strictly true, of course. Shelley has spent a lot of time with me over the last two years and more, walking out, talking, "consoling" me on my misfortunes, sometimes a little more ... why, this very date is ringed in my diary because on 30th December 1814, Bysshe and I walked out to Kensington Park and ... (CLAIRE SIGHS AT THE MEMORY) – when we got back we told Mary and that fool Hogg who was sniffing round, as ever, that the gates of the park had been locked and we had been stuck inside! How I loved him then. It all seems so long ago and that is *not* why I am stuck in Bristol!

The truth is ... I am pregnant, eight and a half months pregnant with Byron's child. In a few days I will give birth to the most beautiful girl, Alba – or Allegra, as Byron will make me call her – but even my mother does not know. Thus I will bring further disgrace on my "poor" parents.

I'm sure you know the story. Byron ... "Lord" Byron as the world knows him ... seduced me heartlessly and when I was pregnant, dropped me like a hot pototo to run back to his half-sister and countless other whores.

SHELLEY:	(UNFREEZING AND APPROACHING HER) Ah, but that is not quite true is it, Claire?
CLAIRE:	It is absolutely true.
SHELLEY:	Did he seduce you? Or did you send him a letter, out of the blue without ever having met, *giving* yourself to him? Then did you not make all the arrangements, where to meet, how to keep it secret...
CLAIRE:	It was just a letter! I did not know he would use me and

	then wander off to Geneva without so much as a by your leave ...
SHELLEY:	Geneva! And who should he find when he got there but ... Claire Clairmont?
CLAIRE:	Not just me! You and Mary too, it was your idea! And then he seduced me all over again.
SHELLEY:	(SHAKING HIS HEAD SADLY) Claire, Claire! Even at seventeen, you knew how it would turn out.
CLAIRE:	I did not know he would abandon me.
SHELLEY:	You were too *forward* ... he would not marry such a girl.
CLAIRE:	I thought he would want to be with me and his child.
SHELLEY:	No, the truth is, you saw what Mary had, with me, and you wanted the same thing, only better. A lord, not a mere baronet. The famous author of *Childe Harold*, not a dreamy failure like me.
CLAIRE:	This is all nonsense! He took advantage of my innocence and used me cruelly. Just as you did!
SHELLEY:	What?! I cannot talk to you when you are in this mood. I must return to my wedding day and my lovely bride.

He rejoins the party which unfreezes.

MRS GODWIN:	Is Claire not well? I have a mother's instinct that something is wrong.
MARY:	She is perfectly healthy, mama. But someone has to look after little William for us.
GODWIN:	I shall spend some time with my grandson from now on. I will teach him Latin.
MARY:	He is a little young for that! Perhaps soon he will have a little brother or sister to play with ...
CLAIRE:	(ASIDE) A mother's instinct? Mary will have a baby girl, Clara, almost nine months from now.
MARY:	... William is a sturdy chap but he does pester me when I am trying to check the proofs of this cursed Frankenstein thing.
SHELLEY:	I'm sure he will have lots of playmates. And the book is

269

	nearly done. You will be famous, Mrs Shelley, and we will be rich.
MARY:	Mrs Shelley ... Mary *Shelley* – how can I get used to *that?* (THEY LAUGH) When we are rich, will we have a little house of our own, just you, me and William?
SHELLEY:	And what of your poor sister, Claire?
MRS GODWIN:	She will always be welcome here. Especially now that Fanny is ... Fanny is *gone* ... (FREEZE)
CLAIRE:	Gone? Enough of weasel words – she is dead. Dead! Did you never hear of Fanny? Fanny Imlay, orphaned daughter of Mary Wollstonecraft and a failed actor, and brought up by Godwin, alone at first, and then as a big "sister" to me and Mary. Fanny was quiet and, let's be honest, very plain. She fell in love with Shelley like the rest of us, but no one noticed. While we gallivanted off to Geneva and set up our little "communities", Fanny was stuck here in Skinner St with her dowdy parents. Fanny wrote to Mary and to me and even to Shelley and begged to be allowed to visit, perhaps even to stay with us. Sometimes I confess we laughed at her behind her back. Then, just two months ago, she sent a desperate letter to us in Bristol, threatening to end it all. Shelley saw her, I think, and turned her down flat, then she journeyed on into Wales to a quiet boarding house. By the time Shelley followed her and found her, she was dead in her little room. Laudanum. Did we grieve for her? No, we were all too busy keeping her identity out of the papers, avoiding scandal. No one knew her, no one missed her.
	And now, fifty years on, how do I view Fanny? As the wise virgin who foresaw the truth – that there was nothing in this vale of tears for her. I wish I'd had the courage to do likewise.
	Do you think it's callous to arrange a wedding so soon after such a family catastrophe? (LAUGHS) Oh but there is more, so much more ...

The party splits into groups of two or three with their drinks. Mary and Hogg emerge at the front.

MARY: Thank you for coming, Prince Prudent. I know it can't have been easy.

HOGG: It hasn't been easy for any of us.

MARY: I think things may be a little bit different from now on. But I just wanted you to know that I remember your kindness to me and our times together with fondness.

HOGG: (STIFFLY) Just as I do. But I don't think I will be calling you "my dormouse" in days to come. Nor will I be your "sweet Alexy".

MARY: (PUTTING HER HAND ON HIS ARM) You will always be my sweet Alexy. Just not in *that* way ... (THEY FREEZE)

CLAIRE: And what way was that we wonder? I think it is time for a little heart to heart with Mr Jefferson Hogg.

She summons him over; he comes forward reluctantly.

CLAIRE: So, Mr Hogg ... we shared a house together, yet I know so little about you. Tell me your story.

HOGG: I met Shelley when we were both undergraduates at University College, Oxford, and our lives have been intertwined ever since, perhaps always will be. I helped him write the pamphlet advocating the necessity of atheism, for which we both got sent down. Then, when he eloped with Harriet Westbrook on her sixteenth birthday, Shelley invited me to share their honeymoon in Edinburgh.

CLAIRE: A strange thing to do ...

HOGG: Well, we both know that Shelley is utterly hostile to the institution of marriage, but it wasn't that. It's more that he was scared of being alone for any period of time with just one person. Even then he talked of a community of like-minded individuals, sharing everything.

CLAIRE: Everything?

HOGG:	Yes, everything. He called it a Godwinian arrangement. Hence the little "misunderstanding" which I'm sure you heard about.
CLAIRE:	Perhaps. I heard that Shelley was called away to London and you propositioned the poor girl.
HOGG:	I shudder to think of it now. She was rightly horrified. I thought Shelley had set the whole thing up that way. Indeed, I'm sure he did, but he just hadn't got round to clearing it with Harriet.
CLAIRE:	He *wanted* you to make love to his bride?
HOGG:	I thought so. I was young and innocent too. And Harriet was heartbreakingly beautiful. I was infatuated. Perhaps she married the wrong man.
CLAIRE:	There is no doubt of that. Poor Harriet! Whisked off her feet at fifteen, then she defended her "honour" until she was safely married. But for her there was no safety in marriage, was there?
HOGG:	Not when he met you and Mary, no. I tried to help her, once she'd forgiven me, but ...
CLAIRE:	But it didn't stop you coming to live with us in Arabella Rd, did it?
HOGG:	I ... I ... Shelley can be very persuasive, can't he?
CLAIRE:	What a cosy foursome that was! Mary was pregnant and for a while Shelley seemed to find me rather better company.
HOGG:	It was the same thing, wasn't it? Shelley was not equipped for monogamy and when he was out with you, he felt it was only fair ...
CLAIRE:	That Mary should find some consolation with you?
HOGG:	Nothing ever happened, you know. And then she lost the baby a few days after it was born and it was never quite the same after that.
CLAIRE:	Oh, bad luck! So you missed your chance with the first Mrs Shelley and then also with the second Mrs Shelley, as she is now. Are you attracted to anyone *apart* from Shelley's conquests?

HOGG:	With Mary I was just playing the part I thought Shelley wanted me to play. I think Mary would say the same thing. Our hearts weren't really in it. With Harriet …
CLAIRE:	You really loved her? Was she carrying your baby when she …?
HOGG:	Now is not the time to talk about it. It's just three weeks. Three weeks! I should never have come today. The whole thing is barbaric.

Hogg rejoins the others, leaving Claire to speak to the audience alone.

CLAIRE:	And indeed Mary was not the last Shelley-substitute in Hogg's life. After Shelley and Edward Williams were drowned in the Gulf of Spezia in 1822, Hogg was just the man to console Jane Williams, Shelley's final paramour. The young widow came back to England and Hogg wooed her diligently until they married and – who knows? – lived happily ever after. Hogg could never have his first love – Percy Bysshe Shelley – but at the third time of asking he got the next best thing.

I have come back to haunt this feast like Banquo's Ghost but really it should be Fanny or Harriet playing this role. How can these people sip their madeira and make polite conversation when it is just *three weeks* since Harriet has been fished out of the Serpentine? Shelley's lawful wedded wife had been missing for more than a month and none of us even *knew*.

Shelley learnt of his wife's death in a letter from his publisher, Thomas Hookham. His publisher! Harriet, pregnant, almost destitute and friendless, left her two children by Shelley and walked to Hyde Park and into the cold, welcoming water of the Serpentine. This was the letter she left for Shelley and her sister, Elizabeth.

Claire takes out a letter from inside her dress, waves it to the audience and starts to read.

CLAIRE:	'When you read this letter, I shall be no more an inhabitant of this miserable world. Do not regret the loss of one who could never be anything but a source of vexation and misery to you all ... (SCANNING DOWN THE PAGE) ... I have rushed on my own destruction. (MORE SCANNING) My dear Bysshe, let me conjure you by the remembrance of our days of happiness to grant my last wish – do not take your innocent child from Eliza who has been more than I have, who has watched over her with such unceasing care. – Do not refuse my last request – I never could refuse you and if you had never left me I might have lived but as it is, I freely forgive you and may you enjoy that happiness which you have deprived me of. Now comes the sad task of saying farewell – oh I must be quick. God bless & watch over you all. You, dear Bysshe and you, dear Eliza. God bless you all is the last prayer of the unfortunate Harriet S—'

And yet here we are, a few days later, going through this charade of a marriage so that Chancery will grant you (GESTURING TO SHELLEY) custody of Ianthe and baby Charles. Could you not even respect her final wishes?

SHELLEY:	(COMING FORWARD TO DEFEND HIMSELF) It is my right as their father and my responsibility!
CLAIRE:	It is your *right*? Then the law is an ass. Byron will use the same words in taking my lovely Alba from me and what will he do with her?
SHELLEY:	I have no idea.
CLAIRE:	He will ignore her and place her in a rat-infested convent – no, *prison* – in some disease-ridden Italian marshland, and ... and ...
SHELLEY:	And what?
CLAIRE:	(COLLAPSING IN TEARS) He will murder her. There, I have said it. He will murder my lovely girl. And *he* had the wealth to look after her properly; you do not even have that. What sort of life will you be offering Ianthe

	and Charles if you win your case?
SHELLEY:	The same as for baby William.
CLAIRE:	Hah! That boy will be dragged across Europe, forced to endure conditions that no child should ever face.
SHELLEY:	Why? We hope to live quietly in Marlow.
CLAIRE:	(SHE BEATS INEFFECTUALLY ON HIS CHEST) Because ... because ... oh, I cannot bear it! But you will not win – this charade will be in vain. Lord Eldon will grant custody of Ianthe and Charles to Elizabeth and Harriet's parents. The children will be spared their father and you will never see them again. Not once. Your lovely Ianthe will grow up happy and healthy and your only grandchildren will be hers.
SHELLEY:	Why are you telling me all this? I who have done so much for you? Mary and I will welcome you and your baby to our new home. To you, Mary has been like ....
CLAIRE:	Like a sister?
SHELLEY:	Like a rock. And from now on I will be like a rock to her. This whole business with Harriet has taught me many things. I will not make the same mistakes again. I shall start right now (he goes back to put an arm round his wife).
CLAIRE:	(SHOUTING AFTER HIM) You can never change! Perhaps none of us can.

She returns to her seat and puts her head in her hands, sobbing silently.

GODWIN:	We cannot wait for ever. It seems that no one else is coming back from St Mildred's. So I'd like to say a few words and then perhaps the lovely bride will cut the cake and we will share that, er, sacrament.
	Ladies and gentlemen, thank you for sharing our happiness with us today. We all hope to show our support and love as Bysshe and Mary start out on their married life together. It will be a long and sometimes difficult journey, I'm sure, but with so much literary talent as well as love to sustain them, and with the

275

support of their friends and family, I am sure they will do the old institution of marriage proud. If they are half as happy in marriage as Mary Jane and I have been, then they will be lucky indeed.

I could not let this moment pass without some words about our dear, departed daughter, Fanny, for whom we all still grieve. I am sure she will be always in our hearts. And it is a shame that little William could not be here on his parents' big day. And our other daughter, Jane, I mean Claire, of course. So let us drink a toast to absent friends.

ALL: (RAISING EMPTY GLASSES) Absent friends!

GODWIN: And now, Mary, will you do the honours?

Mary takes a large knife and begins to hack at the cake, shovelling slices on to plates. The hubbub rises as these are shared round. Hunt and Hogg take their cake to a spot where they will not be overheard.

HUNT: A very pretty speech for one who holds such views as his!

HOGG: Delicately done, I'm sure. I don't think there will be any mention of "free love" today.

HUNT: Godwin was a young man when he wrote *Political Justice* – we can hardly blame Godwin for all this.

HOGG: But don't you see that that was why Shelley hunted out Godwin in the first place – it validated his own instinct for polygamy. And it was a real bonus that Mary and Claire had grown up in an environment where such ideas had been put into practice. He sensed that these two 16-year-olds would be more compliant than Harriet had ever been, and so it has proved.

HUNT: It is a bitter pill for the old man to take, having to try to protect his daughter from exactly the sort of relationship that he had himself advocated.

HOGG: Wait till he hears what has happened to Claire!

HUNT: Some time later today, I should imagine. I don't think

	we should be here to see it.
HOGG:	But can't we have our cake and eat it first? (THEY LAUGH)
SHELLEY:	(tinkling his glass; the others fall silent) I would just like to reply on behalf of myself and Mrs Shelley. You will all know that Mary and I have been living together as man and wife for some time so this is just the icing on the cake, as it were. And delicious icing it is too! Marriage will not change our love for one another or our feelings towards our friends and family. It will be the best of all Godwinian arrangements. We want to thank all those who have stood by us these last two years when we lost our baby and … and all the other events that have befallen us.

They all freeze. The lighting gradually fades until Claire stands alone in one spotlight. A second spotlight picks out each of the characters in turn.

CLAIRE:	Enough, enough! Such hypocrisy! You are all ghosts and you cannot hurt me now! How will all your hopes turn out? I will tell you.
	Leigh Hunt, you face a long slow decline into poverty and isolation. Your journals will fail and the men who might have helped you, like Byron and Shelley, will all be dead. Your domestic affairs are already a scandal in polite society and one day Dickens will make fun of you as Skimpole in *Bleak House*. Your sister-in-law, Bess, will find solace in writing a best-selling book about pot plants but that will not keep you in your old age.
	Thomas Jefferson Hogg, your legal career will be blighted by the deeds of your youth but you will live happily enough with Jane Williams, surviving blackmail attempts and a life of obscurity. There will be no more *Memoirs of Prince Alexy Haimatoff* and your half-written biography of Shelley will be littered with lies and prevarications. You will die, appropriately enough, of gout.

Mr and Mrs Godwin, you too face penury and the scorn of polite society. Shelley will never give you the money that you crave, partly because he never has any to give. You will be the last to hear about my scandalous affair with Byron and the child that will be born a few days from now. You will never forgive me, nor will I ever be welcome in Skinner St again.

Shelley, your fate is well-known. Soon you will come with me to Italy to help me deliver Alba to Byron. You, Mary and I will not return – at least, until you, like Harriet, are drowned. Your little racing boat, the *Don Juan,* will go down not far from our little beach-house on the Bay of Lerici. You will be buried close to John Keats in the Protestant Cemetery in Rome.

And you, sister Mary? Your heart will be broken long before Shelley's death, not just by the pain of exile and your husband's infidelities but by the loss of your children. William will die quickly in the heat of an Italian summer, from malaria. The baby you are now carrying, Clara, will contract dysentery and waste away. Only your fourth child, Percy, will survive. Somehow you will keep going after Shelley's death. *Frankenstein* will bring you fame and fortune. You will dedicate yourself to your husband's literary legacy and the rehabilitation of his reputation. You will never marry again and you will die long before me.

So now I'm the only one left. I never married, never had another child. Byron and Shelley were my only lovers and I could never trust another man after that. I had no money and would have to work as a governess to make ends meet. But who would let someone like me with my reputation and supposed radical views close to their children? I had to go far, far from England, to the ends of the earth where my name was not known. I went to Prince Alexy's fabled home, St Petersburg, and nearly died of cold. I worked in Moscow, Vienna, Paris, gradually closer to the home I could never return to. I did not walk into the Serpentine, my pockets weighted down with stones.

What did I learn in those far off times? Under the influence of the doctrine of free love, I saw the two finest poets of England become monsters of lying, meanness, cruelty and treachery. Under the influence of free love, Lord Byron became a human tiger slaking his thirst for inflicting pain upon defenceless women.

I was a moth singed by that flame. I gave Shelley the best eight years of my life, sharing him with Mary and a host of others. I almost bore his child too, but it wasn't to be. On the very day that I lost the baby, Shelley's Swiss maid, Elise, actually did bear his child. How could anyone forgive him that? But I did. He held us all under his spell.

I was Shelley's creature and, with my creator dead, I had no choice but to wander the earth alone, even to the frozen north, cursed and shunned by almost everyone who knew who I was.

Free love is a destroying scourge which immolates its victims and causes bitter tears to flow, mine most of all. Shelley and Mary's wedding day was a brief moment of hypocrisy and self-serving cant but at least marriage brought Mary a little peace and happiness before the storm clouds gathered once again.

I have trespassed on your patience too long already. Farewell!

The spotlight dies.

Curtain.

AUTHOR'S NOTE

A longer version of this play, written for radio, may be heard at http://tinyurl.com/pkxy8qh (copyright © the author)

Yusupov and Rasputin

based on the autobiography *Lost Splendor*, by Prince Felix Yusupov

Dramatis Personae

Felix Yusupov	A wealthy Russian prince, aged 29 – perfectly groomed, effete and well-educated
Grigori Rasputin	Siberian starets (mystic) and adviser to Empress Alexandra, aged 47 – dark, unkempt and mysterious
Dmitri Pavlovich	Grand duke and cavalry officer, aged 25 – dashing, handsome, rash but ineffectual
Oswald Rayner	An Oxford-educated English spy, aged 27, posted to St Petersburg – meticulous and efficient
Stephen Alley	A second upper-class English spy, recently posted to St Petersburg
Alexandra	Empress and wife of Tsar Nicholas II, aged 44, mother of Alexy – imperious, with a strong Germanic accent
Anna Vyrubova	Best friend and confidante of Alexandra (and Rasputin), aged 32 – silly and manipulative
Prince Alexy	Haemophiliac heir to the Romanov throne, aged 12 – drowning in mother love
Dr Stanislaus Lazovert	GP and conspirator – bumbling, out of his depth
Vladimir Purishkevich	Monarchist member of the Duma and conspirator, aged 46 – crotchety and frightened
Sergei Sukhotin	Injured war-veteran and conspirator, with both arms swathed in bandages – incapacitated but decent man
Policeman	Beat officer – assiduous, dimly aware of the awkwardness of his position
Servant (Ivan)	At the Moika Palace, general dogsbody

Setting

A basement room of the Moika Palace, St Petersburg, December 29-30 1916.

The room features, just above head height, numerous portraits in oil of notable Russian figures, including Tsar Nicholas II, all in full military attire or splendid evening wear. Primitive electric lights enhance the display.

There is a large old wardrobe (with keyholes), back stage, just large enough to conceal two men uncomfortably. It should have a false back, allowing exit to the rear. A guitar is propped up next to it.

As well as the regal furniture, we see a samovar and an aga-like oven. There is also a drinks cabinet with delicate crystal decanters and numerous musty Madeira bottles on top, together with a copy of the Memoirs of *Prince Alexy Haimatoff*. There is a plush divan or ottoman (amongst other chairs), with a bell-pull close by, a small table with a chess set on it, pot plants in a corner, and a tiny circular drinks table with a revolving top.

One "outside" door (preferably up some stairs) is clearly visible stage right. It has a large key protruding.

It must be possible to run a circuit via this door and an exit on the other side, travelling via the front-of-stage area.

Scene 1 (Moika Palace, early evening, 29 December 1916)

As the curtain goes up, we find Felix, casually attired in a dressing gown, installed on an ottoman. He is smoking a long, slim cigarette in a cigarette holder and reading a military manual. He reaches for the bell-pull and we hear the bell sound in a neighbouring room. Enter Ivan, a Servant. Felix puts his book aside.

FELIX:	Ah, Ivan, good man, I have a little job for you this evening.
SERVANT:	Yes, sir?
FELIX:	I need you to bake me some cakes.
SERVANT:	Some cakes, sir?
FELIX:	Yes, twenty small cakes, half-baked.
SERVANT:	Half-baked?
FELIX:	I do worry about your hearing sometimes, Ivan. Yes, half-

	baked. I will finish baking them myself here.
SERVANT:	I will ask Natasha, the cook ...
FELIX:	If I wanted Natasha to cook them, I would have asked her myself. I am giving Natasha and the rest of the staff the evening off. They are not to know about the cakes, or anything else.
SERVANT:	I see, sir. But I have never baked anything in my life! (FELIX GLARES AT HIM.) What sort of cakes?
FELIX:	Oh, I don't know. Use your imagination. Rock cakes? Cherry buns? I am expecting a few people over this evening – Dmitri and some of his friends.
SERVANT:	Very well, sir, I will do my best. (A DOORBELL RINGS) I imagine that will be them now.
FELIX:	Yes, let them in, would you, and then get baking. I am relying on you, Ivan!

Exit Servant, back left. Felix jumps to his feet and fidgets with the empty decanters and glasses on the drinks table. He is looking the other way as the Servant returns, somewhat agitated. Close behind are the Empress Alexandra, Anna Vyrubova and Prince Alexy, all wearing thick winter overcoats flecked with snow.

SERVANT:	Prince Felix, it is her Imperial Highness, Tsaritsa Alexandra and Prince Alexy, and ...
ANNA:	Anna Vyrubova.
SERVANT:	Anna Verybova.

Felix drops a glass on the tray – it may or may not smash. He turns round to greet them.

FELIX:	Good heavens! Your majesty! How nice to see you!
ALEXANDRA:	(ALLOWING HER CHEEK TO BE KISSED, AS HER COAT IS TAKEN BY THE SERVANT) Good evening, Felix. I hope you are not too busy?
FELIX:	No-oo. (TRYING TO CATCH A GLIMPSE OF HIS WATCH) I'm afraid that Irina is not here this evening, your majesty.
ALEXANDRA:	Call me Alex, please.
FELIX:	She has gone to one of our country estates for the New Year celebrations.

282

ALEXANDRA:	Oh, really? Where is that?
FELIX:	It is called the Crimea. It is one of our larger estates.
ALEXANDRA:	(SITTING) It is *you* I want to see, Felix.
FELIX:	Ah. A glass of, um, Madeira?
ALEXANDRA:	No, thank you. I just want a few words. In private. (SHE LOOKS POINTEDLY AT THE SERVANT WHO IS STRUGGLING UNDER THE WEIGHT OF ALL THE COATS)
FELIX:	Ivan, will you leave us for a few moments. We are *not* to be disturbed. Do you understand?
SERVANT:	Yes, sir. (EXIT)
ANNA:	Her majesty has come on a matter of considerable delicacy, Felix.
ALEXANDRA:	Yes, thank you, Anna, I can handle this. Perhaps you would like to play a game of chess with darling Alexy?
ALEXY:	Mother! Auntie Anna is barely club standard!
ALEXANDRA:	Then let her play white! (ANNA AND ALEXY GO RELUCTANTLY TO THE CHESSBOARD AND START TO PLAY) These are difficult times, Felix …
FELIX:	I am well aware of that, your ma … er, Alex.
ALEXANDRA:	The war is *not* going well. I wish it had never been started. Poor Nicky hasn't been home from the Front for months.
FELIX:	I hope that he is not hurt?
ALEXANDRA:	Oh, he is not *that* close to the Front. That would be too awful. His ears would not stand it. But he must be seen to be close by, advising his generals, that sort of thing.
FELIX:	I hope to be there soon myself. I have an Officers' Entrance Exam tomorrow and I have been swotting for it all day. (HE WAVES THE BOOK IN THE AIR.)
ALEXANDRA:	We appreciate your dedication and loyalty, Felix, really we do. But I am not sure that you are really equipped for … for the hardships of battle.
FELIX:	It will be an honour to fight for Mother Russia.
ALEXANDRA:	Yes, yes, I suppose so. Meanwhile, *I* must do what I can to keep the Duma in order.
FELIX:	The tsar could have wished for no more able deputy!
ALEXANDRA:	I have no interest in politics. All my time is taken up with

	looking after poor, poor Alexy.
ALEXY:	I'm quite all right, mother! (TO ANNA) That's check, by the way.
ALEXANDRA:	So I must rely on my most trusted adviser.
FELIX:	Of course you must.
ALEXANDRA:	Look Felix, I know you don't like Mr Rasputin very much.
FELIX:	Rasputin? I … I …
ALEXANDRA:	There is no need to pretend, Felix. But he is a holy man, a good man. Poor Alexy would be dead by now …
ALEXY:	(LOUDLY) Checkmate! Finished …
ALEXANDRA:	Well, start again!
ALEXY:	I'll give her a knight start this time.
ANNA:	I don't need a knight start!
ALEXANDRA:	Yes, poor Alexy would have bled to death by now if it wasn't for the extraordinary healing powers of the starets. That idiot Lazovert was trying to give him aspirin! We owe Rasputin everything. And he tells me that we *can* make peace and a favourable settlement.
FELIX:	What, with the Huns! Never! I'd rather die, or at least be seriously injured, than give up an *inch* of our rightful territory.
ALEXANDRA:	We have given up quite a few inches already. You forget I am German, Felix! These are my cousins we are fighting. And Rasputin says …
FELIX:	Rasputin! Rasputin! My dear Alex…
ALEXANDRA:	Don't say another word, Felix. In fact it is about Rasputin that I have come tonight.
FELIX:	(GLANCING ROUND UNEASILY) Yes, your ma …?
ALEXANDRA:	You must have heard what they are saying, Felix.
FELIX:	I don't think so, no.
ALEXANDRA:	… that there is a plot to kill Rasputin …
FELIX:	Surely not?
ALEXANDRA:	… here in St Petersburg. I have come here to warn you that there are some who are saying … no doubt wrongly and without any foundation at all … (THE DOORBELL RINGS. FELIX LOOKS ROUND ANXIOUSLY.)

284

FELIX:	*What* are they saying?
ALEXANDRA:	They are saying, Felix, that you … that *you* …
FELIX:	That *I* am involved in some sort of plot?
ALEXANDRA:	It is ridiculous, of course. I just thought I should warn you, about what some silly people are saying, that is all.

Enter Servant.

SERVANT:	Prince Felix …
FELIX:	Not now, Ivan! Whoever it is, put them in the kitchen and offer them a drink.
SERVANT:	But … (FELIX GLARES POINTEDLY.) Very well, sir. (EXIT)
FELIX:	I am most grateful to you, of course, Alex, but …
ALEXANDRA:	I *know* I can rely on you, Felix. Find these people and tell them that Rasputin is a good man, maybe even a saint. If anything were to happen, I'm sure that Nicky … I'm sure that Nicky and I would … well, let's just say, it would be very *bad* for whoever …
ALEXY:	Checkmate! Again!
ANNA:	Why, you little … I have played two games. That is enough.
ALEXANDRA:	We are going now, Anna. (SHE GATHERS UP HER THINGS. FELIX REACHES FOR THE BELL-PULL.) Don't worry, Felix, we can see ourselves out. Remember what I have said. Oh and please give my love to my favourite niece, Irina, when she returns from – what did you call your estate? Ah, yes, the Crimea.
FELIX:	If I might say a few words …
ALEXANDRA:	There is no more to be said, Felix. I am sure my meaning is absolutely clear. Good evening!

Alexandra sweeps past Felix, offering her hand for the briefest of kisses. Anna and Alexy follow her hurriedly out, back left. Felix bangs his head against the wall in frustration a couple of times and follows them out.

Scene 2

There is a loud knock on the outside door. Silence. Another louder knock, a pause, then the handle is tried and the door opens. Enter Stephen Alley, in British army uniform, shivering and snow-covered. Oswald Rayner, dressed as an English country gentleman in plus-fours and great-coat, follows him in. Both men are not so discreetly armed with British army service revolvers.

OSWALD: Anyone home? Felix?

STEPHEN: Are you sure this is the right way in, Oswald old bean?

OSWALD: Felix Yusupov told me that if I needed to see him, *this* was the door to knock at. You're shivering, Stephen.

STEPHEN: (SHAKING SNOW OFF HIS COAT) Don't you just love the Russian winter? It's like being back at Charterhouse. Are you *sure* tonight's the night for Operation Mad Monk?

OSWALD: Late tonight, yes. That's what Felix told me. He's a dear friend of mine, but ...

STEPHEN: A bit of a .... (RAISES HIS EYEBROWS)

OSWALD: Of course he is. Wanted me to pose as a dead Shelley once for one of his "drawings". Had to fight him off with a coal scuttle. But there does seem to be some sort of plan.

STEPHEN: What sort of plan?

OSWALD: He and a few pals of his have persuaded Rasputin to come round to the Moika Palace tonight and they're going to ply him with Madeira laced with cyanide. If he won't drink it, they'll shoot him.

STEPHEN: What could possibly go wrong?

OSWALD: Best of all, they really do think it was *their* idea!

STEPHEN: How splendid! (THEY BOTH LAUGH) But surely the Mad Monk smells a rat, Ozzie? Well, you never know, it *might* work. It'd save us a messy job. But your Prince Felix sounds like a very odd bod.

OSWALD: Do you really think this could win us the war?

STEPHEN: With Rasputin out of the way, there's no danger of Russia pulling out of the shooting match, at least for the time being. Germany carries on fighting on two fronts without the manpower to do either job properly. If they could redeploy all the men on the Eastern front to the battlefields of France and Belgium, our brave boys might well be overrun.

OSWALD: Trouble is, Felix and his pals couldn't shoot a fish in a barrel.

STEPHEN: That's why we need to be here too. Just to make sure. But we

	have to do it as discreetly as possible. The last thing we want is a headline round Europe that reads "Rasputin murdered by British spies".
OSWALD:	I hate this spying business, Stephen. Is this what an Oxford education is for?
STEPHEN:	It's your patriotic duty, old sausage. Look, here's the Madeira! (THEY PICK UP AND SNIFF AT THE OPEN BOTTLES.) Smells normal. What we need is a vantage point from which we can survey the action, make sure they pull it off all right.

They survey the rest of the room. Eventually their eyes alight on the wardrobe.

OSWALD:	Are you thinking what I'm thinking?

They look through the keyhole and then open the wardrobe. Inside are a number of ball-gowns. Oswald takes one out and holds it up for inspection. The outside doorbell rings and there are noises off.

STEPHEN:	Come on, old boy, it's the perfect spot!

They panic and clamber in, pulling the doors to behind them. But some of the ball-gown is showing through the bottom. They attempt to pull it in after them.

Scene 3

While the dress is still possibly visible, Felix comes in with Dmitri (in military regalia).

FELIX:	The others are just arriving, you think?
DMITRI:	No sign of Vladimir. The other two are out in the drive. Sukhotin is not moving very fast these days.
FELIX:	(PUTTING HIS HAND ON DMITRI'S ARM) Do you really think it will be all right, Dmitri?
DMITRI:	Our destiny calls.
FELIX:	And perhaps, for us, it will be a … a new start?
DMITRI:	(PULLING HIS ARM AWAY) No, Felix. Not in that way. That was all a very long time ago. I am a soldier now. And you are married.
FELIX:	You will always be my boy, my sweet, sweet boy. You know that.

Enter Sukhotin, an injured officer back from the front, and Dr Lazovert who is carrying a large medicine bag. Sukhotin has both arms in slings and a large bandage on his head. The Servant follows them, carrying a tray of whiteish cakes. He deposits the tray on the table and exits again.

FELIX: So you made it after all, Sukhotin?

DMITRI: (PRETENDING TO KNOCK ON SUKHOTIN'S HEAD) Is there anybody in there?

SUKHOTIN: (WEAKLY) Very funny.

DMITRI: The lengths people will go to to get invalided away from the front. And Lazovert, welcome, you old fool! (SHAKES HIS HAND VIGOROUSLY)

SUKHOTIN: I'm one of only three survivors in our regiment. And I'm half dead. Meanwhile, you two have still been living it up here in St Petersburg.

FELIX: (INDIGNANTLY) I'm doing my Officer Training.

SUKHOTIN: I see. And what about you, Dmitri?

DMITRI: (MAKING HIMSELF VERY MUCH AT HOME ON THE OTTOMAN) My horse is lame. I must look after her.

SUKHOTIN: Oh, bad luck! No Olympics for you this year then?

DMITRI: I can't believe they cancelled it.

SUKHOTIN: Yes, this war is so darned *inconvenient,* isn't it?

FELIX: What's it been like since the Tsar went down to run the show?

SUKHOTIN: (SPLUTTERING) The tsar? Worse than useless. Hiding under his bed, no doubt. He'd be much safer here.

FELIX: He'll need his armed guard if he comes back now. Rasputin has taken over. If anyone steps out of line, Rasputin has a word with the tsaritsa and she banishes them to Siberia. Everyone in court and the Duma has to lick his ratskin boots. The country is ruined.

DMITRI: Worse than ruined. Until now, that is ...

FELIX: Rasputin would have us surrender tomorrow, Dmitri. He'd give the Germans everything they want.

DMITRI: It's hardly surprising, Alex is one of the Huns herself. *She* never wanted to go to war in the first place.

Enter Vladimir Purishkevitch, in a sober suit and tie, looking very nervous.

FELIX: Well, if it isn't Vladimir Purishkevitch, no doubt fresh from a debate in the Duma! We have a quorum!

VLADIMIR: (SHAKING HANDS WITH EVERYONE EXCEPT SUKHOTIN) How are you, Sukhotin, old friend?

SUKHOTIN: A few scratches, that's all.

DMITRI: Ready to do the deed, Vladimir? (LAUGHS) Night night, Rasputin?

FELIX: I have persuaded him to come to the Moika at midnight.

VLADIMIR: You're serious?

FELIX: It is our duty to the tsar, surely? Nicky will be so grateful, when it all settles down and there is no more talk of revolution. (GESTURING TO DR LAZOVERT) Between the four of us we can hardly fail, can we?

SUKHOTIN: *Four?* What about me?

DMITRI: (MANHANDLING SUKHOTIN'S INJURED ARM) Yes, if it all goes belly up, Sukhotin can engage him in unarmed combat. Unarmed combat! (HE LAUGHS LONG AND HARD)

FELIX: It's a serious matter, Dmitri. I do have an English friend who might help ...

DMITRI: Not that Oswald chap you know from Oxford? He's not been sniffing round here again, has he? Can't stand the English. Why should we need their "help"?

FELIX: Oswald seems to be doing some work for the British Embassy, not *quite* sure what it is. Funny chap, named after a character in *King Lear*, he says. Dr Lazovert, have you brought the poison?

LAZOVERT: I have. You've half-baked those cakes?

FELIX: Yes, they are completely half-baked. So, we are all clear on the plans?

DMITRI: Run them past us again, Felix.

FELIX: Rasputin is expecting me to drive up to the back door of his house and bring him back here, no doubt because I've promised he will get to meet my lovely wife, Irina.

DMITRI: Your very lovely wife, Irina.

VLADIMIR:	Except, of course, he won't because she is still holidaying with your family on the Black Sea.
FELIX:	Correct. I will tell Rasputin that Irina is still busy upstairs where a few rowdy friends have outstayed their welcome.
SUKHOTIN:	So you need us to have a bit of a party upstairs. Meanwhile you will ply him with cakes and Madeira. How are the cakes coming along, Lazovert?
LAZOVERT:	(WHO IS PUTTING SOME WHITE CRYSTALS UNDER THE TOPS OF EACH MINIATURE CAKE) Not too bad. I am putting enough cyanide in each cake to kill a horse.
DMITRI:	Make sure you eat a couple yourself, eh? Lazovert, save some for the Madeira, old chap. He might not fancy a cake.
LAZOVERT:	(TIPPING SOME MORE CRYSTALS INTO A HALF-FULL WINE BOTTLE) There, one glass of that should do for Rasputin. Felix, you'll need to remember which bottle has the poison in it and which one does not, in case you need to drink something yourself.
FELIX:	Of course. So which one is which?
LAZOVERT:	This one is the poisoned bottle. (SNIFFING EACH) No, *sorry*, it's *this* one. I think. No, actually, it's *this* one.
FELIX:	Terrific.
DMITRI:	Don't worry, Felix. If you're feeling a bit peaky, you can just send for a doctor. There'll be one upstairs. (LAUGHS) And if you bungle it, don't worry, all the exit doors will be locked. (HE GOES TO THE OUTSIDE DOOR AND TURNS THE LARGE KEY TWICE, THEN CHECKS IT; IT SEEMS TO BE LOCKED.) The four of us can sort him out. We've all got weapons. He won't get out of here alive. Come on, let's get those cakes into the oven – they should be just right by the time you get back. (THEY PUT THE CAKES IN AN OVEN)
VLADIMIR:	What happens once we've killed him? We can't leave a body here.
FELIX:	First Dmitri and Sukhotin will drive the Silver Shadow round to Rasputin's house and pretend to deliver him back. Then they'll come back here and, in the middle of the night, we'll

	take him to the Petrovski Bridge and throw him into the River
	Neva. With any luck, he'll float out to sea.
DMITRI:	What could possibly go wrong?
FELIX:	Indeed, what could possibly go wrong? Right, time for me to get changed, then go and pick him up. The rest of you, upstairs, and make it sound as though you are having a bit of a party.

Felix exits back left, the rest back right. After a short pause, Stephen and Oswald emerge from the wardrobe.

OSWALD:	Tonight is indeed the night then, Stephen.
STEPHEN:	(SMELLING THE MADEIRA AND WINCING) One can but hope, Oswald old son. Fancy a quick snifter, old chap? No, thought not. With any luck, we won't be needed. It's five onto one, after all.
OSWALD:	Do you think any one of them has fired a gun in his life?
STEPHEN:	The Mad Monk is a big target. (NOISES OFF) Best get back in our box …

They go back into the wardrobe. Blackout.

Scene 4

The lights come back on as Felix and Rasputin enter back left. Felix, turning on the lights, is now dressed colourfully and exotically while Rasputin is roughly attired in peasant's smock and breeches. Felix takes Rasputin's greatcoat, etc, and ushers him to the ottoman.

RASPUTIN:	I do like your English car – a Silver Shadow, you call it?
FELIX:	That's right. Now what can I get you to drink, Rasputin?
RASPUTIN:	The samovar seems to be cold. Where is your wife, Felix? You promised that I would meet Irina.
FELIX:	So I did, and you will. But there is a slight problem.
RASPUTIN:	A problem?
FELIX:	Yes, we had some friends to dinner and they have outstayed their welcome. They are still drinking and dancing upstairs.
RASPUTIN:	I can't hear anything.

FELIX:	Yes, if you listen carefully ... (THEY DO, BUT THERE IS NO SOUND). Perhaps they have gone – I will go and check...

Felix exits back right. Rasputin gets up, picks up a Madeira bottle and sniffs it suspiciously, smells the oven more appreciatively and returns hurriedly to his chair as Felix reappears. From this point on, we hear tinkling glasses, drinking songs and other comic effects at inappropriate intervals from backstage – Felix reacts accordingly.

FELIX:	No, they are still here. Irina says she will be down in a minute. Now, what about that drink? Madeira?
RASPUTIN:	No. I never drink.
FELIX:	I see. But perhaps we can tempt you with one of the delicious home-made cakes that Irina has made in your honour.
RASPUTIN:	I am not hungry. Felix, I sense that your spirit is not at peace this evening. What is wrong?
FELIX:	Oh, nothing. (TAKING THE CAKES, NOW BROWN, OUT OF THE OVEN) I'm just a little concerned that you will accept none of our hospitality.
RASPUTIN:	Would you like me to cast your demons out?
FELIX:	Erm, how would you do that exactly, Mr Rasputin?
RASPUTIN:	(TAKING OUT A LARGE CRUCIFIX) You will need to lie down and look closely into my eyes.
FELIX:	(JUMPING BACK) I don't think that will be absolutely necessary. Where is Irina? I will shout to her again.

He goes to the door and shouts upstairs.

FELIX:	Irina!
DMITRI:	(HIGH-PITCHED, OFFSTAGE) Yes, my love.
FELIX:	We're waiting for you, dear.

Rasputin picks up *The Memoirs of Prince Alexy Haimatoff* and examines it.

RASPUTIN:	The Memoirs of Prince Alexy Haimatoff? Don't think I know him.
FELIX:	Oh, it is a kind of prophecy, I think. It is by a man called

	Hogg who was at my college. University College, in Oxford. A friend of Shelley's. The poet? (RASPUTIN LOOKS BLANK.) Blithe spirit, Ozymandias …
RASPUTIN:	Ozzie who? Oxfoot? Shell-ey?
FELIX:	Not to be confused with Mary Shelley, his wife. They got married one hundred years ago this morning. But then he drowned …
RASPUTIN:	And you fear drowning, Felix? I know everything about you.

Felix shrugs, picks up the guitar, carries it back to his chair and starts playing it inexpertly.

FELIX:	You do? Did you know I play the guitar? Would you like me to play for you?
RASPUTIN:	(SHAKING HIS HEAD AT THE AWFULNESS OF IT) Perhaps I *will* have some refreshment after all. A cake, perhaps?
FELIX:	A cake – excellent. We will both have a cake.

Felix gives Rasputin a cake on a plate and takes one for himself. There is an uneasy pause as they consider their cakes. Felix raises his cake to his lips and then puts it back down on his plate as Rasputin watches suspiciously.

RASPUTIN:	Do you not want to eat your cake, Felix?
FELIX:	Um, all that Christmas turkey has left me feeling a little … (RUBS HIS TUMMY) … you know …

Slowly and deliberately, Rasputin begins to eat his cake. Felix watches incredulously as he finishes it.

RASPUTIN:	It tastes a little strange. Rather bitter. (ANOTHER MOUTHFUL) Almondy. But oddly moreish. (AND ANOTHER)

Felix raises his cake to his lips once more but still cannot bring himself to take a bite.

FELIX:	I think I would rather have a drink. Another cake, Rasputin?
RASPUTIN:	(SITTING) I don't mind if I do. (FELIX SERVES HIM ANOTHER ONE.

	RASPUTIN EATS WITH INCREASING SPEED.) Irina is quite a chef, isn't she? What a lot of noise they are making up there!
FELIX:	Are they? How are you feeling now? I mean, in general?
RASPUTIN:	(BETWEEN MOUTHFULS) Never felt better. But the cakes are a little dry. Perhaps I will have a drink, after all.
FELIX:	Madeira?
RASPUTIN:	Is that intoxicating?
FELIX:	Hardly at all.
RASPUTIN:	Very well, I will try a glass of Madeira.
FELIX:	(AS HE WORRIEDLY POURS TWO LARGE GLASSES, ONE FROM EACH BOTTLE) Madeira is from, er, Madeira. It is a fortified wine.
RASPUTIN:	What is "fortified"?
FELIX:	(PLACING THE TWO GLASSES AND A BOTTLE ON THE SMALL REVOLVING TABLE BETWEEN THEIR TWO CHAIRS. FELIX SITS.) It means no alcohol, I think. Although you may find it tastes a little ... *sharp*.
RASPUTIN:	Is that Irina I hear coming down the stairs?

As Felix turns to look, there is just time for Rasputin to spin the table 180 degrees so that the glasses are switched.

| FELIX: | Not unless she is coming from the servants' quarters over there. |

Felix points past Rasputin who turns to look, giving Felix enough time to spin the table again.

| FELIX: | No, perhaps not. Anyway, bottoms up, as they say in Oxford. |
| RASPUTIN: | Yes, bottoms up! |

They clink glasses and raise them to their lips. Felix pretends to sip and Rasputin takes a hearty glug, then another, draining the whole glass quickly. Felix looks on in amazement.

| RASPUTIN: | Mmm, delicious. I think I could manage another cake now. (FELIX FETCHES HIM ONE) And possibly another tiny glass of your Madeira. |

Felix pours him a huge one; he continues to eat and drink. Felix strums nervously on his guitar.

FELIX: How do you feel now?
RASPUTIN: Why do you ask, Felix? Is it because you love me?
FELIX: (SHOCKED) No!
RASPUTIN: Don't worry, I am used to it. You loved Grand Duke Dmitri, but he is not nice to you any more, is he? And now you want to sleep with me. But I think you have brought me here on false pretences. Your wife is not here, is she?
FELIX: Of course she is. Why, I will go and fetch her immediately.

Felix exits back right. While he is away, Rasputin winces and rubs his tummy, as if suffering from indigestion. He pours himself some more Madeira and forces it down, clearly now in some pain. He examines the sediment at the bottom of the bottle. He does not like what he sees. Felix re-enters back right. We can see that he now has an antique musket behind his back. Rasputin rises menacingly and starts to come towards him, but he is clearly in pain now.

RASPUTIN: What have you done to me, Felix?
FELIX: Don't come any closer, Rasputin.
RASPUTIN: Why, are you going to shoot me? Is that a gun behind your back, Felix?
FELIX: I ... I ....
RASPUTIN: Don't you know that I am immortal? (HE GRASPS AND RAISES THE CRUCIFIX ROUND HIS NECK) Look deep into my eyes, Felix!
FELIX: (POINTING THE GUN AT HIM, BUT SHAKING WITH FEAR) I'm not going to fall for any more of your tricks.
RASPUTIN: *My* tricks? I tell you, you can never kill me, Fe ...

At this point, there is a loud bang and Rasputin clutches his chest. The two men stare uncertainly at each other.

RASPUTIN: (GASPING AND TOTTERING TOWARDS FELIX) I can't believe you just did that.
FELIX: No, nor can I. Sorry! But I'm afraid I'm going to have to do it again.

Another bang. Rasputin staggers desperately towards Felix. The other four conspirators come rushing in, all with antique weaponry except Sukhotin. Lazovert goes for a light switch and manages to plunge the room into darkness.

DMITRI: Who's turned the lights out? Turn them back on!
VLADIMIR: Is he dead, Felix?
FELIX: How should I know? I hope so! (THERE IS A ROAR OF DYING PAIN
              FROM RASPUTIN, THEN A THUD AS HE HITS THE FLOOR)
SUKHOTIN: Is that the light switch?
LAZOVERT: No, here it is. (THE LIGHTS GO BACK ON JUST AS DMITRI IS
              TRIPPING OVER RASPUTIN'S BODY)
DMITRI: Ow! That hurt!
VLADIMIR: He is actually dead, isn't he? Gosh.

They each move tentatively towards him, prod him, shake him. He seems to be thoroughly dead. Eventually, Lazovert gets out a stethoscope and places it next to the gunshot wound in his chest.

LAZOVERT: Yes, I can confirm that he is definitely dead. Well done, Felix!
DMITRI: Well done all of us. Now what do we do?
VLADIMIR: You three must drive over to Rasputin's place and pretend to
              drop him off. Felix and I will start to tidy up here.
DMITRI: OK, let's get cracking. Can anyone actually drive?

Dmitri, Lazovert and Sukhotin rush off back left. Felix and Vladimir collapse in the chairs.

VLADIMIR: A drink to celebrate?
FELIX: Why not? But possibly not the Madeira. (HE FINDS TWO BOTTLES
              OF BEER AND PASSES ONE TO VLADIMIR; THEY DRINK) Here's to a
              job well done.
VLADIMIR: A job well done! To be honest, I wasn't sure we'd be able to pull
              it off.
FELIX: Never in doubt, old friend. Although ...
VLADIMIR: Although what?
FELIX: You don't think we should just check, do you? Just to be sure?
VLADIMIR: Can't do any harm. I'll be right behind you with my blunderbuss, Felix.

296

Gun still in one hand, Felix approaches the body tentatively and slaps Rasputin's face a couple of times. There is no response. Then he tries to check for a pulse. Still nothing.

FELIX: (TURNING TO VLADIMIR) Yes, he's defini ...

At this point, Rasputin gives a huge roar and grabs Felix by the throat with one hand and by his gun-hand with the other. Felix struggles to fight back. (Vladimir waves his gun ineffectually but does not shoot.) There is a moment of stillness as the two men gaze into each other's eyes at very close range. Then Rasputin gets the better of Felix, throws him aside, stands up and starts heading for the outside-door.

FELIX: (FROM THE FLOOR) Don't worry, all the doors are locked.

Rasputin tries the door and it opens easily. He goes through.

FELIX: Shoot him, you fool! (VLADIMIR FIRES HIS GUN, BUT A MOMENT
                TOO LATE) We can't let him get away ...

They chase after him through the door. Rasputin soon reappears front right, running round the front of the stage. As he disappears again, Felix and Vladimir appear in pursuit, firing wildly. They all do a couple of circuits, tripping over things as they go. While they are all off-stage, Stephen and Oswald come calmly out of the wardrobe to centre stage, revolvers in hand.

STEPHEN: If you want a job doing ...
OSWALD: You have to do it yourself.

When Rasputin next comes running round the front of the stage, Oswald takes careful aim – bang! Rasputin falls instantly dead.

STEPHEN: I say, good shot, sir!
OSWALD: Time to make a sharp exit.

They melt away through the outside-door just as Felix and Vladimir reappear. There is one further bang, then Vladimir trips over Rasputin.

VLADIMIR: I think we've got him this time.

Felix tries to fire another bullet, but there is just a click.

FELIX: Just as well as I seem to be out of ammunition.

Dmitri and Lazovert race towards them from back right with Sukhotin puffing in the rear. They prod the body tentatively with their feet.

DMITRI: I thought you said he was dead, Lazovert, you old fool.
LAZOVERT: He was! I mean, he is!
FELIX: Not just now he wasn't. All this racket will have woken up the neighbourhood. Is that someone coming? Hide him behind that bank of snow.

They tug him desperately up to a spot which is hardly concealed at all, front right of stage, arranging pot plants in front. They then attempt to form a human shield as a policeman enters front left.

FELIX: Ah, what seems to be the trouble, officer?
POLICEMAN: Sorry to disturb you gentleman, but – how can I put this? I could have sworn there was the sound of gunfire.
DMITRI: Gunfire? I'm sure you are mistaken.
POLICEMAN: It was definitely gunfire.
FELIX: (AFTER A PAUSE) Ah yes, *gunfire.* There *was* a little bit of that.
POLICEMAN: Any particular reason, Mr Yusupov?
FELIX: It's Prince Felix, please.
POLICEMAN: Not for long it won't be. Or so I hear. Anyway ....
DMITRI: You see, the thing is, we were having a bit of a party, a bit too much to drink, you know how it is. High spirits. We were just leaving and this dog was barking. So Sukhotin here shot it.
SUKHOTIN: (WHO PLAINLY DOES NOT HAVE A USEABLE ARM TO HAVE SHOT ANYONE) I did? I mean, I did. Pesky dog. Sorry.
POLICEMAN: I see. And where is this dog now? (TRYING TO PEER BEHIND THEM)
FELIX: It must have got away. Just as well, eh, officer.
POLICEMAN: (WRITING PAINSTAKINGLY IN HIS NOTEBOOK) And the dog got away. Well, that all seems quite, er, plausible. Yes, all quite normal. I won't take up any more of your time, gentlemen.
DMITRI: You won't? No, I should think not. You should be off catching

298

some real criminals, not people like us.

POLICEMAN: Indeed, I'm very sorry. I'll say goodnight then.
THE REST: Nighty night!

The Policeman exits front left.

LAZOVERT: I think we've got away with it.
DMITRI: Right, come on, lads. We need to lug the body into the boot of
             the Rolls Royce. (THEY TRY, BUT HAVE GREAT DIFFICULTY MOVING
             HIM AT ALL) Alex will have to find someone else to keep her warm
             at night now. Come on, Sukhotin, give us a hand!
SUKHOTIN: I haven't really got one.

Eventually they manage to tug him to and through the nearest exit.

LAZOVERT: This is killing my back. Nearly there now.
VLADIMIR: (AS THE OTHER THREE EXIT) I'll stay here and help Felix with the
             clearing up.
DMITRI: (FROM OFFSTAGE) Leave us with all the dirty work, why don't
             you?

Vladimir and Felix get their handkerchiefs out and wipe ineffectually at assorted
bloodstains, etc.

VLADIMIR: Oh God, what have we done? The place is covered in blood!
             We're going to have to get the servants to sort it out.
FELIX: I dread to think what the cleaning bills are going to be like.
VLADIMIR: Still, we've done our duty to the tsar and Mother Russia.
FELIX: Indeed we have. Nicky will live to a ripe old age and there will
             be no more talk of revolution or any of that nonsense. They will
             make statues of us.

There is a knock on the outside-door. They jump in alarm and freeze. There is
another alarming knock on the door.

VLADIMIR: It's Rasputin, isn't it?

299

FELIX: I doubt if he'd knock. (ANOTHER KNOCK) Come in!

It is the Policeman, notebook at the ready.

POLICEMAN: Sorry to disturb you again, gentlemen. But my sergeant has
             asked me to come back and ask a few more questions. You see,
             the thing is, there are reports that Mr Rasputin is nowhere to be
             found.
FELIX: Mr who? I don't know what you are implying.
POLICEMAN: Local residents confirm there were definitely a number of
             gunshots around 2.37 this morning.
FELIX: But this is ridiculous. You realize who I am?
POLICEMAN: I'm really sorry, it's just that my sergeant ...
VLADIMIR   (IMPATIENTLY) Well, you can tell your sergeant that work of
             national, no, *imperial* importance has taken place here tonight.
             The traitor, Rasputin, has been eliminated. Every true Russian
             will drink a toast to our heroic endeavours ...
POLICEMAN: (WRITING LABORIOUSLY) Every true Russian ...
FELIX: (PANICKING) Don't listen to the idiot. He's drunk. He doesn't
             know what he is saying.
POLICEMAN: Are you drunk, Mr, er, Mr ... ?
VLADIMIR: I ... I ... (SLURRING NOW) Yes, I suppose I am.
POLICEMAN: (WRITING) But the suspect was drunk and refused to give me his
             name ... aren't you that chap from the Duma?
FELIX: Officer, I hope you understand the awkwardness of the situation
             in which you find yourself. Are you aware that the tsar himself
             had given orders that ... if it turns out that you and your fellow
             police officers have ... well, I think you know what I'm driving at!
POLICEMAN: I haven't the faintest idea what you are talking about. The tsaritsa
             has given us instructions ...
FELIX: Do you presume to speak for the tsaritsa? I suggest you go back
             to your silly little police station and think very carefully before
             you start making any accusations. Do I make myself clear?
POLICEMAN: (WRITING) How do you spell "tsaritsa"?
FELIX: Good*night*, officer. I don't think we will be seeing you again. (HE
             SHOWS HIM THE DOOR)

300

POLICEMAN:	Well, thank you for your help, sir.
FELIX:	(AS THE POLICEMAN EXITS) No problem, officer. (PAUSE) Are you out of your tiny mind, Vladimir? We'll never hear the end of it now.
VLADIMIR:	I'm sorry. It's been a very stressful night.
FELIX:	Come on, let's clean up this mess. Second thoughts … (SHOUTING) Ivan?

Blackout.

Scene 5

Daylight. The room has been cleared of all incriminating evidence. Felix comes in, back right, ahead of the Chief of Police.

CHIEF:	Ah, Prince Felix, it's so good of you to see me.
FELIX:	Always happy to assist the forces of law and order, Inspector.
CHIEF:	Just a few formalities, really. You understand that the body of that notorious criminal, Rasputin, has been found floating near Petrovski Bridge.
FELIX:	He has? … Had he been for a swim?
CHIEF:	(SCRUTINISING THE EMPTY DRINKS TABLE) He had been shot several times. Now, he *may* have been a traitor and a lunatic, in my humble opinion, but we are, regrettably, forced to investigate the circumstances of his death.
FELIX:	Of course. But how can I help you?
CHIEF:	Rasputin went missing on the night of December 29th or the early hours of the 30th. There are a number of unfortunate reports of shots being fired at the Moika Palace at about 2.30 a.m. this morning.

The Chief of Police strolls around as he talks. He puts his finger to a mark on the wall and then smells it suspiciously.

FELIX:	Yes?
CHIEF:	Although I am sure this was pure coincidence, I have to ask, just for the record, what happened?
FELIX:	As we explained to the constable at the time, one of our guests

	had had a little too much to drink and tried to shoot our trusty wolfhound, Rinka.
CHIEF:	Which guest was that?
FELIX:	I forget.
CHIEF:	(CONSULTING DOCUMENTS) It appears that it was an unknown man with both his arms in slings.
FELIX:	That is, er, correct, Inspector. Luckily, he missed.
CHIEF:	(EXAMINING HIS FINGER) Constable Plovski claims that he saw blood on the snow and also inside on the walls of the palace.
FELIX:	(LOOKING AROUND ANXIOUSLY) Ah, I see ... it wasn't blood, of course. We had a bit of an accident with a jar of strawberry jam.
CHIEF:	Strawberry jam. And then half an hour later we have witness reports of a Rolls Royce stopping on the Petrovski Bridge and three men heaving a suspiciously large object out of the boot and dropping it into the River Neva.
FELIX:	I was not one of those men. I *do* have a Rolls Royce ...
CHIEF:	Awkwardly, it is known to be the only Rolls Royce in St Petersburg. And there are tyre tracks in the snow all the way from this door here to the bridge and back.
FELIX:	Ah. Perhaps someone borrowed it to try to incriminate me?
CHIEF:	To incriminate you? (PAUSE) Yes, I'd say it's the obvious conclusion, isn't it? Especially as Constable Plovski was interviewing you at about the same time. The Constable says there was a man with you, possibly a Mr Vladimir Purishkevitch, who said, and I quote: "the traitor, Rasputin, has been eliminated".
FELIX:	He was guessing. Or drunk. Or joking. If it was him at all ...
CHIEF:	You don't remember who you were with?
FELIX:	It had been a long night.

Alexandra (in full imperial regalia) and Anna burst onto the stage from back left. The servant is just behind, making apologetic hand gestures. Alexandra tries to grab Felix by the throat.

ALEXANDRA:	You murderer! You cruel, cruel murderer!
FELIX:	(CHOKING BUT WARDING HER OFF) I don't know what you

	mean, your Majesty!
ALEXANDRA:	You have killed my one true friend ...
ANNA:	You still have me, your Majesty.
ALEXANDRA:	(SOBBING) My dearest, dearest friend, a holy man, a saint, the man to save Russia from her enemies within and without!
FELIX:	It's a point of view ...
ALEXANDRA:	You will hang for this, Felix! (SHE LETS HIM GO)
FELIX:	But ...
ALEXANDRA:	As will Dmitri, that traitor Vladimir Purishkevitch, Lt Sukhotin and Dr Lazovert. But you *were* the ringleader. Hanging's too good for you!
FELIX:	Your Majesty, while I concede that my feelings towards Mr Rasputin may not have been quite as warm as your own ...
ALEXANDRA:	Warm? What are you insinuating?
FELIX:	Nothing, nothing. But I have just explained to this gentleman why I could not *possibly* have been involved.
ALEXANDRA:	Inspector?
CHIEF:	(FIDGETING WITH HIS PAPERS) It's early days, your Majesty, a lot of investigative work is still to be done. But I'd have to say that my preliminary conclusion is that there is no evidence whatsoever to link Prince Felix with the, er "crime".
ALEXANDRA:	What!?
CHIEF:	I'm sorry.
ALEXANDRA:	The tsar is on his way back from the Front. When he hears about this ...
CHIEF:	Yes, I am in contact with the tsar already.
ALEXANDRA:	(THE PENNY IS DROPPING) You are? I see. I see! (SOBBING AGAIN) Well, I will be having a word with him too! Come on, Anna, I can see it was a mistake to come here....

She storms out, back left, with Anna in tow.

CHIEF:	Prince Felix, if I may, a few words of advice.
FELIX:	Yes, of course, Inspector.
CHIEF:	I have heard that the weather is a little warmer down by the Black Sea – why not go down and join your family? Just until

	the storm blows over.
FELIX:	(SHAKING HANDS) Thank you, you are doing an excellent job, Inspector. It won't be forgotten. December 30th will be a national holiday, you mark my words. History will speak kindly of us.

As the Inspector leaves with the Servant, Felix picks up a glass of Madeira, smiles and toasts the portrait of the tsar.

Curtain.

AUTHOR'S NOTE

This play is based on Felix Yusupov's autobiography, *Lost Splendor*, which may be read at http://www.alexanderpalace.org/lostsplendor/. It has been augmented with a range of other historical evidence, notably the evidence of the English involvement in Rasputin's murder.

This play won the Oxfordshire Drama Network's Playwriting Competition for 2014.

A longer version of this play, written for radio, may be heard at http://tinyurl.com/nz3vc28 (copyright © the author)

Hillary's Term

Dramatis Personae

HILLARY CLINTON: the Democratic nominee in the 2016 US Presidential Election
BILL CLINTON: her husband, the 42nd US President (1993-2001)
CHELSEA CLINTON: their daughter, recently a mother for the 2nd time
ROBERT REICH: US Secretary of Labor, 1993-1997, a family friend

The scene is a large student room in Helen's Court (left), deep within University College, Oxford. While still recognisably studenty in certain ways, it is clear that extras have been added for VIP visitors. There is a TV and DVD player, with a modest collection of well-known films to hand, including *Groundhog Day*. There is stereo equipment and a collection of CDs of '60s and '70s music, including the Rolling Stones. There are newspapers and board games, including Monopoly. There are bottles of wine and glasses, various other drinks, a fridge with beer in it, etc. There are books on shelves, a sofa and two other comfy chairs, a small table, etc. There is a single outside door, through which characters come and go.

It is around 11.45 p.m. on Thursday, 29th December 2016. Whenever the door opens, we hear the cold, wintry wind blowing.

Before the action, we hear the Rolling Stones' 'Sympathy for the Devil', especially these lines:

I stuck around St Petersburg when I saw it was a time for a change.
Killed the Tsar and his ministers; Anastasia screamed in vain.

Bill Clinton, Hillary Clinton, Chelsea Clinton and Robert Reich enter through the outside door, shedding a variety of winter clothes and putting them on pegs. Chelsea has a tiny carry-cot which she parks on a side-table. While talking, the two men pour themselves a beer from bottles they find in the fridge. Chelsea explores the room while Hillary flops down into an armchair.

305

CHELSEA:	(AS SHE DEPOSITS THE CARRY-COT) Aidan is sleeping beautifully but I bet he'll have me up in the night.
BILL:	Do babies suffer from jet lag?
CHELSEA:	We'll find out the hard way. You know, I don't think I've ever seen Oxford so deserted.
ROBERT:	No wonder the college is officially shut between Christmas and the New Year. We should have a quiet night. This was a terrific set of rooms you had, Bill.
CHELSEA:	Weren't all the Rhodes Scholars in Helen's Court, Robert?
ROBERT:	Not me. I had the pokiest room imaginable, right on the High Street, just along from the Shelley Memorial. I was so envious of the folk in Helen's Court, tucked away here, far from prying eyes.
BILL:	Yes, that first year at Univ was quite something.
CHELSEA:	The happiest days of your life, eh, Dad?
ROBERT:	I remember coming to see you one day, round the back of the library, through the tunnel. Like travelling into another world. Mind you, I could already hear the Rolling Stones belting out. I'm amazed you didn't get sent down just for that.
BILL:	Sent down? (LAUGHS UNEASILY) Certainly ideal for us now, security-wise, with a couple of men on the gate and another one on the tunnel. (TO HILLARY) You can sleep safe in your bed, honey.
ROBERT:	It's perfect. You said you wanted to get away from all the razzmatazz, the hoopla, the press scrutinising your every move, Hill. Well, our plane seems to have lost them, good and proper. *No one* knows we're here.
HILLARY:	(COLDLY) Well, that's nice.
BILL:	Are you all right, love? You hardly touched your food…
HILLARY:	I'm still on New York time. It feels like the middle of the afternoon, not dinner time.
CHELSEA:	We can eat when we like, sleep when we like while we're here. Just say no to jet-lag, Mum.
HILLARY:	It's all right for you. I'm 69.

ROBERT:	Well, you've made a big mistake getting that new job, then. You may find there's quite a bit of travel involved over the next four years. You'll be sending us postcards from Moscow, Damascus, Kabul, Beijing…
HILLARY:	Yes, lucky you gave me a new fountain pen for Christmas, Robert. If only I could take the bottles of ink on all those planes!
BILL:	You'll love it, Hill. And I'll be right behind you every step of the way, making helpful comments. Like the Duke of Edinburgh.
HILLARY:	No, you won't. When I'm President, I'll have all past and future leaders and rivals locked away, just to be on the safe side. For you, as an act of clemency, it will be house arrest in Little Rock.
ROBERT:	I see no reason for clemency.
HILLARY:	And don't you think you are safe, Professor Reich, just because you've been hiding out in Berkeley for the last nineteen years. History books tell me you were Secretary of Labor from 1993-1997. How do you plead?
ROBERT:	Guilty as charged. But I'm not planning my own presidential bid until 2044 when I'm 98, so you are safe from me.
HILLARY:	I need you *now*, Robert. Someone on the left who really understands the economic choices we will have to make. You don't have to sign on the dotted line. Just half an hour on the phone once a week.
ROBERT:	At *my* hourly rate? It would bankrupt the economy. But my latest book on saving capitalism is only 20 dollars, now that it's been remaindered.
BILL:	That's capitalism for you.
CHELSEA:	Look we had a deal, folks. No politics. We've come to Oxford to get away from all that. Just for two days. Let's play a game of something, like normal folk.
ROBERT:	Monopoly?
BILL:	No, you'd insist on being the Bank and giving away all the reserves of cash to anyone who said pretty please. I should know…

ROBERT: I think you'll find those history books say that the first Clinton administration set the benchmark not just for social welfare but also for economic growth. It was only in the *second* Clinton administration...

BILL: When you'd thrown all your toys out of the pram...

ROBERT: ... that things started to go downhill. Still, in the *third* Clinton administration ...

HILLARY: The first Rodham administration, you mean? That will be my first decree after Jan 20th.

CHELSEA: You wouldn't ditch the name of the family firm, would you, Mum?

HILLARY: Sorry, Chelse, but you were the only one of us who was actually *born* a Clinton. I wouldn't have minded taking the name Blythe. But Roger Clinton was a step-father straight out of the Grimm fairy tales. Who would want to be named after him?

BILL: You really feel like that?

HILLARY: (GETTING UP) No, I'm just a bit under the weather. I might get some fresh air.

CHELSEA: But you just had some fresh air. It's dark. And it's the middle of winter.

HILLARY: You've talked me into it. (PUTTING ON HER COAT AGAIN) The middle of winter is exactly what I need.

BILL: (REACHING FOR HIS COAT) Yes, a spot of exercise wouldn't...

HILLARY: On my own. I may be gone for some time.

BILL: (AS HILLARY EXITS) Hill! Honey-pie!

CHELSEA: Do you think she's all right, Dad? She was in a funny mood even before we landed at Kidlington. It's not like Mum to go off for a walk on her own at this time of night.

BILL: (BUSY TEXTING) She'll be fine. Dwayne will keep an eye on her. I don't *think* there's any ISIL or Trump supporters waiting to ambush her outside the Radcliffe Camera. Is-is, maybe ...

ROBERT: The river Isis, you mean? I gather it's burst its banks in West Oxford. But we're on slightly higher ground here, I believe. The ox ford. How did these rooms suit you, Chelsea?

CHELSEA:	Just fine. I could lock myself away and stick my head in a book. The porters did a good job of keeping the paparazzi out.
ROBERT:	Surely they left you in peace here?
CHELSEA:	I wish! Serves me right for having a notorious father. It'll be even worse now. I should sue *both* my parents for violation of my privacy. I'll need the pay-out for when my own children sue me.
BILL:	Do you think you'd've grown up a well-rounded human being with a different upbringing?
CHELSEA:	I suppose not. Not with my genes. Say, would you settle out of court, Dad?
BILL:	I'll talk it over with your mother, honey. She's the one to go to for legal advice. Just as soon as she comes back from her walkabout, that is.
CHELSEA:	Being the daughter of the President is not going to make it easy for me at the Foundation. Maybe I should just stay home and look after Aidan and Charlotte. God, I'm missing Charlie already. And Marc, of course. Still, without the Foundation work, I guess I'd have a bit of time spare for my first love. History.
ROBERT:	History? You got that from your mother. Look at the titles of her books – her autobiography, *Living History*, and the one she did about the White House, *At Home with History*. You've got history in your genes.
CHELSEA:	And it's what I did at Stanford. I loved it. This place has quite an interesting history, you know.
BILL:	Not surprising – it's the oldest college in Oxford.
CHELSEA:	I mean in terms of rogues and vagabonds.
ROBERT:	I hope you're not including me in that list, Chelsea.
CHELSEA:	Of course not. As Secretary of Labor, you robbed from the rich and gave to the poor. *Dad*, on the other hand…
BILL:	I gave him the job and the keys to the Treasury. How was I to know he'd take advantage of the trust I placed in him and actually do a good job?

ROBERT:	Did I? I'm not sure you mentioned that at the time. I was just following the example of other great Univ left-wingers like Clement Attlee and Harold Wilson.
BILL:	But England's different. Politics has a left wing here. There's no such thing in America. You're either right or far-right. You were lucky not to get lynched.
CHELSEA:	So how come Mum got elected?
BILL:	Yes, it is a bit of a mystery, isn't it? Congress will have to get a strait-jacket made to measure for the female form.
ROBERT:	She's gonna do great things, Bill. So, what can you tell us about the history of University College, Chelsea?
CHELSEA:	Well, there's Shelley, of course. Have you read any of his stuff? 'Hail to thee, blithe Spirit! Bird thou never wert, That from Heaven, or near it, Pourest thy full heart.'
ROBERT:	Ode to a Nightingale?
CHELSEA:	That's Keats. The blithe spirit is a skylark.
ROBERT:	Do you think Shelley's blithe spirit haunts the college?
CHELSEA:	Blithe? Not after the college sent him down for his pamphlet on atheism. He was not a happy bunny.
ROBERT:	And Blythe was the name you were christened with, eh, Bill? William Jefferson Blythe the third. A happy coincidence?
CHELSEA:	There's more. Shelley's best friend at college was Thomas Jefferson Hogg. Jefferson, as Shelley called him. Are you beginning to detect a bit of a theme here? Hogg too was sent down. Spent the rest of his life propositioning Shelley's wives and girlfriends.
BILL:	Shelley can't have been too happy about that!
CHELSEA:	On the contrary. He encouraged it. It was the women who wouldn't play ball.
BILL:	Was Shelley related to the Mary Shelley who wrote *Frankenstein*?
CHELSEA:	That was his second wife. They got married on December 30th 1816.
ROBERT:	Seriously? Two hundred years ago tomorrow? Cool! We should find some blithe spirit and drink a toast to Univ's most notorious old boy. This English beer sucks.

BILL:	There's quite a selection of alcoholic beverages left for our delectation. What do you fancy, Chelse?
CHELSEA:	(INSPECTING THE BOTTLES) What about this Madeira?
BILL:	Why not? (OPENS IT WITH A CORKSCREW, FINDS GLASSES, POURS AND DISTRIBUTES DRINKS)
CHELSEA:	This was pretty much the only wine you could drink in Shelley's time, thanks to the Napoleonic wars and various trade embargoes.
ROBERT:	(SPLUTTERING) It's a bit sweet for my tastes.
CHELSEA:	That'll be the delicate tang of the bodies of the slaves used to transport the stuff over to England. That's what cask-conditioned meant in those days.
BILL:	Mmm, that's rather good! We'll be blithe in no time.
ROBERT	Blotto, more likely.
CHELSEA:	And, of course, Madeira was used to kill Rasputin …
ROBERT:	So it was! Prince Felix Yusupov, Univ's other notorious old boy!
CHELSEA:	That's the one. Univ is so proud of the murderous plutocrat that they've named an IT room after him. And, by happy coincidence, felix means blithe.
BILL:	I see where this is heading. By being christened William Jefferson Blythe the third, I was destined to combine the names of the atheists and murderers who had darkened these doors in days gone by. The third in the Univ line. I'm deeply honoured.
CHELSEA:	And you are drawn back here on the anniversary not just of Shelley's wedding but also the night Yusupov and his gang murdered Rasputin.
ROBERT:	You're joking!
CHELSEA:	The night of 29th-30th December 1916.
ROBERT:	That's bizarre. Yusupov committed his dastardly deed a hundred years to the very day after just about the most famous wedding in English literary history? Surely there should be some sort of commemoration here in college?
BILL:	I don't think there's anything on.

CHELSEA:	I doubt if the college has even spotted the connection. (PICKING UP A NEWSPAPER FROM THE TABLE.) But it does figure in this crossword in today's *Daily Telegraph*. At least someone has noticed.
ROBERT:	They say history repeats itself, the first time as tragedy the second time as farce.
CHELSEA:	Karl Marx wasn't too far wrong about that. Rasputin's assassination was pretty farcical, for sure, the way they chased him round the snowy grounds of the Moika Palace.
BILL:	Has anyone checked this Madeira isn't laced with arsenic? If the second time is farce, what would the third time be? And I'm beginning to get seriously worried about Hillary. Perhaps I'll head out and find her before she catches pneumonia again, like she did in September. It wouldn't do to be spluttering her way through the inauguration ceremony in three weeks' time ... (STARTS PUTTING HIS COAT BACK ON)
ROBERT:	Does Hillary's term of office start on the first day of Hilary Term? Just a thought. And the name Hillary means cheerful or merry, from the Greek hilaros. Hillary Blythe would have been a tautology. Roger Clinton saved us from that, at least.
CHELSEA:	Fingers crossed Mum will do better than Shelley and Hogg who didn't make it through to the end of their first Hilary Term. The Tea Party certainly view her as a dangerous atheist. When asked whether they'd written the pamphlet, Shelley and Hogg effectively pleaded the fifth amendment of 1791, that an accused person may not be compelled to reveal any information that might incriminate them. It didn't cut much ice in the kangaroo court here in Univ. But America is a more civilised country, of course.
BILL:	It didn't do me much good when I was impeached.
ROBERT:	But you won! Otherwise you might have been in Guantanamo Bay ever since!
BILL:	Well, there's a thought. Don't ever take up politics, Chelsea.
CHELSEA:	You've been telling me that all my life. Too bad you didn't

	tell Mum the same thing.
BILL:	I did, believe me! But you know what she's like.
CHELSEA:	Indeed I do. If she'd been born a man, she'd have been President at least thirty years ago. As a woman, it's taken a little longer to batter down the walls.
ROBERT:	Yes, she was always the one with the brains *and* the balls, if you'll pardon my French. Even when I first met her, back in '66, that much was obvious. She should have been the one winning the Rhodes Scholarship to Oxford, not us.
BILL:	You speak for yourself. I was worth a place on chutzpah alone, telling the Rhodes Committee that I wanted to prepare for life as a practising politician. (THE OTHERS SNORT WITH DERISION) But the Rhodes was open only to men until 1977 so Hillary was at a slight disadvantage in that respect. Do you think it opened doors for us?
ROBERT:	Of course it did. These days the Rhodies risk being thrown on a bonfire. But back then, we felt like ambassadors. Coming to Oxford was the most important moment in my education. Even though I nearly died on the boat crossing.
BILL:	Yes, yes, until I brought you some life-saving soup. And you've been dining out on that soup ever since.
ROBERT:	And so have you! My big mistake at Univ was to spend too much time studying. That was not an error *you* were likely to make while there were drugs to be snorted and women to be chased.
BILL:	It was hard work! The ratio of men to women in Oxford was ridiculous in those days! Just five women's colleges!
ROBERT:	I'm sure you worked your way steadily and alphabetically through all of them.
BILL:	Hang on, didn't you meet Clare here? Didn't you decide to direct a play simply on the off-chance that she would come along and audition and you could give her the part?
ROBERT:	A musical, actually – the Fantasticks. With no women at Univ, what was a poor boy to do? (SIGHS) Clare was just seventeen.

CHELSEA: Cradle-snatching! How old was Mum when you took her out?

ROBERT: Shush, Chelsea, I'm not sure your father knows about that one (THE MEN LAUGH). Let's see … I guess we were about 19, 20 in 1966.

BILL: And he took her to see a film called *Blow-Up*.

ROBERT: Ah, yes, that was a bit of a mistake. At least, for a first date.

BILL: Antonioni, an art-house classic. Just slightly too much nudity?

ROBERT: Possibly. For 1966. I think she's almost forgiven me now. Still, just as well I failed dismally, eh? Or the entire course of Western history might have been different.

BILL: On the contrary. If she'd been your girlfriend visiting you in Oxford, I would have considered it my duty to steal her off you, so we'd have got together a lot earlier.

ROBERT: Did the fact that she was my ex have any bearing at all on your eventual stalking of her? Just asking.

BILL: Ha. Don't flatter yourself, Professor Reich. I stalked her *despite* the fact she'd had such poor taste in men hitherto. I pursued her because she was the cleverest girl I'd ever met.

ROBERT: *And* because she kept saying no.

BILL: Yes, OK, I admit it. It was the thrill of the chase. Hillary was the most unobtainable woman at Yale Law School. Even now I'm still not quite sure I've managed to pin her down.

CHELSEA: I think you've managed to pin her down all right, Dad.

ROBERT: What about you, Chelse? Were any of the callow youths of Univ after you with their butterfly nets?

CHELSEA: (LAUGHING) Seriously! They couldn't get near me. If the minders didn't put them off, the bullet-proof vest was a deal-breaker. I showed up here a few days after 9/11. I might as well have had a bull's-eye tattooed to my forehead.

ROBERT: You felt you were being targeted?

CHELSEA: No, but everybody else did. There were a lot of people saying I should be cowering in some sort of post-apocalyptic bunker, waiting for the crisis to pass, instead of walking the

	streets of Oxford.

BILL: She'd have been in that bunker if I'd had my way. My precious daughter. Who knew what those bastards would do next? If they could target the Twin Towers and actually bring them down ...

ROBERT: An astonishing feat, when you think about it ...

BILL: ... then it wouldn't have been too difficult to sneak into college and ... God, it doesn't bear thinking about, even now.

CHELSEA: Are we any safer now? I don't think so. But you can't live your whole life worrying about who's out there.

BILL: That's the spirit! I remember Robert and I came to Univ a couple of months after the shooting of Bobby Kennedy. Didn't we, Bobby?

ROBERT: I stopped being Bobby in June '68. Robert seemed safer and more grown-up.

BILL: I was just beginning to think about a career in politics. But it was a time when it seemed like the end-game for any democrat was assassination. JFK, Bobby, George Wallace in Maryland ...

ROBERT: Yes, the guy who shot Wallace, Arthur Bremer, is walking the streets today. A cheery thought.

BILL: And yet here we still are. I guess we've been lucky. Or maybe no one takes politicians seriously any more.

ROBERT: I blame it on that chap from Arkansas. What a comedian he was. How did he get in? I guess the Democrats had no one left who hadn't been shot.

BILL: Teddy Kennedy would have been the heir apparent if he hadn't driven his secretary off a bridge.

ROBERT: That was halfway through our time at Univ.

BILL: A few days after the Stones played Hyde Park.

ROBERT: (WITH HEAVY IRONY) I can't believe I missed that. Did they get all three chords right?

BILL: It was a cultural landmark. Half a million people turned up.

ROBERT: That's because it was free.

CHELSEA:	No, Dad's right. It must have been quite an afternoon. Mick Jagger flouncing on and reading a whole page of *Adonais*.
ROBERT:	*Adonais?*
CHELSEA:	The Shelley poem.
ROBERT:	A whole page of Shelley? The punters must have loved that. Even here in Univ, his old college, Shelley was considered unreadable.
CHELSEA:	It was Jagger's way of paying tribute to Brian Jones, the Stones guitarist, who had just drowned. Right, Dad?
ROBERT:	So the guitarist was dead? Maybe three chords would have been a bit over-optimistic in the circumstances.
BILL:	You can mock. I've always had a bit of a phobia of drowning. Ever since my own Dad … you know …
ROBERT:	Sure. Sorry, Bill. It just sounds like there was a bit of an epidemic of drowning in the summer of '69.
CHELSEA:	I wonder if Mick Jagger realised quite how ironic that whole Shelley thing was?
ROBERT:	What do you mean?
CHELSEA:	Well, there he was reciting Shelley a few yards from the very spot where Shelley's first wife was fished out of the Serpentine.
BILL:	Never!
CHELSEA:	Harriet Westbrook. Met her in his Univ days, eloped, had a couple of children, ran off with someone younger and prettier. So she drowned herself there, in Hyde Park. And that's not the only Univ connection.
BILL:	I never realised you were so well up in college history!
CHELSEA:	When the Stones played Hyde Park, Mick Jagger was just in the process of trading in Marianne Faithfull for his new girlfriend, Marsha Hunt. Both women were just a few yards from the stage. You'd have been four million rows back, Dad, but they were VIP guests. But who would Mick go home with that night?
ROBERT:	Bianca? Jerry? L'Wren?

CHELSEA:	Marsha Hunt. Who was married to another musician, Mike Ratledge of Soft Machine.
ROBERT:	The Softs? No! Even I listened to some of their stuff. Jazz-rock. The other end of the musical spectrum from the Stones.
CHELSEA:	… and Ratledge had not long graduated from Univ where he'd read PPP. Just as Jagger himself might have done if he'd been brighter and aimed a little higher than the LSE. Two Kent grammar school boys. Anyway, Jagger made off with Ratledge's wife …
BILL:	And Marianne Faithfull didn't take the news too well, did she?
CHELSEA:	She and Mick flew off to Australia the next day because he was filming *Ned Kelly*. Marianne took an overdose. Nearly died. And he was still sending love letters airmail to Mrs Ratledge.
ROBERT:	Charming. The Shelley of his day, obviously. Except he never quite got round to drowning himself. No, the only time I saw the Stones play was at your 60th birthday do at the Beacon Theater.
BILL:	They were hot, weren't they?
ROBERT:	No, they were not. How much did they pay you to let them perform? Four old men shuffling across the stage with their zimmer frames while a bunch of session musicians created this wall of noise.
BILL:	(SIGHING) It was a shame Ahmet Ertegun didn't have a zimmer frame.
ROBERT:	Does tragedy follow the Stones everywhere they go? Altamont – wasn't that them?
CHELSEA:	The day the music died. Or was that when Jagger went back to Australia and L'Wren Scott killed herself?
BILL:	Give him a break, will you? Mick is a lovely man and a close personal friend.
ROBERT:	Dial him up. Tell him to bring his guitar over. If he can play one, that is. The night is yet young.

317

The college bell sounds twelve times.

BILL: (LOOKING AT HIS WATCH) Midnight! Mick'll have been tucked up in bed with his Horlicks and his bedsocks hours ago. Look, I'm beginning to get a little worried here ...

CHELSEA: Me too. What on earth is Mum doing?

BILL: All this talk has got me very nervous. What if she's slipped on some ice and fallen in the Isis? I wish she carried a phone...

ROBERT: Give Dwayne a call. Make sure he's still got her in view.

BILL: (PRESSING A COUPLE OF KEYS ON HIS SMARTPHONE) Good idea ... Dwayne? ... Dwayne, what's she up to? ... you *lost* her? ... how could you lose her? ... Jeez ... the cunning so-and-so ... (VERY ANGRY) well, *find* her again ... I'm not interested, Dwayne. Find her and bring her back here. NOW! (HE PRODS THE PHONE AND ENDS THE CALL)

CHELSEA: (CLOSE TO PANIC) What's happened, Dad?

BILL: Nothing's happened. She's just given Dwayne the slip, that's all. She's a grown woman, although sometimes I have my doubts. She can look after herself.

CHELSEA: But it's gone midnight and she doesn't know Oxford like we do. What if she's got lost, or ...

BILL: Or what?

CHELSEA: I don't know, do I? I'll go and find her ...

BILL: No, you won't. It's my job. You have a baby to look after. (PUTS ON COAT AND BEGINS TO EXIT WHILE MAKING ANOTHER CALL) Porter's Lodge? ... Yes, Bill Clinton here. Fine thank, you. ... Mrs Clinton hasn't been by, has she? .... Let us know if ... (VOICE TRAILS AWAY)

Robert pours himself another drink and relaxes while Chelsea checks the baby and paces up and down.

CHELSEA: Amazing how she sleeps through anything. So how well did you know Dad while you were here at Univ?

ROBERT: Well enough.

CHELSEA:	But you didn't really hang out together, did you?
ROBERT:	I realised pretty quickly that I couldn't keep up with him.
CHELSEA:	I'm guessing you don't mean intellectually.
ROBERT:	The dope-smoking. The sleeping around. The loud rock music. It wasn't really my "scene" as we would have said. I just wasn't a groovy kind of guy. Bill grew up listening to Alan Freed and I grew up reading Milton Friedman. He had a lot more fun.
CHELSEA:	Not once he got his call-up papers at the end of Hilary Term. That must have been a frightening time. Surely you were in the same boat?
ROBERT:	To Vietnam? I knew what my role would be, a skinny little kid like me – tunnel rat. I'd've been down there under the jungle, trying to sniff out the Viet Cong. Except they'd have sniffed me out first. GI tunnel rats had the life expectancy of … well, of a tunnel rat. Luckily, I failed the medical. But nearly all of us dodged the bullet, one way or another.
CHELSEA:	The Rhodes Scholars, you mean?
ROBERT:	Yeah, the black kids from Harlem couldn't pull the same strings as Rhodies like me and Bill. That's just the way it was.
CHELSEA:	(STILL PACING) Godammit, where has Mum got to? … It doesn't sound like Dad spent much time here in his second year?
ROBERT:	No-o …
CHELSEA:	You don't sound too sure.
ROBERT:	I don't think he spent any time here in his second year. He dossed down at the commune in Leckford Road once in a while but I don't think he set foot in college again after July '69.
CHELSEA:	Why was that?
ROBERT:	You've seen the stuff on the internet. Or that turncoat Gary Aldrich's book. I think your father went a bit off the rails after he got the call-up papers. Felt that nothing mattered because he wasn't coming back. There was a girl, I think,

	and the college would have taken a dim view of all that.
CHELSEA:	You think he was …
ROBERT:	Kicked out? I think he might have been if he hadn't told them he'd been conscripted anyway. But you couldn't simply kick out a Rhodie – there was a lot of politics involved. I think there was just a quiet agreement that Bill and Univ would go their separate ways.
CHELSEA:	Something that could be conveniently forgotten when he became President and arrived back on his triumphal chariot?
ROBERT:	Someone is probably chiselling the white marble statue as we speak. This is a college that has had to eat a lot of humble pie. Especially when Bill came back here in June 1994 as President. That gave him a lot of pleasure, with the college big wigs bowing and scraping before him.
CHELSEA:	King of kings? Dad?
ROBERT:	(LOOKING AT HER QUIZZICALLY BEFORE HE CONTINUES) It was "yah boo sucks, you're not kicking sand in my face now!" It was fifty years to the very day since D-Day and the moment Bill Blythe the second had marched into Rome with the 5ᵗʰ Army. They'd kicked out the Germans and were enjoying the spoils of victory. Bill went to Rome first and then Oxford in the first few days of June 1994. It was like a second triumphal occupation. He gave a speech here about history, saying "history does not always give us grand crusades" but do you know the one thing your father asked for at that second coming? A private session in this very room with the porter, Douglas, who had made most fun of him.
CHELSEA:	Yes, why was that, do you think?
ROBERT:	(LAUGHING) Because Douglas was the only one left who knew where the bodies were buried. I just hope Douglas drove a high price! (NOISES OFF) Is that your mother I can hear?

As Hillary comes in with Bill not far behind, Chelsea rushes to embrace her mother.

CHELSEA:	Mum! At last! You had me so worried! Did Dad find you? Where did you get to?
HILLARY:	(HAVING TO FIGHT HER OFF) Nowhere! Look, I haven't got Alzheimer's just yet, have I? Can't I be trusted to go out on my own any more?
BILL:	(SIGHING) I found her down by the Shelley Memorial. I thought she might have gone there, after our earlier conversation.
HILLARY:	I was just enjoying the silence for a moment. All the lights in the corridor were off but the statue was bathed in light from above. Beautiful.
BILL:	And then I came along and spoiled it. Sorr-ee!
HILLARY:	(LAUGHING) The story of my life. But I had a little time to think. And you know what?
BILL:	I'm not sure we're going to like the sound of this …
ROBERT:	You've decided to offer me the vice-presidency after all?
HILLARY:	In your dreams, Robert. (CALMLY, AFTER A PAUSE) I can't go through with it.

There is a moment of icy silence.

CHELSEA:	Can't go through with what?
HILLARY:	The inauguration.
BILL:	But how can you be President if you don't …
HILLARY:	I mean, I can't be President. I can't do any of it.
CHELSEA:	Mum!

They look at each other for a moment or two.

BILL:	You're joking. After everything you've been through this year? You've been working towards this moment all your life.
HILLARY:	Sorry.
BILL:	Not just you. Hundreds, thousands of people have dedicated a large part of their lives to getting you elected.
HILLARY:	Sorry. I'm grateful, truly I am, but …
BILL:	Your country needs you. The world needs you.

CHELSEA: Dad!

HILLARY: Tim Kaine can do it. Or Bernie. He ran me pretty close in the primaries after all and the public likes him more than me anyway. Or Julián [Castro]. Or even Joe [Biden] – I said history wasn't done with him.

BILL: History is not done with *you*.

HILLARY: I'm 69. I'm too old to be starting out as President.

BILL: 69 is nothing these days – this is the summer of 69. You tell her, Robert!

ROBERT: Sorry, it's not my call.

HILLARY: I'm tired. I thought I could do it. But all that campaigning, all that infighting, the dirty tricks, the debates, the vitriol that enemies like Trump throw at you – it wears you down. I've got nothing left and I'd be letting my country down if I failed to recognise it. This is not some vanity project. I don't care about my place in history or the Clinton "dynasty".

CHELSEA: (AN ARM ROUND HER SHOULDER) You know what, Mum? You're absolutely right. If your heart is no longer in it, it's the brave thing to do.

HILLARY: Thank you, Chelsea. Your support means a lot to me.

BILL: And mine doesn't, I suppose!

HILLARY: Oh, Bill, Bill! I will need your support now, more than ever! A ton of shit will rain down on me from all sides. From my own party who will feel betrayed. From Republicans who want a re-run of the election. From women who feel I have let women down by being weak and feeble. From men because I am a woman and I dared to take on this challenge in the first place.

CHELSEA: You won't have let anybody down, Mum. And all that will pass. You don't owe your country anything. You did a fantastic job as Secretary of State – God knows what a mess the world would be in now if you hadn't. You earned the trust of the American people and now their votes. They will respect your decision. What will you do instead?

HILLARY: Nothing. I'm history.

CHELSEA:	If there's one thing you can't do, it's nothing. You're simply not capable.
HILLARY:	OK, I'll rewrite history. That's what winners get to do, don't they? I'll rewrite my own *Living History*.
ROBERT:	Funnily enough, we were talking about that earlier while you'd gone walkabout.
HILLARY:	Surely, at my age, I've learned the lessons of history. Except we never do, do we? If history teaches us one thing, it's that we never learn the lessons of history. Otherwise it wouldn't keep repeating itself in ever more bizarre and painful ways.
BILL:	If there's one person I know who is strong enough to break the shackles of history and really make a difference, it's you. Besides, you have made history, the first woman President.
HILLARY:	Well, then I can unmake it again. There's been so many times this year when it's felt like 1992 and 1996 all over again. Do you remember, a few days after you got in the first time, we went to see Groundhog Day? Well, this whole year has felt like *Groundhog Day*, ever since I woke up to confirmation of those first Iowa results back on February 2nd. The alarm clock ringing at the crack of dawn and I'm somewhere on the campaign trail, Pittsburgh, Punxsutawney, wherever, saying the same old things, making fun of Donald Trump, singing for my supper. History is *Groundhog Day* without the happy ending. America has had one Clinton as President. Does it really need two?
BILL:	It does. You know I will back you in whatever you decide to do, Hill, but that doesn't seem like enough to make you throw away something you've worked all your life towards.
CHELSEA:	What is it, Mum?
HILLARY:	I think you know, Chelse. You all do. This hasn't been a "normal" campaign. It hasn't been politics as usual. How much humiliation and abuse is one woman supposed to take? You've seen me up there with Donald Trump. That wasn't politics. That was the Roman Coliseum, a fight to the death. He made my skin crawl. Sharing a stage with that

man implied that we were somehow equals. Just shaking his hand was torture. He wanted me in gaol; he wanted me stripped naked and begging for mercy; he wanted me dead and there were times when I wanted to die, right then and there. When he brought those women along, for instance.

BILL: (TRYING TO REACH OUT TO HILLARY BUT SHE BRUSHES HIM AWAY) I'm sorry, love. It's my fault.

HILLARY: I felt his clammy hands on my body, my mind, my very soul. Many women before me have been damaged by contact with that man and I am damaged too. Right now I think I'm in a state of shock. It may take years to come to terms with the shock, the sense of violation.

CHELSEA: Like a rape victim?

HILLARY: (IN TEARS NOW) Yes. The only thing that kept me going was the thought that I had to beat him. God, it was close. Two million votes sounds a lot but do you know what? If we hadn't axed the old Electoral College system, I might even have lost! If I'd failed and that monster had somehow become President, I would never have forgiven myself. But that's no longer necessary. Donald Trump will never be President.

BILL: The whole world is grateful for that. But I beg you not to do anything too hasty.

HILLARY: I've had a lot of time to think about this.

BILL: Not just a few seconds spent looking at a ghastly old statue while suffering from jet-lag?

HILLARY: No, that was merely the moment I felt certain I was making the right decision. Maybe it was reading the inscription: 'Life, like a dome of many-coloured glass, stains the white radiance of eternity.'

CHELSEA: 'Until death tramples it to fragments.' They left that bit out.

HILLARY: Well, eternity will be my judge anyway. What sort of stain would I be if I took this job, knowing I needed to heal myself first and my heart wasn't really in it?

CHELSEA:	You know, if I was going to choose just a few Shelley lines to sum up my life-history, seeing my two parents do all the things they've done, it would be the last few lines from 'Ozymandias'.

The others look blankly at Chelsea.

ROBERT:	Remind us.
CHELSEA:	It's a sonnet about a traveller who comes across the shattered remains of a statue of an old pharaoh in the middle of the desert. He reads the inscription: '"My name is Ozymandias, king of kings. Look on my works, ye mighty, and despair." Nothing beside remains. Round the decay of that colossal wreck, boundless and bare, the lone and level sands stretch far away.'
ROBERT:	(NODDING) Things that seem important now will be but specks of sand in the great scheme of things?
BILL:	But this is bullshit. We only have one planet. The President of the United States is just about the most important person on that planet.
ROBERT:	The king of kings?
BILL:	Whatever. The decisions the President makes matter not just to her and her family and her story, but to billions of other folk. It's not something to be settled by a bit of old doggerel that you might find in a Christmas cracker!
CHELSEA:	Of course not, but history rarely works out quite the way you expect, does it? A hundred years ago tonight, Felix Yusupov and his cronies murdered Rasputin, an act they expected to save the Romanov monarchy, aid Russia's war effort and stave off the threat of revolution. It had exactly the opposite effect. We make our choices. We can never know *what* would have happened if we'd taken a different path. But for what it's worth, Mum, I think you're making the right choice. I for one will sleep a lot easier in my bed.
BILL:	Don't you think that's just a little bit selfish?
HILLARY:	It's part of my thinking – I can't deny it. The worst thing

about our lives has been the world it has created for our only daughter. Me being President would only mean that the goldfish bowl is even smaller, with the world gawping at every little circuit Chelsea and her children swim.

CHELSEA: Mum! It's not so bad. I've never known any other way. Even if you retired to a nunnery, I wouldn't suddenly be able to lead an ordinary life, would I?

HILLARY: I'm sorry, love. Your father and I have a lot to answer for.

CHELSEA: No, you haven't. You're not just my parents, you're my heroes. C'mon, it's time for a team hug, I think! (BILL AND HILLARY MOVE TO EMBRACE HER) You too, Robert! (ROBERT JOINS IN SOMEWHAT RELUCTANTLY). One for all, all for one, right?

BILL: All for one.

HILLARY: So you'll let me do this?

BILL: (SIGHING) It's not for me to ... to lay down the law. This is not about me. But can I ask just one thing?

HILLARY: What's that?

BILL: Sleep on it. You don't have to do anything right now, today.

ROBERT: It's the middle of the night, after all.

BILL: Think about it through tomorrow and New Year's Eve. And if, on Sunday morning, New Year's Day, it's still your resolution, then we'll tell the world and I'll back you every inch of the way.

HILLARY: You promise? But I don't need that long. I will make a final decision by tomorrow morning and, if the decision is to quit, announce it then, before the year-end. Will you still support me?

BILL: I will. I'll even take the blame. You heard it here first – I accept Hillary's terms.

HILLARY: (EMBRACING BILL AGAIN) *My* hero! OK, I'll do just that. I'll give it some serious thought. Who knows, maybe by the morning the jet-lag will have gone, the batteries will have recharged a bit and I'll be ready to face the new year and my new job. If so, history will never know I had this

	little wobble. I doubt it but you never know. Time will tell.
BILL:	I love you, you ridiculous woman. Keep us all in suspense and then tell us the worst. But for now, let us be blithe. (He grabs the bottle of Madeira and starts pouring.) Let us drink a toast to the greatest President that America might – or might not – ever have!

They raise their glasses and drink.

CURTAIN

About the author

Nick Smith studied English at University College, Oxford, completing a doctorate and training as a teacher. In 1989 he founded Oxford Open Learning (www.ool.co.uk) which is now the UK's leading provider of distance learning courses for GCSE and A-level.

As a writer, Nick is best known for his works on bridge, including *Bridge Literature* (Cadogan, 1993) and, with Julian Pottage, *Bridge Behind Bars* (Master Point Press, 2009). He was NPC of the England bridge team in 2016.

He has also made a name as a regular on various TV quiz shows including Mastermind (where he answered questions on T.J. Hogg), Countdown, Only Connect and Eggheads.

As a playwright, Nick was the winner of the Oxfordshire Drama Network Playwriting Competition of 2014 with *Yusupov and Rasputin*. *Drowned Hogg Day* is his first and last novel.

The author may be contacted via nick@ool.co.uk.

Lightning Source UK Ltd.
Milton Keynes UK
UKHW02f1822191018
330853UK00011B/770/P